FLAME

of

RESISTANCE

their dangerous plan could change the tides of war. . . .

TRACY GROOT

Tyndale House Publishers, Inc.
Carol Stream, Illinois

Visit Tyndale online at www.tyndale.com.

Visit Tracy Groot online at www.tracygroot.com.

TYNDALE and Tyndale's quill logo are registered trademarks of Tyndale House Publishers, Inc.

Flame of Resistance

Designed by Ron Kaufmann

Edited by Kathryn S. Olson

Published in association with Creative Trust Literary Group, 5141 Virginia Way, Suite 320, Brentwood, Tennessee 37027. www.creativetrust.com.

The poetry excerpts in chapter 1 are taken from "High Flight" by John Gillespie Magee Jr., "Parachute Descent" by David Bourne, and "An Irish Airman Foresees His Death" by W. B. Yeats.

This novel is a work of fiction. Names, characters, places, and incidents either are the product of the author's imagination or are used fictitiously. Where real locations or historical or public figures appear, any situations, incidents, and dialogues concerning them are not intended to depict actual events or to change the entirely fictional nature of the work.

Library of Congress Cataloging-in-Publication Data

Groot, Tracy, date.
 Flame of resistance / Tracy Groot.
  p. cm.
 ISBN 978-1-4143-5947-2 (sc)
1. Fighter pilots—United States—Fiction. 2. World War, 1939–1945—United States—Fiction. 3. World War, 1939–1945—Underground movements—France—Fiction. 4. Espionage, American—History—20th century—Fiction. 5. Espionage, French—History—20th century—Fiction. I. Title.

 PS3557.R5655F53 2012
 813'.54—dc23   2011052924

Printed in the United States of America

18 17 16 15 14 13 12
 7   6   5   4   3   2   1

FLAME OF RESISTANCE

For Jack, Evan, Becca, Gray, and Riley

and

For John, Tami, Shaina, Phil, Nikki, and Johnny

❧ ❧

I'm not sure I'll write enough books to dedicate
them separately, you people of my heart, so, as Tami says,
I'll do it all in one "foul" swoop.

Whatever happens, the flame of the French resistance must not be extinguished and will not be extinguished.

CHARLES DE GAULLE

———————————◆———————————

Better to die on your feet than live on your knees.

AESCHYLUS

———————————◆———————————

Audacity is a tactical weapon.

AUDIE MURPHY

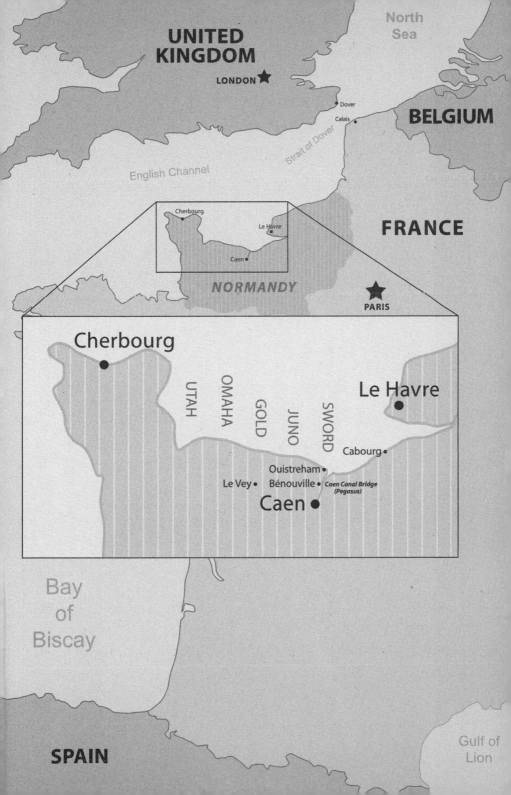

THE SUN CAME warm through the plexishield. The shield squeaked as Tom wiped a patch of condensation. He was no good with words, and he didn't have to be. Plenty of aviators said it for him. One talked of slipping the surly bonds of earth, and of sun-split clouds. Another spoke of rarefied splendor. "Untrespassed sanctity" was a favorite, and those were the words he'd use to tell the folks.

Untrespassed sanctity, he'd say of the English Channel, and of the gut-thrum of his aircraft, of the daily sorties to France, and his placement in the V. It never got old. It was untrespassed. Maybe not invincible, but so far, on his watch, untrespassed.

I know that I shall meet my fate somewhere among the clouds above; those that I fight I do not hate, those that I—

"Angel flight, this is lead." Captain Fitz finally broke radio silence. "Rolling in."

The five Thunderbolts approached the target area, flying in lovely V formation. Tom would ransack his vocabulary for a different word than *lovely* if talking with the guys, but the new guy from Molesworth stayed on his wing pretty as pie. Someday he'd like to hear a liberated Frenchman say, *There I was, getting beat up by a Nazi; we look up and see this lovely V . . .*

"One and two, take targets on the right. Three and four—"

"Captain! We got movement—"

Antiair flak slammed her belly, blew a hole in the front of the cowling. Tom barely knew he was hit before oil pressure plummeted. "Mayday—this is Angel three. I'm hit! I'm hit."

"Angel three, can you make it back?"

"Pressure gauge says no, flight lead. I'm going in."

"Copy. We'll cap the area." Then, "Good luck, Tom."

"Good luck, Cab," another echoed.

"Guts and glory, Cabby," called another.

Bullets stitched the plane as he peeled off the target. Smoke filled the cockpit, burnt oil singed his nostrils. She was flagging the second she was hit, but he gripped the stick and pulled back to get as much height as he could before bailing.

He tried for a look at the ground but couldn't see through the smoke. Where was he? Too charmed by rarefied splendor and the alignment of his wingman to—

"Normandy," Tom coughed. Northeastern Normandy.

Flak exploded and pinged, black patches pockmarked the sky, and as Tom gained altitude, he heard a conversation in the debrief room.

Then Cabby got hit, and that was it, the whole ground opened up on us.

You capped the area . . .

Stayed as long as we could, sir, but it was too hot.

Where was he in Normandy? Caen? Cabourg? Maybe he could—

But the old girl jerked, leveled, and he had no hope of circling back to bail in the sea.

Why do you call him Cabby?

He looks like he jumped outta the womb hollering, "Heil Hitler," but didn't like us calling him Kraut. So we called him Cabbage.

We called him Cabbage.

I ain't dead yet, fellas. I am, however, about to reacquaint myself with the surly bonds of earth.

He waved off smoke, snatched the picture of his little brother, and shoved it down his collar. He jettisoned the cowling, and the plexishield broke from the plane in a *whumpf*, popping his ears, sucking his breath.

There were two ways to bail from a P-47 Thunderbolt. Tilt the plane and let it drop you out, or, in what Tom felt was a more stylish way to go, just stand up, rise into the slipstream, let it carry you away . . .

Listen, Yank. You get hit, you go down, here's what you do: get to Paris, get to the American Hospital. Look up a doc there, a Yank by the name of Jackson. He's with the Resistance. You tell him Blakeney says thanks. He may not remember me. He's helped a lot of blokes. You tell him thanks for me.

"He looks like a *boche*."

"I saw him go down. I heard him speak. He's no *boche*. He flew one of the new planes. You should have seen them. Beautiful."

"What did he say?"

"Not much. Before he came to, something about a flight of angels and a fellow named Jackson in Paris. Now look at him. He's not going to say anything."

"That's what worries me. We have to find out if he's German."

"I'm telling you, he's no German. He sounds like the man from Ohio."

Tom watched the two Frenchmen watching him and tried hard to pick out words. His mother's friend had given him a little French phrase book from the Great War, when she had served as a nurse with the Red Cross. From sheer boredom between flights, he'd sometimes taken it out. It was in his escape and evasion pack, no longer strapped to his back. Either he lost it in the jump, or the French guys took it.

He was in a dark woodshed with a low ceiling. He remembered fumbling for the chute cord the second he left the plane, waiting until he was clear to yank it. He remembered terror at the descent; he'd parachuted many times, none with fear of enemy fire. He'd never felt so vulnerable in his life, not even after jammed gear and a belly landing—Captain Fitz rushed up with a pint of Jack Daniel's after that one. But the float down into enemy-held land, the air thick with bullets, the ground exploding, that was one for the books. He heard himself telling it to the guys, heard Fitz's laugh and Oswald's quick "Yeah, yeah, yeah, and den what happened?"

I don't know yet, Oz.

He suddenly felt for the photo. The Frenchmen leaped back, and one pulled Tom's own .45 on him. Tom held up his hands and pointed to his shirtfront.

"Picture. Photograph." He added, "Uh . . . *frère*. Picture of *ma frère*."

"*Mon frère*," one of them corrected.

Keeping one hand up, he slowly unzipped his flight jacket, unfastened a few shirt buttons, and looked inside. It was stuck in his underwear waistband. He glanced at the men, slowly reached inside, and pulled it out. He held it up for the men to see. "*Mon frère*," he said. "*Mon petit frère*. He's thirteen."

"Oui." The one with the gun nodded, and slipped it back into his pocket.

He looked at the picture. Mother had sent it with the last package. Ronnie wasn't little anymore. The kid was growing up. Still, same old grin, same cowlick, same rascal shine in his eyes. He ignored the rush of pain and affection at seeing the familiar face in this strange place.

"Can't get a word in edgewise even now," Tom muttered. He held it up to the men. "Kid can talk the hind leg off a donkey." He rubbed the face with his thumb, and slipped it into a zippered pocket in his flight jacket.

"Who is Jackson?" the man with the gun said in English.

Tom's heart nearly stopped; had he said it out loud? He'd banged his head good when he came down in a tight place between two buildings. He remembered a gray tiled roof coming on fast; he remembered sharp pain, sliding to the ground, then nausea, vomiting. Then he went into some sort of daze, vaguely recollected being bundled into the back of a horse cart. They covered him up with firewood, and the dark invited him to blank out. He came to in this place. First thing he did was to feel for the gun now in the possession of the French guy.

What else did he say when he was out? He cursed himself. *Don't go to sleep, Cabby; they'll get everything out of you.*

The one without the gun had a sullen, suspicious expression. He paced back and forth, shoulders and arms stiff for a fight, eyes never leaving Tom. The one with the gun had the offhand confidence of being the one with the gun. Both were in their twenties, both were spare built and thin, both had the work-hardened look of factory or farm workers. Who were they? Resisters? The Maquis—French guerrilla fighters? The Brits trusted these collection crews more than the Americans did, maybe because England and France had had little choice but to trust each other. And what choice did he have?

Should he tell them about Jackson? Every instinct said no.

Jackson was a fellow from Maine, a doctor at the American Hospital of Paris. He had a reputation with the British Royal Air Force as a man to trust behind enemy lines. Tom had heard of him more than once from downed airmen given up as MIA. He once witnessed a homecoming at Ringwood, an RAF pilot missing for four months. Once the initial euphoria of his return settled, the guy, Captain Blakeney, had all the men toast Dr. Jackson, "the patron saint of downed airmen."

What if his captors were collaborators? What if they were French Milice? *One peep about Jackson, and Jackson's a marked man.* How much had he said already? The thought sickened him.

Where was Paris? How would he get there? It hurt to even move his head. He'd assess damage later. He needed a plan, and he always favored three-part plans. *Not a word on Jackson. Get to Paris. Don't vomit.*

"Thees Jackson . . . ," the gunless Frenchman asked. "Ees een Paree?"

"Thomas William Jaeger. First lieutenant, United States Army Air Forces. One four oh nine six—"

"This is no interrogation, my friend. We are the good guys." The Frenchman with the gun strolled forward a few paces and sat on his haunches. He pushed his hat up with the tip of the gun. His brown eyes were lively and measuring; his thin face, amused, or rather, ready to be amused. He had the sort of face that invited entertainment of any sort. His English was far better than the other's. "But we do not know if you are a good guy. Tell us why we do not kill you for a spy?"

6

"Tell me why I should trust you," Tom said. "I hear you guys sell out your neighbors. Lot of Jews gone missing, too."

The man wagged his finger. "The question of trust lies with us alone." He gestured toward his face. "Attend this handsome face. Tell me if you see a German. Then I will get you a mirror, and you will wonder why we have not killed you yet. Hmm?"

"Lots of Americans look like Germans," Tom scorned. "Some *are* German. I'm Dutch. I was born in the Netherlands. We immigrated to the States when I was nine. I'm from Michigan. Jenison."

"You are very tall. Very blond. Very square-headed. Pretty blue eyes, too. I am aroused." The man behind him laughed.

"Yeah? Come to Jenison. You'll be plenty aroused. And you're puny."

"I do not know *puny*."

"Petite." He couldn't keep the sneer out. Payback for *square-headed*.

The Frenchman shrugged. "I do not get enough meat. I would be your size, with meat." The other man laughed again. "Perhaps from a great height I am puny. You have legs like trees. Trust me, I had to fit them into the cart. Listen, Monsieur Jenison. I am, hmm—" he gave a considering little shrug— "sixty percent you are not a spy. But we have been fooled before. Some of my friends have died because we were quick to believe a pretty face."

"Where did you live in Holland?" came a voice from the shadows.

A third man emerged from the corner of the shed, and he looked nothing like the other two. This older gentleman was dressed like a lawyer. He wore a fedora. The collar of his gray overcoat was turned up, and he wore a red scarf. He clasped black-gloved hands in front. He had no wariness about him like the others. He looked as if he were deciding which newspaper to buy.

"Andijk. A small city in the northern province."

"Where was your mother born?"

"Apeldoorn."

"Your father?"

"Andijk. Shouldn't you ask me who won the World Series? Or what's the capital of North Dakota? Not that I remember."

The man reached into a pocket and took out a piece of paper and a pencil. He wrote something and held the paper out to Tom. "Tell me—what is this word?"

Tom took the paper. He angled it to catch light from the door. "Scheveningen. My aunt lived near there, in Rotterdam. They bombed it off the map. She and my uncle died in the attack, with my two cousins."

The man took the paper back. "I am very sorry for your family. C'est la guerre . . . to the misfortune of the world." He turned to the one with the gun. "No German can pronounce that word." The gentleman touched his hat, then left.

"We are not the only ones who saw you go down, Monsieur Jenison. But we got to you first. The man who lives in the house you fell on took a beating because he could not tell the Germans where you were. Do you think you can trust us? Hmm? Because thanks to the monsieur, we now trust you."

"I'd trust you more with my gun back," Tom said.

The man grinned. He had a look Tom liked, that of an amiable scoundrel. He knew plenty of his sort; you'd trust him in a fight but not with your sister. The man rose and pulled out the gun, and handed it butt first to Tom. "You can call me Rafael." He looked over his shoulder at the other guy and gave a little whistle between his teeth. "Give him his pack." To

Tom, he said, "Regrettably you will not find your cigarettes. I suggest they were lost in the jump."

"Lucky I don't smoke."

The man with the red scarf, known in Cabourg as François Rousseau, walked rapidly to work. He exchanged pleasantries with his bronchial secretary, suggested mint tea, and slipped into his office. He took off his coat and hung it on the coat tree. He left the scarf on; it was cold in the office, but he did not light the coal in the brazier. What coal the company allotment allowed, he brought home in newspaper to Marie and the children. Thank God spring was coming soon.

He rubbed his gloved hands together and settled down to the papers on his desk. But he could not settle his mind. He finally pushed aside the latest numbers of Rommel's new cement quotas and let his mind take him where it would.

Twice he reached for the telephone, twice he pulled back. He had to work it out in his head, every detail, before he called his brother, Michel. He tapped his lips with gloved fingers. Hadn't they improvised for nearly four years? If there was one thing they'd learned under enemy occupation, it was resourcefulness.

It was a fool's scheme, he knew, but Michel was feeling so very low. The idea could have enough in it to beguile him from the latest blow. And it was an *interesting* scheme. That face? That height?

He thought it through, beginning to end, and picked up the phone. Sometimes, answers to problems literally dropped from the sky. There was only one thing a cunning Frenchman should do with a Yank who looked exactly like a proud German officer. Make him one.

MICHEL ROUSSEAU stared unseeingly out the train window, rousing only at the grumbles and rustling of passengers. "What is it?" he asked of the man in the seat next to him.

"The rail is out from Caen to Paris," the man said sourly, reaching for his package on the rack over the seat.

The journey was over before it began. "All the way?" Michel asked, dismayed. What now? "Surely not all the way. How far can we get?"

"Was it an Allied bombing?" a young woman with a small child asked.

"Probably the Resistance." A middle-aged woman snatched up her basket. "Probably those thugs, the *maquisards*."

"Those 'thugs' aid the Allies," the young woman said indignantly. "Those 'thugs' risk their lives for us. Whose side are you on?"

"I am on the side of France," the woman said, lifting her chin.

"Then I dare you to sing 'La Marseillaise,' you Vichy cow."

"Don't be a fool," the woman hissed, indicating with a

little jerk of her head to the two German soldiers at the front of the car. As if everyone on the train were not aware of them. "However proud you are of your thugs, did they get you where you wanted to go today? There is no civility left in France. No one acts rationally anymore."

"I suppose you think Marshal Pétain is rational," the young woman said, her face flushing, and in his heart, Michel cheered her boldness. "'The trouble with France is you women!'" she mocked. "'You did not produce enough babies to raise a decent army!' First they screech at us for not staying at home to be good little mamas. Then they screech because we are not out there, making enough money to feed our families with so many men in camps. France starves because of us women."

"Do not trouble us with truth, mademoiselle," the man next to Michel cautioned with a sad smile. "We have not heard it for so long, you confuse us."

The people close enough to hear this exchange leaned in, and began to add low-muttered opinions.

"She is right—Pétain and Laval are Nazi puppets. Everyone knows it now."

"We didn't think so in the beginning."

"You live, you learn."

The young woman began to gather up her bags—and hum "La Marseillaise." She caught the hand of her child, lifted her chin, and hummed loudly and proudly. Michel's heart began to fill, and he had to smile. He glanced about discreetly, and others smiled, too. One old man, likely a veteran of the Great War, blinked bright-blue eyes filling with tears.

The national anthem of France had been forbidden for nearly four years. To sing it in public was punishable by imprisonment, or if they thought you revolutionary enough, death. One would hear occasional snatches of it in crowded places, but it was forbidden to gather in a crowd these days unless approved. Even a wedding had to have approval, if the guest list was too long.

Michel found himself humming along. When the song was done and she looked at him, startled, he winked.

"Tiny rebellions keep the spirit alive," he said. *"Oui?"*

"Oui, monsieur," she said fervently. "God bless you, monsieur."

"Oh, no—God bless you, mademoiselle."

"Bless you, child," the old man said.

"I'll add my own as well," said the man next to Michel. "You have made me feel an irrational bit of national pride. I feel French. Old-style French, and for that, God bless you, m'selle."

Michel felt a wave of giddiness. Such an open exchange was beyond reckless. Collaborators were everywhere, people who would turn in their own mothers for wearing a tiny French flag or for doing as this brave young woman had done, humming the beloved national anthem.

This insidious collaboration with the spirit of the devil, this disease throughout France where common sense seemed to have fled the majority—how had it happened?

"We didn't know what hit us," he murmured. *We lost our bearings, and then we lost hope.*

And yet, Michel mused as he followed the others off the train, hope remained if a young woman could hum "La Marseillaise" on a crowded train, right under the nose of a Vichy supporter, right in the hearing of two German soldiers, who pretended not to hear so they wouldn't have to deal with it.

"Tiny rebellions," he mused, feeling better than he had in days. It would change once he got back to his apartment. But the little exchange on the train had been the most heartened he'd felt in a long while, and he wondered if the others close enough to hear felt the same. Today, he too felt French.

The telephone jangled, startling Michel from his thoughts.

"Hello."

His brother's voice greeted him. "You're supposed to be in Paris."

"The rail is down again."

"All the way?"

"Apparently. We hadn't even left the depot."

"You sound cheerful." François sounded suspicious.

"Yes, well, an amazing thing happened today. A tiny rebellion, in which I took part."

"You rebel in ways great and wide, little brother. Tiny is not your style."

"Today I hummed 'La Marseillaise' with a young woman on a crowded train."

François laughed in delight. "You fool!"

"Yes. It was exhilarating. I thought the feeling would leave when I came home but it did not. I feel wonderful. I feel like champagne."

"Did she know she sang with one of the greatest Resistance leaders in France?"

Michel put stockinged feet on the desk. "We didn't sing; we hummed. They'll have to add another clause to the law. But it was far more than that, François. It was what I felt from those around me. I felt hope. I haven't felt it in so long, I think I'd forgotten what it was. I felt, in this tiny collective rebellion, that a far *greater* rebellion lay just below the surface. I can hardly describe it, it was—a gathering of strength. From each other, from angels, I don't know where it came from, but

I felt it, and I know others did, too. You should have heard what the man next to me said—such unhidden truth, spoken in the same air Nazis breathed. I could have danced with him."

"Dancing is forbidden," François said dryly.

"Be quiet. I am at the brink: François, I felt for the first time in a long time a return to *common sense*. That young woman reminded us of who we are. There was a scent of freedom all over the place—above us, around us, it came through the floorboards—as if humming 'La Marseillaise' summoned a holy presence. She will never know what she did for the heart of this worn-out old man."

"You're thirty-eight."

"Today, I feel it again."

"Well, brace yourself, Brother—before I'm done, you'll feel younger yet. If anything, it'll scare the daylights out of you."

"Tell me full on. Today I am expansive and brave."

"I have a plan to infiltrate the German brothel in Bénouville."

"With what?"

"A German, of course."

For the first time, the champagne bubbles went still. Michel took his feet off the desk. "François, if this line . . ."

"I have it checked daily, Michel. It is safe."

"Then what are you saying . . . ?"

"I'm saying it is not too late to gather information on the bridges for the Allies. You told me Madame Vion says one of the prostitutes is sympathetic. My plan is perfect."

Michel rose. "It makes me sick to hear you say this over an open line."

"It is not open. I check it daily, dear heart. Do not worry."

He knew the illusion would not last. He did not expect illusion's truncation to come through his own brother. The last of the freedom trailed away, and he was home again. Back to the real world, and what he did in that world.

"François," he said carefully. "Listen to me. This is not a game. Whatever—"

"Be expansive and brave, my brother, and in two weeks I shall deliver to you Lohengrin himself. It will take that long to heal the poor man's head. He was bleeding and didn't even know."

He gripped the telephone. "You are all the family I have left."

"Is this my own brother? Michel. I have been proud of you for so very long. I have come up with a plan that lets me hope, one day, you will be proud of me."

"I am *begging* you—stay out of it! You have no idea what you're about. Think of Marie. You would be tortured and shot, but your own sweet Marie—she would suffer as Jasmine did. They make examples of the women to weaken the men, and believe me, it works. She was tortured to death. Can you . . . can you comprehend those words? She died in my arms."

Jasmine had made a mistake, and they never learned what it was. Was she denounced? By whom? How did she slip, what had she done to bring about her arrest? They never learned. She whispered one thing before she died, and that with a broken smile: "I didn't talk." Jasmine was the best agent Flame had. She'd worked for the Resistance cell in Caen for three years.

The invasion was coming; everyone knew it. But the closer France got to the whiff of freedom he had on the train, the worse things got. He'd seen plenty of brutality in the past four years, and yes, he could understand the use of some torture to procure vital information to win a war; but what they did to Jasmine wasn't war. What they did to Jasmine was alien.

He had been so strong in the beginning. He wasn't strong anymore. He had flashes of the young woman on the train, humming "La Marseillaise" with her boy. The thought of that brave young woman in Nazi hands made him weak. They knew how to get to the men, as if the devil spoke in their ears.

How could he describe such barbaric cruelty to a man as good and innocent as François? He didn't want the images in François's head any more than he wanted them in his own. Yet not to speak of it betrayed Jasmine. Not to tell it shamed the living for covering up Nazi atrocity. And if it prevented his brother's involvement, he'd tell it in detail.

The telephone cord tethered him; he could not pace. "Listen to me. Must I tell it? I will tell it." Submerged images surfaced, dizzying him. He could smell the untended wounds, he could hear tortured, labored breath. He could feel her in his arms. She was so small, a window broken in place, one nudge and all would shatter. He held her as long as he could. He made her last moments on earth safe. "They pulled out her teeth. They broke her fingers. They burned her, François; between her toes they lit pieces of cloth—"

"Michel, the invasion comes," his brother cut in gently. "You said the Allies need to know about the bridges. We must give them what they need."

"You don't know what you're doing! Stay out of it!"

"I have a plan. It is a good plan. You will see, Michel."

Michel sank into the chair, fingers sinking into his hair. "François, you have not seen the beast."

"Two weeks, my brave little brother. Give me two weeks. You will see."

Several clicks, and the connection disengaged. Michel replaced the receiver. Back to his world, and what he did in that world.

3

COLETTE LAPONSIE had a boyfriend. Brigitte Durand did not. Colette believed Claudio could keep her safe. Brigitte didn't care if Claudio was Milice, the French equivalent of the German Gestapo—Brigitte knew who was in charge of France, and it wasn't the French. Not that the Milice couldn't make miserable the lives of their fellow French. Sometimes they out-Germaned the Germans.

"Where is Claudio?" Brigitte asked, suddenly aware she hadn't seen him in a few days.

"In Paris. On business for the oberkommandant." Colette could make a Milice thug sound like a respected diplomat. She was hemming the frayed edge of a kitchen towel. She bit off the thread and smoothed the towel on her lap, as satisfied with her work as she was with her man.

What sort of man would allow his girlfriend to sleep with other men?

Jean-Paul wouldn't have believed she was doing it, for one. Then he'd have killed every man who touched her, German or not.

You told me to survive, Jean-Paul. She had, but Jean-Paul had not.

He died in the spring of 1940 at the Maginot Line, the place that was to stop the Germans from getting so far. She found out in July of that year, on a hot sultry day when she stood in front of a list taped to a building in Paris. He had occupied her heart, and now he occupied a grave. So this German occupation was nothing to her. It was hunger, it was fear, it was loss of freedom, and it was so very cold, but she saw his name and the world became a different place. The bullet that took Jean-Paul's life did not end one fate; it ended two.

She was hungry. In Paris, alone, and hungry.

The food had had a strange rallying effect. Strange in that, once it brightened and revived, it also filled her with shame for the act that obtained it. Yet days later when the brightness left and hunger came again, no shame remained, only some primitive desperation, and she showed up at the same place she had met the German soldier, at the bench along the Seine near the Notre Dame bridge. He was there, for the bridge was his, and once off duty he came to her again. He didn't say a word. Not that he had any French. He stood with his gray overcoat fluttering in the November breeze, and had the grace, as he had before, to stare at the flowing Seine until she stood and followed him to where he was billeted, at a home on the rue d'Apennine.

The soldier whispered things in German. When it was over, and she waited, eyes out the window, for a handful of francs, she slipped down the staircase and out the kitchen door, past the disgusted glare of the old woman who owned the house.

Paris had fallen. Jean-Paul was dead. And she slept with a German for food. One of those things she never could have conceived, but all three? Three belonged to someone she did not know. Three were a different fate.

"What are those?" Colette asked of the books in Brigitte's lap.

"A Baedeker's and a French-English dictionary. I've decided to be a travel book writer when this is over." She held up a piece of notepaper. "This is the first page of my book. I start out with Ireland."

"How can you write a travel book about a place you've never been?"

Brigitte shook her head at Colette's utter lack of imagination. She held up the Baedeker's. "*This* is misrepresentative. It tells of the Cliffs of Moher in Ireland, but says nothing of the patrolling angels."

"What angels?" Colette scoffed.

"The German officer told me. The expressive one. To speak of the Cliffs of Moher but to say nothing of the angels that press you down before you get to the edge . . ." She lowered her voice to ghost-story stealth. "It's an ordinary day, right? And you're an ordinary tourist. You start for the cliffs, little suspecting what you are about to encounter. You approach . . . and suddenly sense a phenomenon of *caution* in the air. Then it is dread, and then—impending calamity. You creep toward the edge . . . and then you feel the *actual weight* of the *beings themselves*. You are pressed down and filled with a *holy sickness* to *stay alive*. Thus you are preserved, not by what your eyes can see but by what your soul can *feel* . . . the Angels of Moher." She held Colette's transfixed gaze a moment longer. Then, hushed: "This is not in Baedeker's. Who would go for the cliffs? I'd go for the phenomenon of caution."

Colette stared at Brigitte as she sometimes did, with a softened look on the verge of beguilement. It seemed that Colette sat on a fence, and Brigitte always felt the urge to give her the tiniest push and she would topple backward into a far more habitable place—a place, Brigitte fancied, she truly wanted to be. Brigitte long awaited Colette's conversion to humanity.

Colette came out of her daze with more self-consciousness than usual, and contempt fast replaced interest. "You are stupid, Brigitte." She gathered the hemmed towel and the sewing things and shoved them in her basket. "It's your turn to wait in line for eggs today. And if you take any more to the château, I'll make myself an omelet and eat the entire thing."

Colette rose with her basket and left the sitting room.

Brigitte called after her, "You are hopeless, Colette. You have no imagination."

"You're the hopeless one. That German officer was killed by the Resistance last week. So much for 'expressive.'" Colette slammed the sitting room door, rattling a few pictures on the wall. The venom was high today; she must have been close to conversion.

Brigitte regarded the books. So Colette noticed the missing eggs? Colette was a counter. If Simone or Marie-Josette received potatoes or beans for payment, every potato and bean was inventoried with German precision and doled out between the four of them. Colette once broke two beans in half to make sure all was scrupulously equal. Brigitte would have understood her better, and liked her better, if she'd just danced the two beans in the air, out of reach of the others, and then popped them in her mouth.

Maybe it was wrong for Brigitte to take eggs from the others. She had taken the four precious eggs to the Château de Bénouville, the maternity hospital up the road, run by Madame Léa Vion. She brought them not for the women or children, but for the downed Allied airmen Madame Vion hid on her property. She'd left them on the step of the little stone chapel by the river, the place it was rumored Madame hid the pilots. She also left a note: *For the Friends of France. From a Grateful Patriot.*

Brigitte had discovered Madame's secret one day while walking the château grounds, the closest thing Bénouville had to a forest. A few acres of towering trees and bushes and flowers gave grand illusion; no German occupation existed within its silent green realm. At least, not until Brigitte came across the startled British evader. She knew him for British the moment she set eyes on him, and she instantly knew she had to act as if she'd never seen him—Germans were everywhere, and informants, besides. One could be pruning a tree for all she knew. So she gave him a wink and a tiny nod and strolled on, neither slowing nor increasing her pace.

The rumor was true, as she'd hoped it was. Brigitte never told the girls, not with a Milice about. She let Colette think she brought the eggs for Madame Vion, but what did she care about the madame? She'd snubbed Brigitte once in the village. The snub came as a surprise, knowing they were both French, both against the Germans—though the madame would never believe it—and both hungry.

Rolling in baubles and finery, is that what everyone thinks? She'd take a nice Camembert over francs any day. She couldn't remember the last time she'd had a decent Beaujolais.

Brigitte was just as surprised as the madame at what she had become.

Madame Vion had snubbed her as had the man at the café, a French politician who had spit on Brigitte in front of his wife and daughter. Did Brigitte not see him with Marie-Josette last week? Did she shout out what he had done? She did not. She could not hurt his daughter; she was only twelve.

"Brigitte!" Colette called, and when she called like that, there was a customer at the back door.

Brigitte set aside the books and waited a moment before she lifted the needle from the Vera Lynn record. *There'll be bluebirds over the white cliffs of Dover . . . tomorrow when the world is free . . .*

She did not know the man at the back door. He was either scrounging for food or, despite the sign, didn't know this brothel was for Germans only—or for occasional French politicians. This man was no politician; he wore the clothing of a day laborer. He certainly wasn't German.

He pulled off his hat. "Bonjour, mademoiselle."

"Bonjour, monsieur," Brigitte said with a little smile. Such politeness. It reminded her of better days. "Regrettably, we have no food and this establishment is a Germans-only business." She pointed to the sign nailed to the door: *Nur für Wehrmacht.* Only for armed forces. "Perhaps you can try Caen." She started to close the door, but the man put his hand on it.

"You are Brigitte?" he asked quietly. "You are the grateful patriot?"

She stared for a moment, speechless, and whatever she did say, Colette mustn't hear it. She slipped out the door and pulled it shut behind her. She drew her sweater close against the March wind.

"What do you want?" she asked in a low tone.

"I've been sent to see if you are truly a patriot."

"Sent by whom?"

The man leaned against the house and pulled out a package of cigarettes—Lucky Strikes. American cigarettes. It certainly wasn't the stuff they smoked around here, and whatever that was, it was likely more rolling paper than anything else. Occupation tobacco, they called it. Same as Occupation coffee or Occupation tea, shabby imitations of the real thing.

She stared at the package until he pocketed it. He lit a match and cupped his hand around it, lit the cigarette and gratefully pulled it to life. He shook the match dead and tossed it, then offered the cigarette to her. She shook her head, but knew in a moment it was the real thing. It didn't smell like nasty Occupation cigarettes. He smiled and looked appreciatively at the cigarette.

"They came from an American. I like them better than Player's. The British have Player's. The fellow you saw in the château woods was a British pilot."

Brigitte did not answer. The man did not have the same feeling about him that Claudio did. He didn't feel like Milice. He was likely with the Resistance. She felt an odd little tremor of excitement.

"Why do you feed them?" he asked.

She nearly answered with "Because I don't know how Madame Vion can do it with ration coupons assigned only for maternity patients and workers." It would have been a stupid mistake. He could be anybody. Instead, she said, "I don't know what you're talking about."

"Mademoiselle, if I were going to denounce you, I would have done it already."

"What do you want?"

"Help."

"Help from a brothel. I'm sure you realize brothels are state-run."

"Not this one."

She stared at him. "How would you know that?"

"I know it is not registered. It is unlicensed."

"A matter of paperwork. It is fully licensed by the Germans, and in case you haven't noticed, the Germans are in charge." How could this man know her home was not legally registered with the local French government? Brigitte had seen to that. She'd fought to keep it unlicensed. Somehow it kept *her* unlicensed. "We follow the law. We pay taxes. What business is it of yours?"

All of the girls had to be free of disease. Any German soldier who turned up with a sexually transmitted disease was sure to be sent to the Russian front, and the prostitute who gave it to him would be jailed. Brigitte found it ironic. Maybe *ironic* was the wrong word, but even *hypocritical* was too weak a word for a system that would legitimize a brothel but punish any evidence of its sanctioned acts. As with any licensed Parisian brothel, Brigitte saw to it that she and the other three were checked weekly and prescribed fastidious hygienic treatments and preventions. She found these appointments more humiliating than those first "appointments" with customers; the doctor was a kind man. Kindness sometimes shamed her more than any guilty act.

Her eyes narrowed as she thought of the doctor.

"What kind of help do you need?" She said it with enough frosty indifference that the man would not mistake her. This conversation was dangerous. The tremor of excitement now felt more like fear.

"The kind that would mean torture and death if you are caught. Whatever you have in mind when I say torture, make it ten times worse." He pulled on the cigarette, then smiled a rather chilling smile. "I'll never recruit anybody without putting it all on the table."

"It's a wonder you recruit anyone."

"You would be surprised."

Brigitte thought again of the doctor. "You never know who is with the Resistance," Claudio once told her. "Those Communist pigs are everywhere."

"Are you a Communist?"

"Most are not, some are. Do you have a problem with that?"

She couldn't believe this conversation was taking place. She couldn't believe she'd let it go on this long.

"Are you Jewish?"

"Most are not. Some are."

He'd said enough for her to denounce him herself. He could not be an informant, unless he was trying to trick her into betraying her political views. But who would care about the political views of a prostitute? Prostitutes slept with the enemy; therefore prostitutes were collaborators. "Horizontal" collaborators, the joke went.

"Well, are you *French*?"

The man grinned, and it was a lively grin. "Yes I am, and everyone with us. Whatever else they are, they are French. And they want their country back."

"This help you want." She glanced at the house next door. Anyone could be watching from a curtained window. "Will it make a difference?"

"If you are not caught—and the last woman was—yes."

"Then I'll help." The words were out of her mouth before she knew they were there. The tremor became something she hadn't felt since Jean-Paul was alive.

"Then you are a resistant." He took the cigarette from his mouth and made a wry little ceremonial sign of the cross. "The cross of Lorraine, by the way. Our symbol." He held up the cigarette. "Do you know the Americans smoke them only to here?"

"Every nation should have a little taste of occupation, yes?" She folded her arms tightly against the chill, inside and out. "What do you want me to do?"

"On Friday at 2 p.m., you will meet someone at the north café by the Caen Canal Bridge. You will sit at the northeast corner table, closest to the river. You will say not a word of this to anyone—not to your best friend, not to a priest, not to God."

"Who will I meet? A man or a woman?"

"A woman. You may recognize her. Do not act surprised. She will ask if coupon J has been issued for the month. You will say, 'I have no children, I wouldn't know.' When she answers, 'Lucky you, I have three' . . . you will know it is safe. If it doesn't go exactly as I have said, leave the café as quickly as you can, as discreetly as you can. Repeat it to me."

"Coupon J. I have no children. Lucky you, I have three."

"Good. She will give you your instructions. The operation itself will begin in a few weeks."

"What happened to her? The woman who was caught?"

He flicked away the cigarette. "She died."

"What is your name?"

"My *nom de guerre* is Rafael. Someday, when this is over, I will tell you my real name." He glanced up at the house. It was a two-story brick home, built by her grandfather. A little smile attended his inspection, and he shook his head. The smile soon left. "We know of Claudio Benoit."

"I can handle him."

"I do not doubt. But he is Milice. He may as well be SS. Do not change how you act around him. If you treated him with contempt before, continue. If you treated him with respect, continue. One more thing, mademoiselle. I had a friend who served under your fiancé. Jean-Paul Dubois was a good man. He would be proud of you."

"No, he would not," she fired back.

He caught her hand and kissed it. "Yes, mademoiselle. He would." A little louder, he declared, "Such a face, such a body—wasted on the Germans!" He kissed his fingertips and tossed the kiss to the sky. "Say good-bye to a *real* man, m'selle!" He bowed low, replaced his hat, and lifted his chin in affected pride. He gave a quick wink and was gone.

MICHEL'S OFFICE at the Rousseau Cimenterie in Caen was a comfortable, paneled room that resembled a library more than an office. It was a haven for a scholar, and that was what Michel's father had been, when not running the business. On his father's end of the room, a few comfortable wingback chairs stood on an oval rug by the fireplace. There was a small table for coffee and cognac and cigarettes, a desk layered with maps and articles and magazines, and two walls of bookshelves from ceiling to floor, overflowing with books. There was a whimsical display in the corner consisting of suitcases, safari hats, maps, and a pair of binoculars, as if someone were about to travel the world. The file cabinets and desk for running the business were shunted away on the opposite end of the room, near the windows, as if his father did not want business to intrude on real business.

The older he got, the more Michel preferred his father's end of the room, even if the fireplace was always cold, even if his father's amenities of coffee, cognac, and cigarettes belonged to pre-Occupation days. Even if Father no longer sat in his favorite chair, posture correct even in repose, eyes all-knowing, a smile never far off.

At the business end of the room, Michel Rousseau, alias Greenland, received the courier with a curt nod and indicated the chair in front of his desk. He nodded at his secretary, who had shown him in, and she withdrew, closing the door. Into the telephone, he said, "Yes, Hauptmann. He is here now. I'll have him on his way shortly."

"German, please, Rousseau, when others are around," the hauptmann said. "They need to hear you speak it."

Switching to German, Michel said, "Of course. It's hard to go back and forth when you tell me you need to brush up on your French."

"How am I doing, by the way?"

"Not bad. How am *I* doing?"

"You're coming along. Better than when we first met." The hauptmann's voice softened. "It may be a hundred years before German becomes your first language, but I say for your own good you need to get used to it. I'll be honest: I prefer French. I like to speak it. But that's the way it is." More briskly, he said, "You are farther ahead than your countrymen."

"Than *our* countrymen," Michel said with a wink at the courier. Rafael knew a little German, and if he only had half of the conversation, he had enough. Rafael grinned Michel's favorite grin, the deeply amused one, the one he likely saved for the women; his brown eyes shone with conspiratorial promise.

The hauptmann laughed, but Michel's smile drained away at the German's next words. "Honestly, Rousseau, I never know what to make of you. You could be Resistance for all I know. I could be speaking to the great Greenland himself. I am told he operates in Normandy. I think he goes by 'G,' now."

Michel never knew what to say when the hauptmann
baited him like this. Never knew if he was being baited. He
hated these games.

"I certainly wouldn't call myself G," he said lightly, with a
glance at Rafael. "These people have no imagination."

Rafael's grin left him so quickly it could have been comical.
He gripped the arms of the chair.

"What would you call yourself?" the German asked.

"Oh, I don't know. Zippy."

"Surely not. Surely you would come up with something
a revolutionist would be proud of. What is the name from
Hugo?"

Michel rubbed his brows, careful to keep the weariness out
of his voice. "*Les Misérables*? Marius."

"Marius! I will call you Marius from now on."

"I would be ashamed of such a prosaic name. Zippy has
imagination. I heard an American say it once, the one you sent
from Brussels. He said, 'Braun wants this delivered and you'd
better be zippy.'"

"I'll call you Zippy." Hauptmann Braun chuckled. "Agent
Zippy."

"I'd prefer Marius."

It made the German laugh harder, and Michel knew it for
one of his robust fake laughs. Neither man liked this game
once they wandered into it.

"All right, Marius. Listen, my coffee is here, and I like it
hot and in silence, so I will leave you now."

"If the rail isn't out, I'll have André to your office by early
afternoon."

"Very good. Bonjour."

"Auf Wiedersehen." He replaced the telephone into the
cradle, resting his hand on it.

Rafael had wilted in his chair. "You are made of granite."

"It's the first time he's referred to the Resistance since he mentioned Max." Was there a reason for it?

Jean Moulin, alias Max, had died a death not so different from Jasmine's. Moulin was General Charles de Gaulle's right-hand man for the organization of the Resistance in France. He had done his best to unite the scattered groups, which had cropped up in varying degrees of well-meant but ragtag organization since Paris fell. The Gestapo had finally caught up with him. The aftershock of Moulin's death nearly a year ago still trembled throughout the underground. Once Braun had made a comment—whether offhand or not, Michel was not sure—that things could rest a little easier now that the great Max had "retired."

"Do you think he suspects you?"

Michel gave a dismissive little shrug, as if it were not even worth discussing. In truth, Braun had given him a jolt he'd not felt since the early days. But he was long used to concealing reaction, and especially from his Flame agents. "Why do you call yourself Rafael? I've always wondered."

"I thought it sounded virile." He raised his arm. "Look, I can move again. Why do you call yourself Greenland? Zippy is nice. We could call you Z. Sounds more virile than G."

"If you *ever* call me Zippy . . . ," Michel warned. Then he shrugged. "It's Greenland because I'd like to go there someday."

"That's it?"

"That's it." Michel smiled. Then he glanced at the door. It was closed all the way. Charlotte liked to keep Michel's business Michel's. "How did it go in Bénouville?"

"She's in."

It felt like a follow-up punch. Yet he nodded as if all was proceeding well. "Then the madame's intuition was correct."

"She is different." Rafael picked up his favorite paperweight from Michel's desk and tossed it hand to hand. "Not like the other whores I've known."

"Do not use that word. I detest that word. What does she look like?"

Rafael put the glass orb to his eye. He looked through it at the window. "She is determined, she is ashamed of what she does, and she is French to the core. That's what she looks like. I'd marry her if it didn't bother me where she's been."

Brigitte Durand was the key to the entire operation. She owned the brothel the bridge guards frequented, and if she said no, François's plans came to nothing. With all his heart, Michel had hoped she'd say no. Did he show himself in this?

He was tired. He felt old. A year ago, a plan like this would have intrigued him to distraction. He rose from his desk in pretense of giving a last careful inspection to the new set of designs on his desk, the designs Rafael would soon deliver to Braun.

"And the American?" he asked casually.

"He's in, too. Of course, I didn't give him details. I only asked if he was game for a little job to help out the Cause before we get him back to England. Some guys have all the luck. He doesn't know he's about to become the customer of a brothel." He inspected the office through the paperweight.

"He's *about* to impersonate a German officer." Michel riffled through the papers. Rafael examined his thumb with the paperweight, zeroing in and out.

Michel's hands stilled. It was happening too fast. Barely had François brought it up, and it was falling into place. This woman he'd never met, this young American pilot. They had no idea.

"This is ludicrous," he suddenly snapped. "She's a prostitute.

He's a pilot. They're not trained for this. They're not agents. They're not spies. We should move him down the line, get him back in the air to fight where he belongs. It's criminal what we're doing. They're babies. This whole thing—" He broke off. He'd never lost composure with Rafael before, or with any of the Flame agents.

Staring, Rafael lowered the paperweight. "This is a good risk, Monsieur Rousseau," he said, bewilderment in his voice. "The man who recruited me would not hesitate to take a good risk."

Michel went to the windows. He gazed at the courtyard below. It was a cheerless March day, still cold and gray and damp. The cobbled pavement glistened with morning chill. He wasn't strong anymore. He had been compromised through Jasmine's torture and death; he knew it as well as François. The moment a man hesitated in this business, it was time to hand operations over to someone else. Hesitation led to indecision, and indecision was not only no way to lead, it cost lives.

"I had a conversation with Braun a while back," he said quietly. "He noticed my father's copy of *Mein Kampf* on the mantel. He said in a jocular fashion, 'A little light reading, Rousseau?' And I said, 'I used to think my father was an alarmist.' My meaning was unmistakable. I spoke my first self around him, Rafael, the one I am before I am Greenland. I'd never done that."

"What did he say?"

Michel traced his fingertip through the breath on the window. "Nothing."

"I do not judge you, Monsieur Rousseau," Rafael said, in a gentle tone Michel had never heard. "We know who did it to Jasmine. I swore at her side, he will pay. But if you . . . if . . . if you . . ."

Rafael had a hard time saying it out loud, but Michel knew

what he was thinking: *If you've lost your nerve. If you can't stomach one more torture. If you've given up, if you've lost heart* . . .

It wasn't right to confide in this young man. One month ago, the Gestapo had infiltrated Michel's Resistance cell, Flame, leaving one agent dead and one sent to a concentration camp in Neuengamme. Perhaps things had gone so well for so long that dangerous pride had set in: Flame was invincible. Flame was protected because of the rightness of its cause. What should not happen could not happen—a mentality that had plunged France into a stupor from which she did not arouse until jackboots sounded on the Champs-Élysées.

Other than continuing to help other groups move downed airmen down the line in a series of safe houses to Spain, this brothel scheme was Flame's first initiative since Jasmine's death. What was left of Flame still needed leadership. Michel could not afford to speak his first self to Rafael any more than he could to Braun. Yet, from some cursed weakness, words continued to pour out.

"When I made the slip to Braun, I realized how very much it taxes the soul to go along with foolishness, when the heart longs for the simple *freedom*—" his hands made fists, and he drew them to his stomach—"to say out loud, it is foolish. We are born for truth, Rafael, we are miserable for it, and it makes a misery of us."

How he despised Hauptmann Braun, his arrogance, his conceit. He could bear it if Braun were overtly so. His superiority came through in ways that Michel recognized had once belonged to himself, the privileged son of a prosperous businessman, head above the rest, secure, confident, untouchable, and above all, correct. He could bear it, if he hated him. He hated him all the more because he liked him, the righteous, hateful man.

He became aware of the ticking clock on the mantel.

He lowered his fists, smoothing his suit coat. "Everything is all right, Rafael. We are doing good." He cast about for something else just as worthless, innocuous. "It is sometimes hard, because we do not see it."

"Listen to me, Monsieur Rousseau," Rafael said. "You told me this wasn't your idea, it was someone else's. Perhaps that someone can take over and—"

"No," Michel said sharply, half-turning from the window. "It is impossible. He is not with Flame." If a Resistance cell was infiltrated, and an agent broken, he could only tell of the people in his own six-man group. Cells could operate next to each other daily and never know it. But François belonged to no group. And Michel would not have him involved.

Everyone knew François Rousseau to be Michel's partner in the family cement business. They knew the Rousseau Cimenterie had been requisitioned by the Todt Organization to provide cement for Hitler's Atlantic Wall. They knew the brothers were no collaborators; had they been, they would have made a fortune early on by queuing up with other businesses to sell cement to the Nazis.

Rafael had known it was safe to go to François when the pilot was shot down in Cabourg because he was no collaborator. He was a businessman, and had done business across the Continent; he would know if a German was a German, or an American an American. Rafael probably figured François for many a Frenchman, just a man trying to survive this war without undue risk to keep his family safe, without undue collaboration to keep his conscience intact.

For a moment, Michel thought of the young woman on the train. Humming "La Marseillaise" was the first time in a long time he had been happy. He closed his eyes. He wanted to be back in that sacred moment, to feel as if the angel had stirred the water and he had only to fling himself in, and then all would be well, and France would be free, and . . .

She was never coming back.

She'd never burst through that door again, breathless, unwinding her scarf, throwing it on the rack as if she owned the place. She'd never—

Michel opened his eyes.

He turned from the window to his desk. He drew out his chair, his father's chair, and sat down. He looked at the mantel over the cold fireplace. Father's habit was to keep any current books of interest on the mantel, and Michel had kept it up. *Mein Kampf* lay atop a short stack. He tried to remember when it had first appeared on the mantel. Maybe '36 or '37. He wouldn't have noticed, then. While Father and his cronies worried about the rising ideology of Adolf Hitler, the new chancellor of Germany, Michel worried about catching the eye of an American model on holiday, visiting her aunt in Cabourg. Funny. He couldn't remember her name.

The day the cement works was requisitioned, in the spring of '41, had been the worst day of Michel's life.

His secretary, Charlotte, the honest and guileless woman, couldn't stop quietly weeping. Hauptmann Braun, inspecting the office, had acted as if he did not notice. Finally he said to her, "Please, madame; why don't you make us some tea. Perhaps coffee?"

Charlotte, aghast, was startled into protesting that she had no ration coupons for coffee or tea.

Roland Braun was a tall man in his forties, nice-looking and nicely dressed, the sort of decent German who seemed a trifle uneasy, or unhappy, with what his presence did to a room. He tried to make up for it with a briskness that did not seem natural to him. The heartiness waned once he relaxed.

"Not from your personal stores, madame," Braun had said patiently. "Surely your employer . . ." And he looked at Michel, who shook his head. *No,* Michel had thought bitterly, *until this moment, we have not worked for the Nazis—why should we have extra coffee and tea lying around?* And forget about sugar. Michel hadn't tasted sugar on his porridge in a year. Any sugar coupons he got, he saved for François and Marie. They had three children.

"Ah," Braun had said, with discretion worthy of a Frenchman, as understanding came. Then discretion turned to cheerful vigor worthy of a German. "Well, Monsieur Rousseau, things will change for the better around here. You will see. Soon your little cement works will expand. Soon it will make more money than you have ever dreamed."

When the hauptmann left, Michel went to his office, closed the door, and did as Charlotte had done: he wept. His only consolation that day was knowing his beloved father, who had fought the Germans at Verdun in 1916, was dead.

The next day, Michel received a package from the hauptmann. A half pound of pure, real, intoxicatingly fragrant coffee. Not an ounce of burnt, roasted barley. Charlotte wept again.

Rafael turned in his seat to see what Michel was looking at. "Do you actually read that trash?" he said, his lip curling when he saw Hitler's book.

"Know your enemy."

"What's it like?"

"Sometimes it puts me to sleep. Sometimes, because of it, I cannot sleep. It's a lot of things, Rafael. It's tedious. It's grandiose—at times, unbearably so. It is also frightening."

"How so?" Rafael said, intrigued.

"Because sometimes, on different subject matters, I agree

with him. When I do, it depresses me stupendously. I think to myself, *Did I just agree with Hitler?*" Michel gazed at the book, and a small smile came. "But all I have to do is keep reading. Before long, sometimes only a sentence or two, I am in my right mind again when I read a statement so preposterous it is actually splendid entertainment."

Rafael grinned. "I wish I could read German."

"Braun told me it was a great way to brush up on it. He thinks it's good for my soul. Now I wonder if he isn't so sure. It was a stupid mistake, Rafael, that slip to Braun—made long before Jasmine died." He looked at Rafael, whose brown eyes lowered after a moment.

There, my brave young Marius; what do you think of your leader now?

Rafael glanced at the mantel clock. "I'd better be going." He rose.

"We don't have the car today. Get as far as you can by rail, then hire a bicycle or cart if need be. Braun wants these designs by three. If approved, they'll go into production right away. Rommel needs his cement."

"Anything else going?"

"No, but you'll have a pickup for the way back. A fellow who went down over Belgium. He'll be at Clemmie's by now."

"Clemmie" ran a safe house on the outskirts of Cabourg. At any given time the aging widow, whose reputation in the local Resistance rivaled that of Jean Moulin himself, housed as many as five downed Allied airmen. Rommel's recent fortifications of the Atlantic Wall in Cabourg meant a dangerous increase in personnel—mostly conscripts for slave labor, it was true, but also more Germans to supervise them. Try and warn Clemmie about the increased danger. Once her "boys" arrived, the woman acted as if they had crossed St. Peter's gate with hell's breath on their heels and had found immutable sanctuary.

"Good. Another chance to see Jenison," Rafael said, pleased. At Michel's inquiring look, he said, "The American. It's the city he's from in Michigan. I try to visit him when I can. He's loosening up, probably because he's getting bored."

"Any news on how the war is going?"

"He says he's just a pilot; they don't tell them anything. Whatever he gets, he gets from *Stars and Stripes*, and it's old news by the time he reads it. I'm not sure he completely trusts us yet. I don't know what it is with the Americans. You don't get that from a Brit."

"Anything on the invasion?" Michel was part of a friendly pool putting odds on the date of the invasion. He'd consulted an almanac and put twenty francs down on May 8, the day of the full moon for May. Daringly, he asked Braun if he wanted in; Braun put down fifty for May 15. He said the Allies would not attack on a full moon, it was too obvious.

The German seemed to like Michel. "You're not afraid to be yourself, Rousseau," he'd once said quite earnestly, as if he were thankful he had at least one Frenchman with whom he could let down his guard a bit.

Rafael shook his head. "Nothing we don't know. Personnel and matériel buildup, supplies buildup. He said he saw a huge stack of coffins, piled in the corner of some camp in England. They're planning, all right. I wish it was now!"

"It will come, Rafael. We have to be ready when it does. How is his head?"

"Mending. Took some stitches, but there's no infection. Doctor says he's not sure he didn't crack his skull." He shrugged. "He's a big boy, and I mean big. He'll be fine."

"By the way," Michel said, pulling open his desk drawer

to avoid Rafael's eyes, "I have decided to train the American myself. Make plans with Clemmie to have him moved here in a week, if he's up for travel by then. He'll stay at my apartment."

Michel rummaged in the drawer for nothing in particular against Rafael's wordless objection. The mantel clock ticked.

"What is this?" Rafael finally demanded.

"What's what?"

He spread his arms. "Monsieur Rousseau, this is my job. Don't tell me you don't trust me. This is what I *do*. I'm good at it."

"This is what *I* do." Michel slammed the drawer shut. "This is what *I* have done for four bloody long years, before Flame even existed."

"You don't trust me?" Rafael asked, horrified. "What is this?"

"The American's best hope of getting out of this scheme alive is *me*."

"Scheme?" Rafael protested. "What do you mean, scheme? I don't understand. Monsieur Rousseau, you told me something once: Devotion to the objective will answer every detail. The bridges are the objective, and we are devoted. Wilkie and I will train the American with the same—"

"I will train him. I will let you know when we're ready to go."

Michel took a piece of tissue paper from the bottom drawer and positioned it over the designs. He rolled them up, tapped the edges for alignment, and carefully inserted them into a cardboard tube. He sealed the tube and handed it to Rafael. Rafael, his face stony, took it without a word and headed for the door.

"André." This, because Rafael had the door open and Charlotte could hear. He eased the door shut and looked back, face belligerent.

What could he offer? He owed Rafael something. Then, quietly, he said, "Jasmine was her favorite flower."

Rafael held his gaze a moment, his face softening a fraction. Then he left.

Rafael slid the tube into the leather satchel he'd left in Charlotte's office, touched his beret to her, and strode to the Caen train depot.

It was Monsieur Rousseau who had saved Rafael from the labor draft that had stolen thousands of young Frenchmen from the soil of France and sent them to Germany to work in munitions factories. Vichy, the puppet government set up by the Nazis at the time France fell, had lied; they promised the workers good wages, good living conditions. Reports began to filter back, and there was nothing good about it. People starved there just as they starved here. Far better for a Frenchman to starve on his own soil than in hated Germany.

He shook his head in grim admiration. How could Rousseau act so calm when the German officer pulled the name *G* like the pin of a grenade? So cool and suave in a moment like that, vintage Rousseau . . . yet things weren't right.

Greenland knew his agents, knew what they could do; he was a great leader in that he trusted those he led to act as they were trained. Rafael had an idea that whenever a person clamped down with more control, that person was in fear of losing it. Never before had Michel commandeered an operation the way he'd just done.

He purchased a ticket to Cabourg and swung aboard a car. He dropped into a seat, put the satchel between his feet, and settled in to stare out the window.

He loved fighting for his country in the under-the-table way he did, and wondered, at times, if he didn't love the fight more than he loved his country. Yet, he had no fear of becoming a zealot. Rousseau made him a patriot, Flame made him a resistant, and through it all he was André Besson and André Besson he would remain.

When Rafael was a fresh recruit to the Resistance, Rousseau once made him take a walk all over Caen before a training session. It took half the day. When he came back, Rousseau said that *was* the training session and sent him home. For another session, Rafael had to visit a farm, a butcher, a restaurant, a church, and a beauty salon. He had resented such exercises as frivolous.

"What did you notice about these people?" Rousseau had asked the next day.

"The usual. Suspicion. Resentment. Bitterness. Starvation."

"Is that all? What else?"

"What do you want to hear? That I found good French values worth fighting for? I didn't see any of that. I saw people as suspicious of me as I was of them. I will not be the man to die with *'Vive la France!'* on my lips."

He was irritated with Rousseau, who wore a small mysterious smile that irritated him more. He didn't want to waste time with stupid patriotic exercises. He wanted to learn about secret codes and transmitters. He wanted to blow things up.

A few months later, when escorting two crewmen from a downed B-24, a word came to his mind: *overthrow*. The things he saw the day of Rousseau's exercise—the resentment, the hunger—they came from people surprised by *overthrow*.

It set other words spinning in his mind, and one day he asked Rousseau if he could borrow a dictionary. He looked up words like *overthrow* and *conquer*. Words like *democracy*, *republic*, and *parliamentarianism*. He had a vague grasp of what they meant, but he needed to be sure. He looked up *Nazism*, but it wasn't in the book. He tried *National Socialism*, but the term was too new for the edition. He asked Monsieur Rousseau to write out the definition. Rousseau thought it through, even consulted *Mein Kampf* at one point, and wrote it down carefully. On the same piece of paper, under Rousseau's definition, Rafael copied the dictionary definitions of *democracy*, *republic*, and *parliamentarianism*.

He carried the paper around for a week. He studied the meanings, he worked them over in his mind, he set them against what his country used to be and what it was now, and what it might yet be underneath, dormant, until the aggressor was kicked out. He thought about the aggressor, about Hitler and his ideology, and what they meant to France. He came to a stunning realization.

He burst into Monsieur Rousseau's office and rushed up to his desk. "I believe!" he had cried.

Monsieur Rousseau laid down his pen. "What do you believe?"

He was trembling all over. "I believe in a republic, monsieur! I believe in democracy! But it is not so much what we fight for—we have no idea what we fight for, to each his own. It's this: I had nothing in common with the people you sent me to. This troubled me because how could we unite against Hitler?"

He paced the office. "You sent me to see what we fight for. But I needed to know what we fight against—there, Monsieur Rousseau, there we are united! Whatever our beliefs, they are incompatible with Hitler's." He felt a rush of fevered joy. "This unites us!"

Such a smile came to Rousseau's face.

The train car jerked. Smoked-over brick walls began to slide past.

He thought back to the day Wilkie, another Flame agent,

tracked Rafael to a shop in Caen to tell him Jasmine had been dumped in the street in Bénouville. The townspeople had taken the dying woman to one of the river cafés. Someone had recognized Jasmine as a worker at the Rousseau Cimenterie's Ranville plant and had summoned her employer from Caen, ten kilometers away. Rafael had arrived shortly after Michel. By then, it seemed the whole town had turned out. By then, Jasmine was dead.

He came upon the scene, stomach awash in dread, to find his employer sitting on the ground in his impeccable suit, next to the body. Rousseau's face was like nothing Rafael had ever seen. It was as a beach in December—white, cold, deserted.

The Gestapo had dumped her into the street naked. Someone had the decency to drag a tablecloth from one of the café tables and cover her with it. A small bluish foot stuck out, toenails gone, bloody crust where they had been, blackened creases between the toes. Rafael had knelt beside Rousseau, resting his hand on his shoulder, gathering courage to pull aside the tablecloth to reveal her face.

Maybe things would be different today if Rousseau had responded not with desolation but instead with what leaped in Rafael upon that first sight of her—rage. The lovely face was hardly recognizable, lumpy from contusions, mottled purple and gray, spotted with burns. Hand shaking, he drew the rest of the tablecloth aside.

Protestations erupted from the crowd at the sight of the brutalized body. Some clamped their hands over their mouths to prevent themselves from crying out. Some did cry out, in shock and in anger, some called upon God, a few rushed away to empty their stomachs. Men cursed. Women wept and pulled in children to shield their eyes.

Rafael was careful to note every violation done to the petite woman, and he spoke those violations out loud so everyone in the crowd could hear. Resting his head on the train compartment window, his eyes filmed over as images came back. He had no luxury of emotion, then. He had to be a witness, he had to be thorough, and he had to be strong for Monsieur Rousseau. He made himself open her mouth. He made himself open her eyes. He made himself inspect every inch of her body, every private place, front and back, and as he did so, he swore in his heart the deepest oath he could conjure that one day, whoever did this would pay. All the while, he reported to the crowd what he found.

"Stop it!" one woman pleaded.

Another shouted, "No! Let it be known what these animals have done!"

Someone had removed the cardboard notice strung from her neck by baling wire. In French, it said, "This is what happens to the swine Maquis." The notice had been torn in half.

A year earlier, the notice would not have been removed, the body left untouched until picked up by French police. A scalded, fearful feeling of "See what happens if you get involved? You play, you pay . . ." would have prevailed. But something was happening in France, this spring of '44. Whatever your own conscience dictated for personal conduct during the Occupation, no tolerance remained for acts like this, no matter what your political makeup. Fear of reprisal, this spring of '44, began to grow thin. Acts like this . . . incompatible with France.

After enumerating every violation, he gently rewrapped her body in the cloth, covering her face with its edge. Monsieur Rousseau hadn't moved from her side, and some whispered, "Is he her husband? Is he her lover?"

"He is her employer." Rafael straightened from his

gruesome task. "He is Monsieur Rousseau, owner of the Rousseau Cimenterie."

A hush swept the crowd. Some Bénouville residents worked at the factory in Ranville, some in Caen. One thin middle-aged man came forward and helped Rousseau to his feet. Another came and put his arm about Rousseau, murmuring softly. He said something about serving with his noble father at Verdun. A woman came and touched his arm, weeping. "God bless you, monsieur. God bless you for my son."

"They think to manage us with such monstrous acts?" one bespectacled young man in the crowd shouted. He leaped to a café tabletop. "Does this exalt their cause? It only proves why we should resist!"

They looked for German reaction, but the Germans were curiously absent. The only soldiers on duty at the bridge that day were conscripts, soldiers forced into service from conquered countries: an Austrian, a Ukrainian, two Poles, a Czech—few would know their nationalities, but Flame knew. They looked upon the scene with interest from their posts, but did not leave them. Rafael wondered if the Gestapo was watching for reactions close by, writing down names. He wondered about collaborators in the crowd, for surely they were there. He already feared for the brave and foolhardy man on the tabletop.

"What was her name?" he called down to Michel. "We will remember this, Monsieur Rousseau! We will remember her! Tell us her name!"

Rafael quickly glanced at Rousseau. His face was utterly desolate; he was not really there. This loss of composure meant he could blurt out her *nom de guerre*—and more than ever, Rafael was convinced the Gestapo was watching. All Rousseau had to say was "Jasmine," and they would know him for Flame.

Before Rousseau opened his mouth, Rafael quickly called

out the first name that came to him: "Marianne! I think her name was Marianne. She worked at the Cimenterie."

"Marianne!" the young man shouted, raising his fist in the air. "Her name was Marianne!"

The crowd tentatively picked up the name, and soon it rolled and reverberated. Some murmured the name with tears coursing down their cheeks, some crossing themselves. Little children chanted it, glancing up at the adults. Then the French police came, along with toughs who were surely Milice. Yet the people did not disperse as they would have a year ago. They stood firm, chanting the name, and all the while, not a single German soldier to be seen.

"Marianne! Marianne!"

The young man jumped down from the table and knelt beside Jasmine's body. He laid his hand over her cloth-covered head as if in blessing, in benediction. His lips moved, and then he said aloud, tears in his eyes, "We will remember you, Marianne."

Days later Rafael realized the name he had instinctively blurted was the name of the national identity of France, a persona that stood for the republic. Michel Rousseau had been Marianne to him—invincible, proud, irreconcilable to the evil surrounding him.

Rafael sat upright.

"He blames himself for her death," he whispered, dumbstruck. Why hadn't it been obvious? It was the only reason Rousseau would insist on training the American himself.

Rousseau stood at that window, looking down on the courtyard below, and spoke things Rafael had not known. He didn't know how hard it was to tolerate Braun. He didn't know how hard it was to keep his first self separate. It was the unfolding of a man, and he suddenly had an eerie feeling Monsieur Rousseau didn't have much time left.

Much time before what? Before he truly slipped to Braun? Or before someone else in Flame was captured and tortured and revealed the identity of G? All he knew as he listened to Rousseau was that he wanted him to stop. Such honesty would surely attract evil. Framed in that window was a man as suddenly vulnerable as if he'd stepped in front of one of Rommel's panzers. He was a good man, for all the cunning that made him Greenland, and this goodness seemed to beckon evil, perhaps as France had beckoned Hitler. France, naïve in her apple-blossom freedom, flaunting any danger from the East; Hitler, rising all the while like a black lecherous beast.

Framed in that window was an innocent man, unaware of and made very small by the lecherous looming black. At one point Rousseau hummed a few bars of "La Marseillaise," an eerie, skin-raising counterpoint to the darkness.

Rafael pounded his knee. Why didn't he think to remind Rousseau how dangerous it was to hide anyone at his apartment? It was safe in the early days—until the Gestapo moved into the courthouse two blocks over. He'd been so shocked at Rousseau's commandeering the mission he couldn't think straight.

Rousseau had always been cheerful in the face of Braun's arrogance. He'd always moved apart from the oppression of the Occupation. He'd always diminished Rafael's fears with constant encouragement of the imminent Allied invasion. Now he seemed to think and act out of that which surrounded him. Darkness had finally infiltrated the great Greenland.

Rafael's throat tightened, and he felt tears rise. *Let not the darkness consume you. You were never meant for chains, not you, my friend. You have shown me France.*

He watched the landscape slip by. And then another new thought about Rousseau presented itself.

Monsieur Rousseau had been in love with Jasmine.

"No," he whispered in disbelief. Yet all at once, everything made sense.

The way he sat, forsaken, at her side. The way he began to act around her before her capture, stiff and awkward. Rafael had thought it was because Jasmine kept flashing little signals that *she* was in love with *him*, which was no secret to anyone; he thought the awkwardness meant Rousseau was trying to let her down gently, trying to maintain professionalism. Rousseau was not only Jasmine's boss at the Cimenterie, but her commanding officer in the Resistance. Rafael was sure he was too busy for love, too caught up in the affairs of the Cimenterie and the Occupation and the Resistance, too uptight. Could it really be that old Rousseau, who had to be at least forty, had fallen in love?

Then Jasmine's death *had* compromised him. Until now, he'd never commandeered an operation. When a person clamped down with more control, that person was in fear of losing it—and if Rousseau feared losing control, then Flame should fear losing Rousseau.

Could they get him to leave the country, convince him he could be of great use to the Resistance directly under de Gaulle? When Gestapo infiltration licked hot as hell's flames, some agents left the country for London. Yet even as he thought it, Rafael's heart sank. Rousseau would never leave the cement works. He sheltered too many conscription dodgers, forced labor dodgers. Communists, Jews, resistants. He'd never abandon any whom his influence might save. It was no great wonder why Jasmine had fallen for Rousseau.

We will remember you, Marianne.

But who would remember Rousseau?

Who would remember the one who had shown him France?

5

"WHERE ARE YOU GOING?" Colette said from the kitchen, when she saw Brigitte take her coat from the peg near the back door. Colette leaned against the kitchen counter, smoking a cigarette. Brigitte had her alibi ready. She dug into her pocket and produced a brass button.

"I need a match for this. I'll also check and see if there is meat."

Marie-Josette staggered from the bathroom, one hand clamped over her eye. "You're going to La Broderie? Get me some lace, will you? Battenberg. Enough to finish my pillow."

"What happened to you?" Brigitte asked.

Marie-Josette removed her hand to reveal a red and swollen eye. "I used the ear drops instead of the eyedrops."

Brigitte clicked her tongue in sympathy. "Too bad. At least you won't get an earache in your eye. If they don't have the lace . . . ?"

"Tell them I'll spend my money in Caen if they can't stock decent lace." She went off to fetch her purse.

"As if they care about *your* money," Colette called after her.

"Shut up, Colette," Brigitte said automatically. "How much is the Battenberg?"

Marie-Josette came back from her bedroom, rummaging in the purse. "Cheaper than a kilo of potatoes." She examined several coins in her hand with the good eye. She counted some out, frowned, and then threw in another and handed the money to Brigitte. "If you can't get it for that, spit on them and leave."

"If they don't spit on you first," Colette said with an amused little smile, putting the cigarette to her lips.

"Oh, shut up, Colette," Brigitte said. "The doctor will be here at four. I should be back by then if there is no hope for the meat." The doctor came from Ranville every Friday. The doctor in Bénouville had refused.

"Where is the money for him?" Colette said.

"Perhaps he will barter," Marie-Josette quipped. When Brigitte rolled a look at her, she shrugged. "He smells nice. Better than a soldier."

"I'll pay him when I get back. You should have him look at your eye. Wake Simone before too long. It's her day to go to the farms. I'll leave the bicycle for her. Remind her of the farm near Ouistreham. I got a few apples last time." Shriveled, waxy apples to be sure, at the price of tinned goose liver, but it was food. Marie-Josette made what passed for a tart that day, minus the butter, eggs, cream, and Calvados. An Occupation tart. It was a testament to the times that it actually tasted good. It was another testament to the times that they even ate the waxy apple peels.

"You can't get that far anymore," Colette said importantly. She held the cigarette with the feminine grace of a Parisian coquette. Of the four girls, Colette was easily the prettiest. Hazel eyes, sandy-brown tousled curls, and a silky cream complexion. Smoke curled delicately from her nostrils. "Too close to the beaches. Claudio said the area is now restricted." How could she manage to say it with satisfaction in her voice, with some sort of silly triumph; did it not affect her too?

"What about the residents?"

"They're kicking them out." Again, the little ring of triumph.

Brigitte had learned not to show anger over this sick little game; it only gave Colette some perverse satisfaction. Sometimes Colette was so past figuring out that Brigitte didn't know whether to treat her kindly or slap her silly.

"I miss the ocean," Marie-Josette sighed. "To think it's only a few kilometers away. May as well be Paris."

"I miss the chance to lay my eyes on a free country," Brigitte said.

The English Channel separated a country held in a Nazi vise from a country clinging to freedom. Last summer they could still go to the lovely beaches on the Normandy coast. They could gaze with envy at the distant contours of Europe's last holdout, still free, still fiercely hanging on. Just looking at England managed to inspire hope. Some went to the coast to forget the war for a bit and find comfort in the ocean's immensity; Brigitte went to find comfort in England. She sometimes whispered strength to it, and sometimes whispered pleas. Once a strong gust of wind blew south from England; she closed her eyes and filled up on the wind, because it came from freedom.

Strange to think Berlin was farther away than Portsmouth. Yet all of France strained at Berlin's leash, choking on it.

"Remind Simone to keep a lookout for firewood," Brigitte said. Anywhere they went, they looked for dry sticks for fuel. The country was combed clean, but sometimes they got lucky. Coal coupons were useless. There hadn't been a chunk of coal in Bénouville for months. "Back by four, at the latest."

❧❧

Brigitte knew she'd left far too early, but she was too excited to wait any longer. Her life was about to change in ways she could not begin to imagine. She'd heard of the things the Resistance did; she'd seen them. The Milice had the contempt of the French people, while the Resistance had their respect. A wary respect, she allowed, but respect nonetheless. Acts such as blowing up railroad ties to disrupt enemy transport of troops or fuel or weapons might be publicly condemned, but in whispers they were celebrated. To think she was about to—No! And she laughed out loud; she had *already* joined the Resistance! She was already part of the great underground movement to free her country.

She strolled up the avenue, light on her feet, positively inflated with all the things she imagined she could do in the Resistance, and she could do a lot. She could make a place to hide an Ally in the shed—she clapped her hand over her mouth to stifle a giddy laugh. Right under German noses! There was an empty coal bin in the back of the shed, too filthy to use for storing anything but coal; it was as large as the modern bathroom Grandfather had put in the house in '38. It was certainly large enough to hide an Ally.

She could type. Perhaps they would assign her to one of the underground newspapers—*Combat*, or *Libération*, or *Les Sept Fois*. She was good at organizing. She was good at economizing. She wished she knew more about the operations of the Resistance to play with them in her mind. Perhaps she would write about it someday; perhaps she could document the struggle against Germany. What if they assigned her to the Maquis? She thought of the Maquis as sort of the military arm of the Resistance, but she wasn't afraid to learn to use a weapon. In fact, the thought rather thrilled her. Did the Maquis allow women to bear arms? Why not? A woman could die for her country as easily as a man. Wasn't that what she committed to when she joined?

Such a clarifying thought.

Soon she came to the crossroads, but instead of turning right at the Mairie, Bénouville's house of government, which now housed German soldiers, she continued on. She had plenty of time to make believe she was on a stroll to Ouistreham to visit the sea.

The beautiful old church in the tiny village of Le Port, not a kilometer down the road from the Mairie, was the church Grandfather took her to when she was small. Mother was buried in the church graveyard. She had not visited Mother's grave since she'd arrived, more than a year ago. Well, she had no real compunction to. It wasn't Mother she remembered. But Grandfather's grave was there.

Brigitte's mother died of tuberculosis when she was three or four. She'd never known her father. He ran off before she was born. Grandfather raised her by himself, with the help of his sister when a woman's influence was needed. That wasn't very often; Grandfather was a quiet, intuitive man, who had already raised Brigitte's mother after his wife died giving birth to a son, who died at the same time.

She strolled slowly past the gated graveyard, trailing her fingers on the chipped black paint of the iron bars. She could not yet visit his grave.

She passed the entrance to the church, then paused at the bell tower, a tall structure on the left of the church building. The bell had not rung since she had been in Bénouville. The new German government forbade it.

"A pity, is it not?" came a kindly voice at her side.

It was the priest, Father Eppinette. He would not remember her, but she remembered him. He was a small man, eye level with Brigitte. The hair under the fedora now had more salt than pepper. The eyes behind the filmy glasses were kind, if a trifle preoccupied. Hands clasped behind his back, he gazed at the bell tower.

"I have not heard it since June of 1940," he murmured. "How I miss that sound. I miss ringing it. Always made me feel like a little boy." He smiled sadly, then looked at her. "May I be of service, mademoiselle?"

"Oh, no, Father," she said. "I am on my way to meet someone." She looked at the church. "I haven't been here since I was a girl."

"You are Thierry Durand's granddaughter," he said in sudden recognition. "You seemed familiar."

If, in realizing who she was, he made the connection to her profession—and surely he must know—his face never let on. Instead, preoccupation left and he smiled.

"It is good to see you again. Come to church sometime, will you? It will do an old man good to see a Durand in the pew again."

"Is there a place for one like me?" she asked before she could stop it, and could not keep the challenge from her voice.

Brown eyes crinkled. "Mademoiselle, if there is not a place for you, there is not a place for any of us."

"I don't know if I believe that."

"Hmm." He gave a tiny shrug. "Perhaps you should find out."

Brigitte frowned, studying him. Maybe the old man was a little thick. "You know what I am, yes?" Early on, when she had moved back from Paris, the women of the village had let her know just where Brigitte's kind stood. "You know what I—"

"I know." His face remained amiably benign.

"You're saying you'd let my sort just sally on in and have a seat. Without confession."

And still, his face remained benign. There was a challenge of his own in that benignity, as if he dared her to come and find something other than what she expected. Something hopeful.

Fortunately, she had no time for this. She had to get to La Broderie before her appointment. She looked at her wristwatch. "I must go."

"Good-bye, my dear," he said, and he touched his hat while giving a courtly little bow. "Do come and see us sometime."

Us? What did he mean, *us?* Him and the congregation? Him and the two people buried nearby? Him and God?

"Coffee, please, with milk."

"Apologies, mademoiselle. No coffee. No milk. Not this week." The waiter smiled sadly.

"Oh. Well, tea, then. With sugar, if you have it."

"We have sugar—if you produce coupon number 46b. We will, of course, make sure you receive every gram coming to you."

He wasn't kidding. But she'd put that coupon under a rock on the steps of the Allied chapel last week. "What if I produce francs?"

The waiter smiled. "We still take francs, m'selle. Anything else?"

Brigitte shook her head, watched him go. He was nice to her. He obviously didn't know her occupation.

The café was certainly busier than she remembered, because of the garrison at the bridges. Five German soldiers were in this café alone, probably more at the café across the street. She didn't often visit the cafés. When she came to Bénouville in October of '42 to set up business in the old family home, she made a choice not to mix with locals. She went to Caen for her shopping or if she had a spare franc for a café—a ridiculous extravagance that reminded her of Paris, and Paris she wanted to leave behind. She was in Paris on the day France fell, June 14, 1940. Jean-Paul told her to meet him there after they'd thrown back the Germans. He never came. Brigitte knew he was dead long before she saw his name on the list.

She glanced around the café and felt a small wistful pang. She wouldn't have minded waiting tables. In Paris, she'd worked tables before she found a good job at the American embassy. But after France fell, the embassy was gone. She had no job, with none to be found. After sleeping twice with the bridge soldier, Brigitte ran into someone she hadn't seen in months: Colette LaPonsie, her friend who had worked at the flower store not far from the embassy. Brigitte knew the flower store had closed. She asked Colette how she was getting by. Colette took Brigitte home, to a place where she lived with several others, including a girl named Simone. Brigitte learned that what Colette was doing to survive was no different than what Brigitte had done. It was simply . . . organized.

Brigitte rubbed her gloved hands together. Every customer in the café wore his or her coat. It was some satisfaction to know the two soldiers, seated just a few tables over, were as cold as she.

She couldn't stop a smile. She was about to make contact with the Resistance—with soldiers of the Reich in spitting distance! And she knew one of them! She had to calm herself. She had to be discreet. Her blood alternately froze and jumped and ran, since the very moment she left the—No. She would not name her home a brothel.

Grandfather had died in May 1940, one month before France fell to Germany. He never saw a day of occupation. And he never could have conceived what his granddaughter would do to his home.

She casually checked out the soldiers. The one she knew had glanced over but hadn't recognized her yet. He probably never expected to see her in daylight. His name was Alex Tisknikt, from Austria. He was a groom before his country fell to the Reich. Now he guarded the Caen Canal Bridge. He was nice, one of the few who came for companionship as much as for sex.

She glanced at her watch. Five minutes past two. Rafael said two; he said things had to go exactly so. What if someone came at two thirty, with exactly the passwords but not at the right time?

The waiter arrived with hot tea. She tugged off her gloves and put her hands around the small porcelain teapot. *Blessed* warmth. "I wish I could crawl inside," she answered his amused smile as he placed a teacup and spoon in front of her.

"Are you from around here, mademoiselle?" he asked.

Her smile faltered. Just then, the soldier noticed her.

"Brigitte!" he called in surprise, a big gap-toothed grin on his wide lumpy face. "Why you are here? I bet you are not used to daylight, *ja*?" He meant no harm, and thought she'd share his amusement, like she did at her home. "Hey, you try the soup! The soup is good."

So much for discreet. She gave him a little smile, then slipped a glance at the waiter. Whatever conclusions he came to, he kept to himself.

"The soup *is* good, m'selle." His tone was in quiet and arch contrast to the soldier's. He seemed to care far less what the soldier said than how he said it. "Would you like some?"

She shook her head. He nodded and left.

"Foreigners," came a disgusted voice at her side. It was the woman who had waited on her at La Broderie, not ten minutes earlier. Rather—it was the woman who would *not* wait on her. She clutched a Bible and a folded newspaper, glared at the soldiers. "Loud, uncouth barbarians."

Brigitte had asked about the Battenberg lace. But the woman had paused, then folded her arms and said loud enough for the other three customers to hear, "You're the whore. You're the head whore, if I'm not mistaken. Well, I knew Thierry Durand, and he would die of shame if he knew how his granddaughter used his home. No, I'm sorry; you are not welcome here. I protest your presence, in honor of your grandfather." She nodded at the notice in the window: Jews Not Served Here. "I'll add the word *sluts*. You think you're so smart, living better than the rest of us." She chuckled. "You'll get yours after the war."

And Brigitte spit in the woman's face.

It caused a bit of a commotion.

She was hustled to the door by two very angry customers, while another rushed over to the woman, producing a handkerchief. But the woman showed no anger. She only laughed at Brigitte as she left.

A horrid thought came.

No. Please, God. Not her.

She was a beauty just past her prime, with bright-blue eyes and perfectly applied makeup, not too much, not too little. She wore a stylish, immaculately fitted coat as suited the proprietress of a fabric shop. She wore navy pumps, not a nick on them, and, Brigitte could tell, real silk stockings. She stood next to Brigitte's table with her haughty glare fastened on the soldiers and, without looking away from them, smacked her Bible on the table.

"I've decided to convert you. It's the only decent thing to do." She sat across from Brigitte, set down her purse, and began to page through the newspaper.

Brigitte looked at the Bible. It had a lavender leather cover with a gold gilt edge and a gold clasp. Who would have a lavender Bible? Brigitte met this intrusion with a mix of repugnance and relief. She could *not*—

"I can't tell if coupon J has been issued for the month." She paged through the newspaper. "They never put the coupon news in the same spot."

It couldn't be.

Brigitte worked up the words. "I wouldn't know. I don't have children. I'm a slut, you know, not a mother."

"Some are both. But lucky you—I have three. Not easy to feed three huge boys these days. They eat all the time." She scanned columns of print. "They *want* to eat all the time. The war is a pity. I love to cook." The bright-blue eyes stopped and finally looked up at Brigitte. She folded the newspaper and laid it aside, then took the Bible and placed it on top.

"I just spit on you."

"That's why I'm late. I had to redo my makeup."

The waiter arrived with a warm greeting for the woman. "So good to see you, Madame Bouvier. How is your mother?"

"She could not be crazier, Guillemot. Gets worse every day. I love her this way. She's very amusing, and no longer mean."

The way the waiter was smiling, he had a great deal of affection for this Jew-hating, slut-hating woman.

Madame Bouvier eyed him. "You heard what she did the other day?" By his look he had, but he said nothing to encourage her to recount it. "We were at the café across the street.

Right in the middle of our luncheon, she unbuttons her dress. She pulls it apart, looks down at her breasts, and says quite earnestly, 'Do these match?'"

It was the punch line he'd waited for, and he put his head back and laughed. Brigitte was not over the sting of the whole impossible situation to be amused by anything. But this reserved waiter, laughing so freely, made her stare.

Madame's lips twitched. "Imagine my shock. I wasn't sure what to be more upset about, that she'd exposed herself in public or that her brassiere was on backward." The waiter erupted in a fresh wave of hilarity. He had a high-pitched laugh. "I'd been after her about that, Guillemot. She does it on purpose, this backward brassiere nonsense. She has developed a fascinated concern for her breasts. It is disconcerting."

He covered his face with his hand, shoulders shaking with laughter. A few customers looked over, bemused smiles twitching. Finally, composing himself, he managed to say, "Oh, I'd heard it, of course, but knew you would tell it better." He wiped his eyes.

"What a wretch she used to be. If only she knew the things she did now. It's a small revenge. Yes," she said abruptly, "to the matter at hand: I'll take coffee if you have it, tea if you don't, and a bowl of your magnificent soup but only if Adèle made it."

"She did. Right away, madame." He bowed, a smile lingering on his face, and left for the kitchen.

"Adèle is the only one who salts it correctly." She folded her hands. "Now. That was an unpleasant business at my shop. I could not believe it—there you were, when we were supposed to meet in a quarter of an hour. I had no idea what was going on. I improvised, and it has turned to betterment. It created perfect pretense." She patted the Bible affectionately. "When you left, I declared to my customers—one of whom is the wife of the mayor—'What was I thinking? A perfect chance to convert that wicked woman, and pfft—I blew it. What would Father Chaillet say?'

"Well, of course they consoled me, and I brooded, then announced, 'Father Chaillet would have me do my Christian duty. I will go to that house of sin and disease, and I will *remonstrate.*' 'Remonstrate, madame!' cried they, and mousy little Cherise Baton suddenly squeaked from the window, 'But, madame! She did not *go* to the house of sin! She went to the *café*! Whatever will you *do*?' I lifted my chin—" here, Madame Bouvier lifted her chin, and resolution flashed in her eyes—"and said to them, 'As she goes, so goes my duty!' I marched to the back, got my coat and Bible, and strode to the door, shoulders like so. I looked at each in turn, said not a word . . . just raised the Bible, and nodded—like so." She demonstrated. Her expression could not have been more regal. She could have been a figurehead on a mighty ship. Brigitte could not help an absurd flash of admiration. "Cherise opened the door, and out I swept. I stopped and turned once; they were on the doorstep, clutching each other. Cherise was weeping."

Brigitte sipped her tea. "And do you plan to convert me?"

"Heavens, no. I wouldn't know how to go about it properly. The bit about Father Chaillet was inspired. They all know he changed my life. I made it no secret when I came back from Lyon, the summer of '42." She smiled at Guillemot when he delivered the tea. Her eyes followed his retreat to the kitchen.

She lifted the pot lid, gave a single sniff as if that alone determined the perfect brew strength, replaced the lid, and waited a few seconds. Then she poured the tea and stirred in sugar, the teaspoon making a gentle clink on the cup. "We now have a splendid alibi to meet."

"You needed an alibi to meet with me?"

Madame Bouvier looked at her as if she'd said something utterly preposterous. "Of course. You're a prostitute."

Brigitte lifted her cup and took a deliberate sip. The woman's manner was intolerable.

"Spare me your sensibilities and think logically, my little *chou-chou*—why should a self-respecting patriot such as myself have tea with a woman who sleeps with Germans?"

Brigitte set down her cup a bit harder than intended.

"Not only that, you do it for money. Bad enough for good, honest Frenchwomen to consort with the enemy and let traitorous little romances develop; you get paid for it. You also consort with Milice, who have sold out their country. It makes you just as bad as they. You do not deserve to be called French."

Brigitte thought of the sign in the woman's storefront, and shook her head.

"What is that look?"

"So you're a good French citizen? What's that sign in your window? Not that you have any worries; there's not a single Jew around anymore. I used to have plenty of Jewish friends in Paris, just as *French* as you and I, and if . . ." But she trailed off, for a distracting change had passed over the face of Madame Bouvier.

The blue eyes blinked, the nostrils flared, and she slightly withdrew from her aggressive bearing, as if momentarily confused. Her hands went into her lap. Then she composed herself so smoothly, reaching for the teapot and refreshing her cup, her face all implacable serenity once more, that Brigitte wondered if she'd gotten it wrong. Madame Bouvier stirred in a spoonful of sugar and sipped her tea.

The strange little spell broken, Brigitte took the sugar bowl and added a spoonful to her own cup. Regardless if there wasn't

much sugar in the bowl, a preservation instinct made her want
to sweeten the tea far more than she liked.

"Guillemot is resourceful," Madame said, eyeing the sugar
bowl. "He works for next to nothing. They cannot afford
him. This is Bénouville, after all." She glanced about discreetly to make sure no one overheard, then said very quietly,
"Guillemot Picard is a Jew. I brought him back with me from
Lyon, after—" She touched her fingertips to the curl behind
her ear.

After what? So something *had* rattled the battle-axe.

Guillemot arrived with Madame Bouvier's soup. He waited
until she tasted it.

She sipped. She savored. She nodded. "Perfection. Adèle is
a genius. Tell her she has made my day brighter."

Guillemot beamed, inclined his head, and immediately
went to the kitchen.

"Tell me, Brigitte," she said after a few spoonfuls of soup.
"Before we start with your . . . conversion . . . why do you want
to convert? You have a lot to lose."

But Brigitte was still trying to work out a woman who
hung a Jew-hating sign in her window with one who took one
home from Lyon.

She brought her mind to the question. "I have nothing to
lose." She shrugged. "I already lost everything at the Maginot
Line."

"Do you care anything at all for the women at your home?"

Brigitte thought of Colette. She forced her mind to Marie-
Josette and Simone, but it came back to Colette, who deserved
no such attention.

"Yes. Of course."

"Then keep them in mind. They will suffer if you slip up.
Anyone you care for will suffer. And then you will suffer the

most. Wear that on the front of your head, as the Jews do the little boxes."

"Yes, yes, I understand. Rafael told me." Couldn't they get on with it? "Torture, that sort of thing. What is my job? When do I start?"

Madame Bouvier froze with the spoon halfway to her mouth. She set it down. She folded her napkin with precise movements, placed it on the table, and then brought to bear upon Brigitte eyes blazing blue-white fire. Her tone was low, thick with anger. "Listen to me: you may have small regard for your life, but I value mine. Under torture you could name me, and everything we have labored to build will be gone in an instant. Any chance we small pockets had to help win this war—pfft, wasted. You new recruits are a bunch of adolescents. You who have 'nothing to lose' are a trial to me."

What could this vile woman know? Angry tears came, and she hated herself for them.

"We have all lost someone," the madame said coldly. "And we have all lost dignity. We'll grieve later. There is no time now, there is too much to be done." Some of the eye fire eased. She lightly touched fingertips to styled curls, then pushed aside the soup and pulled the Bible over. She undid the clasp, paged through the book, found what she was looking for, and turned it around and pushed it to Brigitte.

"Your conversion begins. Read while I speak, and listen."

"Read what?"

"Anything. Move your eyes along as if they *are* reading. Never forget you are being watched, as am I, every time you step out the door." She opened her purse and took out a slip of paper. She pushed it across the table. "Here is a list of Bible verses."

"For what?"

"If anyone asks, this is what we talked about. You are considering conversion. I am your spiritual guide."

Brigitte snorted. The woman hated Jews and whores. Some guide. Then she thought of Guillemot.

"You are weary of your wicked ways, you are in deep sorrow over the death of your fiancé, and you seek comfort. You'd heard of my famous conversion through the intervention of Father Chaillet, and you are willing to listen. What is that face? Are you going to be serious or not? Did Madame Vion have it wrong?"

"Do you serve the waiter at your store?" Brigitte ran her eyes over the lines of print on the slip of paper.

"He doesn't come in."

"You brought him back from Lyon. What's that about?"

She glanced up when the madame did not answer, and saw again the falter in her demeanor. In the beautiful blue eyes, cold and high like an unforgiving fortress, she caught again the fluctuation to something . . . remorseful. Brigitte knew guilt when she saw it, but this was far more. It was made of the stuff that could unravel a person, should she let it. It provoked an instinctive, unwanted sympathy. But before she could respond in any way, two things happened: the look again frosted over, and Brigitte caught sight of the soldier beyond Madame Bouvier.

The Austrian conscript was staring at Brigitte in alarm. He gazed in an alternating triangle from the madame, to the Bible, to Brigitte. She pressed her fingers to her lips to hide a smile.

"What's so funny?"

"The soldier is afraid I'll convert." Then her smile vanished completely. "Here he comes. What do I do?"

"Act naturally, of course. Always act naturally. Always be yourself. It is your best safety."

Private Tisknikt came and stood next to the table, his hat in his feverishly working hands. "*Hallo*, Brigitte." He nodded at Madame Bouvier nervously. To Brigitte, he said, "Say—what are you reading?"

"The Bible."

"*Ja.* That is what I thought. Why?"

"Am I the sort of woman you would take home to Mother?" she asked.

"*Gott im Himmel*, no. She would kill me." His face colored. "I mean—look: maybe you read when war is over?"

"I protest," Madame Bouvier said in grand disdain.

Brigitte winked at him, then beckoned with a curled finger. She whispered in his ear behind her hand, "Let's make the old bat think she's doing some good. It's the generous thing to do. I'll see you tonight."

Ease came back to his honest face, and he smiled broadly. To the madame, he said, "The soup is good, *ja?*" He bowed to both of them and left. The other soldier got up, and they left for duty. Brigitte watched them go, then glanced out the window to follow them to their posts at the bridge. The one she did not know relieved a sentry at the bridgehead. Private Tisknikt walked across the bridge to the pillbox on the other side.

"Get to know it. That is your mission."

She looked from the bridge to Madame Bouvier. "What do you mean?"

"Your job is to get any information you can about the Caen Canal Bridge out of your bridge-duty customers."

All the anticipation for this meeting, the imagined derring-do . . . an Ally in the coal bin, a typewriter, the thought of placing an explosive on a railroad track . . . of Jean-Paul finally looking her in the face, as he refused to in her dreams . . . it deflated around her like punched-down dough.

"Then I'm not leaving Bénouville."

"Why should you?"

I thought I had a different fate.

"Keep doing what you do best. It's what we all do. Who would have thought *your* particular talents would be needed by the Resistance, eh?" she said, with a look that reminded Brigitte of Colette.

What a fool she had been. She was nothing but a prostitute. Why should they handpick her for anything else? She could feel Colette laugh.

"Courage, my little *chou-chou*. Look on the bright side: now you're doing it for your country." She took out a compact to freshen her lipstick. In that moment, Brigitte knew she despised another person as much as she despised Colette.

Why did the people she hate fascinate her most?

"You will pass on any information you get to an American pilot, who will pose as a German soldier. I hear he looks like the son of Hitler's dreams." She eyed the rest of her makeup, then snapped the compact shut and replaced it in her purse. "He will become your best customer."

"An American," she said contemptuously. "Of course it would be an American." This was getting better and better.

A delicate eyebrow rose. "Do you think the Allies you feed are only British?"

"If America had acted sooner, we wouldn't be in this mess."

So much for the land of the free and the home of the brave. They had cared only for their own freedom, not the freedom of an oppressed and brutalized nation.

If America had acted sooner, Jean-Paul would be alive.

The base of her throat seemed to close, but she refused tears. What had she gotten herself into? Why did she say yes to that Rafael?

Madame Bouvier shrugged. "Who's to say? So many ifs. We deal with things as they are, not as they should be." Her face softened. She looked at Brigitte with interest. "Why do you do it?"

"I don't have to answer that," Brigitte said acidly. She took a sip of cold tea.

"I'm not talking about that. One year ago, Madame Vion from the château told me of a mysterious young woman who would sneak in and stroll the grounds as if they were her own. Every time, she left something on the steps of the chapel for the Allies. From a grateful patriot."

Brigitte's first feeling was mild alarm. All that time, she had been watched.

With less rancor, she said, "I don't have to answer that either." She looked out the window at the bridge. She was no good with measurements. How long did the thing measure across? "What kind of information do they want?"

"Anything. Everything. The Allies need intelligence on all bridges close to the coast. They'll need to know if the Germans rigged this one with explosives in case of attack; they'll need to know how it is guarded; they'll need to know when there are changes, if personnel increases or decreases, if there are any defensive changes around the bridgeheads. Any scrap you can get out of your bridge customers, even if you think it is useless. And they need the information now."

"The invasion is really coming . . ." A tiny flutter of hope rustled. One hardly dared hope for something that monumental, something that frightening, something with freedom attached.

"It's just a matter of when. Any information the Resistance can provide on coastal defenses will save lives. It already has."

Brigitte studied the bridge. It was an odd-looking contraption, a hulking swing bridge that lowered a huge counterweight on the east side to lever the entire bridge straight up in the air for boat passage. Must have been the talk of the town, all neighboring towns, when the thing was put in. "When do I meet the American?"

"His training should start any time, but he's still healing from a head injury. He was shot down near Cabourg. He is another reason you were chosen for this—you speak English."

Bitterness rose. What a day. She couldn't believe her lot. Not only did her Resistance involvement fall far short of her imaginings, but she had to work with an American. An American was only one step removed from a Milice, in her opinion, a Milice being one step removed from a Nazi. The Milice were nothing but French Gestapo. They had the spirit of Colette, some weird anti-French streak, some weird, jeering collaboration of bullies allied with bigger bullies. And the Americans . . . well, they didn't seem to care about bullies.

"How do you know I speak English?"

"You worked at the American embassy in Paris. You were a file clerk, but because you knew English, you were brought in occasionally to help translate, especially in '39 when things got busy and smart Jews were leaving the country. You had a great deal of respect for Ambassador Bullitt."

Respect. You could call it that. It was more of a crush, until she met Jean-Paul. "He was the only American who knew what was going on."

Had Roosevelt only listened to Bullitt's warnings of the rise of Nazi power, of the terrible things that were happening in Germany to the Jews . . . It was Bullitt who raised the alarm when Jews who had fled Germany brought him their accounts of persecution. While others chose not to believe the incredible accounts, or chose to look away, Ambassador William Bullitt listened, and did his best to act.

But Hitler rose, and countries fell in his rising. When the Netherlands fell—just one day after Hitler told them they had no worries of invasion, out of respect for their neutrality during the Great War—then the German army marched on France. The French government fled to Bordeaux, leaving behind what could barely be called a provisional government; and so it was that the lone man in charge of Paris the day France fell was an American, Ambassador William C. Bullitt.

"He did not leave his post," Brigitte murmured. Her tone gained strength. "Why didn't Roosevelt listen? What is an ambassador for?"

"You were in Paris the day France fell. What was it like?"

It was the sort of question a true Frenchman would ask. Paris connected every French citizen, no matter if the citizen had ever been to Paris, no matter his or her station in life—rich or poor, prostitute or shop owner, Paris belonged to every citizen of France.

Not many asked because not many knew she had been there. So many friends were gone. Her Jewish friends, to God knew where. Most of the people she had worked with at the embassy had left the country. She had no one to talk to about Paris, no one who would understand . . . except for Alex Tisknikt, the conscript from Austria. He told her what it felt like the day Vienna fell.

She put her hands around her now-cool teacup. "You walked around in a nightmare, and you didn't wake up. She was dying. She was empty. You cannot imagine Paris empty, but she was, not only of people but of her soul. You could *feel* the absence. The distant fighting you heard was frightening, it was surreal, but it was nothing compared to the emptiness. Someone had slit her veins, and her life drained out."

Tens of thousands had fled when news came that the Reich

had breached the Maginot Line, overrunning it like a mere inconvenience in their surging bloodlust for the beating heart of France. It happened with dizzying speed. No one really believed Germany would overrun the line—it was impossible. No one believed they would march on Paris. Paris? Unthinkable! Who could believe the Nazis would march around the Arc de Triomphe? Who could believe a swastika would hang from the Eiffel Tower? Who could believe France would bow the knee to the foe she had bested not thirty years earlier? But bow she did.

"I hated America. I hated England. We were abandoned. No hope of anyone coming to our aid. You should have seen the people. So few were left, but those who were looked and looked for someone to bring order, give direction—lead. I would have done it myself had I known what to do. There was no one. Ambassador Bullitt did what he could, but he wasn't French. All the misery that followed . . . If Roosevelt had only *listened*, if—"

"If, if, if," Madame Bouvier cut in sharply. "If Roosevelt had listened, if America had acted, if Britain had—Grow up, Brigitte. Look who dies for us, now."

"They do not die for *us*," Brigitte all but shouted. "They die because they finally know the Nazis are a bigger threat to their *own* countries than they imagined. There is nothing humanitarian about their deaths."

"Then why do you feed them?"

When Brigitte did not answer, the woman gave a sour little smile. "So we are back to the beginning." She gathered the Bible and the newspaper and rose. "We will not meet again. Good luck, and be ready. You will know your soldier by this: he will look more German than any you've met, and will say he was referred to you by a Lieutenant Kirsch. Understand?

Kirsch. Until then, observe what you can. Don't be obvious. And whatever you do, write nothing down." She nodded at the piece of paper on the table. "Read those verses. Might actually do you some good." Her tone softened. "I chose a few of my favorites, the ones Father Chaillet gave to me after—"

"Yes, yes, after your 'famous conversion.' Is there a place for one like *me*?"

Contempt rose high on the cold woman fortress. She glared down at Brigitte. "Don't be ridiculous. Of—"

"Just as I thought! At least you are more honest than the priest!"

Without taking her eyes from the ice-blue ones, Brigitte crumpled the paper, rolled it between her palms, and tossed it over her shoulder.

"Very good." Madame Bouvier nodded.

"I wasn't acting."

"I know. We play our part best when we play ourselves. But don't ever spit on me again." She smiled tightly. "Makeup is dear." She opened her purse, laid some coins on the table, and walked away without another glance at Brigitte.

Madame Bouvier shook her head as she left the café. The little tart wouldn't let her finish, and she almost deserved it. Of course there was room for one like Brigitte. If there wasn't room for Brigitte, what hope did Gisèlle Bouvier have? As Father Chaillet had told her when she arrived on his doorstep a mess of a human being, deserving of and desperate for any punishment that could scour away the smallest edge of her guilt . . . yet in holy terror that she would be turned away . . .

"What have you to fear, my child? All are welcomed."

"Then tell me what to do, Father! I do not deserve to live."

And she told him what she had done.

"Tell me *now* that I am welcomed!" she had sobbed. "Tell me how to make *this* right!"

He had laid his hand upon her head. "Acts of repentance will not lead to the mercy you seek, but mercy will lead to acts of repentance. God has mercy on you, child. Look at me. I give you one thing to do: only believe. Redemption will follow."

Perhaps Brigitte had to figure it out for herself. Clearly there was no reasoning with that girl. Madame Bouvier allowed a tiny smile. She rather liked the little hothead.

The smile broadened when she saw anxious little Cherise awaiting her arrival on the steps of La Broderie. How they would gasp when she told of Brigitte crumpling up sacred Scriptures. She relished the thought.

6

THE LOVELY V dove toward the boxcars, and he saw his target on the left, a brick-colored boxcar with a gray top. Bomber boys had nothing on the death stick with the little red button. The power in his grip made his eyes glow. He zeroed in, his hand began to squeeze—

The boxcar roof throws off like a tarp, the train opens a barrage of hellfire.

"Tommy!" his mother called. "Get Ronnie out of the smoke! He can't breathe!"

He snatched the picture, jumped out of the plane. Flak hung like a stairway to the ground. He started down the flak trail, but it led to the Germans. He turned to run up to his plane but his girl is gone, she's gone, blown out of the sky . . .

His own yell woke him.

He was sitting straight up in bed, hand gripping the air to fire the death stream he never did. He never squeezed off a single round.

The flak belonged to another mission, when it was so thick, they later joked that flak protected them from antiaircraft fire. There was no flak the day they approached the rail yard. It was still as Christmas. Looked like a milk run.

The stairs creaked. It was Clemmie, coming to tell him to dream more quietly. He rubbed the back of his sweat-soaked neck. They shot him down without a single bullet of return fire; she wondered why he woke up yelling?

The door creaked open, and in came Clemmie. She went to the dresser to the decanter of whiskey. She poured the amber liquid into a tiny, delicate crystal glass from a set she'd gotten as a wedding present. She came to the bed and handed the glass to Tom.

She nodded at the whiskey and, in heavily accented English, which she thought was much better than it actually was, said, "I could sell for twenty francs that shot alone. Most of my boys would have the bottle gone by now."

"I'm not used to it. It's been warm beer since America." He took a tentative sip, then swallowed the rest down, trying so hard not to cough it made his eyes water. Clearing his throat in a long rumble, he handed the glass back to Clemmie.

"Why 'Clemmie'?" he asked, surprised he hadn't until now.

"Churchill's wife. Behind every great man is a greater woman to put up with him." She reached to smooth his damp hair. "I deserve the name." She lifted an edge of the bandage on the left side of his head, and after inspection gave a grunt of dubious approval. Then she went to the window and pulled back an inch of shade to peek out.

"Another yell like that and I will have explaining," she murmured. "I will tell Old Man Renard I have a young lover; he calls out in his passion." She chuckled, the act gently shaking her frame.

Tom's cheeks flamed at such talk, even as he firmed his lips to keep from laughing. He'd never heard a grandmother joke like that.

"Do you know what *renard* means, in French?" she asked.

"No."

"It means 'fox.' Old Man Fox. That is what he is."

Clemmie wore a neat but worn black dress, loose, as if there had once been more to fill it. She had black-framed glasses, black hair infused with gray, done up in a wispy bun like his mother's, and a mustache you could see in the right angle of light. She had a hairy mole he tried not to notice, not far from a corner of her mouth. Her eyes were large behind the thick glasses. They crinkled with amusement as she watched the neighboring house.

Renard's house was not close enough for him to have heard Tom, even if the window had been opened. But Tom had learned that Clemmie's caution, which he had first thought extreme, had housed a stream of downed Allied airmen without getting caught for three years. She also housed three "residents," which prevented the billeting of any German soldiers. The residents were Jewish, strangers four years ago, now passed off as distant relations dispossessed from an eastern village near Alsace when the Germans invaded France. They were actually from the southeast, Vichy territory, rescued from deportation to the frightening unknown by the Resistance. "Uncle" Anton, "Aunt" Marie, and "Aunt" Tatia.

Clemmie let go the shade, then came to the bed. She pulled up a caned chair and settled in, hands clasped over her stomach.

"So. Your big head heals. I will take out the stitches in a few days. My scalawag Rafael says they have plans for you." She didn't look happy. The mole disapproved. "What are they?"

Tom adjusted the pillows behind his back. "I don't know, but it's not too hard to figure they'll pass me off as a German. My buddies call me Cabbage—"

Her finger came up. "'Little cabbage' is fond title. *En français, c'est 'chou-chou.'*"

"—because I won't let them call me Kraut. Maybe we'll raid a jail and break someone out, maybe a fellow pilot. Wouldn't that be a kick?"

"You are in no condition for mischief. He wasn't sure you didn't break your skull," she said of the doctor who came by, a man who was active in Resistance work—mostly in the treatment of anyone who couldn't risk going to the hospital. He'd operated on Uncle Anton's hernia last spring, in this very room. Clemmie had assisted and said she had the time of her life. "How will I explain this to your mother?"

In the ten days he'd been at Clemmie's, he had learned she held fast to some secret agreement with the mother of every man she helped.

"She will send a grateful letter one day. She will not be grateful if I let you get involved with Rafael. This has not happened before."

"Everything will be fine, Clemmie. I get a chance to do something more than blow things up."

He had a chance for payback he never dreamed, certainly not the day he came home and found his mother on the kitchen floor, next to the stove with a letter in her lap.

His mother had a gentleness he'd not seen in anyone else. Even the weeping was gentle. He was so astonished to see her on the floor that he stood frozen in the doorway. She looked up, and he'd never seen her like that, blue eyes red, face dripping. Her anguish took his breath like someone slammed him onto concrete, and had raised a stone-cold fury he'd kept in his back pocket ever since. It hardly mattered what the news was. Someone made his mother cry.

"My sister is dead, Tom," she had whispered, words staggering. "Her husband. Her children. They are all gone."

He could remember no other image of her, not from the day his parents saw him off at the train that would take him to basic training at Jefferson Barracks in St. Louis. Not when they came with Ronnie to see him off on the troopship in New York. He could not see her, except on the kitchen floor beside the stove.

And now he had a chance to kill a Nazi with bare hands, handed over on a bright shining platter. It was an utterly unexpected wonder, and the prospect made him warm as whiskey. He put his hands behind his head.

"Don't you smile," Clemmie declared. "I am angry. How will I face her if her boy doesn't go home?"

"He'll go home. After he takes care of important business for the war effort. You have important business of your own."

"Yes, and it is you." She leaned to thump his chest. "And you have made it difficult. Oh." She raised a finger, face clearing as a bright new thought came. "You will have company. I get a new boy today. He went down over Le Havre. Rafael will bring him."

He'd spent the first days at Clemmie's sleeping. The week that followed was broken only by a few visits from Rafael, far more interesting than the excruciating work of piecing together a conversation with the "aunts" and "uncle" with his phrase book from the Great War. Boredom began to gnaw his nerves. No music. Nothing to read. Not even visits to the outhouse—he had to go in a bedpan and bear the humiliation of Clemmie emptying it. He could only go out for fresh air when it was dark, and then only if it was cloudy, and only if he did not stray more than two feet from the side of the house. Rafael's visits were bright spots. He was growing fond of the swaggering little fellow.

"You can talk American with him," she said, pleased.

"English. When will he be here?"

"Sometime after midnight." Her bright expression dimmed.

"What's the matter?"

"My scalawag is not himself."

"Rafael?" Tom shrugged. "He seemed fine the other day."

She eyed him. The mole threatened. "You know him so well? I know him well. He was not himself."

He'd had plenty of time to wonder about this woman who put herself in danger every day she housed an enemy of Nazi Germany. Since he was forbidden to go downstairs in case anyone came by, she came upstairs when she could. Sometimes they played cards, a French version of rummy, which Clemmie played with ferocious intensity and won with enough gloating to shame Oswald.

Mostly, they talked. She was hard to understand at first, but even if he wasn't learning French, he was learning the accent, and comprehension of her English came easier. The accent was deeply charming, and she filled it with animation as if animation would make the point if words didn't. He didn't care what she talked about; he just liked to listen.

Sometimes it was angry animation, when she spoke of the latest indignity brought upon the French people by their occupiers; sometimes the animation was intent and patient as she gave Tom the current political lay. It seemed important to her that he, as her Ally, should understand everything the French were going through, as if she expected him to report back to a tribunal of commanding officers. Half the time, though the things she told him were serious enough, he had to make sure she didn't see how much her conversation charmed him.

She wasn't talking now, but he didn't have to fill the silence.

He could sit with this foreign grandmother and feel as easy as if he sat with Fitz or Smythe or Ozzie. War was crazy. If he'd ever pictured himself behind enemy lines, he sure hadn't seen this.

When the silence grew longer, he looked to see the first expression of real worry he'd seen.

He said lightly, "Hey—you said you'd tell me about your granddaughter. You said she's beautiful. Will she date a soldier? Tell her I'm a pilot. Girls like pilots."

"She will not date a German," Clemmie answered. "You are too German." She seemed to realize what she said. She pushed herself heavily from the chair, stood for a moment at his side. "An injured Ally is the worst guest I'll have." She took his empty glass and returned it to the tray on the dresser. For a moment, she rested her hands on the dresser.

"Because we're a pain in the a—ah, keister?" He tried hard not to swear around her. Not an easy habit to break after enlistment in the armed forces. He didn't grow up in a swearing family, but after two enlisted years the words came as naturally as sitting down. Clemmie considered her obligation to save him from corrupt communication to be just as pressing as saving him from the Nazis. Every corrupt word earned a head flick; every near-corrupt word, a glare.

But she was in a different world. She came and fingered the bandage on his head and smoothed his hair. She smiled absently, then went to the door and slipped out, pulling it shut behind her. Her footsteps creaked at the top of the stairs and all the way down.

"You want me to *what*?"

Rafael had arrived with the American crewman at midnight. Tom had no more time than to learn that his name was

Vince Calabrese, a waist gunner from a downed B-17, before Rafael pulled him upstairs to let him know the plan.

Rafael helped himself to the whiskey on the dresser. He glanced inquiringly at Tom, who shook his head. He replaced the stopper on the decanter, started for the chair, then went back for the decanter. He put it on the floor next to the chair.

"Become a customer for a brothel." Rafael shrugged. "What is so difficult?"

"A brothel." The word dropped like a wooden mallet to the floor.

"Don't you have them in America?"

"Not in Jenison." His mind raced at the same time his cheeks warmed. He couldn't think clearly. "Listen, am I supposed to . . . ? Will I have to . . . ?"

"Of course. It's your duty." Then Rafael grinned, though it did not touch his eyes. "I knew we would have fun with this. Relax, Yank—you are to *pose* as a customer. Though I think it might do you good." He knocked back the whiskey. "It's a Germans-only brothel. You'll pose as a German officer so you can come and go without suspicion. Brigitte will pass on whatever information she gets from the soldiers stationed at the Caen Canal Bridge in Bénouville. You'll pass it to me, I'll pass it to my leader; from there it goes straight to London. The war will be won in no time. Home by Christmas." He poured another shot.

Only halfhearted wisecracking, and given the subject, Tom knew he could've had a field day. Dark circles under the eyes made his face appear even thinner. And Tom had never seen him take more than one glass from the decanter, out of respect for Clemmie's desire to save it for her boys.

"Why are you drinking?"

"Don't look at me like that," Rafael muttered, peering into his glass. "Your blue eyes do strange things to me."

Tom grinned. "What's up, Puny?"

Rafael glanced uncertainly at the ceiling.

Funny, the expressions that didn't make it over the Atlantic. He rephrased it. "What's the matter?"

Rafael looked through his glass to the oil lamp on the nightstand. "My boss is in trouble."

"Your boss being . . ."

"Leader of our cell. He is . . . I do not know the English word. I am too tired to think for it." He brought the glass to his eye, then lowered it.

"He's in trouble with the Gestapo?"

"That will come. He is . . ."

Tom pulled his pack from beneath the bed, rummaged through it, and handed Rafael the French phrase book. He thumbed through it, shook his head. "This is no good. It goes from English to French." He paused at a page, wrinkling his nose. "There are no soul words here. What kind of book is this?" He glanced at the cover. It said *Simplest Spoken French*.

"A nurse back home used it in the First War. It was meant for American soldiers and medical staff. Has a lot of medical terms."

Rafael frowned as he paged through it. His expression cleared as he read over a few words. He flipped back a few pages, put a few words together. "His heart has descended. Do you comprehend?"

After a moment, Tom answered, "I comprehend." Mother on the kitchen floor flashed to mind.

Rafael handed back the book. "Four years living where things are upside down, even the best get worn out. Yet I am surprised to see his cracks. I am surprised to see he is human; do you comprehend? You do not think it will happen to you. But it does. Even *I* feel it, and I am superhuman. It is in the air, you see. The air is soiled. We breathe the same air as Nazis."

Tom was getting an idea of what the French had lived through. Things he'd given no thought to were huge issues here. Warmth, for one. Food, for another. His family had gone through hard years, trying to make a farm operate at a profit with a depression on, but being here, in Occupied France, he finally knew what hunger was. The food Clemmie brought never filled him up. He had plenty of time to wonder how she managed to feed her Allied airmen with a coupon ration book designed to allot only twelve hundred calories' worth of daily food. Tom didn't know how much food twelve hundred calories looked like, but he was sure it filled only one plate.

Clemmie kept a tiny garden some distance from the house, in a field behind Renard's home. She had to hide it from the German soldiers, who were as hungry as the French. She told him she hadn't seen real butter in over a year. Often the coupons were for food that wasn't even available. Constant quotas had to be filled for the German army, off fighting Russia. Germany had stripped France starving. Hidden plots of vegetables supplemented a starvation-coupon diet—if the Germans didn't get to them first.

It was one thing to be at an air base in England, feeling occasionally sorry for the luckless French in the Nazi vise; it was another to be in it himself. He'd never again complain about powdered eggs and Spam.

"From what you've told me, your boss sounds tough enough. Don't worry about it. He's just going through a dry spell. He'll find his stuff again. Truth is, I didn't have a lot of respect for the French. I see things differently now."

Rafael's face darkened and his lip curled. "You haven't seen enough."

"I've never met anyone like Clemmie."

Rafael rubbed his thumb on the crystal glass. He said softly,

"I am afraid he will . . . I do not know the word. Take what is within, and show it without."

"Expose himself."

"If he does, it is all over. He will be caught; he will be tortured. I do not think he will talk, but . . ." He shrugged. "If they suspect he is Greenland, they will not stop until he talks or he is dead. This happened to a great man, Jean Moulin. You have heard about Jasmine?"

"No. Clemmie doesn't talk about the Resistance. Who is she?"

Rafael looked at him, surprised. Thoughtfully, he reached for the decanter and poured another round. "She was an agent with Flame. They tortured her, dumped her in the street. She died in Rousseau's arms. I think maybe he was in love with her. I think that is part of why he is in trouble. Jasmine used to escort the Allies, and now it is I. Far more dangerous, since she could pass herself off as a girlfriend going for a walk with her lover. Couples are far safer."

"Easy enough: pass yourself off as my girlfriend," Tom suggested, but Rafael didn't even smile. "I can't promise I won't get fresh." Nothing.

"I used to study the missions. I worked out a plan, you know, and I executed it. That is my job. I am good at it. But my boss has taken over this mission. That is . . . I do not know the word . . . shameful, maybe. But far worse, it shows he is afraid. I have observed a thing when a person is afraid: he reaches for more control than he should. Jasmine died. He does not want you to die."

"Well, there's a pleasant thought. That makes two of us."

"Three." Rafael shrugged. "I would miss your eyes." He smiled a little when Tom chuckled.

"Listen, Puny. Whether it's you or your boss figuring things out, don't worry. I'm a quick study, and the Army taught me to take orders. But I'll tell you something right off. Your plan is no good."

"What do you mean?" Rafael said, in a refreshing switch to indignity. "It is a great plan."

"Don't make me German. Make me a Dutch conscript. Make me some Nazi Dutch sellout who turned in his countrymen for cash and is now in the German army. I know Dutch, not German. I get caught, it's far easier to fake being a conscript than a Kraut."

Rafael tilted his head. For the first time since he arrived, a low light kindled in Rafael's eyes. He nodded slowly. "*Oui.* There are conscripts posted at the bridge." He settled back in his chair. "I knew you were no ordinary dumb American. Have you thought about your *nom de guerre*?"

"Call me Cabby."

"I was thinking Jenison, after your hometown."

"Nope. Cabby."

"What does it mean to you?"

"A God-given chance to get even, *mon petit frère*."

Rafael appraised Tom with new interest. "I cannot push you around, with this face."

He had decided he would kill four Nazis, one each for his aunt and uncle and cousins. He thought about adding one more because they made his mother cry, but he'd not take a drop more blood than he had coming. Four was fair and just. God was watching, through his mother.

"You must promise me something," Rafael said. "Make Rousseau believe you can pull it off."

"Of course I can."

"No, no, I mean it. Make him believe it. He has to believe, and then he will be okay. It is belief he has lost, belief in the good he is doing. It is one thing to be devoted; it is another to believe. Devotion without belief is . . . something ugly. It is religion that is empty."

"What is devotion with belief?"

He rested the glass on his forehead, rolled it back and forth. "There must be a beautiful English word for it. I am too tired." He regarded the empty glass, then got up and took the decanter and glass to the dresser. He put on his beret and stood near the door. "I'll be back in a few days to bring you to Caen. You will stay at his apartment. He will train you not to look like an American, and the mission will begin."

"I thought I looked like a German."

"He will train you not to *act* American. Americans jingle change in their pockets. No European does that. You hold your cigarettes a certain way; you walk a certain way. You whistle. You are too used to freedom. The smallest detail can give you away. It is easier to work with the Brits." He put his hand on the doorknob, twisted it back and forth. "Jasmine was Clemmie's granddaughter. Don't tell her I told you." He opened the door and left.

7

BRIGITTE HEARD LAUGHTER in the sitting room below. The sitting room was a pleasant place that Brigitte had modeled after those USO clubs she saw in movies, a place where soldiers could relax and enjoy conversation and listen to music. Only in the movies the soldiers were Allies, not Germans. And USO clubs were not in . . . establishments such as this.

She leaned toward the mirror and applied a last sweep of mascara. It wasn't really mascara. It was a paste Simone had concocted of coal dust and water, and it actually worked. True, it came off gritty and turned the eyes red if too much was used, but real mascara could only be purchased on the black market. Simone was sure she had a product she could sell after the war was over. Brigitte let her use the woodshed out back to conduct her experiments.

She freshened her lipstick and dabbed homemade rose water on her wrists and behind her ears. She adjusted the silver sash at the waist of her navy dress, then went downstairs.

A staticky Vera Lynn played on the radio. Radios were forbidden, but not even a jealous, indignant neighbor would question a radio in a place frequented by Third Reich soldiers and the Milice. Simone sat in the corner love seat with a uniformed soldier, a dark, brooding man with a day's growth of beard and a paunchy stomach. He took a sip from his bottle of wine. Simone curled up next to him, half-asleep on his shoulder. Her hair was dyed blonde, caught in a red scarf. She wore matching red earrings the shape of large buttons—in fact, they were buttons. Simone's resourcefulness was something else.

Colette was upstairs in her room with Claudio. Brigitte could hear them arguing. They did not often come to the sitting room. Marie-Josette sat on the lap of the German soldier with the lively, grinning face. An officer, if Brigitte wasn't mistaken, maybe from the bridge. She couldn't remember his name. Marie-Josette was his favorite.

She had not known Marie-Josette in Paris. Brigitte had moved to Bénouville with only Colette and Simone. After a week or so had passed, and the town became aware that Thierry Durand's house was now occupied for nefarious purposes, a stream of angry callers came to pay visits. Neighbors came to protest such a place so close to their families, especially neighbors with adolescent boys; the mayor came to tell her that until now, Bénouville was unstained and would she please consider relocating to Ranville. When Brigitte told him she had every intention of paying taxes on her earnings, he left smiling; he knew how many soldiers were stationed at the bridge garrison.

She once opened the door to a bucket of fish guts being heaved at her. She recovered in time to snatch up the bucket and chase the two teenagers down the street, likely sent on their mission by parents. She ran fast enough to bounce the bucket off one of their backs with a most satisfying thud. Once she opened to a grim-faced group of women from Father

Eppinette's parish. She had preferred fish guts to protestations that the neighborhood was about to go up in perdition's flames.

One day, expecting perdition, she opened to a large-eyed, dark-haired young woman with rouge, curves, and a suitcase.

"Good evening, mademoiselle," the girl had cheerily declaimed, presenting a card between two immaculately manicured fingertips. "Are you the proprietress of this establishment?"

"I am."

Marie-Josette Caldecote. Lady of Gentlemanly Companionship.

It was embellished with a border of tiny yellow fleur-de-lys. Brigitte found herself smiling, as much at this bright piece of whimsy in a gloomy day as the fact that this time, no perdition awaited on her doorstep. She looked up at the friendly face.

"You had these printed?"

"I did them myself, pen and ink. I used the back covers of ration booklets."

"Nice job."

"Thank you." Marie-Josette beamed. "I would like to apply for—"

"Can you cook?"

"I can bake."

"You're hired."

Now Marie-Josette looked up from the lap of the German officer and cried, "Brigitte! It is too funny!"

"Let me tell it!" the German begged.

She waved him silent and said, "Remember the apple dessert I made? What do I have in common with it?"

"I have no idea."

"We are both . . . Occupation tarts!" She and the German roared with laughter.

From the corner, Simone smiled without opening her eyes.

Her soldier took another swig from the bottle, gave an impatient jerk of his shoulder. Simone readjusted herself, then settled in again.

There'll be bluebirds over the white cliffs of Dover tomorrow, just you wait and see. There'll be love and laughter, and peace ever after, tomorrow when the world is free . . .

Maybe the man didn't like Vera Lynn's lyrics. If Claudio had been in the room, he would have first made some loud and derisive comment, then would have commanded the station to be changed. Claudio was under the impression that it was he, not Brigitte, who owned the place.

Brigitte went to the radio to adjust the tuner. Some of the static dropped away. She smoothed her hands on her dress, then turned to Simone and her soldier.

"I haven't seen you before. You are new to the area?" Brigitte sat in the chair near the radio, across from the couple.

He eyed her as he took another swig.

"He's from Ouistreham. He's stationed at the bunker on the beach," Simone answered with a yawn. "Doesn't speak a word of French."

He considered Brigitte's face, then her body. There was a time when she never would have suffered a man to look at her so. She should be used to it.

She usually didn't come to the sitting room if she didn't have to, but she couldn't get that horrible woman out of her head. She had to make sure of something. She looked from the brooding man to Marie-Josette.

There was something endearingly ridiculous about Marie-Josette, the way she decorated the German's head with some tinsel left over from Christmas, the way she wore her makeup, as if determined to not only play her part but hold her own in a fashion pageant of chic Parisian harlots. Every detail about

Marie-Josette went one step further: the makeup, the hairstyle, the studied pout of her lips, the clothing and the way she wore it. Even natural details made way for her. She had large dark eyes and full lips and a bustline to make men look twice.

"March is so drab. Now you sparkle." Marie-Josette handed him a piece of tinsel. He began to awkwardly thread it through her dark curls. They could have been a couple on a bench at the Eiffel, giggling and carrying on with life's silly little pleasantries.

Brigitte and Jean-Paul had had no time for silly pleasantries. He came into her life like the crescendo of some march, like a heroic line from an epic poem. There was nothing silly about him because he knew what was going on in Germany in the late thirties. He had been a university student there. She'd met him at the embassy, where he would have long talks with Ambassador Bullitt. He shared the same sort of hero worship she did. He shared the same fear of the things happening in the East, and both were afraid only because the ambassador was afraid.

Marie-Josette's chatter shook her from her thoughts. Marie-Josette's voice had a charming huskiness to it, not like a sultry vamp but like a girl who had cheered her lungs out at a sports event. She was quick to laugh, too quick, most thought. She was a naturally cheerful girl, with an airy way of looking at life that left little room for serious thought. Marie-Josette caught Brigitte's gaze.

"Look at my man! He sparkles! I will put him on top of a cake." She lowered her voice. "Better than the creep in the corner, eh?"

"Don't call him that," Simone said. "He's not so bad."

"He looks angry as a stepped-on cat."

"Why are you so tired?" Brigitte asked Simone.

"I biked to Caen today," she said. "Five farms. Not an acorn to be found. Bruno here brought wine."

"We have wine. What else did Bruno bring?"

She opened her eyes and looked at him. "What else did you bring?" But the man was looking at Brigitte. Simone straightened a little, then said indignantly, "Say . . ." But he didn't take his intent gaze from Brigitte.

"Alex will be here soon," Brigitte said archly, meeting his wine-bleared look with one of subtle defiance. "Poor little Bruno."

Simone pulled away from him, tucking escaped locks into her scarf. "His name isn't Bruno. I can't get it out of him. I think your Alex is in love, Brigitte."

"He's afraid I'm going to convert."

Simone chuckled. "What gives him that idea?"

Always act naturally, the battle-axe said. *Always be yourself.*

"You won't believe this—the woman who owns La Broderie tried to convert me the other day."

"You're kidding," Marie-Josette said. "What did she do?"

"Well. It started when she refused to serve me at her store."

"Oh, that's a nice way to convert someone," Simone said.

"I thought you said they didn't have any lace," Marie-Josette protested.

"They didn't because she wouldn't serve me. She said she'd add the word *slut* to her No Jews sign."

Marie-Josette's soldier pulled the tinsel off his head. "She said that?"

Be careful, Brigitte.

"Yes," she said, and she waved her hand as if it was nothing, "but she came to the café to apologize—and she brought her Bible. Apparently, I'm her new project. Alex had a heart attack when he saw that Bible." The German's stony expression, she noted, had eased. "I assured Alex I wouldn't convert until after the war—imagine his relief."

Everyone laughed except for Bruno. He looked at Brigitte more intently than ever, then took a long swig from the bottle.

"Alex may have to wait," Simone said crossly. She folded her arms.

"Sure he can wait—if your ugly pirate can come up with something other than wine. Wine does nothing for my curves."

"We haven't had curves in months," Simone complained.

"What about you, Stefan?" Marie-Josette asked the German with a pout. "Are you going to convert?"

"Of course—after the war." He buried his face in her neck, and she squealed. He pulled back and looked up at her. "Say . . . what will *you* do after the war?"

"I can make a delicious apple tart out of nothing. Just think what I can do with real ingredients." She lifted her chin. "I will work at a fine patisserie in Paris someday."

"Do you know?" Stefan said earnestly. "I believe you will do it."

Brigitte was glad Colette was not in the room to dim the lovely glow on Marie-Josette's face.

Brigitte loved Marie-Josette because she was cheerful. She had plans for the future. She sometimes gave Brigitte newspaper clippings she thought would help a travel book writer. If Brigitte fed the occasional vagabond who knocked at the door, Marie-Josette would run to find something else to add. Nothing infuriated Colette more than people who asked for food.

Brigitte liked Simone because there was a steadying quality about her. She acted lazy, but was not. She complained, but didn't mean it.

Colette, she couldn't figure out. They had been friends in

Paris, before the war. They sometimes had lunch or coffee together. Colette had an eye for one of the messenger boys employed by the embassy, and she and Brigitte would have fun plotting "chance" encounters. What few real conversations they'd had, Brigitte enjoyed. Now they were apart from each other, some strange abyss between them that Colette would not allow Brigitte to cross. But Brigitte remembered who she used to be. First impressions were hard to shake.

She looked at the tinsel gleaming in Marie-Josette's hair, at the red button on Simone's ear. Hardship did unexpected things. It made friends into strangers, and strangers into friends. The madame was correct. She had a lot to lose.

The German took Marie-Josette's hand and kissed it. His face was troubled. "Your people will not let you get away with what you have done."

"Lucky I won't be around. No one knows me in Paris." She put a kiss on his nose, then pulled him up from the chair and led him from the room.

"You and I have something different, *ja*?" Private Alex Tisknikt asked.

She'd heard it before, more times than she could count.

"Is not such bad idea, Brigitte. To convert after war."

Alex paused on the edge of the bed when she did not answer. He pulled on his trousers, stood, and buttoned them. "You would like my mother. Well—after you know her, *ja*? And after you convert. And baptize. Your clothing—well, I think is okay."

"Do you ever get tired of your duty?"

"What duty?"

"Bridge duty."

"*Ja.* Is boring out of mind. Except when old ladies cross, and we search baskets. They get . . . What is word . . . ?"

"Feisty?"

"*Ja.* Like my mother." He added quickly, "But you would like her. We will not tell what you have done."

"Don't you wish you could do some target practice or something? Shoot some tin cans off a fence? My brother used to do that." She affected interest in the frayed edge of a pillowcase. "Do you have guns in your little foxhole at the bridge? You could do target practice. You wouldn't be so bored."

"Sure we have guns. But we cannot waste ammunition on fun. I used to hunt squirrel on estate where I worked. I miss that place. The smell of barn. The warmth—*Gott im Himmel*, the warmth. My favorite horse was—"

"Topka."

"*Ja.*" He smiled at her, and the smile became dreamy. "What a horse."

Five minutes of silly talk later, things got interesting.

"Do you ever do target practice with that machine gun at the bridge? My, what a big gun. I bet it could blow holes in a—a *wall*."

"Machine gun?" Alex scoffed. "Is no machine gun. *Antitank* gun, little one. Blow holes in *tanks*. Rommel should install more."

Antitank gun. Brigitte kept the unpleasant surprise from her face. "Why should he install more?"

"Because, my little bird," he said patiently, clearly happy to have someone upon whom to bestow knowledge—and Brigitte reinforced it by staying wide-eyed and impressed—"my bridge is *steel* bridge. Is only crossing of Caen Canal along major road to Ouistreham, where empties into sea. Allies attack on beaches, then steel bridge give passage to Rommel's panzer division from Caen—once division is finally *transferred* to

Caen. Panzers go over bridge, go east, then come back around to flank Allies' attack on beaches. Bam!" He flashed his wide grin. "Stop Allies dead."

"My goodness," she said slowly. "Your bridge really is very important. I had no idea." She thought she had believed in what she was doing. She hadn't, until now.

"Is most important bridge in all Normandy!"

A panzer division was being transferred to Caen. Caen! Here, in Normandy! Did the Allies already know about it? Brigitte had no idea how big a division was, but it sounded—frightening. She used the alarm she felt. "Do you really think the Allies will attack on the beaches?" she asked anxiously.

"If so, we throw them into the sea! No worry, darling. *We* do not worry. Not so much about Allies." He wagged his finger importantly. "Resistance, ah, now that is other thing. If Resistance target bridge—"

"God forbid," Brigitte said indignantly. Yes, it was exactly how she would react. "How horrible if we had to resort to ferries! Many people travel to work between Ranville and Bénouville, people who can't afford a daily crossing fee. It is impossible! They would not do such a thing, would they?"

"Say . . . ," Alex said slowly, grasping his chin. "Do you get French customers?"

"Not very often." The skin tingled at the back of her neck. "Why?"

"I get in good with commanding officer if you found things. You know—if Resistance plans anything."

Brigitte shook her head. "You know what the sign on the door says, and we only get the occasional . . . politician . . ."

What if—?

She sat up straight, clutching the covers to her chest. What if she told Alex she'd keep an ear out for anything of interest from French customers? Then, under the guise of trying to get information out of the Resistance, she could get information out of Alex. She could hear a conversation now. *I found out the Resistance thinks you have the bridge rigged to blow. Of course, that isn't so. Right, Alex?*

"What is it, Brigitte?"

"Alex, you are very smart. I do suspect that one of my customers—and I'll not tell who—*may* be helping the Resistance. What if . . . ?" She allowed her countenance to turn a shade wily. "What if I fished about for interesting little scraps? What if I passed those scraps to you?"

Alex's wide face lit up. "And I pass to commanding officer," he breathed. His eyes lit with a hungry vision of glory.

"Exactement." She folded her arms.

"Brigitte! What a girl! My mother would—well . . ."

And while Alex tried to reconcile his mother and Brigitte, Brigitte saw only images of German panzers rolling through Caen, heading for Bénouville.

When Alex was long gone and the doors closed for the evening, she was in the kitchen preparing a cup of tea from overused leaves. She heard Claudio lumbering down the stairs from Colette's room. He was drunk.

He watched her prepare the tea from the kitchen entrance. He was an arrogant buffoon when sober, fond of checking his reflection in the mirror in the hall to make sure his Milice beret showed the silver-circled insignia to the best advantage; but when drunk, he was an arrogant and dangerous buffoon. "Look at you. Making your tea."

Her heart beat a little faster.

She wished he wasn't blocking the only way out of the

kitchen. She didn't answer, because she had learned it didn't matter if she said something or not—either would provoke him.

He lurched forward a few steps. "We had a good time, last time, didn't we? When they were all gone to bed, and it was just you and me?"

"That was a long time ago."

He was drunk, then, too. Her stomach tightened. She calmly poured hot water over the tea, wishing she could hurl the pot at his head and end many little miseries on this earth.

"Colette hates you, you know," she said.

The words stopped his approach. He seemed to work them over in his tiny booze-befuddled mind. "Why should she hate me?" He suddenly lunged.

He wasn't big, but he was strong. He grabbed her hair and jerked her close. The teapot clattered into the sink, the teacup smashed on the floor.

"So proud," he breathed into her ear. "You're not better than my Colette. I'll show you who's in charge. It isn't you, Brigitte Durand. This place isn't yours. No, this whorehouse belongs to the Reich. And so do you."

Once she had come upon Marie-Josette curled up in the sitting room with a swollen lip and a bruised cheek, eating a little packet of raspberries, a tear slipping down her cheek. Marie-Josette wouldn't speak of it. The first time Claudio had cornered Brigitte in the kitchen, he showed up the next day and gave her a small packet of raspberries. Where he got them, she didn't know, and where he came by a conscience, she knew less. She had never told Colette what happened, and gave the raspberries to Simone.

That was last summer, and Claudio had gone from a brute who still had a sense of remorse, to a brute with none. There would be no raspberries tomorrow.

※

When Claudio left, she swept up the remains of the teacup and brushed it into the bin. She took the teapot out of the sink, and while she was examining it for chips, Colette appeared.

"I thought I heard something," she said. "What happened to your lip?"

"I fell."

"Klutz," Colette said, lip raised in a sneer.

"I broke a teacup, too," Brigitte said, trying not to sound cheerful as she examined the teapot. The teacups belonged to Colette.

"You klutz," Colette said again, now angry. "I expect you to pay for it." After a disgusted glare she whirled away and stumped up the steps to her room.

"I did," Brigitte whispered.

She set the teapot down. She ran to the cupboard and pulled it open. On the shelf Colette had labeled *Brigitte* was a packet of Red Cross–issued crackers she'd been saving for a day when hunger was unbearable. Tiny bites of salty food could sometimes fool the stomach. She snatched it from the shelf and ran for her coat.

Curfew had started hours ago. She'd be arrested, if caught.

"Tiny bites of salty food can sometimes fool the stomach," she whispered crazily to herself as she ran down the dark, deserted road to the château.

The gates were wide open because there wasn't reason to keep them locked. It was a maternity hospital, mostly left alone by the Germans. In the summer, men whom she now suspected to be the same Allied airmen Madame Vion hid in the chapel tended the gardens and the walkways.

There were hungry Allies in the chapel. When hard things

happened, when she missed Jean-Paul so deeply it scalded her insides, when she could not bear one more customer, one more humiliation, she came here as fast as she could.

She hurried along a tree-lined walkway. The walkway ended with the massive, imposing château on the left, the chapel, set back nearer to the Caen Canal, on the right. Between the two was a dangerous, open expanse. Usually she skirted around to the far right, came to the chapel from behind.

She looked around carefully. No one was about. No one would be, at five in the morning. She dashed across the open space and crept up the stairs of the chapel. When she reached the top, someone leaped from the shadows.

He shoved her against the chapel door, one hand stifling a gasp, another seizing her wrist.

"What are you doing here?" he hissed. "What is that?" He held up her captive wrist, looking at the packet she clutched. A change came to his face.

"Please, I'm just—"

"You're the grateful patriot." There was recognition in his voice. He let her go.

She was trembling. He was French, he wasn't going to hurt her, and the relief made her a little foolish. "I—Tiny bites of salted food can, you know . . . fool the stomach." She held out the packet.

"No one has ever met you." He pulled off his cap as he took the crackers. "You can call me Sam. I'm a fan of Beckett."

"I like him, too."

"He is with the Resistance. Isn't it funny? I have taken his name, and he has taken someone else's." He offered his hand, smiling. "I am glad to finally meet you."

Brigitte took his hand and shook it, there in the cold March morning on the stone steps of the Allied chapel.

"I'm the lookout." He nodded at the chapel door. "I bring them your gifts. I've only seen you a few times." His tone was wistful. "I sometimes wondered if you were real."

"What is needed most?" Brigitte asked. "Can I do anything else? Clothing?"

He shook his head. "You're already doing it. Food is even harder to come by."

"I bring so little."

"No," he said earnestly. "Whatever you bring is gratefully accepted. But it's more than that." He seemed suddenly bashful. "It's your notes. They help me know I am not alone."

The tears she had denied in the kitchen filled her eyes. She hoped it was too dark to see. "That is why I come, too."

He glanced around. "You better get going. It will be light soon. The first patrol goes by the gate at 5:50."

She started for the steps and said over her shoulder, "My name is—"

"Mademoiselle," he said quickly. "We call you GP."

She stopped, staring at him.

"Please, m'selle," he said, nodding toward the gate. "Sometimes they are early."

She was known. She was known for something other than lying on her back for Germans. The Resistance recruited her because she was a prostitute. Here, she was known for something else.

Her feet flew along the tree-lined path. When she came to the road, she looked both ways for Germans, darted out through the gates, and, coat flapping in the morning cold, ran the rest of the way home, sometimes laughing out loud, sometimes leaping.

8

VINCE CALABRESE, the waist gunner from the downed B-17, reminded Tom, after a few days, of all the things that irritated him about living in close quarters with a bunch of guys.

"You got a girl back home? I got a girl. She's some honey. How many Krauts you taken out? You nail any of them 109s? You fighter pilots, you got some slick deal. You go up in a bathroom. Just you and your business. Me? I go up in a living room. Boy, oh boy, you got it made."

Yet it wasn't *bad* irritation.

"Clemmie says that little guy's gonna pick me up in a few days once they got a route figured out. She says they're gettin' me back through the Pyrenees. Spain. Can you beat it? South enough for a suntan, with England in eyeshot. That's a slow boat to China right there."

It made Tom miss the guys all the more. The way Smythe clacked his dental bridge to drop his front fake tooth—it was funny the first time. The last thing he remembered saying to Smythe was if he did it again, he'd need another bridge. He did it on the spot, face frozen in that gap-toothed grin, and for some reason, instead of making Tom mad, it made him laugh.

He missed Captain Bill Fitzgerald and his annoying ability to drive the English girls nuts with those aw-shucks Gary Cooper looks. He missed Burke and his stupid corny jokes. Missed Markham, how he shared anything he got from home. He missed Oswald's perpetual good humor, and the way he shouted, "Guts and glory!" before any mission.

He missed the swagger, the sweat, the lousy music some of them liked.

"Yeah, well, sometimes I wonder what it's like to go up with a living room full of guys. Some days I'd like that." It was a generous thing to say, and Vince knew it. No fighter pilot would ever swap seats.

"Nah. You guys are the cream. But I was glad to switch to a B-17. Used to be a waist gunner on a B-24."

"B-24's a beast," Tom agreed.

"Froze my lovin' keister off. Waist gunners had it worst. Open windows at the waist. You'd freeze over just like your guns." Calabrese tapped the arm of the chair, and his knee began to bounce up and down. When next he spoke, it was softer.

"Lost my best buddy on takeoff in a B-24. Turret gunner. I was watching 'em go—the thing was headed down the runway like normal, just gettin' off the ground, then all of a sudden the nose goes up, tail goes down, and just that quick you know she ain't gonna make it. Pilot cut the throttle, the thing nosed over, and that's all she wrote—flips over, *blam*. Blew 'em to pieces. Two thousand gallons of fuel. Five bombs. They didn't suffer." He nodded, and the knee bounced. "They didn't suffer."

After a moment, Tom murmured, "Sorry, Calabrese." He wouldn't have had to say anything if it was one of the guys.

Silence worked for them. But he didn't know Calabrese well, and he had a feeling that even if he did, he'd still need to say it.

A brisk three knocks came at the door, and it opened.

"Uh-oh. Here she comes, Tommy boy," Vince boomed. He put his hands behind his head and his feet on the bed. "She's got that light in her eyes, Tommy. She's goin' after them stitches and it ain't gonna be pretty."

Calabrese really wasn't a bad sort. But Tom resented how he acted as though he'd been staying at Clemmie's for two months instead of two days. He treated her with a familiarity that had no basis. Clemmie was Tom's. Not Vince's.

Clemmie took it all in good humor.

She patted Vince's head as she went past with her tray of medical supplies. "We *four* have the light in our eyes."

"Four?" Vince asked with a grin. "You got some mice in your pockets?"

"Me, and Jesus, Mary, and Joseph." She put down the tray. "You should fear me too, Mr. Waist Gunner, with your burn. What a silly thing—*waist* gunner. You gun from the waist?" She struck a pose, holding her hands in the shape of guns at her waist, face screwed into a scowl that all enemies should fear. She looked like a grandma gunslinger at the O.K. Corral. Tom and Vince laughed. She broke the pose to pull back the sleeve of Vince's pajamas. The scowl returned after she peeked under the soiled dressing. She adjusted her glasses. "Jesus, Mary, and Joseph."

"My mother would say that's swearing," Vince said.

She glared at him. "You will know when I am swearing. Then I will speak French so I do not damage you. That was— oh, what is the word . . . ?"

"An invocation?" Tom suggested.

"I do not know *invocation*." Her finger came up as her face cleared. "It is a *calling upon*. Not a swearing." She flicked Vince upside the head. "Telling an old lady she is swearing. Your mother will give me words if I send you back a bad-mannered *cochon*." She flicked him again, more gently. "Say, I have news for you. That fellow made it."

"Posey?" Hope bloomed in Vince's face. He took his feet off the bed.

"He stays in Montebourg. It is too dangerous to move him right now. He broke his leg. But he is well."

Emotion passed over his face. After a moment, he cleared his throat. "His was the only chute I saw, you know, and then comes the antiaircraft fire. You should see what that does to a parachute. Talk about Swiss cheese. Didn't see any others. They didn't have a chance 'cause they cut the beast in half, you know, like a giant kid broke it over his knee. Seventeen missions with those guys." He rubbed his hands together. "I didn't think he had a hope in the hot place. Good old Posey."

Clemmie adjusted her glasses as she took Calabrese's forearm and examined the burn. The mole mightily disapproved. "Some animal put grease on this. Grease is twice as long to heal. What happened to 'you wrap it, then you soak it'?"

But Calabrese didn't hear. His face was far away. Tom was glad for the talkative fellow.

It was another benefit of being a fighter pilot. Sure, you got tight with the guys in your squad, but not as tight as the guys on the bombers.

Clemmie wadded up the old dressing and used it to gently wipe grease from the edges of the livid burn, wincing a little, muttering all the while in French. She rewrapped it with cut strips of bedsheet. Then she flicked him upside the head. "You, waist gunner. Go downstairs and see Aunt Tatia. Tell

her, *J'ai besoin de le tremper dans l'eau froide.* Comprehend?"
She repeated it slowly and made Calabrese say it.

When Vince left the room, Tom said, "*He* gets to go down-stairs."

It was Tom's turn for the head flick. "Old Man Renard is gone. What is more, I need to talk to you."

He had a feeling he knew what it was about.

"We get those stitches out, we free your head." She motioned to the chair, and Tom took it. She rummaged on the tray, selected tweezers and a razor blade, and went to work.

Presently she said, "You can say no to Rafael."

Tom didn't answer.

"He is a good boy. But his business is rough."

"Isn't your business rough?"

He hoped she would not speak of her granddaughter. He didn't know what he would do. A ripple of panic brought the image of his mother next to the stove. He tensed and finally realized it hurt to have stitches out.

"Ouch."

"I take out four, this is your first ouch."

"I wasn't thinking about it then. Ow!"

"Five more. Stop being a whine baby."

"Crybaby."

"Whine, cry, what difference." Clemmie carefully cut through the next stitch with tiny brushes of the razor blade and tugged. New skin had grown into the threads. Tom could feel a sweat begin. The gentle tugging drove him nuts, he wanted to push Clemmie's hand aside and just yank the things out.

She laid a stiff, bloodied thread on the cloth next to the others. "Four more."

"You gonna miss me?"

"Not the whining." Her lips twitched, and the mole lifted. Soon, however, it descended. "I miss all my boys. I want them to come see me when the world is safe. But they will have different lives."

"Clemmie—"

But Tom wasn't used to telling people how he felt. He had been raised by a quiet woman, with the help of a man who believed that to speak of private things was weakness.

"I'll come back," he said with resolve that he hoped she believed.

"Pfft. You will not even remember me."

"No one could forget you," he said quietly. "I'll come back, Clemmie. I promise."

She pulled back to look at him. "Is a promise in America the same as a promise here?"

"Do people keep them here?"

Her face clouded. She put her head over her task again. "They try, Tom Jaeger." She tugged another stitch free and laid it on the cloth.

If she said a word about her granddaughter, he'd have to kill another Nazi. Rage would overrun the dike. He had control because she had control. She muttered in French over the next stitch. He held his breath.

This Jasmine had been tortured to death, a woman from the bloodstock of one who now fussed that his hair was not long enough to hide the wound. Ever since Rafael mentioned it, he had done his best to wall off thinking of it. Yet it moved along the edges like a silent serpent, and every now and then a fearsome thought got through. How could they torture a *woman*?

Women were supposed to be protected. They were to be taken care of, looked after. This was the job of men; that's what he learned from his father, from his uncles, from the men in the town of Jenison, from Michigan, America, *his* world. Yet men here had *tortured* Clemmie's granddaughter. It was unthinkable. What could they have—?

More unthinkable thoughts tried to take shape, and he repressed them with an effort that made him sweat.

"Ouch," he said absently.

"Yes, that one hurt." Her voice was gentle this time, and she put a cloth to the wound. "Two more. I do more damage taking them out than leaving them in." She hesitated. "He will be here anytime. You can say no. I ask you to say no, Tom Jaeger, for your mother."

Oh, Clemmie . . .

"I want you to get married, have babies, and tell them you helped an old lady win a war. You mix with Rafael, you don't know what could happen."

A tap at the door, and Rafael came in. He touched his beret to Clemmie.

"Ready, Cabby?"

Clemmie pulled back to stare down at Tom. The mole towered in high accusation. "You have taken a name."

"Yes, Clemmie, I have taken a name. We won't win the war without doing something."

"You fight in the air!" she stormed, shaking a finger at the sky. "That is where you fight best!"

"I can also fight with my feet on the earth!"

They glared at one another. Then she went back to work, and this time the tugging was not gentle.

"Clemmie, listen to me . . ."

"Stupid youth. Stupid youth!"

He could not say, *I'll get even for you. I'll make them pay for what they did.* He could only vow it in his heart.

Clemmie dropped the razor and tweezers onto the tray.

She reached into her dress pocket and took out a button. She rolled it between her thumb and finger, then took his hand and put it on his palm. She gave a last frown at the wound, checked more closely with her glasses, and blew some debris from it—then she paused, and laid her hand on his head. She gave it a gentle caress.

She took the tray and left the room, pulling the door behind her.

"That was good-bye," Rafael said.

"What do you mean?"

He nodded at the button in Tom's hand. "It is all the good-bye you will get. She will hide in the back of the house until we leave. Do not try to find her." He handed him a brown-papered parcel. "Put this on. A pig farmer wore it. We have to bury everything else."

Tom looked at the black button on his palm. "I have to thank her."

"She knows, Yank."

He took the crinkly parcel. "We have to bury everything? What about my gun?" He hated to part with anything in his pack. The Benzedrine tablets, the compass. The malted milk tablets—those he could leave for Clemmie.

"It is illegal to carry a gun in France, unless you're a gendarme or a German; and they wonder why we starve, when we can't even shoot game. If we are stopped, not even false papers will save you if you have a gun. We will retrieve your things later and put the gun to good use. We have a beautiful weapons cache. It will make a gorgeous addition."

"My phrase book, in case we get separated . . ."

"Nothing could say 'I'm a downed pilot' more."

Tom said nothing about the picture of Ronnie, lest he lose that, too.

"I have to tell her good-bye."

"Good-byes are too hard for her."

"I have to thank her."

"I won't let you."

"Then get me paper! I'll write her a note."

"No. If her home is raided, they will find it."

Tom was silent. "Listen, will you—"

"I will, Yank."

After a moment, Tom put the button in his pocket and said, "Cabby."

"Cabby." Rafael nodded at Tom's pocket. "She has a match for every man she's helped. Keeps them in a jar. It is your photograph to her."

It was the first time Tom had been out of doors in days, not counting the times he sneaked out to pee on the side of the house when it was dark. A man could bear someone taking away his sloshing bedpan only so many times.

"Stop looking around," Rafael said.

They waited in a busy market area, moving around when Rafael got nervous. They were to meet the gentleman he'd met the day he was shot down, François Rousseau. The man was going to pick them up in an automobile, a vehicle commissioned for his cement factory by the Wehrmacht. It was decided not to take the train to Caen. It was too risky since they had not been able to get false identification for Tom. He was far too Nordic for any photographs they had available, a problem they'd never had before.

He put his hands in his pockets, and Rafael told him to take them out.

"You will kill us both," he hissed. "I've never escorted

someone who looks like he should be escorting *me*—to Gestapo headquarters. See how everyone stares? See the woman over there, in the beauty shop? The mean-looking *vache* looking right at us? She doesn't know what to make of you."

Tom felt like a different person, getting a look like that. Though it was a glance quickly subdued when she found Tom looking back, it was one of unveiled hatred. Though he knew better, he felt it personally.

"We're on the same side, lady," he muttered.

It could have been his keyed-up imagination, but as he surreptitiously studied this French neighborhood, he could feel the tension as palpably as the shoes he stood in. Everybody constantly watched everybody else, openly or with quick, thorough glances. The group of men putting in a storefront window, the man selling newspapers, the woman in the beauty shop across the street, who watched more obviously than the others outside, thinking perhaps the window offered less scrutiny of herself—everyone watched everyone.

"Feels strange here," he murmured. "I'm standing in the street at the O.K. Corral." Any minute Clemmie would appear with her waist guns.

"Hurry up, Monsieur Rousseau," Rafael said under his breath. He glanced at Tom. "Will you stop staring at everything?"

"It's what everyone else is doing. What's that?" Tom couldn't help gazing at a metal boxlike contraption affixed to the grille of a truck, which drove slowly past. Holes at the top of the box showed glowing embers below.

Rafael growled between his teeth, then muttered something in French. He took out a pack of cigarettes—Tom's cigarettes—and lit up. "The Germans take all the gasoline. We burn wood and coal to run the cars."

"You're kidding. How does it work?"

"The engines are adapted. Burned coal makes a by-product that goes in the carburetor. The result is rubbish. The engines have no guts."

Tom just barely kept himself from whistling, something Rafael had all but clubbed him for not five minutes earlier. "So this is the embargo on Spain. I wanna get back just to tell the higher-ups it's working." France could no longer get gasoline from Spain, with the embargo on fuel that Congress had slapped on it. Strange to see things he'd only half listened to in action. "Pretty ingenious. Run your car and have a barbeque at the same time."

"I do not know *barbeque*, but it is a pain in your keister. The engines do not run well, and you must forever stop to stir the coal or wood. The worst is this: whatever they burn to run trains and cars is *not* burned to heat homes. France is very cold, *mon ami*. And no one cares. They don't care if we freeze or starve."

"I care," Tom muttered, low enough so Rafael could not hear.

"What if Canada wanted Michigan, hmm? And came and took it? What if all this, in your Jenison—this suspicion, this fear, this hunger? What if Canada turns your Jenison into such a place? Canada steals your food, your gasoline, your men to fight their war or work in their factories . . . what would you do?"

"Same thing I'm doing now."

Rafael nodded grimly. "You would resist. You would be incompatible. You would fight to turn things back to the way they were, even if those things were not perfect. You would know they were far better than this. And you would come to love your country, though you did not love it before, or did not know you did." Relief came to his voice. "*Merci Dieu*, here he is."

❧

Michel slumped at his desk, his father's copy of *Mein Kampf* in front of him. He idled with a corner of it, riffling the edge over and over.

He was supposed to be working on a new gallery design for Braun, who was planning a subterranean command post in Fontaine-la-Mallet, not unlike the one recently completed in Caen for General Richter. He wondered why Braun didn't simply duplicate the Caen design. The Todt Organization typically showed its efficiency in endless duplication of what worked the first time, from bunkers to radar stations.

This particular edition of *Mein Kampf* was the *Volksausgabe*, the people's edition. It contained both volumes. It was navy blue, no dust jacket, a gold swastika embossed on the cover. It was in German, of course. Michel wasn't sure whether it had been translated into French. Not that he wanted it in his native tongue.

Father had been a scholar at heart, and he'd left the running of the business to François once he was back from university. Michel was no scholar, nor did he have any interest in business, family or otherwise. He'd wanted to be an artist of some sort: an actor, a poet, a novelist, maybe all three. He reluctantly fell in at the Cimenterie to make money to fund his dreams. Somehow, he'd never left. Somewhere along the way, he stopped wanting to leave.

When Hitler came to full power, what had been merely another dusted book became Father's companion. While Michel sat at the desk, directing Charlotte, experimenting with new designs for casting and composites, reviewing production and labor reports with François, he'd often hear the mutterings on the other side of the room fan to full-blown diatribe. This he did for the benefit of his sons, Michel privately thought, and it annoyed the sons to distraction.

"*Mon Dieu!* I give up, I tell you. How did this shoddy workmanship make it to print? A work of art, they tell me? Ha! Some work of art! The portrait is nearly as disgraceful as the frame! The grammar, the phraseology . . . his style sickens me. If I must read heresy, for heaven's sake, let it be well-written heresy. I hate him all the more because he wrote his puke so poorly."

Father would snatch off his reading glasses in theatrical display of his contempt, and, protestations to give up notwithstanding, presently replace the glasses in the slow, haughty protest of a thinking man subjected to such a book.

Michel smiled a little. For all the times Father declared he was giving up on it, he never did. He'd read every word. Now the book was Michel's, and the going was hard. He glanced at the bookmark placement; he was only one-third through.

His thumb riffled the edges of the pages again. Hitler's deeds began to match his writings. One man. One wrath. What an absurd horror that Hitler had pulled off all he had so far. One man, and he got thousands to fall in behind—this, the centerpiece horror.

He thought of her at times like these, when all he could think of was escape. The last time he'd seen her as herself, before the Nazis got to her, it was here in this room. She had spoken things he had not known, things he never dared hope for.

She and Charlotte had stood in the doorway to his office, in hushed consultation, occasional looks thrown his way. He tossed down his pen.

"Feminine collaboration," he remarked dryly. "What is it this time? A blanket drive for the POWs? Let's see. We already have boxes at the plants for your book drive, your clothing drive, and your soap drive. Any more boxes and . . ."

But they ignored him. Charlotte whispered something emphatic to Jasmine; Jasmine whispered emphatically back, complete with arms-flung gestures. Charlotte folded her arms, lifted an eyebrow, and with a tiny move of her head, indicated that Jasmine should go in. At that point, Michel got a funny little flutter in his stomach. He suddenly wished there was another exit.

Jasmine set her shoulders, turned from Charlotte, and came into the room. Charlotte, with a long, unreadable look at Michel, slowly closed the door.

At that point, Michel began to perspire.

He rose a little more hastily than intended and started for Father's end of the room, until he saw that was where she was headed, too. He detoured for the windows, made it look like that was where he intended to go all along. He pulled out a pocketknife. He began to chip at a sealed window casement. "This paint . . . it welded the window shut . . ."

She came beside him. She slipped the pocketknife from his hands and set it on the windowsill. She'd never stood so close to him. Her nearness spiked his heart rate.

"I would say that it is time for us to stop fooling ourselves," she said, gazing up at him while he gazed helplessly back. "Charlotte says it is time for *you* to stop."

"Jasmine," he protested gently. "You know I cannot afford to—I run a—large . . ." He was terrified. He couldn't think straight. It couldn't all break down now. He had been strong for so long, enduring all the times he had to send Rafael and Jasmine on assignments as a couple, wondering, heartsick, if they would *become* a couple. "I run Flame. And a business. And I have to—fix this window . . ." She was looking into his eyes as she had never looked before, and he lost speech.

Finally he said, quietly, "Don't do this to me."

She smiled at last, joy lighting her face. "So charming and humble with Braun. So deferential with the Milice. So complying with French officials. They all think they have you in their pocket, when you have them in yours. And all it takes to shake your composure is just an ordinary girl."

"You were never ordinary," he whispered.

"I will tell you when I fell in love with you. We were going over a mission to raid the commissioner's office for ration books. And Wilkie was quiet. It was when his sister and her husband were sent to Neuengamme. Everyone knew they would be executed. Such despair was upon him . . ." Jasmine's green eyes brightened with tears. "And when you finished the details of the mission, you looked straight at him and said, so commanding, 'You are not powerless.' You held up a ration book, and it was then, Michel; that was the moment."

Michel touched her cheek. She caught his hand.

"You told him he had to do something, anything—it didn't matter what it was. You shook that little booklet like it was a ticket to freedom, and you said, 'Any act, however humble or bold, will strike at the same evil that holds your sister in her cell.' You said if to defy evil were to simply stand in front of it, you would do it. Wilkie changed after that; do you remember? You gave him courage."

She kissed the hand she held. "You taught us not that we *should* fight evil, but that we *could*. You taught us not to do *something*, but *anything*. You taught us that the smallest action raised against wrong has dignity, how in raising a hand to save, we are saved. Michel—you taught us what it means to resist."

"You're teaching me not to," he said, eyes traveling her face.

She smiled. "Charlotte won't open the door even for Braun."

And because he was weak, or maybe because he was finally strong, he pulled her close, lips barely touching, and hesitated for a long moment, giving himself one last chance to push her away. Then he kissed her.

He buried his face in her neck and held her close. Someone to share the monstrous burden, someone to share the fear. Even if he never spoke a word. In that moment, he was no longer alone. In that moment, he was no longer one.

And now he was one. And now he was alone. He would be alone for the rest of his life, whether in chains, whether free.

"I remember when your father read it," came Charlotte's soft voice. Her eyes were on his thumb, riffling the edge of *Mein Kampf.* "How he adored reading that book." Any rare reference to his father was always in soft tones. "I don't think anything gave him greater pleasure."

"Pleasure?" His thumb stopped. "Hardly. He hated it."

"Did you ever see him more alive?" Charlotte sat in the seat across the desk. In living memory, she had never done that. She had worked for the Rousseau Cimenterie since he was a boy, over thirty years, and if she ever sat in the office, it was in the tiny fold-up chair she pulled over from the corner.

He pushed the book aside. He did not change his position, however; he remained in his lackadaisical slump, another action that had not occurred in living memory. Not in front of Charlotte.

The look on her face was one he had not seen directed at himself. That motherly anxiety had belonged to his father. Charlotte took care of him until he died in '39.

"Do you like your job, Charlotte?" he suddenly wondered aloud.

The question startled her. She began to rise.

"No, no!" Michel said quickly, motioning her to stay put. "Oh—please, that's not what I meant."

"I like my job," she said a bit warily, easing back in place.

"Good," Michel said. "Good. You do it well. Always have. I don't think I tell you enough. It should be said." Posture restored, his hands sought small details on his desk. He aligned *Mein Kampf* with the desk blotter, he repositioned Rafael's favorite paperweight. "Is anything on your mind?"

"Yes. I don't want you to read that anymore." She looked at *Mein Kampf* as if it were about to sprout hairy black legs and scuttle off the desk.

Good, forthright Charlotte. He firmly resisted a smile. "Why not?"

"I see what it does to you. It does the opposite of what it did to your father."

"I'm not my father."

"No, Monsieur Rousseau. You are not." It was carefully said, and he couldn't guess at what she meant. Her steady gaze gave nothing away.

"Why do you suppose it did that to him?" he said, forgetting himself, wondering aloud again. His hand sought the edge of the book, and his thumb resumed riffling. "It made him angry. It doesn't do that to me."

"I wish it would."

"It is a cheat, you see. I have a fair amount of trust when I sit down to read a book. Some pact with the author, I suppose, a pact I didn't realize existed until this book. With this the mind tries, as it normally does, to latch on to something. There is nothing to latch on to—not quite, not quite, and circling for it doesn't find it. No place to rest. No pact. It is maddening. It makes me uneasy. It makes me—I feel like a caged animal when I read it."

"Then why do you read it?" she asked.

The question surprised him. "Same as my father. I am a

leader, a businessman. I am responsible to know the truth of my times."

"You are quite right, Monsieur Rousseau." Charlotte rose, looking down on him with that steadfast gaze. "I have decided you know enough." She picked up the large book with both hands, tucked it under her arm, and left the room.

A few moments later Michel realized he was still staring at the door.

He noticed a few sketches on his desk, a few photos of the Caen underground post, a list of Braun's ideas for the new one. He touched a photograph.

He took his pencil and sharpened it. He looked in his coffee cup and wished for more coffee. Then he went to work.

An hour later he looked up into the face of a young man for whom Hitler would have shaved his mustache—an immense, blond-haired, blue-eyed German Viking. He put his pencil down, sat back in his chair, and thought for the first time since he'd heard it that perhaps François's scheme wasn't such a bad idea after all.

9

"NO WONDER you couldn't find a photo," Michel said.

"Monsieur Rousseau," Rafael said proudly, "I give you First Lieutenant Tom Jaeger. United States Army Air Forces. He flies the new plane. The P-47."

"Not so new." Tom Jaeger shrugged. "She's been around for a while."

Michel rose and put out his hand. "I confess, my instinct is to hide my Jews."

The Viking laughed with a trace of surprise, as if he hadn't expected to find humor behind enemy lines.

"That *was* a joke," Michel assured, smiling himself. "Charlotte doesn't think it funny. When things get too German, we say, 'Quick, hide your Jews.'" He looked at Rafael. "I'm sorry I doubted you about not needing a photograph. He is far too distinctive. No other likeness but his own will do. It is not just his face, but the force of his presence." His focus went back to the blond monstrosity, where it couldn't help but go. "The kind of attention he will receive means the documents must be flawless. We will make immediate arrangements for a photograph."

"Shall I contact Wilkie?" Rafael asked.

"Who is Wilkie?" Tom said.

"He is a member of Flame," Michel answered. "By day he works with his father at a clothing store, by night he operates our transmitter—and performs other magic tricks, like producing hydroquinone in the middle of an occupation. Only God knows where he will get it." To Rafael, he said, "He'll be dropping by soon. Have him meet us at my apartment tonight. Where is my brother?"

"Talking with Charlotte."

"How hard is it to get a photograph taken?" Tom asked, glancing from Rafael to Michel.

"We must not only be sure we have the right film, we must develop it ourselves. We have the film, but getting the right chemicals is difficult. Some we can order through the Cimenterie, and it arouses no suspicion—sodium carbonate, sodium hydroxide, easy enough. Hydroquinone is another story. The censors would flag it. Everything is black market, my friend. Anything you really want." Michel sniffed. The man smelled awful. His odor certainly didn't match his looks.

"It isn't me. It's these clothes," Tom said, frowning at Rafael.

"The pig farmer was the only man close to your size," Rafael said, openly amused. "You would stand out even more if your pants came to your knees. Quit complaining. They don't smell as bad as they could; there aren't any pigs anymore."

"Magnificent, isn't he?" François came into the room, arms stretched forth in triumph. "A resplendent example of Hitlery." He stood next to Tom, beaming at him. He then called attention to various attributes; he might have had a pointing stick. "*Attendez*: This chin. This jaw. This eye color, to say nothing of this height; is he not perfect? *Et voilà, attendez*—the swelling, gone from his face, the bruise near the cut, diminished.

126

Behold, the Lohengrin of the chancellor's dreams, the one for whom Wagner surely wrote his opera."

"Hide your Jews," Michel agreed.

"Did I not tell you, Brother?" François said sweetly, his face upturned in a comical, supremely satisfied smile. He blinked twice. It was an old face from boyhood, one that never failed to make Michel chuckle.

"You did indeed. And did Rafael tell you his idea?"

François waved his hand airily. "Yes, yes. Make him a Dutch conscript." He gave a courteous nod to Rafael. "But of course, it is perfect. *Formidable.*" He patted Tom's arm. "My poor Lohengrin, to have Dutch blood in those magnificent veins. The Führer weeps at this moment, and knows not why. Now tell me, Michel. Have you come up with his . . . What do you call it? . . . His—"

"Occupation?"

"Surely there is another word," he said, appealing to all the room. "A far more apropos spy word."

"Occupation will do. Yes, we have, and it doesn't concern you."

François's rapture deflated. "But he is my greatest triumph."

Michel came around the desk and put his arm about his brother. "And you are amazing. Your plan will contribute greatly to the war effort. I will see to it myself you are commended by de Gaulle. For now, my brave brother, we—"

Wilkie's very white face suddenly appeared at the door. "The hauptmann!" he whispered, then vanished.

François put a hand on Michel's arm and said quietly, "Quickly, as rehearsed. I will detain him."

Michel stared at the pilot. "François, he will never fit."

"He will have to." François hurried to the door, closing it behind. They soon heard his voice raised in greeting.

Rafael moaned, clasping his head. "He will *not* fit! What about the window?"

"He will be seen. Come." He took Tom's arm and pulled him to his father's side of the room, to the bank of bookshelves along the right wall.

The shelves were built on cupboards fitted with the same library panels that lined the rest of the room. He went to the last cupboard nearest the fireplace and pulled it open. It had long since been cleared of Father's things, during the early months of the Occupation when the need for such a hiding place had been foreseen. They had taken out a dividing insert. It had never been used, and had not been planned for someone almost two meters tall.

"In, in!"

The pilot dove into the small space, shifted about inside, but could not pull in his knees. Michel shoved against the door, but it was no good.

"Mon Dieu," Rafael groaned.

Michel swiftly pulled over a wingback chair to block the jutting door, just as the office door swung open.

As Michel had expected him to, Hauptmann Braun first surveyed the business end of the room. When he turned to look for Michel, Michel was innocently examining a patch of the oval rug with the Cimenterie courier, André Besson.

Michel rose, hands on hips, shaking his head. He looked up at Braun. "Good afternoon, Hauptmann." He looked down at the carpet, flung his hand. "*Regardez.* I long told my father to put down protection discs. What a pity he did not listen."

Braun walked over, hat in one hand, briefcase in the other. "*Quel dommage, n'est-ce pas?* The claw feet clutch brass balls. You see they have tarnished my rug."

Braun shook his head. "Too bad, Rousseau. I share your regret. The rug must be an heirloom; I notice you mix your French with your German when you are upset." He lifted his briefcase, clearly eager to get to the point of his visit. "New ideas, Rousseau! I have not been this excited for a project in a long while. Come, amaze me with what you have done so far."

He went to the desk, put down his briefcase and hat, and to Michel's dismay, he took off his suit coat, folded it, and draped it over the back of the chair. He unfastened his cuff links and began to roll up his white sleeves. He noticed Michel's drawings, and went around the desk to examine them.

Michel turned to Rafael. "André, see if Monsieur Cohen on avenue de la Rochelle is still in business. I do not think this can be cleaned. Perhaps he can find matching inserts."

Braun glanced up, rolling his sleeve. "A name like that, do not hold your breath."

"He had beautiful carpets," Michel said quietly.

Braun tapped one of the drawings. "You are thinking along my lines, Rousseau. Yes, I want a different ventilation system than Richter, but it is more than that. In fact—" He looked at Rafael. "Run along, please."

When Rafael had gone, Braun's gray eyes kindled and his voice gained intensity. "I have an idea, Rousseau. I'm sure all the theoretical strategists have had the same, but I really think it is plausible—after all, this is what I do." He took a map of France out of his briefcase, unfolded it, and laid it on the desk.

Michel strolled over, painfully alert for any sound from behind.

Braun put his finger on the place he had planned for the new subterranean command post, at Fontaine-la-Mallet. "What if, instead of an underground post for command here—" he slid his finger along the coast to Calais—"we begin an underground tunnel here . . . and dig toward England?"

Michel stared where the German's finger rested. At one time he would have called such a notion preposterous. But Hitler had shown the world that nothing was impossible.

"We can give it a working code name: the Trojan Tunnel. Prosaic, yes; but is it not perfect? Oh, I suppose we'll have to change it—perhaps Project Zippy—but can you not imagine? Another way to take England? Not by sea, not by air . . . but by earth? Come in through her underbelly? She is not such an island after all."

On the other side of the room, in a cruelly cramped cupboard where a pig farmer's clothing began to sadistically itch, producing a trickling sweat that also itched, Tom heard himself recounting the story to the guys.

So I crawl into a cupboard the size of a coffin, where I can't move or even breathe because it might move the door, and then I hear German, guys—German. It rattles me good, worse than floating down to the middle of a firefight.

Yeah, yeah, yeah—and den what happened?

And then, Oswald, everything Clemmie said became real. Capture, interrogation, torture . . . and I thought, What if I am caught, what if they torture me—will I say anything? You think, Of course not, I'm tough, I won't say a word. But Rafael said you never know. The toughest talk. The toughest are broken.

And den what happened?

I don't know yet, Ozzie. That German hears a sound and it's all over—for me, for this Frenchman, for Rafael, maybe even for Clemmie. It's real, and I'm not a spy, I'm a fighter pilot. Who am I kidding. I feel like a FOOL and want nothing more than to be

*in the sky where I belong. I can't breathe, I can't move, and this
tiny space will drive me NUTS—I can take a COCKPIT because
a COCKPIT has SKY!*

Think about Clemmie, Captain Fitz said calmly, *and you'll
be all right. Not an inch. Not a sound. Win it in your head,
Cabby. Win it in your head.*

An unprecedented four and a half hours later, during which
Charlotte sent for food and wine, Braun finally left.

Michel waited a few moments, then went to the office
door. He pried it open and listened. Charlotte was gone; she'd
left hours earlier. He at last heard Braun's driver start the automobile and rev the engine. He waited until he heard the car
drive off, then flew to his father's end of the room.

He shoved aside the chair and yanked open the cupboard
door. The pilot's knees fell out. They lay motionless.

"Monsieur! Are you all right?"

Complete silence.

"Well . . . that was fun," came a hoarse croak.

Not an ounce of strength left, Michel sank to the floor. He
began to laugh. Soon the pilot was laughing, too, with a hoarse
dry chuckle, still in the cupboard with his knees sticking out.

Michel laughed until tears came. He was very much afraid
he was going to like this man.

10

OVER A WEEK PASSED before Rousseau was sure Tom could play his part—and play it flawlessly. It took nearly that long for Wilkie's contacts to track down the hydroquinone needed to develop the film.

Tom looked at the picture in the little green booklet with *Deutsches Reich* stamped on the cover, above a spread-winged eagle sitting atop a laurel wreath with a swastika in the center. Below the Nazi symbol were the words *Arbeitsbuch für Ausländer*. It was a labor record book for foreigners and aliens, issued on July 7, 1940.

The green booklet was only part of his identification packet. It told of a civilian employed as a day laborer on a tulip farm, with many rubber stamps and signatures on the pages.

The next booklet, red, with a gold-embossed swastika in the center of a cog, told of the same man now employed at a German munitions factory. There were paper stamps pasted in. No photo for this one; it was some kind of record book. "The German Workforce," Rousseau translated from the first page. On the inside flyleaf was a quote from Hitler. Rousseau translated some of it for him: "You are not allowed to forget that the nation only lives through the work of everyone. Work is creation. Work is discipline."

The third and final piece of identification was a beige booklet with a beige slipcover, the word *Soldbuch* stamped in black, under the eagle clutching the swastika wreath.

He'd had two photos taken. One in civilian clothes for the green booklet, and for that they slicked his hair back, and managed to shadow the wound so that it would not show. He looked younger, as intended. For the *Soldbuch* booklet, he was in a German uniform. He stared at the photo, hardly believing it was him. Proud, unsmiling, maybe a little anxious.

"Your name," Michel said.

Tom put the booklets down. "Kees Nieuwenhuis."

"Where are you from?"

"Andijk, a small town in the northern province."

"Where was your mother born?"

"Apeldoorn."

"Your father?"

"Andijk."

"What were you doing the day your country fell to the Reich?"

"I worked at my uncle's flower farm in Andijk. Good thing, too; we had tulip bulbs to eat when things got rough." That was new, and Michel raised an eyebrow. It was true; it was what his aunt told Mother in a letter.

"When did you go to work for the Reich?"

"When I was rounded up with other men from my village. In the *razzia*, with the other *onderduikers*."

It was another addition with which Tom thought he might be impressed, but Michel frowned. "What *date*?"

"I am not sure of the date. I know it was September 1941."

"How long did you work in the factory?"

"Six months at the first one. Because I had an exemplary record, I soon rose to leader of my section. I was transferred to another factory."

"Where were the factories located?"

Tom hesitated for only a second. "The first, in Berndorf—"

"Unblinking, unhesitating. From the top."

Tom's face flushed. "I can do this."

Michel ran through the questions from the beginning, his tone never varying from that of a probing interrogator.

"Where were the factories located?"

"The first in Berndorf, Austria. The second was a factory called Berthawerk, near Auschwitz."

"What did you make?"

"Artillery fuses."

"At what point were you approached to join the German army?"

"When they saw my talents were wasted on fuses."

"Prior to this, how long were you a member of the Dutch Nazi Party?"

"I signed up in '38, with several friends."

"How do you feel about joining the army that conquered your nation?"

"If you can't beat 'em, join 'em."

Michel wearily rubbed his eyebrows.

"I thought that was a good improvise. It felt natural."

"For an *American*," Michel said, exasperated. "That has an *American* sound to it. You do not respect how good these people are. They will *smell* American on you. My job, Tom, is to make you odor free. From the top. Unblinking, unhesitating, *unimprovising*. Do the drill as you are trained, soldier."

That did it. Soon a little anger and shame produced an

interrogation that put even Michel at ease. After Tom had flawlessly completed the first, Michel started the next.

"What business do you have at the Rousseau Cimenterie?"

"I was transferred here by orders of Rommel himself to survey the Dutch conscripts posted to the Atlantic Wall in the Normandy sector—"

"Put a little more swagger into it. Rommel is a demigod to the Germans."

"I was transferred here by order of Rommel himself. I am to survey the Dutch conscripts—"

"Good."

"—assigned to Normandy construction sites."

"What is Rommel's designation?"

"Marshal Erwin Rommel, inspector of coastal defenses, commander of Army Group B. He has reunited the Seventh and the Fifteenth Armies north of the Loire. I have been assigned as his emissary to the Rousseau Cimenterie to observe and report any signs of subversion within the Dutch conscripted labor. It is suspected that information has been passing from and to the Netherlands through Normandy. Since I speak English and Dutch as well as a little German, I am well suited to secret observance."

"Good. Except I asked you one question. Did I ask about your orders?"

"No."

"Did I ask if you spoke English and Dutch as well as German?" Tom flushed. "No."

"Did I *ask* if you are well suited to secret observance?"

"No."

"*I* speak Dutch, Cabby. I've never volunteered that, and why? Because you never asked. You just volunteered information I never asked; because of this they will suspect you. They

will be unsure of what they suspect, and they will come after
you." Michel rubbed his temples. "From the top. Unblinking.
Unhesitating. Unimprovising. And *terse*. What business do
you have at the Rousseau Cimenterie?"

"I was transferred here by Rommel himself . . ."

*Make Rousseau believe you can pull it off. Make him believe,
and he'll be okay.* Nothing Tom had seen in two weeks made
him think this Frenchman was anything other than capable
and committed. He didn't know what Rafael was talking about,
that the man had shown weariness, that he didn't believe anymore; all Tom had seen was relentless pursuit of perfection, like
Pavretti, his drill sergeant back home.

Tom liked Michel's determination. The repetition could
very well save his life. If Michel seemed tired, he had a lot to
do; if his eyes had dark, puffy smudges beneath them, it was
no different than the other Rousseau, probably a family trait.
And if at times he seemed sad or depressed . . . well, if you
were French, these were depressing times.

Rousseau asked the final question, Tom answered, and the
older man eased back in his chair to study the younger. Then
he smiled a very small smile, and Tom felt a silly wave of pride.
Well, it wasn't easy to please this man.

"Very good. You know who you are, and you made me
believe it. All I have left is this: stay alert at all times. The
moment you let your guard down is the moment something
will happen, and trust me, it will. Here in France, we are under
a cloud of darkness. Anything that has hope in it, anything
that moves toward freedom will attract darkness. In a very
dark place, a little light stands out all the more. Do not shine."

"I will do my best."

"You misunderstand me. I do not want your best. I want
perfection."

It was hard to assent to perfection, but Tom thought of Rafael and nodded.

They sat in the study of Rousseau's apartment, the nicely furnished room of a man with money and taste. Tom had never been in a more elegant setting, actually. Mother kept the home neat and tidy, and there was always the smell of something cooking, which to Tom meant a different kind of wealth; here, the place smelled of tobacco and wood polish and papers and books. It smelled important. Clemmie's place had a feeling closer to home; this place felt wise, and troubled, and on the brink. Maybe because of the meetings that constantly took place here; maybe because Gestapo headquarters was two city blocks over.

In the first days here, Tom had wanted to help out in some way. He wanted action so desperately that one evening he thought he'd surprise Rousseau and cook supper. He scoured the icebox and found a small package of bacon, a little milk, some eggs, and cheese. He found a few potatoes in the cupboard, and an onion. He pulled out a black cast-iron pan and went to work.

That evening Monsieur Rousseau came home to a table set for two, with the splendid black skillet placed in the middle of the table, steaming with Tom's labor, a casserole-hash type of meal that, to Tom's satisfaction, wasn't far from what his own mother could have done.

Rousseau was quiet during the meal. Tom attributed his stiff manner to the fact that Rousseau usually made the suppers, and maybe felt awkward at Tom putzing around the kitchen on his turf. Tom might have felt the same way, if the roles were reversed.

Later, while Rousseau spoke with Wilkie, Tom mentioned the meal he had prepared to Rafael.

TRACY GROOT

Rafael got a funny look. "You used *all* the bacon Monsieur Rousseau had? How much?"

Tom shrugged. "Not much. Maybe a quarter pound."

Rafael made a very small sound. "And how many eggs did you use?"

"Four."

Rafael coughed, cleared his throat. "Tell me. Please. How much of the cheese did you use?"

"All of it. There wasn't much."

The next question sounded strangled. "How many . . . please, how many potatoes?"

"Four."

Rafael whimpered as he clapped a hand alongside his face, a man caught between admiration and another very strong emotion. He finally managed to say, "My dear Cabby—you just used two weeks' ration of eggs and potatoes, and an entire month's ration of bacon and cheese."

Oh no. "On one meal."

"On one meal," Rafael squeaked. "Why didn't you invite *me*?"

It was the last time Tom cooked.

Rousseau's face, this evening, was placid. The fellas would say he was a man who kept his cards close to the vest. It had been so for two weeks. Now he seemed like a man ready to put a few cards on the table. But before Tom could ask a question, and he had many, Rousseau beat him to it.

He glanced at the three booklets Tom shuffled in his hands. "I have found that before a mission, there comes a calm in which everything that can be done has been done. Perhaps this is similar with battles. I wouldn't know. I have not served in the military."

"It's like that." Tom shrugged, thinking of the bunk room in the big house where his squad was quartered. No one would

139

ever talk of the mission the next day, especially if it was a big one.

"The more I get to know you, the more I do not believe what you told me at the first, that this is a chance to do something for the Cause."

Tom paused in shuffling the booklets. "Why is that important?"

"Maybe it isn't. Maybe it is. What is your motive for taking on this very dangerous job?" He took a cigarette from a metal case and lit up.

"My motive?" Tom said, starting to get annoyed. "I'm doing what you want me to do. Why should you care?"

"Oh, I will tell you why." He shook out the match and tossed it in the ashtray. "A mission can depend upon what started it. If my motive is not strong enough, then later I get confused, and I drift; I need to find my way back to the beginning and remember why I got involved in the first place. I need to go back to motive, and find it strong. If it is not strong, then I lose . . . oh . . . what is a good English word. My follow-through." He made a pushing motion. "I lose that which pushes me from behind to follow through."

"Your power."

Rousseau waved his hand, as if that wasn't quite the word but would do. "*Oui.* My power. You must not lose yours. What is the source of your power for this mission? Where does it begin?" When Tom did not answer, he added, "What is your story?"

Tom shuffled the booklets more slowly and finally stopped. "Once upon a time there was a mother. A good mother. And Germany bombed Rotterdam. And the mother's sister died. The end." He resumed shuffling.

"Revenge," Rousseau said, as if he hadn't expected it.

"Sure."

"I hope you find something else."

"She's some mother."

"I do not doubt. Maybe *she* is enough. Revenge is not. It does not have enough in it."

That seemed a ridiculous thing to say. Not enough in revenge? What about Hitler's revenge? This war was supposed to be payback for the first, and so far the world had paid in spades. But, he thought sourly, how could he argue? He was younger, he hadn't lived in an occupied country for four years—to Rousseau, he couldn't possibly have enough credibility for a viable point. He cast about to change the subject.

"I've been thinking about the prostitute. What do you know of her?" Tom looked from the booklets to Michel. He was smoking contentedly. He wasn't used to Rousseau content. "Why does she do what she does?"

Michel breathed out a column of smoke. He gave the little shrug Tom was beginning to associate with all Frenchmen. "You will have to ask her."

"How can a girl—?" He shifted uncomfortably in his seat. "It's degrading, isn't it? Here or in America. I keep thinking about what Rafael said, if Canada invaded Michigan. What if one of the girls I knew from high school did that?"

"You would be disgusted?"

"You bet I would! If Canada's the enemy, and they occupy us like the Germans, and then a girl from Jenison High sleeps with an enemy Canadian . . . that's treason. In my eyes, it is. How is it for you?"

Michel nodded slowly. "About the same."

"At the very least, it's a bad thing to do. Here is what I don't understand: this Brigitte is doing something bad, and now she's doing something good, and brave, something that could save a lot of Allied lives and get her arrested and killed. How do you figure that?"

"What do you mean?"

"How do you explain it? It's suspicious to me. Maybe she's a double agent. Have you thought about that?"

Michel shook his head. "She has been doing something to get herself arrested for over a year. We learned of Brigitte through a woman who runs another cell. Brigitte had discovered that this woman hid downed Allied airmen. Instead of denouncing Madame Vion, she's been bringing the Allies food—once or twice a week." Rousseau smiled wryly. "All the while, running her brothel. Now try to figure her out."

Tom whistled. Rousseau stiffened, and Tom winced. "Sorry."

"Do *not* whistle, Cabby. Ever, ever, ever." He muttered something in French, then adjusted his shoulders, and said more mildly, "So. How do you feel about meeting her? How do you feel about dealing with a prostitute?"

"I'm not sure. It's not like Jenison has—and I've never—I mean, I was seventeen, I quit school to join up, and . . ." He scratched his jaw and chuckled nervously, glad for a moment that the guys weren't around. "I guess that's beside the point, right?" He felt his face begin to warm. He'd had plenty of time to think about meeting her. Since she was a prostitute, what if she expected . . . ? She wouldn't, would she? Of course not, why would she? And would he . . . ? No! He shifted in his seat. Not the first time, with a prostitute. *What she's doing is treason twice—treason to her country and treason to her gender.*

What if she's pretty?

What if she's got a great figure?

What if I'm tempted?

His face flamed. He cleared his throat and said roughly, "So what about you? Have you met her?"

Rousseau shook his head. "No. And I am glad."

Tom nodded grimly. "Because, as a Frenchman, what she does disgusts you."

The contentedness finally drifted from Rousseau's face. He leaned forward to press out the cigarette. "Because I cannot hold in my arms one more woman who has died for freedom. I do not have it in me."

Tom began to shuffle the booklets.

"I guess you'll have to go back to your beginning," Tom presently said.

"Nothing there is strong enough."

11

BRIGITTE RAISED HER HEAD at the kitchen sink. She did her best to keep cool. Anything that came out of Colette's mouth could set her off. But this . . .

She turned to Colette at the kitchen entry. "This is *my* home, Colette." This couldn't be happening. She suppressed a wave of panic. "*I* say who moves in. Not you."

"Well, what can *I* do about it?" Colette said angrily. She rummaged in her purse for a cigarette, threw it down when she found none. "I can't tell him no. Neither can you."

Colette didn't look any more pleased about Claudio Benoit moving into her room than Brigitte did. Brigitte wondered why. They were to marry, one day.

"Why should he move into my home? They have no other place to put their people?"

"It's closer to the bridges. They believe the Resistance is planning something."

"Then why can't he stay in the Bénouville Mairie?" The town hall was much closer to the bridge.

"Not enough room. Too many soldiers, he said."

"When is he moving in?"

"I don't know!" Colette snapped. "Soon! Ask him yourself."

She couldn't stop it. If she tried, they would take away her home. They could do anything they wanted. French ownership of anything was a farce. Property deeds meant only as much as the capricious whim of whoever inspected them.

The operation had to be called off. It was far too dangerous now. Wasn't it? Brigitte began to pace the small kitchen.

From the moment she met Rafael, she had a chance to do something for her country—no, if she was being honest, that wasn't true. She had a chance to hold her head up when the war was over. A chance for personal redemption that no one else had a part of; it was for her, and her alone. She made fists; her nails bit into her palms. That turncoat Milice pig was not going to keep her from it!

She stopped pacing. No. No, it wasn't for her alone.

It was for her stupid, sleepy, whore-hating village. It was for the boys who threw fish guts. For Guillemot, the waiter. It was for her country. She was now a part of something far bigger than personal pride, and with it came an unexpected burden of responsibility. It was not an unpleasant feeling. In fact, it was the opposite, something she wanted to hold tight to her chest. But it was unfamiliar.

It was only fair to send out a warning about Benoit moving in. If they had to shut everything down, if she lost her chance to hold up her head, so be it—but if she didn't warn them, she could never hold up her head again.

She stood very still, then went to the peg and took her coat.

"Where are you going?" Colette demanded. Brigitte paused in pulling on her coat. Colette's disheveled sandy-brown curls framed an irritated face.

She shouldered into her coat, then went over to Colette.

What was it about this girl that provoked as much compassion as anger? "I don't know why you run with Claudio. You hate him."

"It's you I hate," Colette hissed, her face contorting to deeper, ugly lines of contempt.

"Yes, and I don't know why. We were friends once. But you do hate him. You hate everybody. Yourself most of all. And I am sorry for it. And I am sorry for you. I remember who you used to be. I miss that you."

Colette slapped her face.

Brigitte stood motionless until the pain passed.

Colette wanted a catfight in the worst way. So the only way to win was not to fight at all. She went to the door.

"You're going to the château!" Colette shouted, a sob catching her voice. "You always do, when you're upset! What do you do, imagine it's a garden in England? Does that cursed imagination get you out of France? Does it bring back your Jean-Paul?"

"I am going to La Broderie to talk to the witch who wants to convert me." She took out the list of Bible verses she had carefully smoothed out and showed it to Colette. "If I convert, won't it settle a lot of things? You can have the house all to yourself. Claudio can even have my room. Cross your fingers, Colette; let's see how good the witch is at conversion. I could be out of your life for good."

She slipped out. She had not gone three steps before she heard the crash of a teacup against the door.

It was quiet in the shop. Madame Bouvier sat behind the counter, sorting through a basket. There was only one customer, a thin young woman, barefoot, with greasy, unkempt hair and a stained and threadbare dress. The dress was tight and far too short. It looked like a child's dress. Looked as if she'd worn it since the beginning of the Occupation. She fingered the edge of a bolt of fabric, looked at the cloth as hungrily as she would doubtless have looked at a loaf of bread. Brigitte studied cards of buttons on a rack near the back of the store. She occasionally glanced at Madame Bouvier, who took no notice; her disapproving glare was for the scruffy young woman.

"Look," she finally said to her, "are you going to buy anything?"

The girl snatched her fingers from the fabric. Madame Bouvier jerked her head at the door. The girl slowly made her way to the door, touching items as she went, a bit of lace, a packet of thread.

"Shall I make you empty your pockets?" Madame said.

The girl trailed her fingers along the top of a lovely old Hurtu sewing machine for sale. She finally left.

"She had no coat. She only wanted to get warm. Still, I'm glad she's gone." Brigitte went to the counter with several cards of buttons. She took out the uncrumpled sheet of Bible verses and laid it next to them. She glanced at a canister on the counter labeled, "One and a half million Frenchmen in POW camps. They are hungrier than we. Put your change here and make a difference." A card next to the canister said, "Book Drive for the POWs—Bring in a book and receive 10% off your purchase."

"What are you doing here?" Madame said in a low tone.

"Yes, I shouldn't be here, right? There isn't a place for one like me." She continued to study the cards of buttons, in case someone outside was watching. "We have a problem."

"Whatever it is, it's yours, not mine."

"Do you know who Claudio Benoit is?"

"No."

"Rafael does. He is about to move into my home. He is Milice. He told Colette he is to keep an eye on the bridges. Now he can keep an eye on my home. He says the Resistance is up to something."

"The Resistance is always up to something."

"What do I do?"

"Figure it out," Madame Bouvier snapped.

For the first time, Brigitte noticed the makeup wasn't perfect. In fact, she wore hardly any. It made her look older.

"What's with you?"

"Do you know who paid me a visit the other day? A soldier from the bridge." She reached for a pair of crutches that Brigitte had not noticed and used them to walk carefully around the counter. Her foot was bound in cloth. She propped the crutches against the counter, then bent to unwind the cloth. It fell away to reveal the shocking sight of a foot deeply bruised and swollen. The toes were puffy, and a few toenails had turned black.

"He wondered why I had not yet put the word *slut* on my sign. Then he stomped on my foot with the heel of his boot and said if I did, he would break the other one."

Brigitte's hand went to her mouth. Marie-Josette's German. The one Brigitte didn't think was so bad, for a German.

"They wanted to know why I couldn't get the lace," she said faintly. "I told them. You said to be myself . . ."

Madame Bouvier bent to rewrap the foot, but Brigitte swooped to do it. When she finished, she looked up at the madame. "Is it too tight?"

"It's fine," she mumbled.

Brigitte stood. "Claudio moves in soon. The American has not yet come."

The woman's face was pasty gray with pain and lack of makeup. "You want to call it off? Is that why you're here? You want to quit?"

"No! But things are far more dangerous for that pilot."

"What do you want *me* to do?"

"It is only fair to—Can't you tell them—?"

"I won't risk a message just because things got hard." Then the rancor lessened. "What's new? Nothing ever goes as planned. That's the only thing you can plan on." She fit the crutches under her arms. "Do not waste my time with things like that. I'm watched more than ever. Don't you know the Gestapo is in the next building?" She slowly hobbled around the corner of the counter. She settled onto her stool with a sigh of relief, propping the crutches against the shelves.

"I am sorry about your foot."

Madame pulled the basket to her lap and went back to sorting. Brigitte started for the door, remembered a few centimes in her pocket, and slipped them into the canister.

She had her hand on the door to leave when Madame Bouvier said, "I asked myself how the two of us were alike, once I knew I would be working with you."

Brigitte stopped. She did not turn around.

"It is not easy to work with others in the Resistance. There are many with whom I would never ordinarily associate. If I have to work with someone I do not like, or with someone who has a job like yours, one of which I do not approve, I ask myself: what do I have in common with this person? If I find something in common, it is easier."

Brigitte did not move, wondering if there was more, wondering if she wanted to stay around and hear it.

"Your home is unlicensed," Madame continued. "When Madame Vion told me you refused to register your establishment as a brothel with the French government, I thought, *Here is a girl I understand. She doesn't want to be pushed around. She wants to be in control.* But know this, if you don't already: your control is an illusion." Her tone dropped to a low mutter. "Nothing but an illusion."

Brigitte waited, but she said no more.

She left the store, turning right to go home. But she stopped and turned to face the Caen Canal Bridge. She started walking.

She stopped at the end of the street, at the bridgehead, between the two cafés. The café on the right was run by a couple who didn't seem to like to wait on prostitutes any more than they did Germans. She had been there, once, with Marie-Josette. The café on the left employed a Jew rescued by a Jew hater, whose foot had been broken because Brigitte had opened her big mouth.

She looked at the hulking steel bridge. Just past it, situated on the southeast side of the riverbank, was a permanent gun emplacement with a large gun built on a swivel, a gun that was not a machine gun but an antitank gun. On the northeast side was the house of the bridge keeper. Only yesterday Private Tisknikt told her it was due for demolition in a few weeks. When she asked why, he said it would clear the way to see anything coming from the sea.

A salty breeze stirred her hair, and she smoothed a lock behind her ear. The invasion was coming. The Germans prepared, the Resistance prepared, the Allies prepared. She had been in Caen when the Allies had bombed a factory, but it was hard to imagine bullets and explosions in this sleepy little town. Hard to imagine German tanks. Would it come to that? *War*, right where she stood, in this street, at that bridge?

A sentry at the south end of the bridge paused in his

strolling patrol to peer at her. She was standing still, after all, while others passed by. Who stood still these days? The act was as suspicious as running. If you ran, you were guilty. If you stood, you were guilty. She turned and started for home.

She was passing La Broderie when she heard a scream. She froze, staring at the storefront. She took a step toward it and heard it again, an agonized sound to clutch at her stomach. But it didn't come from Madame Bouvier's shop. Somewhere to the right, the pub or the room above it.

The Gestapo is in the next building . . .

The anguished scream came again, then stopped abruptly. A passerby heard, too; he glanced at Brigitte with a heavy, grim look. Had they heard it in civilized times, both would have rushed to aid.

The man walked on and, soon, so did Brigitte.

"Did you convert?"

Brigitte paused, looking through the records. It took a moment to understand what Colette was talking about. She took out Vera Lynn, placed it on the turntable, and set the needle.

Brigitte dropped into a chair and took up the Baedeker guidebook. She stared at it, then put her head back to allow the crooning song to wash over her.

"She wasn't talkative. One of the Germans at the bridge broke her foot. Marie-Josette's German. Stomped on it with his heel."

There'll be bluebirds over the white cliffs of Dover . . .

"Why?"

"Since when do they need a reason?"

Colette was curiously silent. No "She must have had it com-ing" or other acid comment.

Brigitte closed her eyes. She gripped the guidebook. "I heard someone scream today. At the Gestapo building." *There'll be love and laughter, and peace ever after . . .* "I don't want to convert. There isn't a place for me." A tear ran down the side of her face, and she turned her head from Colette. "I want to be a bird."

12

RAFAEL'S EXPRESSION when he first saw the German uniform made Tom's heart sink.

The only uniform they could get to fit had once belonged to a major from an antiaircraft artillery unit, killed in an ambush by the Resistance. Tom wore a light-brown French military shirt under a blue-gray woolen uniform. A Walther P38 holster sat at his waist without a pistol in it—Wilkie was working on that. On the other hip was a leather map case, looped on the same belt. His hat was blue, edged in silver with silver braid over the brim and a silver eagle at the peak in front, clutching a swastika in its talons. Tall, black leather boots came just below his knees. His trousers were bloused and tucked into the boots. The French military shirt was a necessity; they couldn't get the blood out of the original owner's shirt.

On the inside of this German belt, he'd carved four notches. He'd fill in each with ink, like painting a swastika on his plane for every Nazi kill.

"Very handsome," Rafael said with an artificial smile. "Very smart."

"Don't go all funny on me."

Rafael softened. "Do not worry. You will do fine. You've got *me* nervous."

"Would a German wear this?" Tom fingered the French shirt collar, anxiously looking in the mirror.

"Many uniforms are cobbled together these days. They can't afford new ones."

Tom stood back to take in his image at the mirror. "Isn't it funny? Me, a pilot, wearing the clothes of a guy who probably shot one of us down?"

"I do not think it is funny."

"Not funny ha-ha. Funny ironic." He looked at the triangular red patches sewn to the edge of the collar. "I can think of another question they'll ask: how did you make major so fast?" He answered with Oswald's Jersey accent, "Cuz dis is all de uniform we could git, ya dimwit." Rafael liked it when he did Oswald. He glanced, but Rafael didn't even smile.

"You need a rank high enough that anyone will think twice about questioning you, low enough that you will not attract too much attention."

Tom's mission was to visit the brothel in Bénouville twice a week and bring whatever he learned about the Caen Canal Bridge and the Orne River Bridge, a quarter mile past Caen Canal, back to Michel. Otherwise, when he was out in the open, he was to look as if he were on a perpetual errand. If anyone asked, he was assigned to the Cimenterie in Caen to observe and report on Dutch workers to Rommel. And if anyone asked, he was billeted at Michel's apartment. It was the first time in four years someone stayed at Michel's home quite openly.

For now, Tom was to accompany Rafael to the Cimenterie office. There, he would enter the building as Major Kees

Nieuwenhuis, and ask for Monsieur Michel Rousseau. He would present his papers . . .

"Signed by Rommel himself," Major Nieuwenhuis said in English, with a strong Dutch accent, nodding at the papers in Michel's hands.

The major stood near the door. Michel stood near Charlotte's desk reading the papers. His secretary was trying to pay no attention to the exchange over her desk, nervously inserting a thick, carbon-copied invoice into her typewriter.

Two men sat in the waiting chairs, reading newspapers and studiously ignoring the conversation. One man was Charles Belanger. He sold advertisements for the paper he was reading, an outfit that sadly had stopped reporting any real news about four years ago. Real news came from the BBC, if one were lucky enough to own the contraband needed to hear it. The other man was Georges Tenerife, a Belgian, one of the construction site managers for the Todt Organization.

Michel looked up from the papers. "You are to interview my Dutch laborers. May I ask why? They are good workers. I have no complaint."

"Orders are orders," the young officer said, looking about the room with interested disdain. "I do not question them. Neither should you." Charlotte's hands shook as she pulled the invoice from the machine, aligned the carbon, and tried again. "By the way, Monsieur Rousseau, where do you live?"

Charlotte's fingers fumbled on the keys. She could not hide the fact that she knew English.

"At 128 rue de l'Heribel. May I ask why?"

"*Ja*, you may. I am assigned to stay at your home."

After a moment, Michel said, "I see."

"My kit." He nodded at a duffel bag near the door. "Have your courier take it to your home. I will not arrive until late this evening. 128 rue de l'Heribel." He put his hands behind his back and strolled over to the men in the chairs. "Tell me, gentlemen; do you know of a good German brothel in the area? A reputable place, where a fellow will not buy a ticket to the Russian front?"

Charles Belanger looked up, startled. He glanced first at the man next to him, then shook his head, mumbling that he did not speak English. Georges Tenerife, after coolly turning a page of his newspaper, raised his eyes to the young officer.

"There are a few in this city, monsieur, but if you want reputable, you will have to go to Bénouville. So I am told."

"Merci beaucoup," the officer said, trying out his French. He took his papers from Michel. "I will be back tomorrow to interview the first man on my list—Ambroos DeBeers. Have him here at 9 a.m. sharp." He turned back to Tenerife. "Excuse me—how do I get to Bénouville?"

Tenerife lowered his newspaper. "Take the main road north. The road will divide as you leave the city. Bear east. Keep the Caen Canal on your right. Bénouville is seven or eight kilometers."

"And when I am there . . . ?"

"Ask around. I wouldn't know." He went back to his paper.

The officer said to Rousseau, "I will see you tonight," and left the office.

The office was silent. After a moment, Charles Belanger looked at Michel. "So, Rousseau. You will have a guest. Too bad. We have been lucky so far. We had only two young men at the beginning, and that for only a week."

"It was only a matter of time. *C'est la guerre.*" To Charlotte, Michel said quietly, "See to it that Ambroos DeBeers is here at 8:50 a.m. Tell his supervisor I am unsure when he will return. I believe DeBeers is at the Ranville plant. If not, check Cabourg."

Charlotte nodded and reached for the telephone.

He turned to Georges Tenerife, who had risen and folded his newspaper. They shook hands, and Rousseau ushered him into his office.

Michel went to his desk. Tenerife took the chair in front. Both sat. Both looked at one another.

"That went well," Michel said softly.

Tenerife nodded and said as quietly, "Belanger will have it all over Caen by nightfall. The privileged Rousseau is finally put upon. He was wonderful, Michel. Wherever did you find him?"

"He went down near Cabourg. Pilot of a P-47, collected by Rafael's team."

"Even knowing who he was, he made me nervous. You don't think he's a spy?"

"They'd never send someone that Nordic. To Holland, maybe, never France."

"And the brothel?"

"She's with us."

"Can't say I've ever referred anyone to a brothel. Your poor secretary. What she must think of me." Tenerife looked thoughtfully at Michel's face. "You have changed, my friend. You seem . . . tired."

But Michel stopped listening. It had gone well. So well that the moment Charlotte saw Tom, she was as nervous as the first time Braun had walked into the room. She did not seem to connect the rough-and-tumble pig farmer she'd seen briefly a few weeks earlier with the spit-shined Wehrmacht officer in jackboots. *Good. Very good.*

"Do we have any real business to discuss?" Tenerife said lightly.

"Do you have any Dutch conscripts at the radar installation?"

"Which one? I'm working three."

"We service Douvres-la-Délivrande."

Tenerife shook his head.

"Then no. But you should stay a little longer. How are the wife and kids?"

And Michel heard not a word as his mind went on to Bénouville with Tom.

He was alone behind enemy lines for the first time.

In the States, Tom and his best friend, Pete, threw in and bought a beat-up 1926 Cleveland motorcycle. They rigged a second seat over the back fender, bracing it with bars rigged to the back axle, wincing every time they went over a bump that brought it down hard on the wheel. They had fun, but no real speed. They took Ronnie for rides when Mother wasn't around.

He now drove a German-made Zündapp K500. The Resistance kept the vehicle hidden in a patch of woods outside Cabourg. Tom had had to accompany Rafael to retrieve it; the Frenchman would attract too much attention riding a vehicle assigned to the Wehrmacht. Rafael didn't know the year, probably mid to late thirties. It had low handles that made turning awkward, with Tom's long legs. But it had power, and he couldn't resist opening her up on a straightaway to see what she could do. If Pete could see him now. But Pete was somewhere in the Pacific, in a faraway place called Guadalcanal.

Tom took care to keep the speed moderate and to avoid potholes when he could. The past few days had been dry, so the road was reasonably mud free. A few spatters on his boots would clean up easily enough. Once he put the German uniform on, he had the same feeling he did when he wore his USAAF uniform: the alert need to keep it polished and dirt free for inspection. There, the similarities ended.

With his USAAF uniform, he felt pride and he felt power, two feelings he kept in check when remembering something his father told him before he left for Basic, an admonition he didn't understand until he was issued his first uniform at Jefferson Barracks: *Don't let that uniform change you, Son, except for the good.* With this uniform, he experienced a sensation that went beyond the disgust of wearing the enemy uniform. Donning the German uniform felt like slipping into personal falsity. He supposed it was good for his role.

"Don't let the uniform change you, son," he whispered.

Rafael's reaction was bothersome enough, but the reaction of Rousseau's secretary was far worse. The fear he saw in her eyes, and in the eyes of the men waiting, brought revulsion to his gut. In America, his parents had made his height a source of pride. In America, he was considered good-looking. Here, his height and his looks and now this cursed uniform brought nothing but shame.

When he came to Bénouville, he took a wrong turn. The brothel was supposed to be past the Château de Bénouville on the right. But he couldn't find the château, and he was too nervous to ask for directions. When he finally figured he'd driven past Bénouville altogether, he stopped at a church to ask directions of a fedora-topped priest, who told him the tiny village he was in was called Le Port.

He couldn't possibly ask a priest where a brothel was, so he asked for directions to the château. But the priest didn't seem any happier.

"Ees a *hospeetal*," he said in broken English, consternation in his face. "Ees for wee-men, weeth babies."

"Yes, a maternity hospital," Tom answered, then realized he didn't put enough Dutch into it. "*Ja, ja*, I know. I have . . . an errand there."

The priest was unhappy, though he tried to conceal it. Then Tom realized the man might be with the Resistance; to such a man, a fellow who looked like Tom, asking directions to a Resistance stronghold, might just cause a bit of alarm.

"Look," Tom said sheepishly, looking away, "I am trying to find the brothel, if you must know. A buddy referred me. He said it is close to the château."

Relief came. "*Oui, oui,*" he now said, far more agreeably. He stepped away from the church to point down the street. "Past zee Mairie. Zee Mairie ees on zee corner, on zee left. Past eet, four, five 'ouses."

"*Oui. Merci, monsieur.*" Should he call him *mister*? He didn't know the etiquette for priests. He bowed his head awkwardly, then swung a leg over his motorcycle. He started it, revved, and turned the machine around. He glanced, and the priest was watching him go.

Four or five houses. Was it four or was it five?

Just before the Mairie, the German-infested town hall Rousseau warned him about, he paused at the corner for a quick look left, down the street. He'd gotten just a glance when he was heading into Le Port, realizing he'd gone too far. Now he looked at the bridge at the end of the street as long as he dared.

He wished for a spy camera to take pictures. He wished he could motor down there and step off the width, eye the length. Pilot training, that's what that was—he had a clear target to act upon and all he wanted was to get his hands on it. He wondered what sort of intel Brigitte—

Movement across the street caught his eye. The door of the Mairie had opened and out walked three German soldiers.

His heart did a belly flop to his gut. *Three-part plan: Act normal, act normal, act normal.*

He looked right and left for traffic, then eased forward. They'd be watching with the racket a motorcycle kicked up in a sleepy town. Should he look? Should he acknowledge? He suddenly remembered he was a major. The red patches at the corners of his collar demanded respect, and a major would look for it.

He glanced left as he passed, noted three salutes, and casually acknowledged. Even as he returned the salute, a barrage of questions flooded: would a major in the German army drive alone? Or would he rate a staff car?

Did they wonder who he was, what he was doing here?

He barely had time to sort through possible answers when he came to the fourth and fifth houses on "zee" left.

He pulled up on the stubbly expanse between the two homes and shut off the machine. He kicked out the stand, then pulled off the heavy motorcycle helmet and hung it on one of the handles, doing his best to make every movement appear as smooth as if this were not only the third time he'd dismounted. He opened the leather side compartment attached to the backseat and took out the German hat. He put it on, adjusted it, and faced the two houses.

Maybe guys who went to brothels didn't go to the front door. Maybe they went to the back, and maybe that would give Brigitte time to notice that a motorcycle had stopped out front.

"Kirsch," he said under his breath, rehearsing what Michel told him to say. "May I ask for Brigitte? I am referred by Lieutenant Kirsch."

He walked between the two houses and checked the house on the right, first. *Nur für Wehrmacht,* said a yellow sign attached to the back door.

"This is it, Ozzie," he muttered. "Boy, wouldn't you like to be me right now."

Heart pounding wildly, he knocked on the door.

Hello, Brigitte? I'm Tom. I wish with all my heart I had listened to Clemmie because I don't know what I'm doing, impersonating a German officer, knocking on the door of a brothel, acting like someone who—

The door opened, and a girl stood there. She was pretty, and she had a great figure, and she'd been crying.

THE OFFICER took off his hat.

"Bonjour. I am looking for Brigitte."

"I am Brigitte."

"I am Kees Nieuwenhuis. I was referred by a friend, Lieutenant Kirsch."

She studied him. "*Oui.* It's been a while since I've seen him. He must have been transferred." She opened the door wide to let him in.

"Would you like some tea?" Brigitte said outside the kitchen entrance, where Marie-Josette was fixing a late lunch. "I am sorry; we do not have coffee."

"*Ja,* sure. Tea would be nice."

Brigitte went to the counter and turned on the hot plate. She filled the kettle and put it on the plate. Marie-Josette glanced up, then looked again. She looked the German up and down appreciatively. "You sure know how to fill a room, Officer."

"He doesn't speak French. At least, I don't think so." Brigitte looked over her shoulder. "Do you speak French?"

The man held up a tiny space between his thumb and forefinger. "*Très peu.*" Then in English, "I speak Dutch. I am from the Netherlands. But I speak English, too."

"I'm free, Brigitte. Very much so," Marie-Josette said in low-toned French. "I like them tall and blond."

Like the one who broke Madame's foot? Brigitte wanted to ask. Instead, she airily replied, "So do I. He's a little too German for my taste, but do you think I'm giving him up? I usually get ugly oafs like Alex, Ernst, and Josef. Any decent French girl would kill herself first."

"We are not decent French girls. Who would be, around him?" She gave the officer a deep and unmistakably prowling smile. A faint blush rose above his collar, and he glanced away. "He's gorgeous. Dreamy eyes."

"Exactly. I haven't had one like him since Paris," Brigitte said lightly, while her stomach twisted at the memory of the bridge soldier. "Hands off."

"Think of me next time he comes and you are busy." She took her plate and walked slowly to the kitchen table, swaying her hips as she went. Brigitte glanced at the man, who was looking anywhere but at them. For some reason she had expected someone older. He was close to her age, and it made her uncomfortable.

It took a cruelly long time for the water to boil. She wanted nothing more than to get him out from under Marie-Josette's toying gaze, before Colette or Simone showed up.

She poured the water into the teapot, threw a cozy over it, put two cups on a tray, and said, "Come, we'll take it in my room or Marie-Josette will have you for dessert." She turned the corner, and he followed her upstairs.

She pushed open the door with her foot, set the tray on the little table near the window, then went back to the door and closed it. She listened for a moment, told herself time was past for second thoughts, and turned around.

Did she look at him as he looked at her? Did brown eyes reveal the same as the blue—the uncertainty, the doubt? Just when she saw these things, she saw other things in that strong, smooth face. Resolve. Defiance. Then the flash of uncertainty once more.

Two strangers stood in a room. What were they doing? What were they playing at?

"Hello," he said softly, with no Dutch accent.

"Hello."

"I'm Cabby."

"I am—" She had to think for the English letters. "GP. Call me Brigitte."

"I'm no spy. You may as well know it." He took off his hat, as if to complete the admission. "I'm just a pilot."

"I'm—" She lifted her chin. "I used to be a file clerk at the US embassy in Paris."

They studied one another, silent, until Brigitte murmured, "The tea is probably ready. Please—have a seat." She turned to pour the tea.

He wasn't what she expected. None of this was. And what was that? She couldn't remember. She only knew, looking into those frank blue eyes, that this American was far more human than her imaginings. When reality did not match the imagination that gave it shadings and flourish, it never failed to surprise her.

When she turned around with the teacups, he hadn't sat down. Then she realized he did not want to sit on the bed. The only chair was next to the table where she had set the tea.

She felt a stir of annoyance. Was it so loathsome to sit there? She had taken pains to make her room a pleasant place. It was neat and tidy, with warm, comfortable tones. The bedspread was chintz, with a pattern of tiny roses, the head of the bed piled with artfully placed pillows and cushions. The curtains were a lovely burgundy, with an inset of cream-colored crepe, perfectly matching the cream in the bedspread. A braided oval rug covered much of the wooden floor.

Near the window was the little table with a pretty doily and a chair with a burgundy cushion that matched the curtains. A wardrobe was on the other side of the room, her grandfather's wardrobe, an antique made of bird's-eye maple; the grain had a beautiful, satiny patina, and there were rosettes carved in each corner. It had a tall cabinet on one side and four drawers on the other. A tilting mirror in a frame carved with the same rosettes topped the drawers. It was the loveliest and likely the most valuable thing she owned.

He was looking around, too, and his eyes rested on the wardrobe. "I've never been in a brothel before." He put his hands in his pockets, then took them out. "This looks like a regular home."

"It *is* a regular home," Brigitte said icily.

He glanced at her, then came and took his cup. "Thanks."

"Do you have a problem sitting on the bed?"

His face colored in earnest. "No. Well—that chair is fine. I like natural light." He went over and sat, and huge as he was, looked like a man sitting in a child's chair. He took a sip of tea, clearly uncomfortable, and turned toward the window.

A new atmosphere tinged the room, and she regretted it. Perhaps it wasn't what she thought. Maybe he had no problem with what she did. He was here to get information, not to judge her. But she felt judged. She took her cup and, with dignity, sat on the edge of the bed.

"I am sorry for the weakness of the tea. I am also sorry I can offer you no sugar. Or milk."

"Don't worry about it. You folks have had to put up with a lot." He looked both ways out the window. "I can only imagine what it's been like," he said, half to himself. He turned to her. "What do you have so far on the bridge?"

She told him about the antitank gun placement on the east bank. She told him about the twenty soldiers, French gendarmes included, stationed at the bridge for the different shifts, and that she knew next to nothing about the Orne River Bridge, on the other side of the Caen Canal Bridge, other than that it pivoted in the center to allow boats to pass.

"Alex also told me about a division of panzers. He said it was being transferred to Caen. Is this already known?"

"I have no idea," he said slowly, taking this news with more gravity than the rest.

"How big is a division?"

"It depends," he said, still lost in troubled thought. Then he said, "What else?"

"That is all."

"That's it? That's all you have so far?"

"Alex hasn't been in for a while. The doctor told me he's getting over pneumonia. I only see two other bridge soldiers, and they don't talk much. Alex is the best source I have."

"Only three customers?"

"There are others," she said stiffly. "From different placements around Ouistreham, Ranville. They have nothing to do with the Caen Canal Bridge."

"Oh." He finished off his tea and put the cup on the table. "Well. Very good. See what else—"

"Wait! The bridge keeper's home. It is due for demolition, for the purpose of—" What was wrong with her? She spoke perfectly fine English, yet found herself fumbling for words. "For the purpose of—seeing."

"A clear sight to the sea?"

"*Oui!*"

"Okay. That it?"

"*Oui.*"

"Very good. Well, then. See what else you can find out." His tone had gone brisk and a little more superior, a little more take-charge than Brigitte liked, especially since he was her own age. "Get the dimensions. They especially want to know if the bridge is rigged to blow. With charges." His hands made a gesture like a bomb going off. "You know—charges placed at intervals along the—"

"Yes, I know," Brigitte cut in. What did he think she was, some ignoramus?

"Okay. Well, then. I'll be going." He rose and put on his hat. "See you next time."

Brigitte stared up at him. "You cannot leave yet."

"Why not?"

She couldn't stop an incredulous smile. "Because we are not . . . finished."

"You have more information?"

"We are not—*finished.*"

At his blank look, Brigitte politely pointed out that "The time elapsed for this little chat will not coincide with the time it takes for an appointment with a real customer."

His face turned a flaming sunset. He quickly took his seat, bumping the table and jostling the teapot, which he hurried to right. Brigitte bit back a smile.

"You must think of these things," she murmured. "You must be aware."

He snorted ruefully, and the superiority vanished. He

leaned forward, twirling his hat with his finger inside the brim. "Yeah, that's what M—Greenland said. And I almost messed up again, with his real name. He said to be alert at all times. Some spy, huh?" A glance flickered at the bed. "So . . . ah, how long is the usual . . . session?"

Suddenly she found herself giggling. She put her hand over her mouth, but couldn't stop. And the big man, far from being embarrassed, first grinned a sheepish half grin, then laughed, too, a warm, rolling sound.

"You won't tell anyone, will you?" he said, blue eyes glinting. He twirled the hat with his finger. "The guys would have a field day. Especially Ozzie."

"I won't tell." Then her amusement vanished, and his because of hers. "I have to tell you about Claudio."

"Rafael says he's someone to avoid."

"That won't be easy anymore. He's moving in."

Cabby straightened. "What? When?"

"I don't know. Soon. He's moving in with Colette. Her room is just down the hall. He is assigned to keep a closer eye on the bridge." In case the pilot wasn't sure, she added, "If this was dangerous before, now it is . . . perhaps perilous."

"I wouldn't go that far," Cabby muttered. She could tell his mind was working quickly by the slow way his fingers moved the hat in a circle.

"He will wonder about you."

"Yeah? Well, I wonder about him. Why here?"

"Because the Mairie is filled up."

"Doesn't make sense. Why not one of the cafés by the bridge? Why not one of the shops? If he's supposed to keep an eye on the bridge, they'd post him by the bridge. They'd kick a soldier out to make way." He looked at her. "Maybe it's you he's supposed to keep an eye on."

She stared. That never occurred to her. Who was the spy now?

"They must suspect you. What about the other girls? Are they Resistance?"

"No. Colette is Claudio's girlfriend. Marie-Josette . . . well, she's my friend, and she's never spoken of it."

"Have *you* said anything?"

"Of course not. But I'd read it in her eyes, and I do not see it. Neither is Simone. Simone is a survivor. As a general rule, survivors do not join the Resistance."

Floorboards creaked in the hall. They shared a frozen gaze.

"Shall I make some noise?" Cabby presently whispered, his deadpan face belying the glint in his eyes. "Customer noise?"

She clapped a hand over her mouth.

"What kind of noise would I make?"

She warned him silent with a fierce wave.

"Do they whoop it up?"

She bent double from the edge of the bed, shaking with muffled laughter.

"I'd probably whoop it up," he said, in that relentless, innocent whisper.

She snatched a pillow and plunged her face into it.

When at last the creaking passed, she looked up at him, face sticky and hot. She brushed hair from her eyes and said fiercely, "This isn't a joke!" The pillow fell to the floor. She smoothed her dress in a huff. Then she rubbed her stomach and chuckled helplessly. "Oh, that hurt. I have not laughed that hard since—"

But no, not even Jean-Paul made her laugh that hard. In fact, he never made her laugh, though he always took her breath away.

The pilot had a self-satisfied look. He twirled the hat,

smirking, until the problem of Claudio came upon them once more. The hat stilled. She picked up the pillow and put it back where it belonged. She tugged her dress a little lower over her knees.

"What do you miss the most?" he asked softly. "From pre-Occupation days?"

"Soap that smells good and lathers."

"Not freedom?"

"Soap, I tell you. Nothing but soap. Freedom is for the birds."

A smile twitched. "What else?"

"I miss our flag."

"What else?"

"My fiancé."

"Where is he?"

"Buried near the Maginot Line." She took a bolster to her lap. "I miss everything. I miss the way things used to be. Life, work. You are suddenly out of the routine you were in for years, and all is different, cruelly so, because it is an inescapable different. Nothing will ever be the same and you cannot comprehend it. It is a death. Death is difficult to—" she rolled her hand for the word—"mold to."

She rolled the bolster back and forth. "We kept waiting for everyone to come to their senses. 'Come now, enough of this war stuff. Back to Germany you go. It is just a big misunderstanding.' But no one came to his senses. I saw a memorandum on Ambassador Bullitt's desk. Someone told him, 'The game is lost. France stands alone. The Democracies are again too late.' At first we were sure Britain meant France to fight the war alone. Let the French fill the casualty lists, while England sits on her panzer-free island. And America . . ." She glanced at the pilot. "If you'd come to our aid sooner, if you had believed the reports—"

"You're gonna pin the war on me?"

She looked into his eyes. "Not anymore. When I look into someone's eyes, it changes things. Sometimes against my will." She was talking too much. "After four years, it seems we are fallen into a haze of endurance. I am astonished at what we have come to put up with. And I am astonished to discover the profound indifference of the average citizen to another's fate. People once kind and personable, now cold and gray, dead to another's suffering. I never would have believed it. It's every man for himself in France. No one cares. No pity." Her voice dropped to a bare whisper. She rolled the bolster on her lap. "I was starving. And no one cared. No pity."

"It isn't true."

She looked up, shocked to find his eyes hot, his face intent.

"You can't think your entire nation has abandoned pity."

"What do you know, *Cabby*?" she said indignantly. "I was nineteen! I was—"

"You dishonor a remarkable woman with this talk." He rose and pointed out the window with his hat. "If you speak against your nation, you speak against her, and I won't hear it. You wanna talk about how awful your people have been, fine—not around me."

He glared at her for a long moment, then he lowered his hat and began to halfheartedly twirl it. "Are we done? Is it time enough?"

She nodded, senses stinging.

"I'll see myself out."

"Wait—you must pay me," she said very quietly.

He paused at the door. He put his hand in his pocket and pulled out a handful of francs. He looked at the mess of bills and coins helplessly, then held it out for her to pick out the right amount. "I'll be back in a few days."

"Hopefully I will have something more." She added, "Do you play chess?"

A little surprised, he nodded.

"It will give us something to do."

His apparent relief annoyed her.

He stepped into the hall and looked toward Colette's room, slowly turning the hat in his hands. Then he put it on his head and settled it. He turned for the stairs, ducking under the low-slanted ceiling, and descended without a backward glance.

She shut the door. She went to the table and tossed the bills on the tea tray. She sat very still on the edge of the bed. The motorcycle started, and she listened long after it had faded into the distance.

Tom took off his hat and hung it on the coat tree near the door. He stood in the doorway of Rousseau's study. The Frenchman sat at his desk with a glass of cognac and a very dark look.

"You're late."

"When was I supposed to be back?"

"Don't be stupid. Hours ago. As planned."

"I went for a drive."

"You went for a drive," Rousseau said, nodding. "You used up Resistance-obtained Occupation petrol to go for a drive. I hope you had a good time."

"I did, in fact. I went to the coast and walked around. Visited an installment. Listened to a guy play the accordion on top of a bunker."

Rousseau softened a little. "Rommel is fond of handing out accordions to deserving soldiers."

"He should give them to people who can play."

"Unnecessary exposure is foolish. Coming home late instead of when you are expected is unacceptable. Did anyone talk to you?"

Tom's belligerence faded as he remembered the reactions he'd received. "Why should they? They're too scared of me. You should have seen her face when she first saw me." He stared at Rousseau. "Do you know the only place I feel at home is with the Germans? Nazis! I blend in with Nazis."

Rousseau was silent. Then, "Are you hungry?"

"No." Then, "Yes."

"Charlotte made some stew."

They sat at the small kitchen table and ate without conversation. Charlotte had not only made stew, she had also brought a baguette and some coffee from the office, the latest gift from Braun. She seemed distressed that the Germans had inconvenienced her boss, and she apparently felt personally obliged to answer for his indignity, although she and her husband had put up with two soldiers for years.

When they finished eating, Michel made coffee and brought it to the table. Something made him think Tom needed a small and comfortable kitchen, not a large, cold study.

Tom held the cup under his nose and inhaled the aroma. "Where did you get this?"

"Hauptmann Braun. I suspect he gives it to us because he hates to come to our office and be without."

"You two seem to get along okay."

"He's not bad."

"Hauptmann. He's an officer, like me?"

"Not exactly. His is a civil commission. He's an engineer

assigned to certain installments along the Atlantic Wall. His official title is a little difficult to manage. Take the word *Festungspioniere* and add about five syllables. He told us to call him *hauptmann* to make things easier." Michel breathed in the fragrance of the coffee. He was suddenly sent to cafés with his father when he was a boy, to cafés with François during school breaks.

He took a sip, but was not sure he enjoyed it as much as the transportive fragrance. "What is she like?"

Tom didn't answer, just took a gulp of coffee.

Michel winced. "You need to *savor* it. I beg you, savor it, for my sake." Michel took a hopefully exemplary sip.

"So," he finally asked. "How did it go?"

"It went all right."

"And what could she tell us?"

Tom told him the few details of the Caen Canal Bridge that Brigitte knew.

"What about the charges?"

"She doesn't know yet. The guy who talks the most has been sick. She should be able to learn more soon. She did say something about a panzer division transferring to Caen." Tom looked at Michel. "Know anything about that?"

He kept the alarm concealed. "We know Rommel had reformed the Twenty-First . . ."

"Right here? Here in Normandy?"

"I don't know." Well, this was something to talk to London about. Surely aerial photographs would reveal something as large as a panzer division on the move. "Did she say when the transfer would occur?"

"I don't know." He amended and said, "She didn't know." Then he muttered, "I made an idiot of myself." Some of the same belligerence as when he arrived came to his face. Michel slowly took a sip.

"I hate it when you people talk yourselves down. So far, I've seen a lot of brave stuff. From Clemmie, from you, from Rafael. Sure, every country has bad eggs, some more than others. But there's good, and she—it was wrong, what she was saying. No pity, no one caring. It was like spitting on Clemmie." Tom looked up. "Claudio Benoit. He's moving into the brothel."

Michel sat back. First a panzer division on the move, now this. "When?"

"She doesn't know. Soon. It means she's being watched. What's the deal with him?"

"He was in prison in Paris, on pimping charges. The Milice got him released."

"What exactly is Milice?"

"It started as a Vichy police force to maintain order in the Unoccupied Zone. Now it's nothing but French Gestapo. A man named Joseph Darnand is in charge. He's a zealous fascist. He drove the Milice to become what they are today. All they represent is authorized pillage, murder, and rape. They give convicted felons a choice of enlisting in Milice rather than serving a prison term. Things are even worse now than they were a year ago. The Milice have license not only to arrest, but also to interrogate. Above everything else they are determined to crush the Resistance."

"And they are French," Tom said contemptuously.

"They are French. Perhaps you can understand Brigitte a little better, regarding how she feels about her countrymen." Michel sighed. "I am sorry the work is not as . . . satisfying, surely, as flying your plane."

Tom didn't answer.

"We play what we're dealt, Tom. Some are dealt an ugly hand. They play it best as they can." *How do I play this one? Do I keep Tom on the job, with a Milice over his shoulder?*

"I've had a good hand. Flew a beautiful plane. Blew things to smithereens. Went back to England to have a beer." He raised his eyes to Michel. "What happened to Clemmie's granddaughter?"

Michel studied his coffee cup. "I cannot talk about it."

"I'm sorry I asked," Tom said quietly. He finished his coffee and pushed back from the table. Before he got up, he said, "In the bathroom, there is a dish with little soaps in it. Paper-covered soaps. Would it be all right if I took one?"

"Take two."

There'll be bluebirds over . . .

"I'm sick of that tune," Colette complained. She was fixing a shirt for Claudio. "Does anyone have a thinner needle? This material is too thick."

"You can use my thimble. Or you could go to La Broderie," Marie-Josette said, adding slyly, "Wait—they don't serve sluts." She giggled and took another sip of wine.

"They do now," Brigitte murmured, holding a pillow to her growling stomach. "Thanks to your German soldier."

Marie-Josette lowered her wineglass. "What of him?"

"He broke the owner's foot," Colette said with relish so discreet it was worse than if she'd triumphed openly. She loved to tell bad news. "He said he'd break the other if she put *slut* on her sign."

Marie-Josette's amusement faded. "Stefan did that?"

"She had it coming," Colette said.

Brigitte groaned, "Colette, you are such a—" but she pressed the pillow over her face and told it exactly what she thought of Colette. Marie-Josette giggled. Then Brigitte yanked the pillow off and snapped, "Why don't you grow up, Colette? You can be such a—" and she buried her face again.

Marie-Josette giggled again, then suddenly exclaimed, "Oh, oh! You should have seen him, Colette! Ooh la la, what a pastry." She rolled her eyes and fanned her face. "What's his name, Brigitte? Your own German soldier?"

Brigitte yanked off the pillow. "Cabby," she spat, glaring at the now-content Colette. Always playing her sick little game. When could Brigitte tip her from the fence into humanity? *Do not make me give up on you!*

"Cabby," Marie-Josette sighed.

"Cabby," Colette said, pausing with the needle. "What an odd name."

Brigitte's stomach lurched. Panic raced hot in her veins. *Calmly. Calmly.* "Or was it Kees," she mused. "Something with a *K*." She snapped her fingers. "Yes, that's it, Kees. Major Kees, with a long and ridiculous last name. And he's not German; he's Dutch."

"Did you see him, Colette?" Marie-Josette said dreamily, resting the glass on her cheek. "I'll trade you for Stefan, Brigitte."

"I'm not interested in oafs who stomp on old ladies' feet."

Marie-Josette drew herself up. "He is not an oaf. He believes in my dreams."

"Dreams." Colette smirked. She pulled the thread taut and bit it off.

"Even you must have a dream, Colette," Marie-Josette said.

"I dream of a foreigner-free France. No Communists, no Jews."

Marie-Josette lifted an eyebrow. "Finally, the ice queen has an opinion all her own. Or is it Claudio's?" She raised her glass. "Sounds like vintage Milice to me."

For answer, Colette gave Marie-Josette an odd look. Her eyes had a strange light in them, and she gave a vacant little smile. The playfulness in Marie-Josette's face faded, and she took a sullen sip of her wine. Then the look slid to Brigitte, where it seemed to want to go in the first place. Such a strange, considering look.

She resumed sewing.

By the feeling in the room, Colette had fallen from the fence and had not landed on the side of humanity.

14

THREE DAYS LATER, Major Kees Nieuwenhuis knocked on the back door, and soon two heads nearly met over a chessboard. The table was small for a game table. The tray with the tea things lay on the braided rug.

They fell easily to discussing business over something as distracting as chess. It helped to avoid looking at the bed, that big centerpiece of the room, which provoked disruptive thoughts.

Captain Fitz was a chess player and taught Tom to fight for the high ground, which, he said, was the center of the board. Apparently Brigitte knew of this strategy, too. She'd lunged for the high ground from move one. He glared at her two pawns, a knight, and a bishop, neatly entrenched in the center. He wished one of his pawns could lob a grenade, wipe out the whole smug squad.

"When will he return to duty?" Tom asked of Private Tisknikt, keeping the frustration from his tone. He wanted intel. Something he could squeeze in his fist, something worth this awkward charade. Nothing like playing chess at a teeny tiny table next to a great big bed with history.

"Soon. He's doing better. But I do have news. One of my customers is an engineer stationed at Douvres-la-Délivrande. It's a radar station about ten kilometers west of the bridges."

"That's a long way to come for a brothel," Tom commented. "Don't they have any closer?" He hesitated over his knight, then moved it.

"Not this kind," Brigitte said. She immediately took his knight with her bishop.

"What kind?" he asked, scowling as his knight joined the other POWs. He didn't care for the game because he liked chance better than strategy. Then he could blame it on a poor roll, not a poor choice.

"Will you let me finish? I learned something from him. He's talkative, like Alex. I said something about the twenty soldiers stationed at the bridge, that they didn't bring me much business, and he said, 'Twenty? Not anymore. That garrison's been beefed to fifty.'"

He looked up from the board. "That's a big change. What do they know that we don't know? Did they find something out? A panzer division on the way. Now this?"

"My thoughts precise."

"Anything else?"

"No. But Alex will be back soon, and I have a ruse with him. He wants to get in good with his commander, so I told him I would pass on any information if I heard the Resistance is up to something. That way I can fish for more information." She presented a proud, charming little smile. "Pretty good, don't you think? I'll make a spy yet. It seems they're more afraid of the Resistance than the invasion."

"Well, they're certainly preparing for it."

TRACY GROOT

"You can't move that—it blocks your king. You will be in check. They seem to think it will come east of here. That is what Alex said. That is how they are prepared to defend. Do you think it will come from the east?"

"No idea. The Pas-de-Calais area is closest to England, easiest to resupply. But that's why we won't invade there. Too obvious on our part, too heavily defended on theirs." The ratty little pawn was what he wanted to move, but her hateful bishop pinned it to the king.

"Where do you think they will come? We've talked of nothing else for two years."

Now this was the kind of talk he liked. "Well, thinking like a fighter pilot . . ."

He picked up the chessboard and carefully put it on the floor. He took a spoon from the tea tray and held it up. "Here's the coast of France." He positioned it on the table and took another spoon. "And this is England." He placed it parallel.

"I'm air support, right? I not only do target missions, I escort bombers. B-24s, B-17s, troop transports." He picked up a pawn and a queen, flew them side by side over the spoons.

"But I don't have the fuel supply the bombers do. They won't invade where we can't fly back and refuel, and this kind of invasion has to be the whole shebang—air, ground, and sea. Once we get that foothold on the Continent, we'll refuel from there, then support an overall press for Germany. But we must get that foothold. Flying from England, my range is from about here—" he pointed with the pawn to the tip of the France spoon, indicating the tip of France's west coast—"to about here."

He brought the pawn far over and tapped the imaginary map. "The west end of Germany. Now. The Allies are not gonna risk an invasion there, too close to the Luftwaffe bases. And on the other end, too much chance to get bombarded by

Atlantic storms. That's why this whole area is the hot spot." He moved his finger along the middle part of the France spoon. "Stoutly defended, sure. But here we can give the Allies strong air support."

He gave a quick glance to see if she was with him, then looked again. Her attention was so keen, he looked at the spoons to see what she was seeing.

"It is really coming," she said, incredulous. She lifted her gaze to his, brown eyes full of disbelief that sorely wanted to believe.

"Yes," he said simply, putting as much as he could into that little word. "Yes, Brigitte. It is."

She looked at the spoons. "Tell me more. Tell me true things. There is a buildup." The coast within eyesight, yet they were so isolated. They were so duped, they were so . . . jailed. An entire country imprisoned.

"Like you wouldn't believe," he said earnestly. "The number of personnel is getting close to a million."

"A million," she breathed. "That's not just English propaganda?"

"I've seen it with my own eyes. Acres and acres of tanks, and jeeps, and trucks, and planes, and . . ." He didn't mention the piles of coffins he'd seen at one camp. "Crate after crate of ammunition, tents, blankets . . ."

"All ready to come here."

"Ships like you would not believe, putting into harbors all over England, ready to haul it all over. I wish you could see what I've seen, Brigitte. Hundreds of thousands of soldiers just over that channel, ready to light up the whole earth." He suddenly dug for coins in his pocket. He held one up. "See this? This one coin—ten thousand men. Ten thousand, picture it." He placed it behind the England spoon. Then he showed her the rest of the coins in his hand. "All of these? Ten thousand men each." He slowly drained the coins onto the table, onto England.

She drew upon the sight, discovering the armies the coins represented. She picked up a coin and held it even with her eyes, studying it. Then Tom saw the truth take hold and felt a little thrill.

She looked past the coin to Tom. "I believe it now. Not from the BBC, not from rumors."

"You can listen to the BBC?"

"The Germans like their music. When they are gone, and when Claudio is not around, we listen. We hear messages of hope, that the invasion is coming, and it helps some. But after four years, we are fed up with hope. We need action, Cabby. We need it for the sake of our souls." She looked at the spoons. "Where would you invade?"

Tom didn't hesitate. He put his finger on the center of the French spoon. "This is that nice little chunk of peninsula called Cherbourg. I'd put my money for a foothold right here. It's three times the distance to Calais, but still in easy range for our planes. It must drive Hitler mad, wondering where and when."

The talk had invigorated him. He put the spoons on the tea tray and carefully replaced the chessboard. He rubbed his hands together and settled into the stance of a chess-winning man. "That's it. I'm gonna win."

Brigitte squared herself, too, and took to the board with such fierce focus, Tom chuckled. She smiled, eyes testing out potential moves. "Too late. The invasion is coming. I am revived."

"Anything about Benoit moving in?"

"Colette hasn't said and I haven't asked. He was here the other day, but didn't stay. He gave me a nasty, superior look, though. And Colette's in a better mood, which I don't trust. Who is the remarkable woman?"

Her eyes narrowed as she tested a move, and he took the chance to study her face. Smooth, sloping cheekbones, brown and bright eyes, lovely, full lips. He couldn't stop the sudden image of men kissing them. Lots of men. He shook it off. How could she do it? She was so reasonable.

Then the words reached him. "What remarkable woman?"

"The one you yelled at me for. It's your move."

"Clemmie. She hid me in her house when my plane went down. She's hidden lots of airmen. She had a granddaughter who worked for the Resistance, in the cell I'm with. The cell we're with. Flame."

"Flame," Brigitte repeated. Then she said softly, "Did she die?"

"Yes." Then, "The granddaughter, not Clemmie."

"Rafael said a woman died. I wouldn't move there, you're two moves from checkmate. You can still save yourself."

Tom scowled, scratched his head, and then placed his rook on the same rank as Brigitte's queen.

"Good. Now you will make me think." She put her chin on her fist.

"What's it like, living in a jailed country?"

Brigitte lined up her captured pieces alongside the board. "It surprises me what you get used to. I can hardly remember life without queues. Or the worry that they will run out the moment you make it to the front. Yet I am used to it." She rearranged the pieces by rank, and then, as if it had helped, reached for her queen on the board and decisively plunked it down. "Voilà. You are in trouble. I never thought I would get used to ration coupons. Even then, you have to be on good terms with the butcher or the fishmonger for even a carp's head. Prostitutes aren't on good terms with anybody. Except soldiers. And they don't bring carp."

Tom wrinkled his nose. "What do you do with a carp's head?"

"Soup. Always soup. We are supposed to get one liter of wine every ten days, but only if the store has been supplied. Some of our ration coupons are worthless."

"What's the worst about it all?" He left off studying the board. He rested his head on his fist.

She considered the question with surprise. "It seems rolled into one. Hunger, I suppose. After that, loss of freedom. But food first, since really, the only real freedom we have is to die of hunger. I think when you are filled up, you deal with things better. Food gives perspective. I am grateful to get whatever I can, when such a notion would not have brought forth any such gratefulness before." She smiled wryly. "The Occupation has taught me to be glad for what I do get. Before, I was never grateful."

"Are you always hungry?" he asked, wishing he had brought something from Michel's.

"Not always. But I miss not having to think about it. It can be very distracting." She tilted her head to one side, in a movement Tom was coming to know. "Every now and then you have panic, but . . . What is the English . . . ?" She snapped her fingers, summoning the word. "I cannot think of it, but you take charge of yourself and say, 'This is how it is, *chou-chou*. Have courage; it will not always be this way.' Sometimes—" and her face went sly—"you save up your food, enduring the hunger so you can spend it on one gorgeous meal, knowing you will be magnificently full." Her eyes sparkled, and she kissed her fingertips to the ceiling. "Sick with food."

He smiled. The expressiveness reminded him of Clemmie.

"I have an excellent imagination when it comes to food. Weak beef broth becomes beef stew. A piece of bread sprinkled with sugar becomes a fine pastry from the best patisserie." She leaned forward and said, "I can put chocolate on it with my mind."

"What food do you miss the most?"

"Butter!" she exclaimed. "Not the fake stuff, this margarine. It is a devil invention. Butter is . . ." Her expression went dreamy. "Voluptuous."

He'd never heard the word applied that way. He couldn't help a chuckle and, before he had to explain himself, said, "It helps to drink a glass of water before you eat."

"Pfft. I don't want what helps. I want food to fill my belly, not water. That is where imagination is—" her fingers fluttered for the word, and she brightened when she found it— "my ally. You see, in the beginning of the Occupation—" she warmed, eager to talk about it, something he'd noticed about Clemmie—"less food was taken with far more courage and dignity. It was a novelty in the beginning. The ration coupons were a novelty. As it went on, we were less amiable to endure hardship; less patient with the food queues, more suspicious of others. There is anger and envy when you know your neighbor eats better than you because of her connections.

"Hunger shows the Occupation best, because you deal with it every day, and it tries your character. You don't always deal with the cold, or the fear, or the feeling of chains; you can dream yourself away from some of that. You can stand under the stars, because there is always the free expanse of the sky, and that freedom will lift your heart if you let it, sometimes sail you over the white cliffs of Dover. But you cannot dream hunger away. Not until you develop a stupefying imagination."

"Stupefying . . . ," Tom murmured, liking the word on his tongue. "You have quite an English vocabulary. I speak it better than my parents, but you speak better than me." The accent was charming, too. In fact, it was . . . it was effervescent.

Effervescent? Was that even a word? He must have heard it somewhere. If it meant "soft and alluring," the way he once saw a woman wear a silky lavender scarf, then that was the word for her accent. Maybe "rarefied splendor." The way she spoke sometimes blew a mist around his senses. The way she infused expression into her speech . . . it made her so carefree, so unaware of her charm.

"I studied English in school. But more useful than that, I worked for an eloquent man. Ambassador Bullitt. His words always sent me to my dictionary. If I do not become a travel book writer, I want to teach English. I love it! I love to read Hardy and Dickens and Gaskell in English, not French."

Impulsively, he said, "Brigitte, why . . . ? Was there no other way?"

The delicate features became still as stone.

"I'm sorry—it just came out," he said quickly. Then he decided to crucify himself. "Look, I can't figure you out. You're so smart, you talk better than anyone I know—why do you do it? It seems the resort of someone cheap and stupid, not you."

She did not answer. She sat motionless for a time. Then she looked out the window. "You have a strange way of making me forget myself, then making me wish I'd never been born."

Tom closed his eyes. *You—idiot!*

He hurt her. He owed her. He cast about desperately to make it right.

"I want to show you something." He rose and unbuckled his belt. He slipped it off and found the notches. He showed them to her. "See that? I get to color one in for every Nazi I kill with my own hands."

Her features hardened at the sight of the notches. "Good for you."

"One each for my aunt, my uncle, and my little cousins, Caspar and Klaas. They died at Rotterdam."

Her cold look went back to the window.

"I'm doing it for my mother."

"You are doing it for yourself."

He snatched the notches from her view.

He shouldn't have told her. He had an idea that any plan weakened if he told about it before he put it into action. Something corrosive in the air did it. Plans had to stay secret until they built and grew and burst into action.

It was a very personal plan. He'd owed her, but he'd paid too much. He turned away and put the belt back on. He took his hat from where he'd tossed it on the bed. "Is it time enough?"

She nodded, still staring out the window.

He went to the door and remembered. He pulled out some francs, picked out what she had the other day, and went to the table to put them on the chessboard. He hesitated. He reached into another pocket. Next to the francs, he placed two little paper-wrapped soaps.

"I don't know if they lather," he said roughly. "They smell good." He put on his hat and went to the door.

"Wait." She came to the door. She rubbed a little lipstick from her lower lip, then reached up to rub it onto Tom's neck. His traitorous skin tingled at the touch. Then came a mental flicker of her lips leaving the mark instead of fingers. His face warmed. "In case they see you when you leave," she said, noticing his discomfort.

"I know," he snapped, then seized her hand. "Do you think I'm stupid?" He glared down at her.

He didn't know how long he'd locked with the brown eyes. He realized he still gripped her hand, released it like it burned.

※ ※

It was close to 11 p.m., and Rousseau was not yet home. He had a late meeting at the office with site managers over some collapse at a new installment.

Tom sat with Rafael in Rousseau's study.

Rafael sat in Rousseau's chair and had helped himself to Rousseau's cognac. "If he asks, you were thirsty. You needed a good drink after your hard day's work at a brothel." Rafael took the silver case of cigarettes and offered one to Tom, who shook his head, then took one for himself.

"If he asks . . ."

"I had me a smoke."

Rafael winked as he lit up. Drink in one hand, cigarette in the other, he draped his arms on both sides of the chair and grinned. "I could get used to this. Monsieur Rousseau has a nice life. How did it go today?"

Tom put his head back to stare at the ceiling. "I can't keep my mouth shut. I say such stupid things. You know something? I'm figuring this out just now: I can separate who she is from what she does. I couldn't do that before. I don't respect her *occupation*. But I respect *her*. Does that make sense? It's . . . stupefying."

"Bien sûr." But Rafael paid more attention to the cognac. He raised the glass to look through it. "I believe I can now tell the difference between the cheap and the good." He took a sip, nodded. "This is good."

"Would Rousseau have anything less?"

"Times as they are, you never know what you will choose to give up. Did you get more news?"

"Not much, but relatively significant. They've upped the garrison to about fifty men. She found out from a different guy. Her main source is still sick."

"What do you *do* when you are there?" Rafael asked, a grin on the rise as he drew from the cigarette. He was far less interested in the intel.

"What do you think we do?"

"Make whoopee," he said with a gleam. Tom chuckled, and Rafael shrugged. "Is it not slang for sex?"

"It's not like that. We played chess today."

"Who won?"

His smile faded. "She did."

"That is wise." More soberly, he said, "She is pretty."

"She is."

"Are you not tempted?"

"No. Yes." Clearing his head, *"No."* Then, quietly, "Yes."

Rafael's face crinkled as he grinned like an amiable scoundrel. Then he said with true interest, "What is her story, Cabby? Hmm?"

"I don't know it yet. Not all of it."

"Rousseau told me about Benoit. That is not good. It does not sound right."

"He hasn't moved in yet."

"I still do not like it."

"Me either. How's Clemmie doing?"

"The same. Her airmen can do no wrong, but she bullies me."

"Then she treats you like a son." Tom hesitated, then asked, "What did they do to Jasmine?"

Rafael was about to take a sip, but he put the glass down. "Terrible things."

"Does Clemmie know what they were?"

"I hope not." Rafael looked at Tom. "Why do you want to know?"

"I've asked myself that."

"You are looking for a fight, my brother." Rafael looked at

the light through the amber liquid. "Do not make me recall what I will spend the rest of my life trying to forget." He raised red-stained eyes to Tom. "Now. Tell me about Jane Russell. I have seen the uncensored version of *The Outlaw*. How can I meet her?"

15

AT FIRST TOM had dreaded the meetings with Brigitte. Now the days between began to drag. Not that he wasn't without occupation. Rousseau gave him the occasional errand to keep Tom coming and going so his presence in the neighborhood would be noted. Once he made Tom go to the cinema.

He also had Tom keep up a minimal pretense as Rommel's watchdog of Dutch conscripts. Rousseau provided him with a list of benign questions, and twice he had been to the Cimenterie office to interview conscripts—twice, he met with men whose open hostility baffled him at first, until he put himself in their shoes. Anyone who spoke fluent Dutch and wore a German uniform had to be a traitor. They themselves were slaves, conscripted to labor for the Atlantic Wall. They had no choice. Major Kees Nieuwenhuis had a choice. He should have chosen hard labor. He chose to lick Hitler's boots.

This morning Rousseau decided Tom needed to be seen with him. They would walk together as if Tom had asked Rousseau to show him the sights. A tall blond in a German officer's uniform and a short well-dressed Frenchman provoked looks quickly averted—just the sort of thing Rousseau said he wanted. Let them pity poor Monsieur Rousseau, those who knew him, let them wonder what had happened that he should come under what was surely unfair scrutiny. It was exactly the sort of diverting nuance some Resistance cells needed; summon a bit of attention in order to deflect it. It didn't make a lot of sense to Tom, but this was what was explained to him when they set out on an excursion Rousseau would later come to regret.

They had been walking for an hour in the city of Caen, strolling through winding narrow streets, Rousseau pointing out historical landmarks, mostly abbeys and very old churches: the Church of St. Pierre just outside the Château de Caen in the heart of the city, dating to the thirteenth century, the Church of St. Gilles, the Church of Notre-Dame-de-Froide-Rue. He was just pointing out another when they came upon a scuffle beside an awning-covered newspaper stand in a marketplace.

A German soldier and two men wearing Milice-insignia caps stood around a man on his knees in the gutter. Each time the man tried to rise, one of the three booted him down. He had a bloody nose, a bloody lip, and a bloody scrape on his chin, as if he'd been shoved face-first into the pavement. After one final kick he stayed on his knees in the gutter, dripping spittle and blood.

"What are they doing?" Tom whispered, horrified.

"Keep walking."

Tom tried, but he couldn't. He stopped even with the group, watching openly while everyone else—some gathered at the newspaper stand, some standing in doorways, some at windows above—watched furtively.

"Keep walking," Rousseau hissed.

Then came a thin wail, and attention went to an old man with no coat, wispy gray hair lilting in his rush to the group. Anguished, he tried to get to the man in the gutter, but one of the Milice pushed him back. When he tried again, the Milice backhanded him. He staggered, fell, and sat weeping on the sidewalk, holding his bleeding mouth.

It wasn't just that the Milice had backhanded him; it was the *way* he did it, with form, with style, like a tennis shot, knowing all eyes watched. It was all about the power he had to do it and how he'd made it look.

Tom barely felt Rousseau's hand on his arm. He shook it off, and before the Milice knew what had happened, a tall blond officer had him by the throat and against a newspaper rack. The rack toppled backward, and Tom followed him down. He clutched a handful of collar and flesh, hauled him to his feet, and slammed him against the newsstand counter, scattering customers and papers.

The other Milice and the German didn't know what to do. Perhaps Tom's size and rank silenced them.

Rousseau came to Tom's side, but Tom didn't take his eyes from the shocked and reddening face of the gasping man who scrabbled at Tom's hand.

"Major Nieuwenhuis, please," Rousseau said in Dutch, "I would suggest these three know their business."

His fingers dug deeper, the man began to choke. He clawed frantically.

"I would suggest you are endangering this man's life, and that you will not make your superior officer happy with this behavior. Your superior will be angry."

Tom released him. The man gasped and twisted away from the counter, bending double to cough and clutch his throat. Breathing hard, Tom looked at the Frenchman on the street.

The elderly man was now quietly weeping at the younger man's side, smoothing his hair, helping him to stand.

"We must go," Rousseau said urgently.

Tom leveled a look at the other two men. He kept the gaze on them while he adjusted his hat and smoothed his coat, and, for final effect, brushed off the rank insignia on his shoulder. Rousseau touched his elbow, but Tom wouldn't budge, not until the elderly man led the younger away.

Rousseau set a nonchalant pace until they took the first corner; then he picked up speed, taking corners and turns and curving alleys until they came to a small stone church flanked by apartments built into its sidewalls. They ducked inside, Rousseau absently crossing himself at the threshold. They went into the sanctuary, a cold, echoing chamber that smelled of incense and mildew. Rousseau knelt and crossed himself again before entering a pew. Tom slid in next to him, hat on his knees.

They sat in a frozen silence until Tom finally said, "You're not happy with me."

"I blame myself. I blame myself!"

"How can you take credit for what I just did?"

"I have not put enough fear in you. I have not shown you the beast." And Rousseau told him what they had done to Clemmie's granddaughter.

The horror Tom had felt in the marketplace was nothing to this. Nothing to the tears in the eyes of Michel Rousseau, this great, iron man Tom had come to respect as much as he respected Roosevelt and Churchill. For the first time, Tom understood Rafael.

"She was so very brave," Rousseau whispered, lips trembling. "Right until the end. I thought I knew what I had. I did not know until then. I have been alone ever since."

They did those things to *Clemmie's granddaughter?*

Electricity on his skin, breathing hard, Tom got up and paced the aisle. A priest appeared to the right of the altar, saw Rousseau and then Tom. He hesitated, then came toward them. Tom waved him off with a growl. Taken aback, the man paused, then slipped away.

He wanted—he needed to be in a P-47 dive, bearing down on target, stick in his hand, red button under his thumb, a never-ending stream of death.

Tom stood next to Rousseau's pew. He finally sat down.

"You have not seen street massacres," the older man said, his face vacant. "You have not seen bodies piled up on each other, like sacks of fertilizer. You have not seen devastating retribution for a simple act of defiance. A woman who protested the billeting of a soldier was shot in the face. Boom, her face exploded, she was gone. You have not seen Jews herded into the Vélodrome in Paris, you have not seen their children torn from their sides. I have seen these things." His breath caught. "They are in my eyes and they are in my chest. You are no longer in civilization, Tom. Everything around you is a false front. It hides hell."

Tom's imagination, fed by Rousseau's words, showed him all.

"Who knows what that man had done," Rousseau said bleakly. "Perhaps he looked at one of them the wrong way. Perhaps, and most likely, they only thought he did. What shocked you so is commonplace to us. After every fresh atrocity, the shock wears away, and you get used to everything. Your true self, your first self, is hidden away under numbness, waiting for the long night to be over."

"No one helped him."

"They want to live." Rousseau looked at Tom. "They could be Resistance and know that to prevent one man's beating may put other lives at stake. It is just another kind of hell."

〰

Cabby did not want to play chess today.

He sat at the window in a slouch, idling with a black button he'd taken from his pocket. Brigitte sat on the bed with her workbasket, embroidering a blue pillowcase with bright-red poppies. She had begun to look forward to these visits from Cabby. Even if he sat sullen and silent, his presence was strangely comforting. She felt as if she had in her room a little piece of Vera Lynn's song.

She hated to tell him there was no news on the bridge. Ernst, one of the bridge soldiers, told her Alex was still on the mend. There was no getting information out of Ernst. He never talked. Cabby took the news with indifference.

"People are afraid of me," he finally said. "I'm not used to that."

Brigitte glanced up from her work.

"I went to the cinema in Caen. I go to buy my ticket, and the ticket girl goes white as snow. I go take a seat, and the whole place goes quiet. I try to hunch down, hide my height, but it's no good. Greenland says I have to wear my uniform everywhere, or I'll be asked for my papers. I only felt better when it got dark. I'm not used to frightening people. I hate it. I worse than hate it. It's evil."

"Some like it. Claudio likes it."

He didn't answer.

"Even if he doesn't move in today, he's sure to come. Today is the day he meets with his superiors in Ranville. He always comes here after." She watched for a reaction. He only studied the black button.

"It gets to you, the feeling here," he murmured. "Hacks away at you. I finally feel it. I feel trapped, like I'm in that cabinet, like I'm in it wherever I go. Sometimes I close my eyes, and I'm with my girl again. I'm back in the air, stick in my hand, man on my wing. A clear target, a mission accomplished. We head home, and I land and taxi, shut her down, talk with the ground crew. They cuss me out if she took a shellacking. We go to debriefing, then mess. If it's a good day, and everyone came back, then Oswald does his guts-and-glory shtick, this crazy song and dance, and we all sing with him, and pretty soon Captain Fitz gets sick of it and starts yelling, and Smythe is already halfway to oblivion with that English beer . . ." A faint smile came.

"What if it is not a good day?"

"Then it's quiet."

"That is how it was when you did not come back." She smoothed the work on her lap, murmured, "It has been time enough, Cabby."

"I don't feel like going. Do any guys . . . Is there ever—" he jerked his shoulder and shifted in his chair—"round two?"

"Sometimes," she replied archly.

"Hey, you wanna see a picture of my little brother?" He dug in the pocket of his jacket, hung over the back of the chair. He took out an identification booklet, took it out of its slipcover, and paged through it. He winged a picture at her, like a playing card.

She caught it and studied the boy. She smiled. "He looks naughty."

"He is. Gives my folks a heck of a time. Teachers, too. I was a good boy."

"I don't believe that." She grinned.

"I was," he protested. He was about to say something else, but his face gained a curious expression, and he went quiet.

"What is it?"

He didn't answer for a time.

"I controlled my patch of sky," he said quietly. "I was *in* control. I had firepower, with my girl. Now I got nothing. This gun?" He leaned sideways to show the Walther P38 on his hip. "No bullets. That's me."

Brigitte handed back the photo. "Did you name your plane?"

He put the picture carefully back into the booklet. "A name never came. She was just 'my girl.' We have a couple of RAF pilots in our squadron. You should hear them talk about their Spitfires. One guy told me it was the most charismatic plane ever built. *Charismatic*, what a word. Well, he never flew a P-47." He dropped the booklet into the pocket. "Twenty-three missions with my girl. She took care of me, then took one right in the heart. I couldn't watch her go down. I couldn't bear it. They were beating a man today, Brigitte."

The needle and thread stilled.

"His father came running. He was an old man, and one of them hit him in the mouth, and in that second, I was caught between Kees and Cabby and Tom. My name is Tom."

"Which of you won?"

"Tom." His shoulders came down. "I could have killed him. Greenland told me how stupid I was. There were a lot of people watching. But I couldn't just watch. Did I give away who I am?"

"Yes!" Brigitte exclaimed, setting the sewing aside. "I am glad that is who you are."

"I don't want anything to happen to Greenland," he said, gloom filling the blue eyes. "I can't stop who I am. I'm no spy. I—reacted instinctively, like a pilot, like I'm trained. What was I thinking? I was so arrogant, thinking I could pull this off. Who am I kidding? I'm a pilot, and that's what I'm good at, and that's where I want to be. I want to be back where I belong, with the guys, fighting from the sky." He noticed he still had the button in his hand. He pocketed it. "I'm worried about Greenland. There he sat, powerless. I never saw him powerless. It's like it drained right out of him. The stuff he's seen would unhinge—"

A tap came at the door.

Her eyes flew wide. She stared in alarm at Cabby. No one ever knocked with a customer inside. That's what a closed door meant.

Cabby swiftly unbuttoned his shirt and pulled it off. Brigitte pushed the pillows from the bed, swept aside the workbasket, and jerked back the bedspread. In two strides, Cabby was in the bed and under the covers.

Brigitte mussed her hair, then went to the door, complaining loudly in French, "Someone better be dying." She opened it a crack, standing behind it as if she were not dressed.

It was Marie-Josette. She came close to the crack in the door and whispered, "Claudio is here. I thought you'd want to know." She slipped away.

Brigitte eased the door shut. She turned to Cabby.

"What did she say?" he whispered, throwing off the covers.

"Claudio is here. Why would she warn me?"

"What do we do?"

Brigitte put up her hand in warning and went to the door. She laid her fingertips on it, then her ear. Soon she heard Colette and Claudio quietly bickering as they came up the stairs. It stopped when they reached the top. All was silent. Then a creak of floorboards as they continued down the hallway, until Colette's door clicked shut.

"You must leave."

She tossed him his shirt. While he put it on, she grabbed his jacket and held it at the ready. He slipped into it. She handed him his hat. She went to the door, ducked out, and waited motionless as she stared down the hall at Colette's door. Then she beckoned Cabby. He went down the stairs before her, trying to be quiet. They slipped into the hallway at the bottom of the stairs, and she saw him to the back door. He gave her a fleeting look in good-bye, then was gone.

She hurried to the front room, where the phonograph played Glenn Miller. The front room was directly under Colette's.

She heard Cabby's motorcycle start and listened very hard for any movement upstairs, tilting her head toward the ceiling. There it came—a quick trample to Colette's window, where Claudio surely watched Cabby drive away. Brigitte's fingers crept to her stomach.

Marie-Josette sat on the sofa, paging through a magazine.

"Thank you," Brigitte said quietly.

"Don't mention it."

Brigitte's mind raced. Why should Marie-Josette warn them? She wondered what to say, if she should say anything at all.

"I overheard them last night," Marie-Josette said softly, flipping pages. "They were in the kitchen. Thought everyone was asleep. Claudio was excited about something, I don't know what. But I heard him say the name Cabby."

Brigitte clutched a handful of her skirt.

Marie-Josette raised her large eyes to Brigitte. "I don't know what you're involved in, and I don't want to. But I know you don't have sex with him."

"How do you—?"

"Please," Marie-Josette scoffed. Then her face became more serious than Brigitte had known, showing the lines of humanity she had longed to see in Colette, because she thought Colette was deeper, smarter, more able for it; here it was in Marie-Josette. She had silenced all traces of silliness and frivolity and joie de vivre. It left her grave and forlorn, and somehow prettier than ever. "Oh, Brigitte," she whispered. "Be careful. Whatever you are doing, please be careful. You're all the family I have."

Brigitte sat beside her on the sofa. She put her arm around her shoulders. "Marie-Josette, I am finally happy. I am doing something. It's not much, but it is something. I'm in secret accord with the unseen force about us. It's a force for our good, that wants our freedom, and I am moving with it."

Marie-Josette's eyes filled with tears. "I want to move with it, too. But I am so afraid. What will happen to us? Is there no saving who we were? I am so tired, Brigitte." The tears spilled. "I'm tired of hunger. I'm tired of men. I grieve for the children who have lost their papas. I grieve for the Jews. I grieve for us, who have turned them out. I grieve for good people who have become what they don't want to be."

"The invasion is coming, Marie-Josette." The words felt worse than useless; they felt like a parody. *Oh, God—please. Help her to see what I saw! Help her to believe!* "Look at me. They are coming. Men, guns, a force like you wouldn't believe. Thousands of them, *tens* of thousands, right on our doorstep! Any day. Any moment."

Tears mingled with Occupation mascara and left a dusky trail on Marie-Josette's face. She brushed a hand under her nose. "He told you that?" she asked, dubiously hopeful.

"I have seen it with my own eyes." She cleared the coffee table. She took a stalk of dried flowers from a vase, broke off two stems. She snatched Colette's workbasket, rummaged for buttons. Then she laid a stalk on the table and opened the world to her friend.

"This is England. And this France. . . ." She held up a button. "This? Ten thousand men! . . ."

16

MICHEL SAT MOTIONLESS at his desk, hands folded over papers.

He should have never listened to François. He had to pull Tom from the Bénouville mission. The lad was too thinking, too feeling.

He did not know how the young pilot would react. He did not know what Rafael would think. It did not matter, he would leave them to it. He should never have listened to François.

With the decision came clarity. He'd contact London and arrange for a pickup in a small Lysander plane. Downed airmen didn't usually rate a Lysander; they reserved those dangerous midnight flights for British SOE agents and other spies, for either insertion or extraction. But it was too risky to get him out through the usual channels for downed pilots. He attracted too much attention.

He opened the lower drawer and took out the almanac. Lysander flights needed to be scheduled around moonlight for navigation.

Wilkie would transmit the message tonight: *Agent needs*

extraction. Michel felt no apology. Tom had become an agent the moment he put on that uniform. They'd have an answer in the next few days through the coded "personal messages" at the end of every BBC broadcast.

It had been some time since G had received a message. His contacts in London knew he was lying low after the infiltration of their group, through Jasmine's death. They'd likely think the agent would be himself.

He paused and made a mental note to also have Wilkie relay the rumor of Rommel's Twenty-First Panzer Division. Was it true? Was it en route to Caen?

He was paging through the almanac with the eraser of his pencil when the door opened.

"Hauptmann Braun," he said, surprised. He laid aside the book and rose. Behind the man she'd just let in, Charlotte's face showed a quick glimpse of alarm before she closed the door.

Michel had not seen him since the day Tom hid in the cabinet. He had been called away to Berlin because his wife had health problems. Something about her kidney. He tried to recall the details. It always pleased Braun when Michel remembered personal things.

"How is your wife? Did the operation go well?"

"Yes, yes, excellent," he boomed in French. "She had the best physicians, the most excellent care. She is convalescing at a wonderful château on Lake Geneva. It was hard to leave. Did you enjoy the olives I sent?"

"We certainly did. Charlotte cried every time she ate one. I wept in private."

Normally, Braun would have laughed. Instead he declared, "Good, good. A pleasure. I am glad you enjoyed them." He strode to Father's end of the room. This part of the room always seemed to interest him. He liked to look at the book titles on the shelves. He liked the jumble of maps and magazines on the desk. He liked the whimsical display of suitcases and safari hats. Michel saw him glance at the carpet, where the chair's claw feet rested, and he clicked his tongue. "The Jew is no longer there, eh? What a pity," he murmured. He put his hands behind his back and looked at the stack of books on the mantel. Surprised, he glanced at Michel.

"Where is your book?"

"My secretary borrowed it."

"How goes the reading?" He had switched to German, unconsciously or not, Michel was not sure.

"That's a difficult question for a Frenchman to answer." Michel smiled, as if making it light. "I'm sure you understand. Were I Jewish, it would be very difficult."

"Do not be too free with me, my friend," Braun said, briskness fading. He picked up a book and looked it over. "Already, this is difficult."

Michel's stomach lurched. "What is difficult?"

He did not answer for a long moment. Michel became aware of the tick of the mantel clock, the soft staccato of Charlotte's typewriter.

"I like my job. That job is cement, the way I make it stay in the air, the way I make it conform to the picture in my mind. I like to make Rommel happy. He is a hero to us Germans, Rousseau. A brave man, a good leader. I wish you could see him not as a German, but as a man. Then you would know my admiration for him is just."

This wasn't Braun at all. Rather, it was exactly what he expected out of Braun's first self.

Braun replaced the book and started for the business side of the room, hands behind his back, face deeply thoughtful.

Michel lowered himself into his chair. "What is this about, Braun?"

"They made me part of their investigation because I know you best."

Michel drew a concealed breath and let it out slowly, just as concealed. "This is news to me," he said affably. "I had no idea I was being investigated."

"For some time now, since the death of one of your workers. Claire Devault."

"What about her?"

"You were with her when she died."

"Yes. In Bénouville. I was summoned because I was her employer."

"Were you her lover?"

"No." *No, not soon enough. I was too obtuse. Too busy. Too late.*

"She was a known Resistance operative. If you were not her lover . . . what were you to her?"

"Her employer."

"Is it usual for an employer—? I am told she was in your arms when she died." Braun stopped in front of the desk. Penetrating gray eyes looked down into Michel's.

Anger rustled, and he rose. "I wanted her last moments on earth to be safe." He wasn't as tall as the German, but he felt his ire equalize the difference. "What is wrong with that? It was human decency. Something she was grossly denied."

"What did she say to you? She said something to you."

Michel studied him. "I thought it odd there were no Germans about."

"What did she say?"

"Do you know what they did to her?"

Braun's steady gaze faltered. "She was Resistance."

"She was a woman! A small, delicate woman. Did they tell you what they did?"

"I don't want to know," Braun said quickly, his face settling into unhappiness. He sat in the chair in front of the desk. After a moment, Michel sat too.

Braun traced his fingertips on the wooden armrest. "What will we do when the war is over, Rousseau?" he finally said. "Will we be friends? In Germany, I think you and I would have been friends. Two years ago, I was certain Germany would win the war. Now it feels fifty-fifty. A fifty-fifty chance the world will speak German a hundred years from now."

Michel let him talk while he considered his answer. He would ask again; it was why they had sent him.

Truth was best whenever possible. But how could he tell Jasmine's last words? *I didn't talk.* Why should she say that to her employer, Michel Rousseau?

Make it close to the truth, and beat him to it.

"She said, 'I did nothing wrong.'" That was truth, too, in the broad scope, and in the time it took for Braun's faraway gaze to come to Michel, he devoted himself to the trueness of those words. It wasn't hard to feel the indignation of them. She *had* done nothing wrong; on the contrary, she had done what was right. Many of his countrymen simply put their heads down to wait out the war, to stiffly ignore anything and everything unpleasant, to determinedly live in an ever-shrinking sphere of unreality. Not her. She looked full on and would not look away.

"Between us? Man-to-man? What they did to her could turn *me* into a resistant." Michel let some teeth show. "What they did was unholy. You have made a terrible name for yourselves."

"I am not of the Nazi movement," Braun said, and something strong flickered in the gray eyes. "You know I am not.

213

Not every German is. There are different parties, you know. I am not of that party."

"I know."

"You cannot know how it is. You cannot understand. You do not know what it's like to—" He broke off. "We are two men from very different nations. Yet I feel kinship with you. I felt it the moment I walked into this room, and not because I wanted to feel it, not because I—"

Braun looked down at his hands for a moment, then looked up. "I have found you to be honest. Someone with whom I can be a little of myself. I've told my wife about you. We could be friends when this war is over."

"Yes? Well, Hitler is doing his best to turn me into a racist. I don't want to assign you with the Nazis, I don't want to hate you because you are German, and I don't think I do. But . . . he makes it hard." His throat tightened. "She was a lovely girl, Braun. She did nothing wrong."

Surprisingly, a tired smile broke over Braun's face. Michel couldn't read it. "These things I will remember years from now, Rousseau. Whatever the language, and whether or not we are friends."

They rested in a less tense silence.

Braun rose, put on his hat, adjusted it. Some briskness returned. "I will tell them the truth. You know nothing. And the girl said nothing of consequence."

He played it to the end, because Braun would expect him to: "Nothing of consequence to a Nazi, perhaps. But if she said, 'I did nothing wrong' and suffered the death she did . . . it means a great deal to a Frenchman."

Braun inclined his head. Then, not looking into Michel's eyes, he said quietly, "Leave revenge alone. Nothing good comes of it. God will take care of it, in the end."

"What do you know of revenge?"

"Are we not living it?" he said sadly.

Michel tilted his head a little, unready for such words. He waited, hoping, daring to believe for more.

"Such times might not have been," Braun said, "if the nations had not cast upon defeated Germany reparations too humiliating, too impossible for her to bear. We were not shown mercy in our defeat, and such a thing from once-noble adversaries was unbecoming. One man's pride could not bear it. One man's rage came to represent my nation. I couldn't finish the book, Rousseau. There is too much truth in it. Too much ugliness. No decent German wanted to see these horrifying unconcealed places of the heart. Once the man laid bare these places, we did not need someone to lead us into the revelations; we needed someone to save us from them. I couldn't finish the book. Not every German can."

"Charlotte didn't borrow it," Michel impulsively replied. "She took it from me. She said it wasn't good for my soul." And he saw enough in the gray eyes to know that if they survived, they would be friends when the war was over.

Braun started for the door. When he got there, he paused.

"It may interest you to know they arrested the woman's grandmother. It turns out she has been housing Allied airmen. Perhaps it was the grandmother they were after all along. They believe she's a ringleader. They're still trying to sort it out. Who knows—perhaps *she* is the great G." He touched the brim of his hat, then turned to go.

Under the wash of suddenly rushing blood, Michel drew another concealed breath.

"Yes, I met her once," he said quickly. "She was at the Rousseau Cimenterie picnic last summer, with Claire. Hard to believe, an old woman a Resistance leader." Then he made the next words sound newly thought, and spoke them with the fresh concern he made to appear on his face. "Hauptmann. I hope for the sake of decency she is treated well. You can understand my concern."

"I wish I hadn't told you," Braun muttered.

"Why is that?"

"You did not need to know. Now it will upset you."

"Only if she is mistreated. If she is Resistance—" and Michel gave a careless shrug—"she knew she could get arrested. That was her choice. But she is an old woman. Innocent or guilty, if she is treated in any way like her granddaughter . . ." Michel rose from the desk, fingertips resting on it. He mastered the trembling. "Like I said, Braun; it could make a resistant out of me."

"That has an unwelcome sound to it . . ."

"It is a plea. I ask you to see to it personally this woman is not mistreated. I ask on behalf of the kinship you feel. You are right; you shouldn't have told me. But now I know, and now I must follow my conscience."

"I wonder that about you. I wonder how often you really do follow your conscience."

Michel didn't answer. The moment became long.

Finally Braun said, "I'll inquire."

"That is not good enough. You know it isn't."

"I'll visit where she's being held," he said with deliberate patience. "I'll make sure I see her myself." When Michel did not respond, he added, "Today."

Michel released a breath and nodded gratefully, as if he fully trusted Braun would not only visit but also prevent any mistreatment. "I will wait here until I hear from you."

Mild surprise came to Braun's face. "I may not know anything for some time."

"I'll be here when you do. Please call."

After a moment Braun nodded and then left, leaving the door ajar. The clack of Charlotte's typewriter filtered in.

Michel had no idea what sort of weight Braun carried with the SS. Braun was a civil engineer. It was like a high school principal presuming to use his authority to interfere in a military court case. But for now, Braun was all Flame had.

They believe she's a ringleader. They're still trying to sort it out.

Michel had seen how they sorted things out. He sank into his chair, put his head in his hands.

Had she been careless? Not Clemmie. Did a neighbor denounce her? What about the three Jews? Were any Allies arrested? Any couriers?

What about Rafael?

He had to slow down and think. He had to make arrangements; he had to act. Tom's life was now in danger—if she knew, Clemmie could tell where he was. Other lives: couriers and airmen could be en route to Clemmie's, they could be walking into a trap. He had to get a message out. He had to find Rafael. He reached for the telephone and froze.

What were they doing to her? Would they subject her to the same interrogation as Jasmine?

"Monsieur Rousseau?" came Charlotte's soft voice, cutting through the void. "Clemmie has been arrested?"

Michel gazed up at his secretary.

"Did he say where they are holding her?"

He shook his head, the motion jerky.

"We will have to move quickly. They've been transporting all resistants straight to Fort de Romainville in Paris. It will be too late then. I will have my people inquire and inform you when I can."

"Your people?" Michel said weakly.

"My dear Monsieur Rousseau," was all she said with a fond smile. She turned on her heel and left.

Michel came home late that evening, around ten. Tom called a greeting from the study. Michel slowly unbuttoned his coat, hung it on the coat tree.

No word from Braun. Until Michel returned, Lily Dechambre, Wilkie's sister-in-law, would sit at Charlotte's desk in case Braun called. Whatever happened, he could not tell Tom about Clemmie.

Part of the day's ordeal had an unexpected benefit; he did not have to tell Tom they were taking him off the job for any other reason than this investigation of the Rousseau Cimenterie. It would spare the man some pride.

The transmitter-receiver, an instrument Wilkie fondly called Heloise, was hidden in Michel's office, in the innocent guise of a decorative cloth-covered suitcase. The suitcase was part of the display near the bookshelves, with the other objects artfully arranged to look like a travel adventure. François had come up with it. Until Tom, it was his greatest triumph.

With Lily keeping watch in Charlotte's office, Wilkie had gone to work as quickly as he could. He sat on the carpet to avoid being seen through the windows and set it up. The suitcase was an OSS affair, outfitted with a set of headphones, a telegraph key, and an antenna coil. Within an hour of Braun's departure, they had passed the word to the cells in Caen of Clemmie's arrest. Wilkie consulted a new cipher table that had been tightly scrolled into a hollowed-out fountain pen and passed word to London, both of the arrest and of the need for a Lysander pickup. At the last moment, Michel remembered to pass on what they had picked up about the panzer division. They waited and soon received acknowledgment of the transmission.

If all went well, in a few days they would receive a personal message over the BBC for Greenland with the coded pickup time. The almanac said the next full moon was April 8, ten days away. A half-moon was best; the pickup could be scheduled for any time a few days before or a few days after. Even in half moonlight, the Lysander could land safely enough without the need to track down enough resistants or *maquisards* to light the airfield with flashlights.

With Clemmie's arrest, every safe house Flame had used was in jeopardy. They had forty-eight hours, the golden time for action after any arrest. A pact existed between every resistant; for forty-eight hours they pledged to hold out under torture as best as they could to allow others to escape. They had to get Tom out of Michel's apartment.

No news of Rafael. No word on the three Jews. And Charlotte had disappeared. She had left the office moments after she spoke to him and hadn't returned.

Tom looked up from the desk, closing a book. "You're late. Have you been using Occupation petrol—" He broke off. "What happened?"

"We have been compromised. We must get you out immediately. Braun came to my office to tell me I am under investigation."

Tom's face went white. "Is it because I—?"

"It has nothing to do with you. I've been under suspicion as Claire Devault's employer. I could be arrested for interrogation anytime, and their favorite time is evening." This was all true, although Braun had defused it. The least of his worries was himself. "You must leave immediately for Bénouville. Go straight to the brothel."

"I was already there today. Won't that get attention? Wouldn't it be better to send me to Clemmie's?"

Michel had an answer ready. "Cabourg is twice as far. The brothel will be safe. We are making arrangements to get you out of the country, and our current airfield is much closer to the brothel."

"But—what about the bridges? What about the intel?" Tom shook his head, as if clearing it. He firmed his jaw. "No. Wait. I can do this."

"There are other cells in Bénouville. The bridges will be covered. But you are connected to the Rousseau Cimenterie, and a spotlight on me is a spotlight on you. We are arranging for a Lysander to pick you up, within days of the next full moon. Perhaps five to eight days. You must stay hidden until then."

"What about Benoit?" Tom said. He went to get his jacket on the sofa. "He's moving in soon. He may have already. He was there today."

"If things get too hot, go to the Château de Bénouville. Madame Vion will hide you, but only if you give her this word: *century*."

"Sensory?"

"Cen-tu-ry," Michel enunciated.

"You don't speak English as well as you think you do. If this is the last time I see you, you might as well know it." He seemed to be waiting for Michel to smile, but he couldn't. Tom paused in pulling on his jacket, eyeing him. "There's something else."

"We cannot find Rafael."

When Michel had told Wilkie about Clemmie's arrest, he had shot out of his chair, blindly pacing the room. With tingling foreboding, Michel asked what was wrong.

A B-17 had gone down east of Houlgate, not far from Cabourg. Rafael and his team were sent to do what they could. The only Flame safe house close to Houlgate was Clemmie's.

"A B-17 went down. Rafael went in for collection. We have not heard from him." *Because maybe he stopped at Clemmie's to visit.*

Tom finished pulling on the jacket. "Don't worry about him right now; worry about yourself. Rafael's a cagey little guy. He'll be fine."

"Listen, this is very important. We know the brothel has a radio. You need to listen to the personal messages given after every BBC broadcast for the next several days. Listen for a message for Greenland. It will give the date and time for your pickup. I will have as many ears on the broadcasts as I can, but if I cannot get to you, you need to get to the rendezvous on your own."

"How will I decode it?"

"The date and time will be in a simple Caesar cipher."

"A what? I fly planes, I don't break codes."

"Find someone who can. They will code it to your hometown, Jenison."

Tom tucked in his shirt. "Caesar cipher, coded to Jenison . . ."

"Listen: the airstrip for the Lysander is in a short clearing near a tiny crossroads town called Le Vey."

"Le Vey."

"It's thirteen kilometers due west of Bénouville."

"Thirteen kilometers west . . ."

"Once there, take the crossroad north. On the right, where the wood begins, keep looking for a path wide enough for an automobile. Go in. Keep going, the woods will open to an airstrip. Do not leave the brothel if—"

"It's not a brothel, it's her home."

"—you can avoid it. Stay put until you hear from the broadcast or me. And if the broadcast, then do precisely as it says. If you—"

Tom was adjusting his belt, buttoning up his jacket, checking his ID. He glanced over. "If I . . . ?"

What would become of this man, François's Lohengrin?

Three years ago this towering boy was in high school, wondering what he was going to do with all that height and breadth for the rest of his life. Now he fought with the Allies, was shot down behind enemy lines, and, from ignorance or bravado, took on a dangerous intelligence mission. He brought a prostitute two paper-covered soaps. He spoke of Clemmie as if she'd personally win the war. He defended a bullied Frenchman as if kin and, in that moment, won a foothold in Michel's heart no Ally had occupied.

He was naïve, he was inarticulate, he could not cook to save his soul, and he had a fair amount of that odious American swagger. But the boy was first-rate. First-rate, indeed. He was in trouble only because Michel—if only Michel had not—

He lifted his chin and put out his hand.

"What is it with you French?" Tom muttered, then shook his hand firmly. "This isn't good-bye. It's see you later. I promised Clemmie I'd come back. I'll look you up when I do. Tell Rafael to lay off the sauce. Good luck, Greenland."

Michel did not trust himself to speak. He went to the door with Tom. Tom smiled, tipped a little salute off his hat, and trotted down the steps. Michel watched until he disappeared around the corner.

"Good luck, Cabby," he whispered.

The motorcycle started. He waited until it faded into the distance, then left the apartment to hurry back to his office.

17

"MISS ME?"

Brigitte stared at the man in the doorway. She pushed him aside to look both ways out the door, then seized his arm and dragged him in.

"What are you *doing* here?" she hissed.

"I felt like chess." A grin came and went. "Trouble in paradise. Looking for a place to hole up."

Brigitte seized his coat lapels and stood on tiptoes to whisper in his ear, "You *cannot* stay here! Marie-Josette told me—"

At that moment, Simone came out of the kitchen bearing a tray. She stopped, looked up at Tom. Brigitte released the coat lapels, smoothed them, and eased down.

"So you're the one," Simone said in English, flicking an appreciative glance at Tom.

"Simone—Major Kees Nieuwenhuis. Did I say it right? Kees, this is Simone."

"Nice to meet you," Simone said.

Cabby smiled and said with his Dutch accent strong, "*Ja,*

nice to meet you." To Brigitte, he said, "No, you do not say it right. You must make it bold. *Nieuwenhuis.* Make your lips like this. Say, *Nieuw-en-huis. Nieuw . . .*"

"My lips will look silly like that," Brigitte said, trying to tell him with a discreet death glare that Claudio was in the front room.

Cabby turned to Simone and announced, "So—*ja*, I was here already today." He leaned in conspiratorially and wiggled an eyebrow. "I am here for round two. Maybe even . . . round *three.*"

Simone smiled a bemused little smile, shot a quick look at Brigitte that could have been sympathetic, and continued down the hall with the tray. "Bruno brought coffee, Brigitte. Join us, if you want."

"Did you have to say that?" Brigitte rounded on him when Simone was gone.

"I was trying to sell it."

She whisper-shrieked, "You do not have to sell it!" She stamped her foot three times. "Listen to me! You cannot stay here. It is impossible. Marie-Josette heard—" She looked down the hall. She grabbed his arm and pulled him around the corner to lead him upstairs, muttering in French, "Of all times for you to show up. You cannot come when you're the only person I want to see. You have to come when Claudio and Colette set up shop in the sitting room like a queen and her consort. *Something* is going on, and I *don't* know what it is, and it has to do with *you*, and does she *ever* go to the sitting room? No! The one time is *now*, when—"

Cabby gently pulled her sleeve, and she stopped and turned. She stood a few steps up, eye level. He looked at her in that dim stairway, and oddly, her stomach gave a little flutter.

"I can't understand you," he whispered.

And quite suddenly, he was handsome. No man had been handsome since Jean-Paul. Earnest pale-blue eyes, smooth and broad cheek planes, dropping flush to a strong-lined jaw. Were he any more handsome, his face would parody itself. But the truth was, he was simply . . . friendly. His earnestness bordered on a familiarity she did not resent; she was simply unused to it. He was a man with nothing to hide, and no wish to. Was it him, or was it the freedom from which he came?

"I think it is you," she murmured in French. "The freedom is incidental."

"Clemmie saved the French for cursing," he murmured. Anxiousness clouded the pale-blue sky. "Was I wrong to come? I can go to the château."

"I . . . I . . ." What did he say? "I did not curse. I scolded."

"Oh, Brigitte!" Marie-Josette called in a singsong from the back door. "Alex is here!"

Brigitte clapped a hand to her forehead and let fly a fine display of the seamy underbelly of the French language.

He nodded. "I've heard some of that from Rafael."

"What do I do?" she whispered, a hand to her cheek. "He is expecting me! What do I tell him? What have you done?" She reached to clutch his head but instead clutched her own. "Claudio is right downstairs!" she groaned. "He and Colette are like some—Oh, I cannot explain it now. Go, go!" She grabbed his arm and pulled him up, pushed him past. He paused at the top to glance down, then slipped into her room and closed the door.

What was she going to *do*?

Oh, how she wanted to scream the biggest scream she could muster, one to put freckles on her face.

Instead, she crossed herself.

She had said something fascinating to Marie-Josette, hadn't

she? That she now moved with the unseen force for good? With angels, perhaps? Oh, that the force for good should attend her now.

She smoothed her dress. Somehow, someway, she'd go down those stairs, she'd open that door, she'd face that Alex . . . and tell him—what?

Whimpering, she started down the stairs.

Tom couldn't sit still. He got up from the little chair and took off his coat, suspiciously sniffed his armpit and grimaced, and tossed the coat and hat on the bed. Terrible timing—duck into hiding with the shirt he meant to wash several days ago and no spare. He'd walked out of Michel's apartment with nothing but the clothes on his back. Well, what was new? He left as he had arrived. At least he didn't smell like pig.

He started a tour of her bedroom, but his steps slowed. Brigitte had grabbed the front of his coat, pulling him down as she pulled herself up, and when she breathed into his ear, his skin prickled in a rushing sweep from ears to toes. He smelled her perfume, that light rosy fragrance, he felt the closeness, and his head spun. He wanted to pull her in.

He smacked his face and went Oswald. "Shake it off, Cabby, attaboy. Whatsa mattah, some broad got ya rattled?"

She sure has.

You should see what she can do with a piece of bread and a little sugar, Ozzie. I tasted the chocolate myself. Her face . . . it flashes, it douses, it tells me everything, keeps everything from me. I'll meet a current if I touch it. When I'm near, I feel it. Some . . . force, something alive.

Tom resumed a slow stroll. He felt heady, like he was breathing her fragrance.

Oswald warned, *This ain't no ordinary broad, Cab. You know what she is.*

Tom touched a picture frame on the dresser part of the wardrobe, picked up a seashell. He leaned on the dresser, idling with it.

She is, and she isn't. But what does it matter? If I even touch her, she'll see me no different from any other guy who shows up here. He looked at his reflection in the tilting mirror. *Why should she? Especially when I look like that. Especially when I say stupid things, and douse her face like I pulled the shade on the sun.*

Tom heard a door slam below, then steps on the stairs. He felt oddly guilty. He dropped the seashell and ran for the chair.

The door opened. Brigitte slid in and closed the door with her back.

Her face was odd. The cheeks had a high flush, and the brown eyes were huge. She had a look of disbelief, or incredulity, Tom didn't know what.

She stood wordless, pressed against the door.

"Sooo . . . ," he said, rolling his hand to encourage her to start. "You got rid of him?"

She nodded.

"And it went . . . good?"

She shook her head.

"It went bad."

She nodded. She shook her head.

He smiled. "You don't know if it went good or bad. You want to sit down?" He went and put out his arm to escort her to the bed. She allowed him to lead. She sat down straight-backed, folding her hands primly in her lap. Tom went back to his chair.

"I told him I converted," she suddenly said.

"You—?" He shook his head a little. "What?"

"I crossed myself before I went down. It must have inspired me. It was the only way I could think to get rid of him. I am afraid I am rid of him . . . permanently." Her face finally let down. "He is my source for the bridges. What have I done?" She looked at Tom. "If someone says she has converted, but she really hasn't, what sort of sin is that? A remarkable one, *n'est-ce pas?*"

Tom opened his mouth to answer, but shook his head helplessly.

"I will have to ask Madame Bouvier," she said thoughtfully. "In a way, I *have* converted."

"In what way?"

"In the way I now move with the force around me, instead of wishing I did."

"What force?" His skin tingled. The precise word he'd used to describe her face to Ozzie.

"The force for freedom and good. The force that wants the liberation of France." Then, speaking the words as they came, "And . . . and . . . the liberation of me." A delicate softening came.

She rose from the bed and walked over to the wardrobe, where she touched a carved rosette. "Show me a liberation that . . ."

Tom waited.

And waited.

"Erases it all?" he said tentatively.

"No! Show me a liberation that . . ." She turned her back on him, pressing her forehead against the wardrobe.

"Changes everything?"

"Quiet!" she snapped, forehead still against the wardrobe.

The moment became long. Tom could hardly stand her agony as she fought for the words. This was no matter of finding them in English. He suspected she didn't even know them in French.

Then the fierceness stilled. "I want a liberation that means a place for me," she whispered, cheek against the wardrobe.

"Why wouldn't there be?"

"He can say whatever he wants. They came to my door and wanted me gone."

"Who can say whatever he wants?"

"Father Eppinette. He says there is a place for one like me."

"Sounds like a safe bet," Tom ventured, hoping to be helpful.

"All they care about is my past. The bad I've done. They seem to think I am unaware. I do not need the church to tell me prostitution is wrong." Tears came, and she tried so hard for control, Tom wanted to go to her.

Then her face changed in a flash. "I am so *angry*! How could he know that I do not want to be flogged forward? I want something there to *bring* me forward."

"It sounds like he is on your side."

"That is what makes me angry." Her face turned away as she put her forehead on the wardrobe again. Her hands came up, she brushed fingertips and palms over the surface of the wood. "God has a place for me. That is what he is saying."

"Do you believe it?"

Her hands stilled.

"What's it worth if you don't believe it?"

She looked over her shoulder. Tom didn't expect a face ready to hatch a storm.

"Well? Is it true for you or not?"

Anger, then something else, then anger again, and then a helpless little sob. Tears spilled, and in a sudden burst of fury she pounded the door of the wardrobe, and the veneer of golden bird's-eye maple cracked.

She stared in horror. "The only thing of beauty I have!" She tried to put her arms around the whole wardrobe, sobbing, and Tom looked down. He wanted to go to her in the worst way. He made fists.

"It doesn't mean a thing if you don't believe it," he said. "What good is it, then? Oh, don't listen to me." He reached for his hat, set it back down. "I wish my mother was here. She'd say it better."

"I am not fit to be around her," Brigitte spat, digging at tears with a fist. "Just like Alex's mother. He has to clean me up first."

Tom shook his head. "That's not who my mother is." A thought came. "That's not who God is. Brigitte . . . you just gotta have faith that he's good. I think you do. And I think he never wanted to flog you forward, but get you there by setting out the good. You just have to go. When you do, I guess you'll leave the rest behind. I think that's the deal." He thought about what his mother would say, then nodded. "He has a place for you."

She traced her fingers along the crack. Fresh tears spilled. "Look what I've done . . ."

"Say it, Brigitte," he said softly. "Just say it."

Fingers stilled. Lips trembled. And a crack came to beautiful veneer.

"He has a place for me."

When she remembered there was someone else in the room, she looked over her shoulder, dark hair wispy, face flushed with leftover storm, and Tom didn't think she had ever looked lovelier. "Why are you here?" she said.

"They're pulling me off the mission. Rousseau is under investigation."

"Oh no," she breathed. She brushed hair out of her eyes. Then, tentatively, "Monsieur Rousseau . . . he is Greenland?"

He hesitated, then nodded.

"Has he been arrested?" She came around the corner of the bed and sat on it.

"Not yet. Were you there the day they dumped Jasmine's body near the cafés?"

"No. Marie-Josette was," she said quietly. "She cried for days. She didn't even know her. It seemed as though a blanket of grief had fallen over the city, for this woman we did not know. I lit a candle for her." She looked at him. "What will I do with you here?"

"Tell them I'm your boyfriend. Tell them I'm moving in. Rousseau says word will come through the BBC of my pickup. They're sending a plane to a little airstrip in a place called Le Vey. It'll be sometime in the next several days, around the next full moon."

"What sort of hiding will this be? The girls will wonder if you don't come and go."

"I don't know. We'll work it out."

"So the mission is over."

They were silent.

"Some adventure, huh?" Tom said quietly.

"What about the bridges? What about the charges, what about—?"

"It's out of our hands. Rousseau says other cells operate in this area. They'll be on it."

Her face became blank. "I didn't do anything real. Nothing that mattered."

"Sure you did. You opened your door."

They looked at one another until a faint pink came to Brigitte's cheeks. She said with a slight smile, "You did not have to sell 'round two,' but we will have to sell you as my boyfriend. I think it wise if we march straight down there because they'd never expect it." Her face sobered. "Something is going on between Colette and Claudio, and we do not know what it is. Marie-Josette overheard them in the kitchen last night." She hesitated. "She heard the word *Cabby*."

Tom straightened, speechless.

Brigitte flushed. "It is my fault. The other day Marie-Josette asked your name. I wasn't thinking. Colette was in the room."

"What a pair we make," he said in awe.

"Why would they talk about you?" Brigitte wondered aloud. "How could they even suspect you? It does not make sense. Colette has never met you."

"No idea." Such an eerie thought, a Milice and a woman he'd never met using his code name. "What could have happened? It can't be Flame. No one would—Well, what do I know. I only know Michel and Rafael. Clemmie isn't with Flame, and—Wait; there's that Wilkie. I've only met him once, when he took my pictures. But they trust him completely."

"We must—Oh, what is the word . . . ? *Defuse* this."

"Go straight down there, set 'em back on their heels. Get 'em thinking."

"Exactement." Brigitte clasped her hands, bringing them to her chin in quick thought. "If you are moving in, if we will make you my boyfriend, we must keep everything close to the truth. That is what Madame says. So we keep you working at the Cimenterie. But . . ."

"Life at Michel's apartment is dull."

"And now you heard he was a bad boy, and there is an investigation . . ."

"And I wanted to get out of the way. I thought, hey, I'll bunk here for a while since I'm your new boyfriend."

"Oui." She looked a little uncomfortable. "But they know me. I have not been interested in anyone since—We will have to 'sell it,' as you say. They are watching."

"Seems a national occupation." Tom shrugged. "Easy peasy. How did you act with—?" He suddenly wondered if that was precisely what he shouldn't say. Was any time with Brigitte complete if he didn't stick a jackboot in his mouth?

"I will have to sit in your lap," she said gloomily. "We will have to hold hands."

"Well, don't let it wreck your day," Tom snapped. "Back home I'm not half-bad. Nobody here believes it. Sorry I'm so distasteful to you."

Indignation flashed. "That is not what I—*You're* the one who wouldn't even sit on the—" She snatched a pillow and shrieked a few words into it, or just shrieked in general, Tom could not tell.

"Occupation angst," he said.

She pulled the pillow away with dignity, then smoothed her mussed hair. "We cannot go down there like this. We are in *love*." She flipped the pillow aside, got to her feet, and pulled on his shirtsleeve to make him stand. He felt obstinate. She pulled harder, declaring, "Oh, don't be a child!" He got to his feet.

She looked up at him. "Look into my eyes. Oh, do not be a—a *dope*, Cabby. This is real. This is your life. Outside my door is nothing but peril for you. Do not give them a reason to think twice about you. They know the name Cabby? What of it? You are Kees."

He looked into her eyes. The longer he looked, the more he felt flippancy drain away. She made it real. She made it life and death. And she didn't want him in peril.

"Put your hands on my waist."

He settled his hands on her waist, and did not feel awkward, not looking into her eyes.

"Touch my hair," she said, less stringently.

He reached to smooth a dark strand of hair alongside her face, and his finger lingered on her cheek. He was right. He met a current and it went straight into him.

"Voilà, here is our story: We are going to marry. You are going to take me away. You know I want to write travel books when the war is over. You want to take me to America, show me all the glories of America so I can write a travel book in French for the French." Her eyes went a trifle distant, and she smiled a little at what she saw. "I will interpret the glories. That is a travel book worth reading."

"Travel book . . ." The lingering finger moved to trace her lip. He pushed the lip lower, gave a little examination, said, "Nice teeth." She smiled against her will, and he grinned. He felt suddenly lighter. "You'd make a good leader, you know that? You could lead a whole Resistance cell. You should talk to Rafael, he could—"

"Cabby, you must be serious."

"Don't call me Cabby," he said, quite serious. "Not when it's just the two of us. It's Tom."

Alarm leaped in the brown eyes. "No! I will not even *think* your name. You are Kees, you are Kees."

"I wouldn't take you to America." When she blinked, he said gently, "I'm not from America, remember? I'm from the Netherlands. You'll interpret the glories of the Netherlands."

She pressed a palm to her forehead and muttered in French.

"Don't worry. You'll do fine. I'll do fine." He slipped his hand from her waist. "Whatever we say, we'll think twice before we speak. The minute we step out that door, I'm Kees, you're my girl, and we're in love."

He tried to give her as steadying a look as she gave him. He took his coat from the bed. She reached up to put on his hat. He put out his arm, she slipped hers into his, and they went downstairs.

They paused just outside the sitting room. Tom's gut felt like a couple of fighting rats. He ground his teeth. He'd put aside fear for Michel, for Rafael, for Clemmie, for his own sweet skin; he'd blank it all out.

He was a Dutch Nazi. He was on the winning side, proud, to be feared. Hitler did not conquer his nation, he liberated it. Hitler gave him a reason to hold up his head. Hitler showed him what to do with defeat: ball it up, hurl it back.

"Nice to hear Glenn Miller." He seized Brigitte's hand, cold as his own, and smiled at her.

She looked up at him and whispered doubtfully, "We are in love."

He squeezed her hand and whispered, "Mad crazy love, sweetheart."

"Do you have a sweetheart?"

"Only you, darling."

"I mean, back in . . . the Netherlands."

"I left behind a brokenhearted nine-year-old named Greetje."

"What about . . . ?"

He shook his head. "My girl went down over Cabourg."

She smiled. "I will fill in for her."

"Tall order. She took one through the heart for me."

He looked away, pushed down the rats that tried to climb up his throat. Brigitte on his arm, he swallowed hard, stepped through the doorway, and when he did . . .

Fear left.

He made his gaze proud and austere; it swept the room as

if he expected and received fanfare. He gave the dark blinking man who was surely Claudio no more than a condescending flick of the eyes, resting them instead upon the girl on his lap who had to be Colette, whom he deigned to give two uninterested seconds. The gaze swept on, acknowledging Marie-Josette as if they were old friends, taking in her soldier customer with the cool politeness of higher-ranking comrade meeting lower-ranking comrade, and moved on to Simone. He gave her a slight smile and gave the glowering creep at her side a small indifferent nod.

Every move was effortless. He filled his uniform, he filled his own height, and filled it with a sense that had eluded him these past weeks: duty. It came in a rush of comfort; it had not forsaken him, and he had not forsaken it. He'd not blow this. He'd sell them on everything—on his rank, on his affection for this girl at his side, on all that made Kees Nieuwenhuis a Dutch Nazi.

He had duty to America, the country he and his parents had come to love; he had duty to the girl at his side, to the man who couldn't say good-bye and now worried about him in Caen, to an old woman in Cabourg who had fussed over his wound and given him a button. Most of all—and this feeling gripped his middle—he had duty to the guys in his squadron, to make it back and fight once more at their sides.

He might have lost his girl, but he felt like he was flying now. He would survive this, he would get back to England, and when he returned, he'd come as part of a mighty horde, the biggest military invasion in history that would liberate not a godforsaken country, but a country God had not forsaken.

He led Brigitte to the center of the room.

"Ladies and gentlemen," he announced in courtly fashion, every English word spoken in the Dutch brogue of his father, "please, to have your attention: My name is Major Kees Nieuwenhuis. I have pleasure to announce: today I asked this lady to be my wife." He gazed down at her. Some aiding force made his heart swell as he took in the brown eyes. "And she has said yes."

He heard whistles and applause and well-wishing, mostly from Marie-Josette and her soldier, but it seemed to dim the longer he looked at Brigitte. And before he knew it, he was selling it good and found out her kiss could light the room as much as her face.

He hardly knew where he was when it was over. His hands were in her hair. He was breathless, disoriented. He wanted to be anywhere else with her instead of a room filled with people. He wanted to know just who had done the kissing: Kees or Tom.

18

MARIE-JOSETTE was brilliant.

Sure, she said she didn't know what Brigitte was involved in, said she didn't want to know. She knew Cabby had to be an Ally, after Brigitte told her what he had said about the coming invasion. She knew something was up with Claudio and Colette, after overhearing the name Cabby from the kitchen. And of all the girls, she knew Brigitte could not give her heart to another after Jean-Paul Dubois. And she was absolutely brilliant.

She stood in front of Brigitte, hands clasped dramatically to her heart for a moment of dire sentimentality, then flapped her hands and shrieked and did a little dance in place and threw her arms around Brigitte.

"Oh, I am so happy for you!" she cried, hugging fiercely, rocking back and forth. She released Brigitte, then stood on tiptoe to grab Tom's lapel and pull him down for a kiss on the cheek.

"Champagne!" she cried, appealing to the room. "We need champagne! Do we have anything bubbly?"

"I have a bottle of Badoit," Simone offered, grinning. "I was saving it for the invasion, but . . ."

"We couldn't possibly," Brigitte protested, hands clasped about Cabby's arm.

"Don't be ridiculous," Simone said briskly on her way to the door. "I haven't seen you this happy since I've known you. It is time to be happy."

"I look happy?" Brigitte wondered with a smile. She glanced up at Cabby, and oh, how easy this ruse. That breath-stealing smile, those blue eyes, like the sky from where he came; she found herself looking at his lips and suddenly grinned. He'd certainly played *his* part, and it helped her to play hers. Daringly, she lifted her face for another kiss, and she did not miss the answering sparkle of mischief as he bent to slowly accommodate. An appreciative whistle came from Marie-Josette's soldier.

No, she had not been this happy since Paris.

How could he kiss her like this unless . . .

She pulled away. *No, Brigitte,* she told herself gently. *It is a ruse. He is not Jean-Paul.*

I don't want him to be.

"I didn't see this coming," Colette said mildly—for her, as gracious a comment as if she'd just offered a bouquet of felicitations. She sat on Claudio's lap near the radio. Claudio's face, always dark with a five o'clock shadow, was hard to read. His wary attention was on Cabby.

For that matter, despite her civil comment, Colette's face seemed to mirror Claudio's wariness. Brigitte could read Colette better than Claudio; there seemed to be a trace of doubt in those hazel eyes. Doubt about what? Did she doubt their engagement? Did she doubt Cabby?

"Let's get to know your man!" Marie-Josette cried. She

waved them over to the couch. She and her soldier brought over chairs. Simone's soldier, Bruno or whoever he was, was the only one unsure of what was going on and not happy about his uncertainty. He muttered something in a language Brigitte couldn't place, something Slavic, got up from the couch and left the room. The back door slammed.

"Oh, good riddance to that old sack of cheer," Marie-Josette said. "He could depress Saint Peter." She cleared the coffee table of magazines, just as Simone came in with a tray. On the tray were little glasses, a bottle opener, and the bottle of Badoit.

"You are from Holland, Major?" Marie-Josette's soldier asked Cabby with a glance at his rank patch. He said hopefully, *"Sprechen Sie Deutsch?"*

"Nein, nur wenig," Cabby answered, holding up a small space between his thumb and forefinger. *"Ik spreek Nederlands.* And English."

"He's a blond Matterhorn," Marie-Josette said in French, with a sly up-and-down look at Cabby. "You sure know how to pick 'em, Brigitte."

She and Simone handed out glasses, then Simone opened the bottle of Badoit. She threw the bottle cap at the ceiling, to a round of chuckles. "There—there's your champagne, Marie-Josette."

"Occupation champagne," Marie-Josette said merrily.

Though Brigitte felt a trace of guilt that Simone had spent her saved bottle on them, it warmed her to watch Simone carefully divide out the precious sparkling mineral water. She caught Simone's eye and kissed her fingertips to her. Simone smiled.

Marie-Josette raised her glass. "To Brigitte and Kees!" and Brigitte called out, "In English, please, Marie-Josette!"

Marie-Josette gave a charming little nod, and continued in English. "To Brigitte and Kees! To love in the middle of war!"

"Hear, hear!"

"To love in war!"

Glasses lifted, clinked, and the happiness Brigitte felt should have been artificial. Cabby seemed to be enjoying himself, too.

"Thank you!" he said to them all in Dutch-accented English. "Brigitte tells me of the good people here. I am honored." He gave a little bow of his head. He and Brigitte took a seat at the couch, while the others sat in a semicircle of chairs. Colette resumed her position on Claudio's lap.

"Tell me about yourselves," Cabby urged. He took a sip from his glass, eyeing Colette. "You must be Colette. Brigitte tells me she knew you in Paris."

Colette summoned a smile. "I worked in a flower shop across from the Hôtel de Crillon. She worked at the US embassy nearby."

"What is Paris like, eh?" Cabby said wistfully. "I have not been. I want to see the Eiffel, very badly."

She glanced at his rank insignia. "You cannot manage a transfer?"

"Oh, do not be fooled," Cabby said. "I am Dutch Nazi, not German Nazi. They regard my party, but not yet my blood. May as well be corporal." He glanced at the bridge soldier. "No offense."

The soldier looked to Marie-Josette to translate. When she did, he waved in a broad gesture of goodwill. He spoke rapidly to Marie-Josette in German. She translated, "Yes, there is prejudice, and that is regrettable, but it is not for long. Soon all will be regarded as one blood for the Reich." It softened a little of her cheer.

"Where are you stationed?" Colette said.

"Rommel stationed me," Cabby said proudly. "Oh, I do not mean to—what is word?—boast. My mother says watch my pride." He cracked a little smile. "But to confess, it is an honor, *ja*?"

Brigitte watched Claudio's attention sharpen at the name Rommel. He glanced at Colette, who translated since Claudio didn't speak a word of English. He told Colette to ask where Rommel had stationed him.

"I am to interview Dutch conscripts at Rousseau Cimenterie. I am to . . . detect. Understand? I am to detect if they work with Resistance." He shrugged. "But now the owner himself is . . . How do I say it? . . . Detected. Perhaps Rommel was right, *ja*? Something funny going on there."

"Rommel himself . . . ," Colette said, her tone impressed. Or was it confused?

"You want to see papers?" Cabby said, eagerly. "I take them out just to look. To confess—" and here he gave a slight shrug—"I have not met him. It is a wish like Paris." He took them from an inner jacket pocket, produced them, pointing to the signature with pride. "I will keep these orders, *ja*? I will show my grandchildren."

Colette and Claudio leaned forward. The other three crowded in. Cabby pointed to Rommel's signature. Respectful murmurs came, especially from the German soldier who now regarded Cabby with something bordering on awe, but it was Colette and Claudio whom Brigitte watched carefully. And she did not miss the subtle exchange of glances as they resumed their seats. But what was *in* that exchange? It seemed as though each felt doubtful of something. That had to be good.

"Is Tommy Dorsey, *ja*?" Cabby said, pointing enthusiastically at the radio. "*Wat prachtig!* Is *wonderful* to hear! The place where I stay—no radio!" He groaned and clapped a hand over his heart. "Forever since I hear good music!"

"And now you can hear it all the time, darling," Brigitte said, smiling at him. She looked at the others. "Ladies, I must tell you—I have invited Kees to come live with us for a while. Just until the unpleasantness is over at the Rousseau Cimenterie." She leaned against Cabby, walked her fingertips up his arm. "*Mon cher*, you have music to your heart's content."

"I had music the day I met you," Cabby answered, settling his hand over hers.

She smiled a genuine smile, simply because this was fun.

They were looking into each other's eyes, sharing amusement, when Colette's voice came clear.

"Tom."

The word launched like artillery into the air, rained down invisible freezing fallout, for everything froze—their eyes, the smiles on their faces, Brigitte's heart.

How to pull out of this, how to act naturally, yet even as Brigitte's mind raced for the proper reaction, she knew it was too late. She felt a squeeze from Cabby's hand, to encourage, to comfort, to steady. To console.

They searched each other's eyes, and both knew the game was over. Both, as one, looked over at Colette.

The tension in the room snapped and popped like a downed electric wire.

Colette's face was flushed, triumph in her eyes, and yet a triumph that seemed to frighten her. Her eyes were on Cabby, but they flickered once to Brigitte; what was in it? She could not tell. Brigitte tried to take in both of them at once, and it was Claudio who had her dread attention.

The triumph did not frighten him. He grew with it.

His eyes glowed as if a bonfire leaped high. And the way he looked at Cabby made Brigitte want to throw herself between them.

Claudio and Colette rose. He seized her hand, and they walked out of the room.

"What just happened?" Simone said, perplexed, holding her glass.

Brigitte sat at an angle where she could see into the hallway to the back door. And the silly little thing she noted frightened her most of all: Claudio took his Milice hat from the top of the coat tree, put it on his head, and left—without checking his reflection in the mirror.

Brigitte breathed, "Something awful has happened."

It was past midnight. Not long after Colette and Claudio left the room, Tom and Brigitte left too.

Where had Claudio gone? Was he going straight to the Milice? Though they heard occasional crescendos of music from the room below, the rest of the house was silent.

They sat on the bed. Tom wanted to put his arm around her, calm her fear. He would not allow himself to touch her. Not here, not when he needed her this much, not when she needed him.

"What do we do?" Brigitte said softly, her tone as hollow as Tom felt.

"I don't know."

"You must leave. Sooner the better."

"Where do I go?"

"I could take you to the chapel. But I do not know if it is safe. I do not know if they trust me enough to bring someone like you. You could be shot before we make it to the steps."

"I have a password. They will trust it." He shook his head slowly. "Where's the leak? Did it come from Flame? Wilkie? He didn't sell us out, did he?"

"No, wait! Not the chapel—Colette knows I go to the château when I am upset, and maybe she knows why. After all, she knew your name is Tom." Her voice dropped to a hush of incredulity. "What is she? A spy? *Colette?*" Then she said, very softly, "Who kissed me? Tom or Kees?"

"Kees," he lied.

A gentle tap came at the door, and before either could move, the door opened. It was Marie-Josette.

"Brigitte . . . ," she whispered, then stepped aside. Behind her was Rafael.

After a staring moment of astonishment, Tom sprang from the bed and pulled him into the room. Marie-Josette withdrew into the hallway, drawing the door closed.

"Rafael, what—?"

"Rousseau did not want me to come," Rafael said, his face lost, his voice toneless. "He did not want you to know. But we owe you the truth. Clemmie has been arrested."

Tom took a few steps back. Brigitte came to his side.

"Where is she?" he said hoarsely.

It took some time for the question to register, and when it did, Rafael shook his head, still lost. "Some jail in Cabourg. It does not matter."

"It doesn't matter? You mean you're leaving her there? That's all Clemmie gets?"

"You don't understand. There is nothing to be done." He lifted his hands in a hopeless gesture and let them fall. "They will transfer her to Fort de Romainville in Paris, with the three Jews. We learned it from Rousseau's secretary, not an hour ago. Rousseau is . . . in a state."

"Wait a minute, wait—all the men she's saved? All the, the, the—pilots? The gunners? You won't even try? If she goes, the whole war goes! The whole war!"

"It is an SS jail, Cabby."

"My name is Tom!"

"Please keep your voice down," Brigitte pleaded.

"Michel told me what they did to Jasmine."

"They won't do it to an old woman," Rafael said.

"Who in this country can convince me of that?" Tom shouted.

"Tom, please!" Brigitte hissed. "They will hear you."

He shook her off. "It's too late—you know it."

Brigitte gave three stamps and a shriek of frustration. "We are wasting—"

Marie-Josette burst in. "They are coming! The Milice and the gendarmes!"

"It's too late," Tom said, numb.

"It is *not* too late, but now it is *twice* as difficult," Brigitte growled. "Come with me. Both of you." She snatched Tom's coat and hat. To Marie-Josette, she said, "Tell them I took him to the château! Quickly!"

Marie-Josette nodded, face white, and started to leave.

"No!" Tom said sharply. "Send them anywhere but there!"

Marie-Josette nodded, then fled.

Brigitte grabbed Rafael's arm, pushed both men into the hallway. She hurried them to Colette's room.

Colette's room had been Brigitte's when she came to stay with Grandfather as a child. It had a decorative window ledge that led to the corner of the gable. From there, though they couldn't go down, they could go up and over the gable. On the other side of the gable was a drainpipe that ran from the eaves trough to the ground. The drainpipe was outside the front room. The pounding she heard was in the back.

Brigitte had done it many times when she was a girl. Whether the drainpipe would hold the weight of one the size of Tom, she did not know. They had no choice but to try.

She yanked open Colette's door—and in the darkened room was Colette, pressed to the window like a peering sentry. She whirled.

"What will you do now, Brigitte? They are right at your door!"

"Oh, Colette. Why couldn't you take me for a friend?"

"You betrayed Jean-Paul!" she spat. "Do you know how many times he came in to buy you flowers? You did not deserve them! He would have *died* for you, Brigitte! The least you could have done is lived for him. With every single customer, you have betrayed him."

Brigitte stared.

"How many men come along like that?" Colette said, lips trembling, tears rising in the hazel eyes. "Forty-seven times, Brigitte. He bought you flowers forty-seven times. I'll bet you didn't even know." She put her arm over her face.

Oh, Colette.

Storm-tossed, uncomforted.

How could I know you were in love with him, too?

Pain seared her heart, grief for Colette, and Brigitte squeezed her eyes shut. *Oh, God—please . . . let me land on the side of humanity.* "You are right, Colette," she whispered. "I betrayed him. I did not deserve him."

Whatever Colette expected, it wasn't that. A little despairing sob escaped, and her lips parted, but she said nothing. She quieted. Her arm came down. She looked at Brigitte, and Rafael, and then Tom. She said in a dull monotone, "Don't go to the château." She walked out of the room.

Brigitte yanked up the window and leaned out to look down. She heard Marie-Josette's voice at the back door. She turned to beckon them. "They are at the back door. Get to the corner of the gable. Go up and over. There is a drainpipe on the other side."

Rafael went first, carefully finding a foothold before they watched his fingers slip from the casement. They heard the muffled brush of his progress along the wall, and soon a scrabbling overhead. Then they heard a soft and short whistle. Brigitte turned to Tom.

"Go up the road toward Le Port. Go right at the Mairie. A shop called La Broderie is on the left, just before the café near the bridge. Tell Madame Bouvier Brigitte sent you." She added, "Use the code 'Lieutenant Kirsch.' Go!"

He started to duck through the window, then paused and looked back. "I kissed you."

And he was gone.

19

IT WAS 1:15 A.M. The clock on the mantel ticked, the only sound in the room other than the occasional pop and rustle in the fireplace.

Michel and Charlotte sat in his father's end of the room in the chairs by the fireplace, watching the glow of slumbering embers. Charlotte's husband, Gerard, paced along the bookshelves, hands behind his back.

"You should go," Michel said, surprised at the sound of his voice. He had fallen into some stupor.

"We will not leave you, Monsieur Rousseau," Charlotte said.

"Clemmie is in trouble, not me. Braun took mine away. I think he is a good man, Charlotte. Hard to tell, with Germans."

"I know he is."

Michel looked over and saw her for the first time since she had arrived more than an hour ago. She had turned on the lights. She put a coat about his shoulders. She made coffee. Gerard started a fire.

His eyes wandered the room. Father sat in that chair.

François cleared out the cabinet for a hiding place. Wilkie sent and received transmissions. Rafael received orders. He and Braun played whatever game they played, and Charlotte took dictation, did the payroll, ran errands—and coordinated a Resistance cell called *Sept*. Seven. "It is the number of times a righteous man falls, and rises again," she had told him an hour ago.

Sept specialized in information, the printing and distributing of underground newspapers. The name of her newspaper, printed by Gerard on an old printing press in the boiler room of a church, was *Les Sept Fois*. *The Seven Times*. Michel had read it often, never knowing its anonymous pen was that of his secretary.

During the early days of the Occupation, the first efforts of those who felt compelled to do something generally focused on providing the French public with truthful, accurate information on what was going on with the Allies and the Axis. The information connected them and gave hope. Speeches from de Gaulle, unheard at the beginning of the war by those who had had no access to the BBC—and that was most of the public—were printed in its pages. Speeches from Churchill, from Roosevelt; words of hope from Catholic priests and Anglican ministers; advice columns on how to resist without looking like you were resisting; practical information on how to use fuel more efficiently; recipes to make food stretch or taste better—it was all in *Les Sept Fois*, and had been for years.

"I should have known," Michel now said.

Charlotte gave a small, acknowledging lift of her brow. Her lined face, sliding past middle age and heading to elderly, was weary. Yet a satisfied sparkle shone in the deep brown eyes.

"Some things sounded familiar," Michel mused.

"Some came straight from your mouth."

"The idea to make coal balls out of coal dust and newspaper . . ."

"That was you."

"It was actually Marie, François's wife. And you quoted a woman as saying, 'Defeat we can accept; collaboration, never.' It surprised me. I was encouraged to see others felt the same as I."

"I liked it coming out of a woman's mouth."

"What did you do with the book?"

"I was going to burn it," she admitted. "But then I thought, if things go very badly, then someday, years from now, people need to know. They need to find it in an attic, read what your father wrote in the margins. Have some idea where the madness began."

"Did it begin with Hitler?" Michel wondered.

"Perhaps not. His is not a unique evil. Just a very old one."

The remarkable thing about Charlotte was that she was, in fact, unremarkable. The diminutive woman was plain of face and quiet in manner. She was even a bit boring. She used to be plump in pre-Occupation years, and she wore her new thinness with a forbearance of spirit that Michel suspected she rather enjoyed. Some undertook to endure the indignities and inconveniences of the Occupation with grim relish, and Charlotte was one of these. Yet nothing in her stoic manner so much as hinted at the unlawful events that lay beneath, much less the acumen that flowed from her unlawful pen.

She noticed a tiny spot of some offense on her blouse, brushed at it, examined the results, and glanced at the clock on the mantel.

"Charlotte, please," Michel protested. "Go home. Get some rest. Gerard, take your wife home."

"You think she listens to me?" Gerard grunted.

"I wonder how it went with Rafael," Charlotte mused.

Charlotte's role was still quite new to him. "You don't even call him André. I told him not to go."

"If I were the pilot, I would have wanted to know."

"Me, too," Gerard said.

Michel shook his head. "He would have been happier. It would have been mercy."

Rafael was at the office when Michel had returned from sending Tom away to Bénouville. The boy had learned about Clemmie in the worst way possible: he had been there.

The B-17 had a catastrophic landing, no parachutes, no survivors, and in fact had killed an unknown number of civilians when it plowed into a farmhouse outside Houlgate. After being hit inland, the pilot had come about and seemed to have made a valiant effort to ditch into the sea. Rafael came to the site as neighbors sifted through the smoldering wreckage for survivors. There was nothing to be done, so he decided to visit Clemmie on his way back to Caen.

For the first time, the kitchen curtain was drawn over half of the window. Had it been fully drawn, it would have been safe to go in. Rafael nearly did not check. When he did, incomprehension froze his feet. There could not be trouble with Clemmie. Anyone but Clemmie. It was impossible.

He ducked across the road into a hedgerow and waited for hours, watching the home. Just when he was ready to come out, armed with a good tongue-lashing for Clemmie's lapse in protocol, he caught a glimpse of a German soldier through the front window. There was no lapse. Clemmie was taken.

It was so unthinkable, he could not remember how he made it back to Caen, only that, by the time he did, word had already reached Wilkie that Clemmie and the three Jews had been arrested.

The telephone jangled, and all three jumped.

Michel rose and hurried to his desk. "Hello."

"Rousseau?" It was Braun. "You are still there."

"I am here."

There was a pause. Michel gripped the receiver.

"I am afraid I have bad news. The grandmother is dead." He added quickly, "She died of a heart attack. Or perhaps a stroke. Natural causes, Rousseau."

The telephone nearly slipped from his hand.

So goes a rose of France.

The wind came and took her away, bore her to a place where her beauty could be unveiled. Yet how sorely they needed her beauty here.

"Rousseau?"

Michel found his voice. "You are sure she is dead?" He was vaguely aware of a stifled exclamation from Charlotte, Gerard hurrying to her side.

"I am just from the hospital. I saw her myself. She was to be transferred to Paris in the morning. Before they finished the paperwork, she had a heart attack."

She had not suffered as Jasmine had. Yet she was dead.

Rafael would take it very hard.

"Any news of the other three?" Michel asked.

Silence. Then Braun said in cold anger, "Is it not enough that I saw to the old woman? Is it not enough for you?" A moment passed. He hung up.

Michel replaced the receiver and said softly, "Oh, Tom."

When the blond behemoth appeared at her door, Madame Bouvier believed her time on earth was up. Was this how the Christians in the Colosseum felt after living in the dark in the catacombs, hunted down, seized, thrown for sport to gladiators and lions? Relief that it was finally over? Exhilaration that they would soon be in heaven? Fear of the pain of getting there?

"I must consult with Father Chaillet," she had said crazily.

Then she saw the face of the comparably tiny Frenchman behind the behemoth. She knew that face. It was he who, on that terrible day, had called out the wrongs done upon the young woman thrown into the street. It was he who took tender care of Monsieur Rousseau.

"Kirsch," the behemoth said breathlessly. "Lieutenant Kirsch."

"Please let us in, madame," the Frenchman said, with a backward glance.

That was an hour ago.

Gisèlle Bouvier spoke little English, and because she hated to do something unless she did it admirably, she chose not to speak it at all. She ignored the handsome young pilot and kept her attention on Rafael. He explained the situation, and a terrible one it was. Somehow she was not surprised Brigitte was at the heart of it.

The pilot sat at a bench in the kitchen, head in hands. He pulled from his melancholic stupor to rattle something in English, then sank into it once more. Gisèlle looked at Rafael.

"He is worried about Brigitte. He does not know what they are doing to her."

"Nonsense. She can think on her feet. Tell him her reputation is not all mirrors on the ceiling." At Rafael's wondering look, she said crisply, "I stayed at a brothel in Paris last year. They hid me for two days. They had mirrors. Brigitte will be fine; it's him I'm worried about. Look at him." She shook her head in grave respect of Greenland's now sadly defunct plan.

This man was cut from the fabric of Germany like Hitler never was. "Hide *him* under a bushel, no . . ."

"But he needs a place to hide until we hear from the BBC."

"He has it, God help me; but do you suppose, with the Gestapo next door, that I can use a radio at my leisure? A daft mother can answer many things, but it cannot cover the sound of a radio."

"We will listen. We will bring word as soon as we hear anything." Then Rafael said, "We are grateful, madame."

The pilot said something. Wearily, Rafael nodded and, at Gisèlle's look, said, "He is very worried about Clemmie. The old woman who hid him in Cabourg. Her home was raided. She was arrested."

"That is too bad," Gisèlle said gently. "I am sorry."

The pilot rose and began to walk the kitchen floor. He said something, to which Rafael responded sharply.

"Gentlemen, you will have to keep quiet. My crazy mother has not yet begun to speak English in a man's voice."

The pilot seemed to pick it up, quieted. He spoke urgently to Rafael, who argued strongly back. The pilot declared something quite vehemently; Rafael flung his arms in an angry gesture, then, face dark, fumbled in his pocket for a pack of cigarettes. He offered one to Gisèlle, who took one only because they were Lucky Strikes. While they sat at the table and smoked, the pilot continued his restless prowl of the kitchen, back and forth, back and forth.

"He wants to go tonight and break her out," Rafael muttered. "He says he can do it with his rank."

"Perhaps he can."

"You do not understand. He looks the part, but cannot play it. He would be arrested." He chuckled bitterly. "That is why we are here. He gave himself away. It was not his fault.

I . . . *We* did not have enough time to train him. He would have done well, I think. He is angry because I will not guide him to Cabourg."

After a moment, Gisèlle said, "Tell him I can at least inquire about Brigitte. Word has spread I have undertaken to convert her." She glanced ruefully at her wrapped foot propped on a chair. "Tomorrow I will go to the brothel with my Bible, and it will not be questioned."

Rafael passed it on to the pilot, who nodded gratefully, looked directly at Gisèlle, and said, *"Merci."* But he resumed his restless tour.

"What can be done about this Clemmie?" she asked, watching the unhappy man.

Rafael pulled on his cigarette, jerked his shoulder. "I lied and told him we would figure something out." He spoke rapidly, she knew, so that if the pilot did have any French, he would not pick it up. "But it's over for her. She will be sent to Paris. The Jews will be sent to Germany."

"Jews?"

"She hid three. They were taken."

Three. It had to be three. "Was it a mother and two children?" Gisèlle asked faintly.

Rafael glanced at her, shook his head.

Perhaps God forgot confessed sins, as Father Chaillet suggested; Gisèlle Bouvier had a better memory than God. She had no right to forget.

It was 1942, July. Paris, the Vélodrome d'Hiver—the bicycle racetrack and stadium. A year earlier, Gisèlle had turned in her Jewish housekeeper and the housekeeper's two children. They were sent to Paris, and then, Gisèlle was to learn, they were sent to the Vélodrome in the Jewish roundup.

Hannah had brown corkscrew ringlets. Mother had made

a wide satin bow for her hair. She loved Mother, and Mother loved her. She was three years old.

"This cannot be my Hannah," Mother had said of the photograph on the front page of the underground newspaper *Les Sept Fois.*

But it was.

She stood in a group of children behind a chain-link fence. She was not the smallest child—no, little Hannah was holding a baby, a real baby. Who the baby was, Gisèlle did not know. Where Hannah's older sister was, Gisèlle did not know. The caption read, "Jewish children taken from their parents."

Mother knew her by the bow. Gisèlle knew her, and every child in the photograph, by the monstrous guilt.

For a time, Gisèlle Bouvier went a little crazy.

To this day, she could not remember how she got to Lyon, seven hundred kilometers away, in Vichy territory, the Unoccupied Zone.

"Formidable!" Mother sang appreciatively of the young Allied pilot, arms outstretched as if to conduct a song.

She shuffled into the kitchen, slippers flapping, dressing gown quite open with no clothing beneath. Not a stitch.

"Rafael, my foot hurts. Could you . . . ?" Gisèlle nodded at Mother.

Rafael, mouth sagging in horror—*and who would not be horrified,* Gisèlle thought; *please, God, take me before I am a walking prune*—roused himself and went to the old woman. He put his cigarette in his mouth and, holding himself back as far as he could, awkwardly pulled Mother's robe together. He found the sash and tied it.

Mother had rapt attention only for the pilot. After waiting for Rafael to finish the trussing, she went straight for him. Gisèlle hid a smile.

Age-filmed eyes dancing, the tiny old woman stopped in front of the pilot, who had stopped, too. She gazed with her head far back, as when Gisèlle had taken her to the Eiffel Tower. She was as delighted now as she was then. She clasped soft and wrinkled hands to her cheeks, then beckoned the pilot down.

He bent low, and Gisèlle saw the deep anxiety in his face, fear like a fog within. At the old lady's admiration, he mustered a smile and began to withdraw. But Mother wasn't finished, as Gisèlle knew she was not. She took his cheeks in the soft, wrinkled hands, and declared in her high trill, "Do not be distressed, my dear! So goes a rose of France, to the bouquet from which she came!" Beaming, she patted the cheeks, and the pilot withdrew to his height. "This one is a keeper, Gisèlle. I'll have Eloise set another place for tea."

"Tell him she talks nonsense," Gisèlle said, pleased that the pilot's face was a trifle less worried.

Rafael spoke to the pilot in English, then asked, "Who is Eloise?"

"She was our housekeeper. Mother thinks every 'guest' is a potential beau."

"You let this one go, and you are crazy," Mother declared.

"I won't, Mother," Gisèlle reassured.

"You will have huge babies," Mother said thoughtfully. "I worry about your milk."

"Don't translate that," Gisèlle said with a stiff smile.

"Don't worry," Rafael muttered.

20

IT WAS CLOSING on 5 a.m., and Brigitte was so tired. She pressed a cold, wet cloth to her bloody lip. She would not let her eyes close. The last time she did, the man hit her.

They were assembled in the kitchen, Brigitte seated at the kitchen table, Colette across from her. While Tom and Rafael had crept over the roof in front, the squad of Milice had burst into the door in back. They'd acted as though they'd raided a Resistance headquarters full of weapons, instead of a home with four women.

"I don't know what else we can do here," the man who'd hit Brigitte said to Claudio. "Do you want this to go all the way up to Rommel? Not me."

The man's name was Laroche, a brisk, authoritative man with streaks of gray in hair so thick it stuck up from his head like a bristle broom. "If we pursue it, that is where it will have to go. Is it worth it?"

"But it is true," Brigitte said plaintively. "He worked for Rommel himself! Please don't look at me like that, Colette. I am sorry I did not tell you everything. I am in love."

Colette said nothing.

"He did not tell you he is working with the Allies . . . ," Laroche said once more.

"No! I told you, I do not know why he left. Is he guilty of something? Perhaps. We all are, I think. But I make no excuse for how I feel." She drew herself up, declared passionately, "So what if he is guilty of something? I am in love!" Suddenly she gasped, then clapped a hand to her cheek.

Laroche said quickly, "What is it?"

"Nothing," Brigitte said.

"I can even out your mouth, my dear," Laroche said.

"It is nothing, it is ridiculous." Then, unwillingly, in a small voice, "His motorcycle. He says he borrowed it . . . but now I wonder . . ."

"Borrowed it from who?"

"Rommel."

"Rommel?" Laroche barked, incredulous. He turned to Claudio. "You say his papers were signed by Rommel? He was assigned to the Cimenterie by Rommel? And now he borrows a motorcycle from his best friend, Rommel?" He frowned. "I wonder if we are dealing with a simple lunatic. Certainly the papers are forged. Maybe he stole them from someone. Perhaps his only crime is that he is a braggart who wants to impress a whore."

"Oh no, monsieur, he is on very good terms with Rommel," Brigitte assured.

"Terms?" Claudio exploded. "He said he never met him! Didn't he, Colette? He said he'd pass his papers on to his grandchildren! He'd never met him."

"That is not true!" Brigitte hotly declared. "He told *me* he is Rommel's confidant!"

Claudio swooped in, pushing his face into hers. "He knew

he could lie to you, but not to us." He withdrew, leaving a sour wake of wine-coated breath. He turned to Laroche. "I'm telling you—"

"Enough." Laroche had the look of a man who had figured it all out. He put his hands behind his back. "If we go to the Cimenterie, we will find there never *was* a Major Kees Nieuwenhuis. Perhaps he is the very Dutch conscript he was sent to 'investigate,' just a man who filled himself with grandiose thoughts." He shrugged. "You are enslaved on the wall twelve hours a day, what else can you do? Your country is flattened by the Reich, you have lost all pride . . . you imagine yourself to a better place. He is nothing but a con man."

"What about the name Cabby?" Claudio demanded.

"Yes—and when have you ever cared about the transcripts, Benoit?" Laroche turned a glare on him. "I know what you do with them. You use them to wipe your backside. How many times have we handed them out, hmm? You read *one* transcript and suddenly you are an expert on Allied evasion tactics."

"It was *her* idea," Claudio said, pointing at Colette. "She read it and—"

"*She* read the transcript?" Laroche demanded, voice high. "You pass out the weeklies to your friends?"

"It was just sitting on the table with—"

"What else has she seen, hmm? Oh—perhaps I should be talking to Mademoiselle Colette, here. Maybe she should have *your* job!"

"But the way he looked when she said, 'Tom'—"

"The way he *looked*," Laroche mocked. "He probably looked the way I would have: 'Why is this crazy broad calling me Tom? Doesn't she know my name?'"

"What transcript?" Brigitte asked.

"Go ahead. Show her. Everyone else has seen it."

Grimacing, Claudio reached into his back pocket. He unfolded a piece of paper and tossed it on the table. Brigitte reached for it, smoothed it out.

—Angel flight this is lead. Rolling in. One and two take targets on the right three and four

—Captain we got movement.

—Mayday this is Angel three I'm hit I'm hit.

—Angel three can you make it back?

—Pressure gauge says no flight lead. I'm going in.

—Copy. We'll cap the area. Good luck Tom.

—Good luck Cab.

—Guts and glory Cabby.

"It was part of a transmission intercepted at the radar station at Douvres-la-Délivrande," Laroche said. "Benoit believes your man is this pilot. Yet I have questioned everyone, Benoit; all say he was Dutch, no question about it—especially Private Müller, and a German should know, in particular one who lived near the border of Holland."

The paper sat in Brigitte's hands. It was supposed to mean nothing to her.

"I have had enough of this. I am sorry I struck you, mademoiselle. You were falling asleep. It was rude." Laroche's look lingered on Brigitte, and his eyes narrowed. He turned to Claudio. Half to himself, he said, "Could it be that you are jealous?"

"What? Me, jealous? Pfft. I can have her anytime I want. Trust me."

It was supposed to mean nothing to her.

Mayday this is Angel three I'm hit . . .

"You never brought me flowers."

Attention went to Colette. It was the first time she'd spoken since Laroche had questioned her in the sitting room hours ago. Brigitte saw a fleeting look: the hazel eyes went from the transcript to Brigitte. They flashed away to land full upon Claudio.

"Major Kees brought Brigitte the loveliest little soaps. They know each other a few days, he brings her soap. You?" Her lip curled. "At least you brought the others raspberries."

Claudio could not have been more pathetically found out.

"Flowers even once?" Colette shouted. "And we are supposed to be in love? Not a dandelion!"

Laroche rolled his eyes. "Enough. This matter is closed. Benoit, you will apologize to the men you roused. We will keep an eye out for this Kees, we will confiscate his motorcycle—which he likely stole from a garrison—and we will forget this silly debacle. He is long gone, ready to impress the next credulous oaf. Or—" he looked to Brigitte, smiling thinly—"the next, ah, young lady."

Colette had revived Brigitte to her role.

"But I am in love," she said miserably, leaving off the transcript, twisting the bloodstained cloth in her fingers. "You must find him! Please! You must bring him back to me!"

"You are in love," Laroche softly mocked. "A whore does not know the meaning of the word. Love is . . ." He drew a long, filling breath, eyes misty and distant, and then apparently decided not to throw his pearls before swine. With fatherly kindness, patting her arm with the same hand that had struck her, he said, "I advise you to forget him, mademoiselle." He glanced at the gendarme standing near the door and gave a motion to go. He left the kitchen, Claudio on his heels, leaving Colette and Brigitte alone.

The soiled piece of paper lay upon the kitchen table. Colette reached for it, slowly folded it. She held it for a moment and then handed it to Brigitte. She walked out of the room.

Brigitte held the paper to her stomach. When she could, she slipped it into her pocket.

She went to the back door to lock it, then opened it wide. In three desperate wrests, she yanked the sign off the door, *Nur für Wehrmacht*, and winged it into the yard. She shut the door, locked it, and headed for her room.

At the foot of the stairs, she stopped, gasping, a hand on each wall. He was gone. He was gone. She would never see him again. She bowed, until her head touched a step.

He would live. He would live. He was safe.

She lowered her hands. She rose, smoothed her dress, started up the stairs.

It was closing on 5 a.m., and Monsieur Rousseau had fallen into an exhausted sleep, head resting in the wingback. Charlotte fetched her gray wool sweater and covered him, tucking him in. She tenderly caressed his head, something she'd never dare if he were awake.

"So much like his father, don't you think?" she whispered.

Gerard nodded. She slipped her hand into Gerard's, and they left.

It was closing on 5 a.m., and Hauptmann Braun was trying to sleep. He liked Rousseau, and the man's concern for an old woman was commendable. The treatment of the old woman was not.

Rousseau had said it could turn him into a resistant, and though Braun could hardly blame him, he'd not lose his only friend in the country. The woman was dead, and that's all that really mattered. Wasn't it? Maybe she did have a heart attack. He turned over and tried to close his eyes. Whenever he did, he saw the empty eyes and the bruised and swollen face of an old woman.

It was closing on 5 a.m., and Tom listened to Rafael slip out the back door.

He heard the halting creak as Madame Bouvier hobbled to her bedroom. He waited until he was sure the woman was asleep and then slipped out of bed.

He pulled on his trousers and tucked in the shirt Madame had said she would wash in the morning. He slipped on his coat. He settled his bulletless gun on his hip and put on the German hat. He looked in the mirror, but could not make out his reflection. He knew it was a German he'd see, and he'd sell every square inch of this German real estate to get Clemmie released. He didn't know how. He'd figure it out as he went. The truth was, it was now or never. If he stayed, he'd lie to himself just as Rafael had lied, that somehow, someway, the Resistance would figure something out.

Immediate three-part plan: Get a weapon. Get an ally. Get going.

He'd go to Madame Vion at the château. "Century," he whispered as he slipped out the back door and closed it soundlessly. "Greenland sent me."

She was head of a Resistance cell; surely she could get him a weapon . . . and perhaps far more. A maternity hospital must have access to a vehicle. He could get to Cabourg, maybe in an ambulance. For now he only had to worry about getting to the château.

He pressed himself against the door. Two ways to get to the château: take the main road, or follow the Caen Canal. Both were rotten options. On the road he'd have to pass Brigitte's, and who knew if the Milice were still there or if he'd encounter them on their way back to the Mairie. If he followed the Caen Canal, he'd pass too closely to the Caen Canal Bridge, heavily guarded and garrisoned.

What if he crossed the street and took backyards to the château? A straight crow-fly shot? He glanced at the sky. Though dawn was fast approaching, at least there was no moon to betray—And a sudden thought came. He'd take Clemmie with him. To Le Vey, to the airstrip where the Lysander was due in just a few days' time. He'd take Clemmie with him to England. He grinned.

At least you gotta plan for after *Cabourg,* Oswald said snidely.

He squeezed his eyes shut. The Mairie was in eyeshot of Madame Bouvier's. Crossing the road was the first and worst part. He'd have to do it for either route. He'd cross the street and get a feel for which route once there.

"Come on, Cabby. Now or never."

He unpeeled himself from the door, crouched low, and made his way around the house to the front.

Laroche paused on the first step of the Mairie. Something wasn't right. He turned and faced the street.

"What is it?" Paget said, a few steps ahead.

"I saw something." Laroche peered across the road. Something did not belong. What was it? He half turned and almost retraced his last few steps. He was coming around the corner of the Mairie . . . he'd swept a cursory look across the street . . .

"There—in the hedge by the gate across the road." False dawn had given the streets the barest gray illumination. Yet he wasn't sure. He could see a shadow on the periphery, but not if he looked straight on.

"Paget, go out back and circle around. Take Janvier and Russo. One of you come from the right, one from the left, and put a man at the back in case he gets through that gate. Be careful; whoever it is may be armed."

There was no reason a shadow should freeze in a hedgerow. Unless of course that shadow was a lunatic braggart whose best friend was Rommel.

21

WHEN BRIGITTE AWOKE, it was only quarter past ten. She usually slept until noon, like the others. What had woken her?

A soft knocking at the door downstairs, that's what.

She rose and grabbed her dressing gown, pulled it on as she hurried downstairs. She opened the door, and on the step was a small, homely young woman with large, fearful eyes. She clutched her coat beneath her throat.

"I have never been to a house of sin," she squeaked.

Brigitte opened her mouth to answer, unsure what to say, but the girl blurted, "Madame Bouvier has a message for you. She regrets that she cannot meet for your spiritual journey at eleven. She will meet you at noon." Despite the girl's apprehension, she glanced past Brigitte, large eyes flitting for hints of sin. "She says to bring the verses." Her eyes went to Brigitte. "If I were you, I would have them memorized. She is in a temper, mademoiselle."

Something had gone wrong. Had she refused to take Tom in? Yet Brigitte had felt sure . . .

"Tell her I'll be there," Brigitte said.

※ ※

Though it was only a fifteen-minute walk to the café, Brigitte left the house earlier, while the other three were still sleeping. She didn't want to explain. She walked past the Mairie and kept walking to Le Port. She came to the church and stood in front, staring up at the bell tower. What could have gone wrong?

Someone informed.

Someone denounced.

Madame Bouvier had not taken him in. She had called for Brigitte to tell her off.

Tom never made it there. He was shot along the way. Only Rafael made it to tell the story.

Tom made another mistake. They were beating a man and—

"Tom," she whispered.

He came from the sky and brought the sky with him.

The patch of freedom in her room, this *entity*, this marvel—he came from a place where there was still free will, and of his free will, he came.

"Mademoiselle?" said a kindly voice at her side. "May I—? Why, hello again, Mademoiselle Durand."

She stared into the face of Father Eppinette.

"Father? Pray for my friend Tom. He is in trouble."

Father Eppinette inclined his head. "I will pray, child." He looked at her, concerned. "Is there anything else I can—?"

She hurried away.

He was safe. He had to be safe. The sight of the Caen Canal Bridge gave comfort. He was like that steel bridge. He was strong, he was resilient. She would not fear unless given reason. She would act like the resistant she was, and the core of the word was *resist*. She would resist bad thoughts. She would resist fear.

Guillemot, the waiter, recognized Brigitte and favored her with a smile as he approached her table, same as before, in the northeast corner.

"Bonjour, mademoiselle. How pleasant to see you. Will the madame be joining you?"

"Yes. Any minute."

He sighed. "Alas, Adèle did not make the soup today. That brawler, Rondeau, did."

"Rondeau uses too much salt?"

He sniffed. "Rondeau uses too much everything. He has the subtlety of a jackhammer. The soup should be finessed—but no. Rondeau assaults the soup. You will taste it to believe it, no charge, just enough to taste. You seem a sensible young woman. I collect witnesses to verify the violence done upon the soup." He started to leave.

"How long have you known Madame Bouvier?" Brigitte said.

He paused and sent a swift glance about the café. It had only four or five other customers, all seated at the front.

"I know who you are," Brigitte said softly. "What I don't know is why she did it."

The waiter wore a crisp, spotless white apron, out of place in folksy Bénouville. His black hair was perfectly oiled and groomed, his thin mustache precision trimmed. He stood for a moment, gazing out the window at the café across the street, whether in the grip of a distant memory or simply trying to decide how to answer, Brigitte could not guess.

"I do not know her story, mademoiselle, and I have not asked. I only know she saved my life." He started away, then hesitated. "War does strange things, does it not? People come forward to show who they are in war." He left for the kitchen.

Brigitte looked out the window at the bridge, and fell into a sort of daze, keeping her thoughts blank. Before she knew it, a small bowl appeared on the table.

"Voilà," Guillemot said. "Taste, and be objective."

Brigitte hardly dared to be objective. She could not bear to let him down. Tentatively, she took a sip of the red slurry with a swirl of orange froth and frowned in concentration. She looked up in surprise.

"Salt," she said, wrinkling her nose.

"Yes!" Guillemot cried. "Go on."

She took another taste, shuddered. "Garlic."

"I weep. Continue."

"Enough tarragon to flavor *two* pots, and an unwelcome presence of . . ." She tasted another sip and said, perplexed, "Fennel." When he did not comment, she looked up.

Guillemot clasped his hands over his heart, held them out to her, pressed them on his heart again. When he found his voice, he said, "I am surprised you do not smash the bowl and denounce Rondeau a heretic. You gladden my heart." To Madame Bouvier, who had appeared unnoticed, he said, "She gladdens my heart. Her sensitivities are your own, madame. 'Unwelcome presence of fennel . . .'"

Madame Bouvier looked at the soup and said grimly, "Rondeau. Why can you not chain Adèle to the stove?"

Guillemot shook his head in dark agreement. "We have tried." He then said briskly, "Tea?"

"Coffee?"

"No."

The madame sighed. "Tea."

With a last admiring look at Brigitte, Guillemot whisked the offensive bowl from her sight, then went to the kitchen.

Madame pulled out a chair, propped her cane against the wall, and sat. The blue eyes glanced at Brigitte as she settled in, arranging her lavender Bible and pocketbook. She wore the makeup of their first encounter, but beneath it was the pale, taut weariness of the last.

Brigitte said, "What happened?"

"The gladiator went to rescue the Christian. He was gone this morning."

They were beating a man today . . .

"How very like him." A swell of relief replaced dread, and she briefly closed her eyes. But when she opened them, nothing had changed on Madame Bouvier's face. "Tell me," she breathed.

"This morning a man came to my shop to bring a book for the book drive," Madame said quietly. "He is stationed at the Mairie, Resistance posing as Milice. Brigitte . . . the gladiator has been taken."

. . . Mayday, this is Angel three. I'm hit.

"I wish I could tell you he is in French custody. Vile as they are, as little faith as we owe them, the Milice are still French and one cannot but hope they will remember it. But I am afraid he was turned over to the Gestapo. He has been transferred to headquarters in Caen. I am very . . . Brigitte?"

Guillemot!

The poor creature! How white!

Get some water. Brigitte, look at me. Take hold of yourself. She has had bad news, Guillemot.

Here—she must put her head between her knees.

It is undignified . . .

It works, madame, when one is faint. There you are, my dear. Breathe deeply, mademoiselle.

I will not let him die.
Of course you won't, my dear.
I will get him released.
Of course you will. A woman with such a palate can do any-
thing. Breathe deeply. There you are, my dear . . .

Brigitte set out her best navy-blue dress with the silvery sash. It was no Coco Chanel, but it was classically cut, stylish, and fit perfectly. She set out blue pumps, pearl earrings, a pearl necklace, and an original—if worn—Elsa Schiaparelli jacket. She'd worn this on her last day at the American embassy. She had no stockings—silk, nylon, or otherwise. No matter. She had dyed her legs last week, and it had not yet faded. Marie-Josette had penciled in a seam on the back of her legs. The faded line was enough to trace over.

Wearing her slip, she went to work in front of the mirror. Light makeup soon hid most of the pallor and the bruise at the corner of her mouth. She styled her hair, coaxing dark curls into place, and dabbed her wrists, temples, and neck with rose water. She slipped into her clothing and surveyed the effect.

Colette appeared in the reflection of the mirror, at the bedroom door. "Marie-Josette told me of his arrest. Where are you going?"

Brigitte applied lipstick, rubbed her lips together, and tucked the tube into her pocketbook. She went to the top drawer of her dresser, rummaged beneath lingerie, and found Grandfather's old, black leather purse with the clasp. It was all the money she had: 277 francs and some change. She put the purse in her pocketbook.

"I am going to Caen. I will not be back. Not unless I come back with him."

"What will you do?"

"I don't know. I will start at the Rousseau Cimenterie."

She picked up the small suitcase she had packed, tucked her pocketbook under her arm, and passed Colette as she left the room.

Marie-Josette waited at the back door. She wrapped her arms around Brigitte. "Be safe," she whispered. "Tell the Matterhorn we said hello."

Simone stood with arms folded in the kitchen doorway, looking on with a half smile. "Good luck, Brigitte."

"I love you all," Brigitte suddenly said. "Go to Father Eppinette for me, will you? Have him light candles. Have him say prayers."

Colette appeared at the bottom of the stairs. "I will go. Good luck."

22

THIN STRIPS OF CABLE were surely not as comfortable as standard-issue handcuffs. He shouldn't complain; at least his wrists were bound in front. The vehicle pulled up to a tall building draped with an immense swastika. Tom had passed this building with Michel early yesterday morning on the very walk that might have bought this trouble.

You shoulda kept going.

Shut up, Ozzie.

But Oz was right. He'd stepped into the open and was half-way across the street when the Milice hit squad came around the corner. He froze right in the middle of the street, then dashed back toward Madame Bouvier's, diverting left at the last second when he realized that if he was caught there, he'd draw attention to her. He had some idea to ditch into a hedge-row only to find that there was no ditching into a hedgerow. The thing was impenetrable, and he was in the wide blaring open. So he pressed himself in as far as he could, then held very, very still.

It almost worked. Nearly the entire squad had emptied into the building, when the last man paused.

A guard opened the door, pulled him from the car, and that's when he heard it. His heart jumped. He looked up, he looked around. No mistaking that sound—it was the radial engine of a P-47.

And there they were, like some beautiful soaring miracle in the noon-blue sky, a formation of three gorgeous Jugs on the way back to Ringwood or Stoney Cross or—

"Beweg dich," the soldier said, then shoved him forward.

"Neem gemakkelijk, joch," he muttered in Dutch. *Take it easy, buddy.*

They had passed Rousseau's house, a few streets over, but Tom was careful to let his eyes run over it as impassively as the rest of Caen. He'd had time on the way from Bénouville to come up with a plan on how he would conduct himself during the interrogations. He'd tell lies based on facts. They knew he was Cabby, and they knew he was Tom, though how they knew he could not fathom. But it didn't mean they knew he was an American pilot, or that Rousseau was Greenland, or that André Besson, the courier for the Rousseau Cimenterie, was Rafael. He'd keep them away from Rousseau and Rafael and Brigitte.

Yes, he was assigned to the Rousseau Cimenterie—by the Dutch underground, not by Rommel. He was Dutch, after all, and had never lost his love for the country. His parents stayed in contact with family and friends after emigrating, and when the Netherlands fell, they went into action. They set up a covert network of "Friends of the Netherlands," an organization whose front was to aid the country after the bombing of Rotterdam; they actually worked with London to supply the Dutch underground with arms, forged documents, ration

cards, guilders, and schematics for radar installations and
other public works for Resistance targets.

He smiled a little; his dairy farmer father would be surprised to know he was the head spy in a ring of spies. Code
name for this Dutch Resistance group: the Indians. Father's
nom de guerre: Chief Joseph. Mother: Pocahontas. Ronnie,
who would not be left out even in an imaginary scenario:
Geronimo. Tom was Crazy Horse.

The RAF and the USAAF had no idea he bled Orange—
not even his pilot brothers. He had crashed his plane on purpose, parachuted to where he was collected by his contacts,
and the plan was set in motion. Provided with papers and a
uniform, he was to make contact with Dutch conscripts and
see what he could do to get them free.

He memorized the story, and interrogated himself as if he
were Rousseau, until he could rattle off the details flawlessly.
He even began to fashion his thoughts in Dutch, not English.
When he spoke, though he spoke little, it was in Dutch. Every
word.

He paused in front of the building to gaze at the huge
swastika hanging from the balustrade far above the steps. It
was made of heavy material, and when the wind blew, it did
not ripple as much as it rolled like an ocean swell. The pause
earned him a shove, and he stumbled forward.

He was taken through a large and busy reception area,
under a portrait of Hitler to a hallway, through the twisting
and turning hallway to a set of stairs, and finally to a basement,
where a warren of doors lined both sides of a long corridor.

The corridor jangled with noise. Groans, cries, snatches
of conversation waxed and waned as he passed the doors. He
figured a jail for a quiet place, the occupants pondering their
fates. This place sounded as loud as an orchestra tuning up,

and nothing came to resonance. One of his escorts unlocked a door and pushed him in. He saw a disheveled man sitting against the back wall, squinting against the sudden light; his face was reddened and shiny, as if it had been scrubbed raw. It was all the glimpse Tom had before the door closed, cutting off the light. He saw enough to know the cell had no window and was no bigger than a closet. Unless he sat where the other man was sitting, he could not stretch out his legs.

I am sure Monsieur Rousseau mentioned that you are not to talk to anyone in your cell. He could be a Gestapo plant. It was one of the many carefully worded asides beginning, *I am sure Monsieur Rousseau mentioned . . .* that Rafael had slipped into conversations over the past few weeks. And most of the time, no, Rousseau had not mentioned it. Rousseau's focus, now that Tom thought about it, always seemed to center on having his story right. In fact, Rousseau's focus was always in a defensive posture, not offensive. Getting intelligence on the Caen Canal Bridge was not as important to Rousseau as a perfect alias.

Tom wouldn't have hesitated to see if the man was all right, to try to strike up a conversation no matter what the language might be, especially in extraordinary circumstances like these where two scared strangers were all each other had; yet he was Tom no longer—he was Kees Nieuwenhuis—and these circumstances transcended the extraordinary. He rested his back against the wall and, after a moment, slid down.

It was cold in the cell, but the concrete floor was colder; he wished for his jacket to sit on. In Bénouville, they had stripped him of the jacket for his effrontery in wearing a German coat with rank insignia. They'd taken away his belt, his papers, and the picture of Ronnie. He had only the little button in his trousers pocket they had either missed or didn't think worth taking.

The cable handcuffs began to rub into his wrists. Maybe they forgot to take them off; a cuffed man in a locked room seemed redundant. His stomach growled. He hadn't had anything to eat since yesterday, and nothing to drink except a cup of lukewarm coffee from one of the Milice.

So far, things aren't so bad, Tom thought, keeping his mind from the future. Deal with the now, and three small miseries he could handle: an empty gut, sore wrists, and a cold butt.

One day atta time, Cabby, Oswald said with a wink.

Out of the darkness came a hoarse, thin voice. *"J'ai acheté au marché noir une bouteille de Bordeaux pour mon anniversaire. Une bouteille. Pour cela, ils . . ."*

Tom closed his eyes. He couldn't understand a word, but any decent man would have responded in some way.

"Une bouteille!"

There was no need to translate the despair. Tom bit back a sympathetic murmur.

"Je ne sais pas ce qu'ils ont fait à ma femme . . ." The voice trailed into thin, ragged sobs.

We're on our way, pal, with an army you wouldn't—

He caught himself and, with a vague pull of apprehension in his gut, shaped the thought in Dutch. *We zijn onze manier, met een leger zou je niet geloven . . .*

The train did not run on the time-honored schedule it had in prewar days, and it no longer went to Ouistreham; Ouistreham was too close to the Atlantic Wall for German security tastes. It ran to Bénouville and to one station past, but only a few times a day. Brigitte had to wait at the little depot near the bridge for an hour before a train came. By the time she made it to Caen, it was nearly four o'clock.

She asked for directions to the Rousseau Cimenterie office. It was only a kilometer from the depot, so she decided to walk.

She had not been in Caen since autumn. Then, Allies had bombed an electric station, and the collateral damage was grave; errant bombs had fallen on a nearby neighborhood, destroying four homes and killing eleven civilians. She looked for recent damage to buildings as she walked along, but saw none.

I have never been to a house of sin, the girl at the door said.

She would never return. Let the Reich have her home, let them swallow it up. They'd not swallow her.

When she came to the Rousseau Cimenterie office, with a placard announcing Todt Organization above the business sign, she brushed her suit free of city dust, arranged her hat, and firmed her grip on the little suitcase.

The door opened to a bright, tall-ceilinged outer office where a rather dour, graying woman sat clacking away at a typewriter. She finished a word, untangled two keystrokes, and looked up. Brigitte gazed at the typewriter. How long since her fingers had poised over the keys at the embassy . . . Next to her typewriter, she'd had a little cobalt-blue vase, a gift from Jean-Paul. It always held a bud or two. Behind the vase was a photograph of her and Jean-Paul at the racetrack in Chantilly.

"May I help you, mademoiselle?" the woman inquired.

"I am here to see Monsieur Rousseau."

"You do not have an appointment . . ."

"I must see him."

"I will see if he is available. Your name?"

"Brigitte Durand."

If the name meant anything to her, the secretary did not let on. She got up and went to the door past her desk, knocked once and entered, closing the door behind.

She was gone less than a minute. "He will see you. May I take your hat and coat? Would you like some coffee?" She added in a mildly conspiratorial tone, "Real coffee?"

Sturmbannführer Ernst Schiffer pulled slowly on his cigarette as he looked over the file labeled *Kees Nieuwenhuis*. His secretary, Krista Hegel, noted there was not much in it. A thin, paper-clipped report that looked like a transcript, three pieces of identification, a school picture of a boy, and a paper with a few handwritten sentences from the Milice station in Bénouville.

"You know Dutch, Krista," Schiffer stated more than he asked.

"I haven't used it in a while. But yes."

"You will be present for the provisional information interrogation, as well as any that follow. We will be clear on that now."

Krista did not answer. It wouldn't matter if she protested. Worst of all, she had requested this assignment, never dreaming what it would mean. She had merely wanted to get out of Berlin; she wanted to see a little of the world. They sent her first to Italy, where she worked for a man who ran a camp in Trieste. After only two weeks, she was reassigned to Schiffer in Normandy, when he lost his secretary to tuberculosis. She hadn't worked for Schiffer long before she figured his former secretary likely gave herself the disease to escape.

As an interpreter and a secretary, she had to be present for certain interrogations—the "stricter" interrogations, Schiffer called them—to translate if needed and to take notes in shorthand, to be typed into a formal report later. Once she realized what sort of interrogations they were, she refused to be present for them. It was not a matter of translating; it was a matter of witnessing at close hand the torture of human beings, then writing down what was wrested from their brokenness.

When she refused, Schiffer laughed in her face and told her a German woman had to be hard where enemies were concerned. But there wasn't anything German about the way these men, and sometimes women, were treated—not the way Krista was taught and raised. And the more she saw of the SS and what had been unleashed upon the world, the more she clung to those precious things she had learned in childhood. *Love your neighbor. Be gentle and kind. Help people.*

It was not Schiffer who persuaded her to obey, think what he might. It was a still, small voice that asked, *Krista, will Schiffer's cruelty be the last thing these wretches know? Will you not be courageous and offer what you can?*

The only way she could endure the interrogations was to pray in a silent, steady stream the entire time, and she made it her habit to begin the prayers with her first footfall in the room. *Oh, God, if I can do no more than witness the atrocities that I may testify one day, then make me strong; and if I can do more than witness, then give me a chance to help.*

There were days she could not take it. She did her best to hide it from Schiffer, who loved to make fun of her "weakness." But some days the cruelty made her weep long into her pillow at night. Yet she did not want reassignment. What if the woman who came after her was as cruel as Schiffer, like the secretary in Trieste? Would she take the opportunity to fetch the poor wretch some water when Schiffer went out? Would she whisper words of comfort or encouragement, sometimes destroy hidden evidence, or even take a message to a loved one?

Would she offer last rites to an old woman?

Krista was Lutheran. She was not Catholic, let alone a priest. Yet the old woman on the cot in interrogation room 3 had feebly called for last rites.

"I see . . . you are not like him," the old woman rattled, laboring for breath. "Soon I am gone. I need last rites."

Schiffer had left the room. One guard remained; the other had left to summon stretcher bearers from the infirmary. All knew the woman would not last the night.

Krista had gone to the old woman and knelt at her side. She glanced at the guard, who averted his gaze, then whispered, "I am sorry—I am not Catholic. I do not know what to do."

"I need . . . I do not know English word," the woman fretted, clutching her sleeve.

"A priest?"

"I need—I do not have the word! *Dieu, je t'en prie,* give me the word . . ."

"Absolution," the guard quietly supplied.

"Oui!" the woman cried, pathetically grateful. Her head moved in the direction of the guard, but Krista doubted she could see him. Schiffer had taken away her glasses.

"Have you been so very wicked that you need to be absolved?" A tear slipped down Krista's cheek. Today was a bad day, and today she was very weak. She pushed away the tear with a fist, wishing, dear God, she could push away all misery. "You confessed that you hid people. You helped people. You fed people." She touched the bruised, swollen face. "For which of these should you be absolved?"

"Did you hear . . . the French I spoke?"

Krista nodded.

"I called him . . . bad things." The old woman smiled a swollen smile.

Krista smiled, too, and another tear slipped down. She caressed the old woman's brow. "For this, I will not absolve you. No priest would. Jesus our Lord would call him whatever you did."

"Humor me," the woman whispered, her smile fading, her eyes losing strength of spirit. Krista had seen it too often. The woman was not long for the earth.

"I absolve you," Krista said softly and, not knowing what else she should do, drew the sign of the cross on the woman's forehead. Relief came to the battered face.

"Do you know the Lord's Prayer?" Krista asked.

"*Certainement,*" she said faintly, with a rustle of indignation. "Always seems to . . . surprise you Protestants."

Krista took her hand. "Let us say it together."

The woman did not live past *hallowed be thy name.*

Krista had rested her head on the edge of the cot, too full of despair to move.

God trusts me with this terrible job, she told herself, sobbing into her pillow that night. *He must trust me very much.*

Mother, may they know your kindness through me.

Mother, may they know a different Germany through me.

Mother—did you ever imagine you would raise your daughter to witness such things?

Krista picked up the school picture of the little boy, then looked sadly at the blond young man in the identification booklet. He looked nice.

"Brigitte Durand," Charlotte announced.

Michel looked up at Charlotte. It took a moment to recollect the name, and then he had to stifle a groan.

He tossed down the pen. It could only mean something

had gone wrong. What new unforeseen misery would he learn? Rafael had stopped in earlier to report that Tom was safe, if unhappy, at Gisèlle Bouvier's home—and then he launched into an idea for a rescue attempt for Clemmie, and Michel had to break in and inform him that Clemmie was dead.

Michel rubbed his temples. Why so many *feeling* people in this Resistance? Why could they not unplug all feeling until the war was over? Was it not enough, to labor under this cloud? Rafael had wept, and Michel had, too, for the tower of strength in Cabourg who had fallen.

And now, Brigitte Durand, the child he had stolen to the Cause. Foreboding plundered his heart, a discordant measure of "La Marseillaise" plinking in some darkened corner.

"Send her in." *Michel,* he sternly told himself, *take charge.*

The door opened. He rose, summoned a smile, and came around the desk. Charlotte announced that coffee was on its way and slipped out.

Michel shook the woman's hand. "It is a pleasure to meet you, Mademoiselle Durand. A pleasure and an honor." He showed her to the chair in front of the desk and went to take his own.

The woman's fair face was grave.

"How may I assist you?" Michel asked, when she did not speak.

She glanced around the large room as if sure to find someone to overhear. "It feels strange . . ."

"I assure you, it is quite safe," Michel said. "And my secretary is with us."

The young woman's uncertain gaze came back to Michel, and her face seemed to clear. "By now you have heard the news," she said tentatively. "I am here to help. I'll do anything, Monsieur Rousseau. Anything."

He tilted his head slightly. "You refer to the news of Clemmie . . ."

She shook her head. "I know of her arrest. It's—"

"No, mademoiselle," Michel cut in gently. "She is dead." At her shocked expression, he added, "We learned it very late last night."

"I am sorry. I did not know her, but—" she added quite softly—"but Tom did."

"Yes. But you must *not* tell him. Not now; it would be most unwise. Once we get him to England, we can send a message through—"

"But, Monsieur Rousseau," Brigitte exclaimed, "Tom was arrested this morning."

Michel stared.

"I thought you would have heard . . ."

He found his voice. "Where is he being held?"

"Right here in Caen. He was transferred to Gestapo head-quarters from Bénouville this morning."

The door burst open, and Rafael rushed in, Charlotte behind him. Michel rose.

Rafael stood breathing hard, sweat shining on his face. It was a face that knew what Michel had just learned. It was a face stone cold with decision. He walked slowly to the desk, eyes hard on Michel. "Not him."

Brigitte rose. Her self-possession faltered. Though her voice was steady, her lips trembled. "A piece of the sky cannot be caged."

"Not him," Rafael repeated, daring Michel to tell him differently.

"We would risk . . . everything," Michel said heavily. Did it mean to them what it meant to him?

"Sometimes you must," Charlotte said quite clearly. "Stop

being so responsible, Michel." She turned on her heel, muttering about extra coffee.

The interrogation room was not spread with a drop cloth. There would be no blood for the PII, the Provisional Information Interrogation.

The prisoner sat with bound hands folded on the table. When Schiffer and Krista came in, he looked up with the same expression Krista had seen dozens of times. She'd seen it on the faces of the French, the British, the Americans, the Belgians, the Italians: the same fear, the same determination, the same courage, the same alarm, all schooled to one expression Krista had come to call the Provisional face.

Later this face would change. As the days of interrogations went on, the face would become haunted, no matter how courageous the individual. Each new summons would bring a face newly learned in pain. When she saw this face next, it would know the pain of hunger and thirst. When she saw it again, it would know pain far worse. She avoided eye contact with Kees Nieuwenhuis as she set up her station with pencils and pads of paper and three dictionaries. Every new, bewildered prisoner sought a scrap of comfort against well-founded fears and hoped to find it in a young woman armed only with office supplies. He must not find it yet.

"Do you speak German?" Schiffer asked the prisoner as he settled in the seat across from him with the file.

The prisoner shook his head, then shrugged and said in German, "Very little, I am sorry." The Dutch accent was strong.

"Do you speak French?"

"*Nee.*"

"I am Sturmbannführer Schiffer. I do not speak Dutch. Fräulein Hegel will translate, and you will answer truthfully. It is custom, as you may know, to wait ten days or so into your incarceration before beginning our talks. You are a special case."

Krista translated Schiffer's opening statements, settling her mind to the Dutch language, and the PII began.

Schiffer opened the file and took his time to look over the radio transcript.

"Hmm. Do I call you Kees, Cabby, or Tom?"

The prisoner stared at the transcript. Schiffer faked surprise. "Oh, this?" He pushed it across the table. "This is how we discovered you are not who you say you are. Have a look."

The prisoner slowly read the transcript. Schiffer feigned disinterested patience, as if his mind were elsewhere, but Krista knew he was watching the prisoner like a bird of prey.

Krista watched too. Pale-blue eyes ran over the words, and after a few moments, she looked away. She now had a fair measure of his type, and her heart filled with sorrow. Schiffer had the measure, too.

Though the prisoner had done his best to conceal all emotion, she had watched the eyes take in the words first with disbelief, then belief, then resignation, and finally, defiance. The young man was better than others; the flow from one emotion to the other was subtle enough that it took someone who had done this for a long time to recognize the four emotions. She always held her breath when the resignation came, for what followed next determined the entire course of Schiffer's interrogations: if despair followed the resignation, things went better for the prisoner. He would break easily, suffer less. If, however, defiance came—as she knew Schiffer hoped it would, for he loved a challenge—then the prisoner was in for dimensions of hell he knew not existed.

So she turned her eyes away from this young man, and while defiance filled his heart, despair seeped into her own.

Courage, Krista, the still, small voice said.

The prisoner pushed the transcript back with bound hands. He had taken as much time as he dared to buy time for his own course of action. The blue eyes now raised to Schiffer were impassive and steady.

Courage . . .

She reached for a pad and a pencil, and the interrogation began.

That wasn't so bad, Tom thought as they escorted him back to his cell. The corridor held the same jangled cacophony, as if someone opened and shut the reception room of hell. His French friend was gone when he returned. He noticed the stench for the first time, vomit and urine and mildew. The door slammed behind him, and he went to take the Frenchman's seat, but changed his mind, deciding to pace out his thoughts and keep his butt warm a little longer.

Things weren't so bad, and in fact they were better: they had replaced the handcuffs with much softer rope and even left a few extra inches between his hands. Still only three things to deal with, not counting the stench: no food, a cold cell, and handcuffs.

Mentally he'd slid into his Dutch Resistance story after he read the transcript, glad he had it ready; he also became Captain Fitzgerald's ambassador for radio silence. If ever he got back, he'd sell it like war bonds.

A scream tore the air, and Tom made fists until it died away.

Schiffer had not asked a single question about his mission.

The interrogation lasted only one hour, and to Tom's surprise, he asked mostly about the P-47 Thunderbolt. When he asked questions for which Tom figured he already had the answers, he spoke truthfully. The fuel capacity, the caliber of the guns—surely they knew that from recovered wreckage. But when asked about maximum altitude, maximum bomb load, the rate of fire, Tom lied easily about the Jug. When asked how many were manufactured, he shrugged and said offhandedly, as if it were common knowledge, "Thousands." He had no idea.

Schiffer got folksy, or thought he did, asking Tom companionably about his early days of training. Tom answered, feeling all the while that there was nothing companionable about Schiffer. He came off as an actor who spoke the right lines with a determined delivery that was off-kilter for the very reason of the determination. He thought he was good at what he did. Tom encouraged his illusion by easing into a seemingly relaxed posture, talking a mile a minute and saying nothing important.

"I couldn't wait to fly. Early days, I learned on a PT-17, then a BT-13. But once I got into a P-40—" and here, Tom let his face go smiling soft with remembrance—"then I knew what torque was."

"Ah, yes," Schiffer said importantly. "The P-40. And did you train on a P-39?"

Tom looked at him as if surprised. "Sure did. Two hundred hours."

"And what do you think of your Thunderbolt, your Jug? How do you feel about her? Why is she superior to you?"

"She's a warhorse, lemme tell you. She can take fire that would easily knock out others. She's slick in a dive, she's—" Then Tom made as if he'd said too much, and finished with a mumbled "She's not glamorous, but she gets it done."

Schiffer had smiled a kindly, superior smile. He rose to go and then made a parting remark about radar detection, saying with a wag of his finger, as if the Allies had been very naughty, "We found ways around your aluminum strips for jamming." He smiled mysteriously. "You can fill the sky with that trash. It does not matter."

It was an odd comment dropped into a conversation that had no place for it, and it meant nothing to Tom. Schiffer moved to a tune he thought Tom heard.

Tom paced the tiny cell. Four steps to the wall, four steps to the door.

The blonde secretary seemed a cold little thing, not much older than he, all business. She refused him the courtesy of eye contact, and when he made a joke, she did not attempt to smile.

Tom had felt a subdued shock when he first saw the double lightning bolts on the lapel of Schiffer's coat. At first he seemed affable enough, for an enemy SS commander; as the hour-long chat wore on, he got a feel for Schiffer. He knew things would get ugly.

Tom sat down and put his head against the wall. This day, this minute, he was okay. *Attaboy, Cab—*

He didn't want Oswald. He wanted Clemmie.

I hope you're okay, Clemmie.

Jesus, Mary, and Joseph—it's you.

Calabrese would say you're swearing.

Pfft. It is a calling upon. Say—that big blond head made a promise to come see me.

Sit tight, Clemmie. I'm taking you home with me. I'm gonna get you out of this place.

Ten days before the average prisoner was interrogated. Clemmie had to fall into that category. That meant he had seven, eight days. First he'd get out of here. Then he'd get to Cabourg. And then he'd get her free.

He rubbed the black button between his thumb and finger. "Sit tight, Clemmie," he murmured. "Not gonna let my girl go down."

Hauptmann Braun strolled down the street, grateful for the coming of spring. It was late afternoon, and he paused to lift his face to the last warmth of the sun. He wondered how Lisette was doing. He wondered if her thoughts went as his did to their apartment in Berlin, to springtime there, and the flowers, and Franz and Erich home for Easter break, and the lovely way life used to be—

He opened his eyes at the sound of footsteps rapidly descending the steps of the Gestapo headquarters.

He smiled. *Speaking of Berlin* . . . "Krista!" he called. But the girl didn't hear. She reached the bottom of the stairs and kept on. "Krista Hegel!"

The girl stopped and turned. She gazed blankly at Braun. He came closer. "Is everything all right?"

"Herr Braun." A perfunctory smile came and faded. "Yes. Fine."

"Are you well?"

"Perfectly." But the lovely porcelain cheeks, reminiscent of her mother's, were quite pale. Gone was the healthy rose hue she'd had when she came to Caen last autumn. They'd had coffee, then, when they ran into each other in a café near the depot, mutually delighted to be in familiar company so far from home. She was excited about her transfer, glad to be quit of Trieste, she confessed, for the camp in Trieste was a bad place.

They hadn't had coffee since, but they saw each other on occasion as Krista was billeted in the same apartment block as Braun. Now that he thought of it, the girl's natural effusiveness had waned over the past several months. But, Braun thought a trifle guiltily, he had been too busy for coffee.

"How is your family?" he asked. He and Lisette were good friends with the Hegels. Krista's father worked in police administration in Berlin and had managed to get Krista a job when she was sixteen.

"Fine. I am terribly sorry, Herr Braun. I must—I am late. Good day." She hurried off at a trot.

Braun watched her go. He glanced up at the massive tapestry-like hanging of the swastika on the building. It lifted with a slow filling of the wind, then settled against the wall, as if the building were breathing.

The last rays of sun disappeared, and the wind came chill. Braun turned up his collar and walked on.

23

THE SCRAPE OF THE KEY in the lock woke Tom. A guard ordered him to his feet.

He must have finally slept. He had the sense of a passage of time. It had taken a long time to get to sleep. He had to shut out the groans of other prisoners in other cells and the occasional distant screams. He had to stop thinking about water. His body was stiff from sleeping on cold concrete, and now that he stood, he felt sick from lack of food. Thirst had become some demon thing. His tongue felt thick; his lips throbbed. How long since that coffee? Yesterday morning? What time was it? Was it day or night? He had not seen daylight since—

"*Gehe, schnell,*" one of the two guards said with a prod.

"You wouldn't happen to have a beer on you?" Tom asked hoarsely in Dutch. "Tomato soup?"

"*Sei still!*" the other guard said.

They went through the doors at the end of the rabbit warren corridor and turned down the same hallway as yesterday. There were no thrown-together cells in this hallway, and it was far brighter. The building was fairly modern, maybe ten to twenty years old, and the rooms in this hallway were labeled in French, with the German names beneath. He figured out what the *archives* room was for, and there were two of those, but he didn't know what *chaufferie* meant; the German word below, *Kesselraum*, was close enough to the Dutch, *ketelruim*, to make it the boiler room.

They turned right again into another hallway that felt less like a basement and more like a high school corridor. Last door on the right, if they headed for the same room, interrogation room 3.

They did. But the room was different this time. They had a welcome wagon.

"Looks like things are about to get ugly," Tom said with grim cheer when he saw the steel ladder. His heart rate jacked a notch.

It was bent to the form of an A without the peak, centered over a stained drop cloth. Chains dangled in the middle space. A few metal rods lay on the table. One of the guards pointed to the chair by the rods.

Tom sat and noticed the leather whip next to the bars. It looked like a long, braided riding quirt. It was caked with dried blood. His heart rate jacked again, and a bulge of fear rose low in his throat.

Schiffer was not yet in the room, only the secretary and the two guards.

Tom turned from the welcome wagon. "I'm very thirsty," he said to the secretary, who sat at the opposite end of the table with her notepad and pencil.

"Do not speak to me," the woman said coldly, with only a flick of her eyes. "You will address yourself to Sturmbannführer Schiffer."

"I don't think he cares if I'm thirsty. You might."

She did not answer. She glanced through the notes taken yesterday.

"No dice from Princess Ice," he muttered in English, a familiar barracks phrase. He looked over his shoulder. "How 'bout you fellas? Anyone got a hip flask?"

"Stick to Dutch," the secretary said very quietly.

She went over notes with a competent air, filling something in, striking something out. After a moment he was unsure if she had spoken at all.

"*Schön—nicht wahr?*"

Sturmbannführer Schiffer filled the doorway, tugging off his gloves. When the secretary did not translate, he looked at her and barked something in German.

"Beautiful, is she not?" the woman said tonelessly.

"I prefer brunettes," Tom said slowly in Dutch, glancing from her to the man.

Schiffer rattled off a long speech in German, gazing at the woman.

"I think of her often," the secretary said softly, and Tom saw the first crack of composure. Color bloomed in the white cheeks. She blinked and, when Schiffer barked at her again, said, "I—I think how lovely to have her in my arms. My wife is in Munich. France is my playground. I—I want her . . . for my . . ." The cheeks turned crimson.

Tom glared at Schiffer. "You son of a—"

"Where is Greenland?" Schiffer said in perfect English.

Tom's gut plunged.

At a motion from Schiffer, the guards hauled him from the chair and dragged him to the steel ladder. Fear fluttered wildly, like a rush of startled bats. It wasn't happening. It couldn't be happening. They shoved him to his knees on the drop cloth, pushed him over, pushed him to his back. One of the guards took the metal rod and hooked one end to a dangling chain. They brought his knees together and pulled his bound hands over his knees.

"Oh, I get it," Tom said. "You weren't being nice."

The extra inches made it possible for his knees to fit between his arms. They slid the rod behind his knees, in front of his elbows, and hooked the other dangling chain to the other end of the rod. Then the two guards hauled on the chains and hoisted him into the air.

He dangled in a ball several feet from the ground in the empty space of the steel ladder. His head hung back and filled with pressure, his hands and the back of his knees took the job of holding his body aloft. It already hurt.

A ferocious surge of panic came and he tried furiously to struggle, but could not move. He could not even swing himself. He could only dangle and turn slowly in place. He could only watch them upside down, the man and the guards and the girl, whose head bent over her pad.

Schiffer pulled out a chair and sat, crossing his legs. He took the braided whip and laid it in his lap. Sweat sprang to Tom's scalp.

"You are asking yourself how. How did he know?" Schiffer said musingly. He had reverted to German. The girl began to translate in Dutch, but Schiffer gave a sharp command, and she translated in English.

"I will tell you how. Your impeccable papers have been traced to the same forger who worked for Greenland." He let it sink in. "We picked him up last week. A pity he did not survive. You could have reminisced."

The secretary translated in a dull but clear murmur.

"I have broken men tougher than you. You think your size means toughness? You think physical beauty is a sign of strength? I have learned much. Size matters not at all. Beauty will no longer serve you."

What now? Tom couldn't think. He had no plan to fall back on. He had only his carefully plotted story. He had nothing else.

He could barely breathe, scrunched up like this, and if he lifted his head to ease the pressure, it put more painful pressure on the back of his knees.

Stick to the story? But if his papers had been traced to the same forger . . . what did that mean for him? For Rousseau? He couldn't think; he couldn't *think*!

He had no plan, no place to fall back to except one, the last resort of any captured soldier.

"Where is Greenland?" Schiffer asked.

"Thomas William Jaeger," he said in English, then paused for breath. "First lieutenant, United States Army Air Forces." Pause. "One four oh nine six . . . five two six."

The secretary wrote it down.

"It was a radio transmission," Brigitte said. "Picked up at Douvres-la-Délivrande. I saw the transcript. They passed them out to the Milice."

"They know he is Tom," Monsieur Rousseau mused at the window, gazing at the courtyard below. "What story will he give them? What will he do?"

"What will *we* do?" Rafael said morosely, slumped at the desk in Rousseau's chair, resting his head on his arm and idling with a paperweight. Charlotte sat in a wingback near the fireplace.

It was a new day, and nothing had changed since the previous night. They were back in the office with nothing new.

Yesterday they had gone over idea after idea, some plausible, some preposterous—as the evening wore on, the more desperate they grew, the more preposterous the plan.

Brigitte and Rafael had gone home with Michel. Brigitte stayed in the same room Tom had; when she slipped out of her clothing and into the bed, she caught his scent on the pillow. This morning, she took a careful look around the room, searching for some trace of him. She did not find it until she washed up in the little bathroom and saw a decorative bowl arranged with small paper-covered soaps. She took one of the soaps and held it to her nose, closed her eyes.

This is France . . . and this is England . . . and this is ten thousand troops . . .

He was part of the sky, bird-flown and sun-streaked, sometimes clouded and angry, sometimes star-luminous.

"What are they doing to him?" she suddenly asked.

The others were silent, until Charlotte murmured lightly, "We will not think of it, my dear. It will not give him aid."

Monsieur Rousseau stood at the window, hands behind his back, the same place he had long stood yesterday. Brigitte had already learned he thought best when he was very still. Rafael, like Tom, preferred to pace his thoughts. The fact that he sat in Monsieur Rousseau's chair, his face empty of yesterday's passionate determination, meant he had nothing left to pace.

Brigitte learned that for Tom, there would be no transfer to Paris. Caen was close to the Atlantic Wall; some of the prisoners at this Gestapo headquarters were captured submarine personnel on reconnaissance missions, or Allied engineers, or Navy men, or airmen. Most Gestapo commanders hated to give up prizes like captured Allies. Monsieur Rousseau had told Brigitte that airmen were always sent away to a different interrogation place, likely some Luftwaffe base. But Tom had crossed over to Resistance. His uniqueness gave him VIP status. Some Caen prisoners were kept as potential exchanges, some for the information they might know, and some until their usefulness came to light. Tom was likely all three.

Plans for Tom's rescue ran the gamut from staging a prisoner transfer, a tired trick now seldom considered, to blowing up a portion of the building. But the Gestapo headquarters in Caen was heavily guarded twenty-four hours a day. One of the more stately buildings in Caen, a courthouse renovated shortly before the Occupation, it stood apart from other buildings; an approach could be seen from any direction.

"So many unknowns," Monsieur Rousseau murmured. "So many variables. We do not have someone inside, not there." He paused. "And yet . . ."

Rafael lifted his head.

"I suspect your thoughts, Monsieur Rousseau," Charlotte said from where she sat near the fireplace. "It is far too risky."

"You said yourself he is a good man."

"I *think* he is. We cannot be sure, and we put far too much at risk to find out."

"You're the one who said to stop being so responsible," he said, rather sharply.

"Who is he?" Rafael asked, looking from Charlotte to Rousseau. "Don't tell me you're thinking of Hauptmann Braun."

"He helped us learn about Clemmie."

Rafael leaped to his feet. "Helped? It would have *helped* if he got to her on time! It would have *helped* if he got her free! What did he do? He told us she was dead. Does this mean he is our ally?"

"No," Charlotte said firmly.

Rafael began to pace, staring hard at Rousseau as he did. "Oh, I know you, Monsieur Rousseau. I know once you have an idea, you will stay with it. Well, I don't like it. And I don't like him. You get a measure of a man, don't you, by the way he treats others? He treats me like a stupid peasant. 'Run along,' he said to me the other day. He is just another arrogant, conquering German, and I hate him. He probably played the big man, doing you a grand favor; let me tell you, he will make you pay for it. It would be far better to storm the place in a full frontal assault than trust him."

"I agree, Michel," Charlotte said quietly. "We simply do not know him."

Rousseau glanced over his shoulder at Charlotte, then at Brigitte. "She called me Michel." He gave a little expression of mock fright.

"He can't be trusted," Rafael declared. He gazed at Rousseau with such intensity he did not notice all attention on him. Then he flushed, resumed stride.

"It was just a thought," Rousseau said mildly.

"His appointment is at one," Charlotte said, a trace of warning in her tone.

"It was just a thought." Rousseau went back to the window.

"But what can *I* do?" Brigitte said, agitated. She had not the self-possession of the man at the window. She had not Charlotte's poise. "I feel helpless. I want to *do* something. It is maddening."

Rafael stalked the office. He paused when he came even with her chair and said bitterly, "Welcome to the Resistance, m'selle." He flung a hand in the direction of Gestapo headquarters. "While we try to hatch our grand scheme, he is—"

"Rafael," Rousseau said sharply.

Rafael turned a face of innocence to his boss. "I was only

going to say he is probably taking a bath." He looked at Brigitte and smiled a garish smile. *"La baignoire."* He stalked on.

"What is he talking about?" Brigitte said, fear in her throat.

"Oh, why don't you just go home," Rafael snapped.

"I don't live there anymore."

"Then go someplace else. You're right. You're useless." He reached the fireplace and began his return patrol. Charlotte watched him warily.

"I came here to see him free," Brigitte said evenly. "After that . . . I need a job. I worked at the US embassy in Paris." Her chin rose. "I worked for Ambassador Bullitt. I used to type, and I was good at it. I can speak English, I can—"

"You can bed Germans," Rafael said, sauntering past. "I'll bet you're really good at that."

Charlotte's hands flew in the air, Rousseau spun from the window, and Brigitte declared above their protests, "You have no idea. They line up for kilometers."

"So business is booming," he said when he reached the wall. He turned and leaned against it, taking out a pack of cigarettes.

"Like a run on a bank."

"They leave your place quite satisfied," he suggested, lighting up.

"You are mistaken. They leave transformed."

The barest suggestion of a smile touched his lips, and while Rousseau and Charlotte took in this exchange with astonishment, Brigitte took in a drawn face that had not slept, red-stained eyes, dark, puffy circles beneath them. He pulled on the cigarette, daring her to see more, and when she did, he looked away.

"Braun will be here soon," he said after a time. "You want to get some soup?"

"Sure."

He went to Charlotte's office and returned with her coat and purse. He helped her into the coat and looked over at Charlotte, who now exchanged perplexed looks with Rousseau.

"You want to come, Charlotte? I heard they have Camembert. Wilkie said it's a vicious rumor, but some rumors play out." He looked at Brigitte. "A pity there are not male brothels for German women. I would sacrifice myself for Camembert."

Brigitte sniffed. "What makes you think they would come?"

"Mademoiselle." He displayed himself, turning in a slow circle, arms outstretched. "Reacquaint yourself with French real estate. Though I have a feeling you'd prefer the States, hmm?" He grinned at her quick glance. Then he looked at the secretary. "Coming, Charlotte?"

Charlotte said haughtily, "Of course I cannot come. I am on duty." She hesitated. "But if it is true about the Camembert . . ."

Rafael bowed. "For you, madame, I will ambush the kitchen." He held out his arm to Brigitte and escorted her from the room.

24

THE FIRST BLOW flayed not his skin as much as his senses with the simple surprise of pain. The ferocity stunned him, took the breath from his lungs, made him feel like a bewildered child whose playmates were not playing right.

Words came into his hearing. They had been there for some time.

"Who is Greenland?"

"Thomas William Jaeger," he gasped. "First lieutenant, United States—"

The second blow sent spatters to the drop cloth. He stared, upside down, at the drops, bright red over brown, new over old, and wondered about the poor guys who first decorated the cloth.

The third blow produced the first involuntary scream.

The idea of the underground tunnel had freshened Braun's mind play. The new ventilation system arrested his thoughts in particular. The scope of it dazzled, appalled, and confounded

him, providing some of the best diversion he'd had since he left
Lisette at Lake Geneva. He nearly pulled out the latest sketches
from his briefcase just to admire them, but refrained. He would
see Rousseau soon enough, and until then, he'd let his mind run
nimbly along kilometers of intake ducts. Fresh air was the key
to the entire operation, the very first consideration—

"Reinhart, stop the car," he called to his driver.

Krista Hegel was running along the sidewalk, the distress
in her comportment obvious enough to attract attention even
from within a moving vehicle.

"That girl—pull ahead of her, then pull over."

The corporal complied, and Braun quickly opened the
door and got out of the car. She approached in blind haste,
and he knew she would not hear him. He stepped into her
path and, when she came close, called, "Fräulein Hegel!"

She stopped short, breathing hard.

"Why, Krista," Braun said, astonished. "Whatever—"

Instead of bolting away as he feared she might, she ran
straight for him, threw her arms around his middle, and began
to sob most pitiably.

Braun froze. He had no daughters; he had two grown
sons, and neither had cried on him since they were small.
Awkwardly, he patted her arm, and then, seeing a distressed
Lisette in his mind as surely as he had seen intake ducts not a
moment earlier, put his arm around the sobbing girl and held
her close. Lisette approved.

"Come now," he said gently. "Let's go get a cup of tea,
shall we?"

Her nose was swollen, her eyes red-rimmed but clear. She was
quiet. It relieved Braun somewhat, but her silence was almost

as disconcerting. She wasn't the vibrant young girl he'd had coffee with last fall.

They sat in Braun's favorite café not far from the Château de Caen. He seldom came for tea. It was the only place in Caen he could get something resembling beer. The French might be known for wine, but they were not known for beer.

Krista put her chin on her fist and looked out the café window. She looked so very much like her mother, and she had the same qualities she'd possessed since she was a girl. Sweet, and gentle, and kind. She had a purity of loveliness that had him and Lisette exchange occasional glances, thinking of their son Franz. Then the war came, and all young people in Germany went in opposite directions—Italy, North Africa, Greece, France, Norway, Denmark, Holland.

"Thomas William Jaeger," she said softly. "First lieutenant, United States Army Air Forces. One four oh nine six five two six. I write it over, and over, and over."

A cloak descended on Braun's heart.

She gazed unseeing out the window. "Schiffer would be surprised to know not all the guards are as cruel as he."

Schiffer, he thought grimly. Braun had been introduced to Schiffer when intelligence wanted him to put a toe in the political waters of the Rousseau Cimenterie.

"The pilot is to—" A spasm of anguish crossed her face in the first falter since she had contained herself. "He is to remain in his state of . . . incarceration . . . for the day. Schiffer left the room for lunch. I had a bottle of water concealed in my sweater. I went to him and tried to—" She broke from her outside gaze, blinking back tears as she looked down at her hands. "I tried to give him a drink, but the angle of the . . . He couldn't swallow, you see . . ."

Then she raised wondering eyes to Braun. "And do you

know? One of the guards came and helped. He held up the boy's head while I gave him water." Hope freshened the reddened eyes, and he saw a little of the girl he used to know. "I felt as though *I* were the one, Herr Braun, that someone came and gave *me* a drink."

A strange compression came to his middle.

She had seen what he had heard and ignored, strolling on the sidewalk past Gestapo headquarters. That this . . . child, this daughter of his friend should be subjected to such—he wanted to crush the teacup in his hand and welcome lacerations.

"To find a kindred spirit in such a place, that is a gift." He had a brief image of Michel Rousseau. "I am glad for—" He broke off and said in surprise, "The prisoner is a downed pilot?"

She nodded. "He flew a P-47."

"Then why is Schiffer interrogating him? He should be sent to Frankfurt." A Luftwaffe interrogation center was just north of Frankfurt. It was the initial processing and interrogation center for all captured Allied Air Forces personnel.

The brief visit of the sun left her face. She looked at her hands in her lap. "I wish it were so. With all my heart I wish his interrogator were Hanns Scharff. Father wrote to me about him, to let me know I am not alone. He doesn't hurt the POWs. He doesn't even raise his voice." Though she sent a few cautious glances around the café, she seemed less concerned about divulging secret information. Unburdening her soul had loosened her up. "Schiffer wants Greenland, and this pilot is connected to the Resistance. His identification papers say he is a Dutch Nazi, assigned by Rommel to the Rousseau Cimenterie—"

"To where?" Braun said sharply.

"The Rousseau Cimenterie. The paper says he is to interview Dutch conscripts there. But he was caught in Bénouville—"

Bénouville. Where Rousseau had held the dying body of Claire Devault. Braun's eyes narrowed.

"—by the Milice, who had connected him to a radio transmission, intercepted weeks ago. It said his name was Tom. Thomas . . . William Jaeger . . ." She drew a quick breath, but instead of tears, bleakness filled her eyes. "Do you know? I told him to let his head hang, and it would help him pass out. You don't dream of these things when you are a little girl. You don't imagine that the kindest thing you'll say to someone for the day is the way they can best pass out."

"Krista, I will write to your father," he said quickly, pushing aside new thoughts of Rousseau. "We will get you out of there."

"No!" she said, alarmed. "No, please, Herr Braun. If I go, someone may take my place who will not give them water." She sat up straighter, and her hands unconsciously sought small actions, righting a teaspoon, smoothing a napkin. Her hands sought order. "I am better now," she said, trying to convince him. "You've helped me. The guard helped me." The hands stilled. "You have no idea what it meant." She looked earnestly into his eyes. "I know what water can do for the soul. More than ever, I know God wants me for this job."

He filed it away to tell Lisette he had found a wife for Franz.

"So. The pilot is being interrogated as a spy . . . ," he said.

"Schiffer said his papers were traced to the forger who worked for Greenland. And Schiffer wants Greenland. Very badly."

"Everyone wants Greenland."

"Not as badly as Schiffer. I heard him say the other day, 'Klaus Barbie shows me up.' He is the one who captured the famous Resistance leader last year."

"Jean Moulin." He added, "Barbie didn't just capture him; he tortured him to death."

"Greenland will be Schiffer's Moulin."

Whispers of Greenland from Dunkirk to Brest had a centering whirlpool in the Caen area. Though G might have operated earlier, reports had begun to surface of his or her existence in early '43. That was what Schiffer had told him.

"What happened to the forger?" Braun asked.

"He killed himself after the second day. It was a cyanide capsule, wrapped in cellophane, sewn into the hem of his coat. I was glad for him." She sent him a little look to see what he thought of this admission.

"I believe Schiffer interrogated Claire Devault," Braun said darkly, more to himself than to her. Rousseau had offered to tell him what had been done to her, and Braun had quickly declined. "Her code name was Jasmine."

At the name, fresh pain appeared on Krista's face. Her lips trembled.

That such innocence should be in the presence of such evil and bear this burden. He felt some of Reinhold Hegel's heart toward her and wanted to make things right as if she were his own daughter.

"I wish you would leave that place," he said stiffly. "It is not good for your soul. I do not want it to change you."

She put a hand on his arm. "You have done me good, Herr Braun. I have said far too much. I should not have said anything at all—I could lose my job—but it has taken some of the poison from my heart. If . . . I am the last . . ." Her eyes filled. She took a moment to compose herself and looked at him with such firm resolution it prickled the back of his neck. "If I am the last decent human being they will see, I will be there for them to see. It is all I can do. I will do it."

"Please tell me you were there for Antoinette Devault," he said impulsively.

Her blue eyes lowered. She nodded.

Somehow he had known Schiffer had murdered Antoinette Devault, Claire's grandmother. He had no proof, but he knew it for truth the moment he saw the old woman's battered face under the sheet at the Caen hospital. Krista Hegel worked for this monster.

"Can you take me back to headquarters, Herr Braun?" Krista asked in a small voice. "I must report back by two."

"Certainly," Braun said.

She dried her eyes, wiped her nose. "Thank you," she said fervently. "Thank you, Herr Braun. You will never know."

She was thanking *him*?

"I have done nothing," he said with strong self-remonstrance, all of a sudden painfully aware of his lack of worth in the whole human scheme.

"Nothing?" She looked at him in surprise. "You stopped your car."

He shepherded her to the waiting vehicle, accompanied by the new and troubling thoughts of Michel Rousseau.

But now I know, and now I must follow my conscience.

I wonder that about you, Rousseau. I wonder how often you do follow your conscience.

They rode in silence back to Gestapo headquarters. The corporal pulled the vehicle to the curb in front.

As she trotted up the stairs to the door, he looked at the breathing building, with the great black-slashed crimson stain like a wound in the center. He'd never again walk past this building and deafen himself to a scream. Krista was in that room.

Braun was late. Ten minutes. Fifteen. Twenty. It wasn't like him. Michel tossed down his pen and rubbed his forehead.

The last thing he wanted to do was discuss Braun's crazy ideas for the tunnel. He wished the hauptmann would stick to the plans for the new bunker at Fontaine-la-Mallet. Rommel was due for an inspection soon. He was all over the Normandy coast of late. And he would expect more progress out of his favorite engineer.

Last fall, Michel was supervising a delivery to a site for a long-range artillery battery when he met Marshal Erwin Rommel, strolling along in deep discussion with Hauptmann Braun. Braun stopped and introduced him, and though he only briefly shared their conversation, he clearly saw not only the respect Braun had for Rommel, but also that which Rommel had for Braun.

Michel touched Rafael's favorite paperweight. Not long after Rafael and Brigitte left for lunch, Charlotte came in with the distressed look she wore all too frequently these days. She had learned from Wilkie's sister-in-law, Lily, who worked for Charlotte's cell, that the forger Flame had often used was missing. His *nom de guerre* was Diefer. There was no sign of forced entry at Diefer's apartment. No one had seen anything. It did not look as if he had gone on a trip. He was simply gone. Diefer lived alone and was a loner. No one could guess how long he had been missing. Maybe a few days, maybe a week.

Twenty-five minutes. Thirty. Michel got up and went to the window. He clasped his hands behind his back, but after only a moment he pulled himself away. He could not think of Tom. He could not think of any rescue plan. He had not the heart. A visit to the window, which often shaped his thoughts, also invited the shapeless. Fear ever crouched on the periphery, and doubt, fear's companion, ever to wither thoughts and ideas, ever to smother hope.

He came to his senses at the desk, could not remember

sitting down. He was so exhausted of late. It used to be the darkness merely pressed him down; now it came from all directions. He could almost feel the wind of its passing.

"Truth," he called for thickly.

He needed truth to steady him, and the truth was that every resistant agent knew sooner or later his work must end in disaster. Michel relaxed a little, feeling a little warmth. Facing truth was clarifying. The resistant agent knew he was already dead; to prolong burial, now, that was the game entirely.

But warmth began to fade. Death wasn't the worst anymore, not his own death, anyway. Tom was *not* an agent. Tom had been talked into it. Clemmie's death was easier to bear than Tom's arrest. She was a resistant; she knew she was already dead.

Back to the beginning, his mind urged weakly. *Go back to the—*

Nothing there was strong enough, and this the hardest truth of all, that Michel Rousseau had abandoned leadership of Flame. He had given in to François, and in that moment he had abdicated authority. The most important thing his father ever taught him about leadership was, quite simply, to lead.

Your one weak moment will cost a man his life because you said yes to François when you knew, you knew in your heart, you should have said no.

One weak moment? No. There were many. Flame's current state of impotence might have been a matter of attrition. Perhaps, as the Occupation continued, he had gradually allowed Flame to tatter away into nothing but an empty suit of armor.

He used to be good at what he did. He did not stay disciplined of mind; he'd let up bit by bit. One could not let up for one second under this kind of oppression.

Did you think yourself so strong?

What a grand reputation the great G enjoyed in London, respected by MI19, trusted by de Gaulle—and Clemmie dead. Jasmine dead. Diefer missing. All Flame had left was Michel, Rafael, Wilkie, and two others, Tom and Brigitte, conscripted to service as surely as if seized by Germans. Wrested to the cause by Greenland.

He fell back in his chair. He'd spent the last four years sheltering conscripts. Now he made them.

"Dear God," he whispered in wonder. "I am no better than a Nazi."

"Monsieur Rousseau!" Charlotte cried. "Come quick!"

25

BRIGITTE, RAFAEL, AND CHARLOTTE stood in a half ring about Charlotte's desk, gazing at something upon it. Michel shouldered in—and stared.

No one spoke. When Michel finally ventured a comment, his tone was unsuitably loud. He quickly lowered it. "So it is true."

"You see that it is," Rafael said, mesmerized.

"Shh," Charlotte admonished reverently.

A newspaper lay on the desk. It had a bold headline.

The office door opened, and in came Hauptmann Braun. All four at the desk gave him no more than a vague glance and turned back to the newspaper.

The newspaper had a bold headline nobody saw, for upon the newspaper was a proclamation bolder yet, harking back to gentler days and civilized times.

Braun joined the gathering at the desk and looked over their heads to see. He finally ventured, "It's cheese."

"It is Camembert," Rafael breathed.

The glorious wedge, rimmed in chalky white, sat upon a

plate that began to receive the satiny ooze from the recently cut middle. Michel had unconsciously placed his hand on Rafael's shoulder.

"I have Red Cross crackers in my purse," Brigitte said faintly.

"I have a knife," Rafael whispered.

"Saucers," Charlotte said. She went to get them.

Michel reverently swept his fingertip along the top of the cheese. The chalky rind was silken, downy, like talcum. There were tiny red flecks in the silken shroud, and the slow ooze of the center meant it was perfectly ripe, and at perfect room temperature. He touched the chalk to the tip of his tongue and closed his eyes.

Charlotte appeared with five saucers. Rafael pulled out his knife and scored the wedge into five small parts.

"No, no," Braun protested. "I couldn't possibly—"

"I assure you, Hauptmann Braun, we sin against God and country if we share not this . . . miracle with you," Michel said.

"Come," Rafael said, motioning to Michel's office.

Rafael hastily arranged chairs near the fireplace, positioning the two wingbacks, dragging over Michel's chair and the desk chair. He hurried to the corner for the little foldout chair Charlotte sometimes used, then with a flourish indicated the wingbacks to Braun and Michel. He set the tiny chair in front of the coffee table. Charlotte came, bearing the Camembert as if it were a crown nestled on a velvet cushion. Brigitte brought the saucers. She produced the packet of Red Cross crackers and laid them on the table.

Charlotte centered the plate perfectly, stood back to gaze, hands clasped to her chest. She lowered herself into the chair next to Braun, who, with a small smile, gazed with equal mystification at the cheese and the awestruck people around him.

Rafael straddled the tiny chair. He produced his knife. He squared his shoulders, then began to slice the cheese along the scored lines. He transferred each wedge to a saucer with the flat of the knife. Brigitte nervously opened the packet of crackers. She counted out three crackers to each saucer, with an extra cracker for Braun. She took the saucer and handed it slowly to Braun. She handed out the rest of the saucers and settled down with her own.

No one spoke. Each gazed at the cheese on his or her saucer, Braun occasionally glancing at the others.

"Beaujolais," Michel murmured fondly, eyes glowing as softly as if he were staring into a hearth fire.

"Bordeaux," Brigitte sighed.

"Calvados," Rafael said, as if it couldn't be anything else.

Each small wedge began the outward bulge of ooze. Michel looked around, and something happened.

A little shiver ran through him—anticipation, yes, of this fine cheese peculiar to Normandy, but something more attended this gathering, something greater. And now other looks went from saucers to faces, as if yes, they felt it too. How extraordinary, this gathering: the German, the businessman, the secretary, the courier, the prostitute. A tiny snapshot of humanity. How capricious, this otherworld attendance, for there came to the room the presence from the train, the stirring of the pool, one had but to fling himself in . . .

He gazed at this cheese, this form of communion, surely on the brink of transubstantiation. This thing of earth, this substance, it bound them together in some holy enchantment, Braun no less in its thrall than Charlotte, Rafael no less than Brigitte.

Communion. Community. Every plot of God, always about people. He looked at the faces looking at him and felt a swell of love, felt caught in God's plot for humanity, God's scheme to bring human beings together, and Michel wanted nothing more than to aid and abet God. And he felt a great swell of pleasure, as he knew in this moment that he *had* aided and abetted the scheming God of humanity, and felt, in fact, God's pleasure with *him*.

And he could not tell them of nearby angels stirring the pool, of the joyous ache in his heart. They would think him mad.

They waited for Michel. He took a cracker and scooped some of the cheese sliding from the wedge center. He waited until the others had secured the same.

He lifted the cracker, for it was wine as well as bread. "Absent friends."

The others murmured in kind, including Braun.

Not a word was spoken as they ate. When the last crumb was gone, still they lingered, no one desirous to disturb the mood.

At last, Rafael stirred them to their immediate and varied realities with a fitting farewell to what they had shared: he slid his saucer onto the table, looked them round, and then laughed.

Michel stared in wonder. He had never heard the young man laugh, not this kind of laughter. It was a sound sent forth from a moment of pure happiness. Soon Braun chuckled, too, and Brigitte began to laugh. Charlotte, hand ready at her mouth as if to suppress something irreverent and unbecoming, finally dropped her hand, gave in, and laughed.

The contagion welled around him. Michel joined in, and when Braun's chuckle fanned to outright laughter, theirs became all the merrier for his.

When it finally subsided, and tears were wiped from eye corners, and the room at last became quiet, Charlotte let loose a traitorous titter. Laughter revived in a common burst, and all was silly, glorious hilarity.

"What nonsense," Braun said at last, wiping his eyes. A smile lingered, along with an inward glow. Then he declared, "Weihenstephaner."

"That doesn't translate," Michel said, wiping his own eyes.

"My favorite beer. I think it would go nicely with the cheese."

"With the Camembert," Rafael corrected, considering Braun with a far less restrictive eye. "What is it like, this Wei . . . ?"

"Weihenstephaner. It is very refreshing. I like it cold enough to hurt my . . ." He pointed at his mouth, unsure of the French word.

"Teeth?" Brigitte asked.

He shook his head.

"Fillings?" Michel asked.

And Braun snapped his fingers and said, "Yes, yes, fillings." Trying out the word, he said again, "Fillings. I shared it last with my son Franz, before he went to North Africa." The inward glow dimmed a fraction.

In the first personal question she had ever asked the man, Charlotte ventured, "How many children do you have, Hauptmann?"

"Two sons," Braun said brightly, rousing himself. "Franz was in Tunis until '43. He was transferred to a division in Italy, the Fourteenth Panzer Corps. We last heard from him at Monte Cassino. My youngest, Erich, is still in school. He is fifteen." Braun smiled a little. "Oh, how he wants to fight. His mother won't let him. It is a strange twist of fate, Erich the fighter who cannot fight, Franz who can, who would far rather build things. We sent him to the States to study architecture at Taliesin, in Wisconsin. Frank Lloyd Wright's school. He was there only three months when recalled to serve." Braun's smile faded.

"You must be proud of him, Hauptmann Braun," Charlotte said.

He glanced up, appearing a trifle bemused at such a sentiment from a Frenchwoman. "I am. He is a good boy." He added dryly, "A good man. Only yesterday, he was a boy."

"I wish him the best," Brigitte said suddenly. She seemed a little surprised at her own outburst. Cheeks flushing a little, she said, "I admire him for going all the way to the States to learn."

"He loved it. I hope to send him back one day."

"How goes it for him, where he is in Italy?" Brigitte asked.

Braun noticed the saucer he held. He absently dabbed at cracker crumbs with his fingertip, touched them to his tongue.

"He was wounded at Monte Cassino in January. We last heard from a field hospital in Pontecorvo, which has since relocated to we know not where. Someplace remote. As we say, *Dort, wo sich die Füchse gute Nacht sagen*, where foxes say good night." He slid the saucer to the table. He rubbed his hands together, and for a moment, his expression was vacant. "His tank took a direct hit. Franz was a loader. All four of the rest of his crew were killed. His injuries were . . . extensive. When last we heard, he was . . . What is the French? *Im Koma.* He sleeps." His hands stilled. "I told you, Rousseau, that I went to Berlin because my wife had a kidney operation. It is not true. . . . Lisette is at a sanatorium on Lake Geneva. She and Franz are very close." He suddenly flashed a quick and tight smile. "But he is alive. Yes? We will take what we can get. Yes?"

He had left his first self, back to the Braun with whom

Michel was most familiar, all clipped and hearty sentences. "And what of you, young lady? Where are you from? Do you have a beau?"

But Brigitte did not answer.

Michel felt a twinge in his chest. A gravely wounded son, a broken-down wife, all with Rommel's relentless cement campaign for the Atlantic Wall.

He gave him all he could give, a piece of honesty that would cost something. "The girl who died, Hauptmann Braun," he found himself saying. "You asked if she was my lover. She wasn't, because I was too late. We shared a kiss, and the next time I held her, she died."

Braun rustled in his seat. He looked at Brigitte and said, hearty and false, "Come now, answer my questions, young lady! Where are you from? Do you have a beau? Lovely girl such as yourself? They must camp on your doorstep."

But Brigitte did not want Braun to transition any more than Michel did. She leaned forward in her chair and rested her hand on Braun's arm. His lips parted, he blinked. He gave a tiny movement as if to pull away, but remained, submitted to her concern. She gave his arm a gentle squeeze and, after a moment, withdrew. A raw vulnerability came to Braun's face, and Michel dropped his glance.

"I wish the best for your son," Rafael finally muttered. He added wryly, "It is the first time, and likely the last, that I will wish a German well."

"Then it is a potent wish," Braun said gallantly, with a smile less false than it was brave, "and will do my son good."

The Camembert gathering had come to a close.

Brigitte began to gather the saucers. Charlotte took the plate. Rafael pulled the two desk chairs back. Braun and Michel stayed in the wingbacks.

"Back to our worlds, and what we do in those worlds," Michel murmured.

"Yes," Braun said, a little distractedly. He watched Brigitte carry the plates from the room, following Charlotte. "Who is the girl?"

It was unexpected, and he had nothing ready. Rafael was folding the little chair. He glanced at Braun. "She is my girlfriend. Brigitte."

"Hang on to her, André."

Alarm surged in Michel's stomach at the mention of Rafael's real name. He had become so comfortable with the Camembert gathering, he could have easily slipped and called him Rafael. Michel glanced at Braun. He'd never seen him so thoughtful. Not even when they'd talked of *Mein Kampf* and Braun told of Clemmie's arrest.

Rafael had replaced the fold-up chair, nodded first to Michel, then to Braun, even giving him a small smile. He left the office, pulling the door shut.

"André despises you less," Michel observed.

"Camembert will do that."

"You were late today," Michel said. "And even now you are distracted."

"Camembert will do that."

"You have never been late. Not once in the course of our association. What happened?" Michel dared to ask.

Braun wore an impenetrable frown. Folded hands rested in his lap. His gray eyes were somehow icy and hard and vulnerable at the same time. So very still, so very austere. He could have been posing for a portrait painter.

"I was detained by a matter that has brought to my attention a distressing . . . What is the word . . . ?" But instead of conducting a word search, he seemed to come to a decision.

"There is a man who seeks Greenland, and he is a man not unlike Klaus Barbie. You have heard of Barbie?"

"The Butcher of Lyon," Michel said unhesitatingly.

"Schiffer seeks to rival him. He seeks a prize and will find it in Greenland."

"Why should this concern me?"

"He thinks to find Greenland through a young man he is currently interrogating." Braun's distant look found Michel. "A man who has been linked to the Rousseau Cimenterie."

He did not know how long he looked into Braun's penetrating gaze.

Long enough for Braun to see things. Long enough for Braun to come to private conclusions. Heaviness came to his handsome features, and he looked away.

Time passed. Both men sat motionless in the wingback chairs, staring into a cold fireplace.

"How is he?" Michel asked thinly.

"She didn't say." He hesitated. "She was, however, upset."

"He was a mistake." The atmosphere felt repressive, unwilling to receive truth because unused to it; it wanted to keep the words unheard, push them back, but there was no going back. "He is innocent."

"I do not wish for you to say any more."

"We both know it is too late for delicacy."

"It's all going to be over soon. You just had to wait it out."

"Such conflict in this air . . . ," Michel murmured. "Do you feel it?"

"Why couldn't you wait it out?"

"Oh, I think you know the answer. You who could not read the book, any more than I."

Braun rustled in his seat.

"He is innocent," Michel said.

"That depends on your point of view," Braun snapped.

"Not this time. The boy fell from the air and had the misfortune to fall into my hands. Let me ask you something: Is Schiffer willing to deal?"

Braun looked at him.

"Is he?"

"Rousseau . . ."

"She did not have a heart attack."

Braun lowered his eyes.

"And Tom is in his hands. He is in the hands of a monster who would torture the old and the young."

"An angel attended Antoinette Devault in her last hours, Rousseau. She left this earth in the presence of an angel."

"I don't want an angel." Michel leaned forward. "Will Schiffer deal; will he consider an exchange—will he follow through, no double cross?" He smiled, heart pounding, wishing for a cigarette. He gave a little shrug. "I want it to count."

Braun seemed to wilt into the chair. After a long interval, he said thickly, "You expect me to act as your liaison."

Michel reached for the metal cigarette box on the coffee table. It was empty. He got up and went to his desk. He took a cigarette from the case, lit up, shook out the match, tossed it to the desk. He went to the window.

"You expect me to deliver you up. Kiss your cheek."

Michel chuckled. "Oh no. Class me with Pilate. You start listening to the multitude, you may end up condemning an innocent man. In a moment, in one *moment*, I abandoned leadership. I made a terrible mistake. You are the only one who can help me make it right."

He studied the courtyard below. Spring was coming. Green was beginning to show, and some flowers in the green. How his eyes thirsted for color.

"There was a mayor in a neighboring town who was arrested when they found excerpts of de Gaulle's speeches in his office," Michel said. "He was foolish enough to write them down. Yet I understand. There is something holy about forbidden words on a piece of paper. Truth wrested from the air, shaped by ink, trapped on a page, right there in your hand, laid bare for another sense to affirm—and when the eyes see what the heart feels, truth is truer. Yet this one weakness cost the man his life. I allowed myself one weakness. I wish for the mercy to pay for it myself. I wish for the mercy that an innocent man will not have to die for my action. I ask this boon, Hauptmann Braun."

He wasn't sure when Braun had come to the window. He stood in the next window frame, gazing at the courtyard.

"Once, I visited an installment with Rommel," Braun said after a time. "We heard an explosion on the beach. Some mine or shell had gone off, killing the slave laborer who was installing it. And such a look passed over the marshal's face. He cursed, but he did not curse the action of the slave, or the fate that made it go off. He cursed the war."

"Do you think Rommel would have prevented the shell from going off, if he had a chance?"

"I believe he would have."

"Will Schiffer deal?"

After a long moment, Braun said, "For Greenland, he will deal."

"I have presumed upon your friendship, yet I must presume a little further. Will you see it through to the end? Will you get Tom to safety? I ask only that you get him into the hands of André."

"I will do my best."

"I do not ask your best. I ask perfection."

"It will be done."

How often did one have a chance to pay for one's own sins?

It came again, the presence of the train, through the floor-boards, through the windowpane—it passed through his soul. The color for which Michel thirsted shone all around, for all was red-rimmed in glory.

He placed his fingertips on the pane.

"Jasmine . . . ," he breathed. *Is this what you felt at the end? A release from it all? Meet me, my brave, my beautiful girl. I will see you soon. I am free.*

"I must study the best course," Braun was saying. "I have never arranged a prisoner exchange." He added bitterly, "Not many engineers have."

Thoughts came clearly. He had to act quickly. Michel left the window and went to the corner of the room near the fire-place, to the world-traveling adventure display that Braun had admired. He removed the safari hat from the small suitcase on top, removed the small suitcase, and set them aside. He took the next suitcase by the handle, brought it back to the business side of the room.

He set it on the desk. Braun turned from the window, his face as gray as his eyes.

Michel suppressed a pang of guilt, because he had never felt freer in his life. He could dance on snowflakes. He flipped the two latches and opened the case. "Here is your proof. But I need a little time. I have to—"

"Enough! No details!" Braun came to the desk, looked over the transreceiver with eyes that didn't seem to take it in, or didn't seem to care what they were seeing. "I need to think things through. There is no field manual for this."

Michel lightly hooked his fingertips on the edge of the suitcase. "The longer we wait, the longer Tom—"

"Enough!" Braun thundered. He snatched his briefcase, then paused and looked at it. He said bitterly, "Such a ventilation system, Rousseau. You would have been impressed." He headed for the door.

"When will you—?"

"When I am ready," he snapped. Then, running his hand through his hair, he growled, "One hour." He left, and Michel saw him snatch his hat from the coat tree in Charlotte's office. He heard the subsequent bang of the front door.

Charlotte came in, mystified. "What on earth—?"

Michel came to her, holding up his hands. "Many lives depend on what happens in the next hour. Is Rafael here?"

"No. He took Brigitte to the ration coupon bureau. She's going to transfer—"

"You still have the telephone installed at your home?"

"Yes. The Germans—"

"Telephone Gerard, tell him to get here immediately. Then I need the employee roster for every plant. Go, quickly."

"Does this have to do with Tom?"

"Yes. Say nothing to Rafael. Wait—if he returns before I am gone, send him immediately to my brother with this message." He went to his desk. As he scrawled lines onto a sheet of paper, he said, "Tell Rafael the telephone lines are down, and this needs to be delivered."

"All the way to Cabourg," Charlotte said slowly.

He folded the sheet of paper, stuffed it into an envelope, and sealed it.

"Michel, what is this about?"

He hesitated, then placed the envelope in his pocket and went to her. He took her hands. "I have reached an agreement with Braun," he said gently.

Her wide eyes searched his, and at last she gasped, "Michel."

He squeezed her hands. "I go to my appointment a little sooner than yours. Swear to me that you will not tell Rafael. I need you to swear it, and all will be well in my soul, in every last part."

Her face aged in shades before him. At last, she nodded. He gave her the envelope.

"Telephone Gerard, and then bring the rosters. Haste is everything."

Braun climbed into the back of the car. He stared out the window.

"Where to, sir?" the corporal finally asked.

Take me anywhere. I do not belong here. I do not know where to be.

"Sir?"

Braun said in French, "Do you know of any place in this godforsaken land where we can get a cold Weihenstephaner? Cold enough to hurt my fillings?" But the corporal did not know French, and Braun muttered in German, "Take me to my favorite café, Reinhart. They have some miserably passable ale."

"Yes, sir."

After a moment, Reinhart said, "I heard *Weihenstephaner.* That's the only decent French I've heard yet."

A capricious laugh escaped the sorrow pressing upon his heart, and he saw the corporal grin a small, satisfied grin.

A crash of light opened the universe, cascading a shower of sparks.

"Open your eyes."

He struggled to open them. He saw a brown band. No, it was a belt. No, it was his belt, with four carved notches.

"What do these marks mean?"

"Will you look at that," a voice croaked. He had a suspicion it was his own. "Forgot about that. Nazis."

"What do you mean?"

"Nazis I'm supposed to kill. Four."

"Who ordered it?" A pause. "Greenland?"

He didn't answer.

A crash of light, a shower of sparks. Schiffer wasn't using the long riding quirt; he was using his fists. Tom had enjoyed a time of unconsciousness when he did as the girl suggested and allowed his head to hang back as far as it would. He woke to the rattle of chains as the guards lowered him to the ground. The relief for his aching hands and knees was short-lived. He'd learned that any mercy was an exchange for something worse.

"Who ordered it?"

"I did." He tried to swallow. "Payback. They made her cry." He wet his parched lips with fresh blood. Irony, that; finally some liquid to soothe his dry lips, and it was his own.

Schiffer shook out his fist. He reached for the blood-caked riding quirt. Tom couldn't decide which hurt worse, the quirt or the fist. He had better chance of unconsciousness with the fist, though Schiffer probably knew it and therefore switched to the quirt.

"Your papers were forged by a man who worked for Greenland. Who is Greenland?"

"I left her on the floor. She didn't stay there."

The quirt hurt worse, Tom decided, after his mind cleared enough for thought. And into that cleared space came an image he had not seen in years.

Tom could see his mother again. She was not where he left her.

She was at the train station to see him off to Chicago. Ronnie was in school, and Father wouldn't come. Mother made an excuse for him, saying he had to pick up feed at Drenthe; Tom knew the truth. He could not bear to see his son leave for war. So strong, such a firm disciplinarian, such a towering I-run-the-house figure, yet that morning he'd left very early so he wouldn't have to say good-bye. Loving cowards, every one. Father. Clemmie. Michel. He loved them, he loved them so.

He had looked at his mother on the platform at the station, and she did none of the hair or face fussing he had dreaded. She simply looked up at him with that brave smile, eyes shining and full of trust, said she loved him, said she'd pray for him, said she was proud.

"Who is Greenland?"

The quirt sang in the air. Tom heard a perfunctory scream and went back to his inner visions.

This was the mother he had missed, the one trying to get to him, trying to show she wasn't on the floor. *Leave vengeance to God, Tommy. He is the only one who knows how hard to hit back.*

Because he loved her, he wanted to kill four Nazis, and because he loved her, he never could. He left her on the floor, but there she would not remain. He hadn't been able to see her until now. Though he wouldn't mind a go at Schiffer, just this side of death, he suddenly knew he didn't want to kill a Nazi with his bare hands, though a Nazi was killing him. Irony, that.

"There must be something to flagellation," he quipped hoarsely. "I've had an epiphany." He chuckled, and it loosed some blood from his mouth.

Schiffer did not appreciate his sense of humor. It didn't matter. He could see her again. It was his one wish before he died. Let him see her risen, not bowed; let him see her as she always was, strong and quiet, content and purposeful, not locked in that one moment of time.

I've missed you.

I've been right here, Tommy.

"Who is Greenland?"

An explosion of sparks.

"Thomas William Jaeger. First lieutenant . . . and proud son of Johanna Alberta Jaeger. United States . . . one four . . ."

A cascade of brilliant light.

The pencil of the secretary faltered and, through a newly dampened spot on the page, scribbled, *and proud son of Johanna Alberta Jaeger.*

26

WERE IT NOT OBVIOUS in that rigid white face that Brigitte's thoughts were only for Jenison, Rafael would see to it he left enough impression for some thoughts to be for himself. Alas, it was not to be, and though he was certain he had what charm it took to beguile Brigitte from Jenison, he could never do it to his friend. He found himself thinking hopefully of the other girl at Brigitte's place, the one with the large eyes and generous figure, who listened when he said Tom was in trouble, who acted, like Brigitte. That's the kind of girl he wanted.

He remembered with surprise that she was a prostitute. He'd have to set her straight on that. He felt a warm flush of virtue at the thought of persuading her to give up her wicked ways.

They walked along a steep and curving side street in one of the old parts of Caen. It would soon empty onto the main street that led to Gestapo headquarters. Brigitte insisted on walking past it.

"When we walk past," he warned, "keep on walking. Do not stop in front; do not even pause. You will attract attention."

He dreaded seeing the place. Too many people he knew had died there. "Why do you want to see it?"

She did not answer. Her heels made a crisp, feminine sound that echoed back from the walls. The more the afternoon wore on, the less she spoke, and the less she seemed to hear him.

They walked slowly past the former courthouse, claimed and bedecked by the enormous swastika. She reached for his hand when they did. He knew she was straining to hear something, anything, and by the tightness of her grip, she was bracing for it; but they heard nothing.

Rafael had hoped the errand to the ration card bureau would clear his head for a plan, but he had nothing. Surely by now Monsieur Rousseau had come up with something.

Ten minutes later they were back at the office. They were not two steps in the door when Charlotte rose swiftly from her desk.

"Thank God you're back!" She held out an envelope. "The telephone lines are down. You must deliver this to François Rousseau immediately."

Rafael took the envelope. "What's going on?" He looked past her to Rousseau's office. The door was closed.

Charlotte said, "Go, quickly!"

"But—if the lines are down here, are they down everywhere? Can we not—?"

Charlotte's husband, Gerard, burst from Rousseau's office with a sheaf of papers. He stopped short at the sight of Rafael, then continued to Charlotte's desk. He handed her the papers.

Monsieur Rousseau appeared. He pulled the door closed, glancing at the envelope in Rafael's hand. "Well? What are you still doing here?"

"What's going on?"

"Gerard has a plan. It's a good plan. We are summoning

my brother." Gerard, a bit surprised, glanced at Rousseau. Rousseau said quickly, "We'll talk when you return with him. I can't give you the car. Take the train. You can catch the 4:45 if you hurry."

"Do you want me to go with you?" Brigitte asked Rafael. She was as pathetically eager for action as he.

"Sure." Rafael poised at the front door, hand on the knob. "Does Wilkie know?"

The three looked at him blankly. It lasted only a second. Then Rousseau said, "He is on his way."

Something wasn't right. He had known these people too long. But he had no time to speculate. He felt only a gush of relief that action had come at last. Tom had a chance. There was at last a plan, and if it involved François Rousseau, all the better. He could run Flame himself.

He touched his hat, yanked open the door, and left. Brigitte hurried out behind him.

The room was still.

Then Michel observed, "You did not take the receiver off the cradle."

Charlotte said darkly, "I wanted to kick myself."

Michel looked at the papers in Charlotte's hand. "That's all of them. Every third name—" But the way she held the papers, forgotten at her side, made him raise his eyes to her face.

How desolate. How betrayed.

"No time, dear one," he said, then gave her shoulder a quick squeeze. He slipped the papers from Charlotte's hand and showed them to Gerard, who was no happier than she. His thick lips began to tremble, and his face contorted as he tried to bring himself under control.

Michel tapped the sheets to get his attention. "Every third name is one with papers forged by Diefer. Understand? Every third. Get to them immediately. They need to vanish. Tell them to head southwest and meet up with the Maquis in a forest north of La Rochelle. Assure them this group is under orders from London, de Gaulle himself. Once they get to the forest, the Maquis will find them. Have them say, 'Greenland sent us.' Their leader is Willet Garnier. If you are caught, destroy these."

Gerard took the papers. Michel put out his hand, but Gerard took his face, kissed both cheeks, and went out the door.

"Charlotte, you need to get to Wilkie," Michel said. "Tell him our cover is blown. Tell him he has been reassigned to Madame Vion, at the Château de Bénouville. Tell him—" But the words caught in his throat.

"All I have done to watch over you."

Michel pressed his lips together, nodded.

"All I have done to keep you safe." Tears spilled over. She slowly dragged the heel of her hand over the tears. Then, face newly aged and puffy, she looked in bewilderment at her desk. "My purse. It's around here somewhere . . ."

Michel took her purse from where she always kept it, on the top of the file cabinet. He handed it to her and took the sweater draped over the back of her chair.

He helped her into the sweater. She stood for a moment next to the desk, then came to herself and went to the front door. There she hesitated, as if she would turn around. But she pulled open the door and left.

He paused at his office door to collect himself, then entered.

Braun sat in the chair in front of his desk exactly the way he had left him, still as stone, legs crossed, chin on his fist, face hard and empty, eyes staring out the window. Michel took in the room—the desk and his window on this end, the fireplace, the wingback chairs, the books on his father's coffee table.

He walked over to Braun. "I am ready. What do we do? Should you rough me up a bit? Black my eye?"

Braun's hard gray stare slid to Michel. He said witheringly, "We do not need to be as dramatic as that."

"Shouldn't you tie me up? Gag me?"

Braun's eyes returned to the distance outside.

"What about your driver? Did you . . . ?"

Braun reached for his briefcase and rose from the chair. He seemed especially tall next to Michel, and for a moment he seemed to tower over him.

"Have you worked out a plan for Schiffer?" Michel said.

"No, I haven't," Braun said coldly. "And I've tried. I can't think how to hand over an innocent man to a man like Schiffer."

"I am not an innocent man. That should make it easier." Michel gave a little sniff, then wrinkled his nose. "I can tell you tried."

"Your French ale is disgusting. All of this, and French ale, too. God hates me."

"Hauptmann Braun . . ."

Braun tilted his head. "If you try to thank me, I'll bloody your mouth." He firmed lips that trembled slightly from anger. "I plan to 'wing it,' as you say. I have no other course."

"'Wing it' is not ours. Perhaps it is British."

"What difference does it make?" he snapped. "I will make it up as I go." He looked him up and down. "You *are* an innocent man."

"The only innocent man is the one Schiffer now tortures." He hesitated. "Braun—"

Braun swung away and headed for the door.

Michel looked at the transreceiver on the desk. "Don't you want to bring the proof?"

Braun's impressive profile filled the doorway, backlit by late-afternoon light. The cut of the German uniform, the hat in his hand, his carriage, tall, broad, proud. He looked at the trans-receiver with a scornful curl of his lip, as if to say, *Why should I need proof?* He took his hat from the coatrack, swept it to his head, and adjusted it. Michel was sharply reminded of the day Braun and Rommel had strode along at the bunker placement. The way Marshal Erwin Rommel seemed to defer to him, the great respect Rommel had for this man and his work.

He felt a strange mix of he didn't know what—humility, and awe, and shame. He followed Braun from the office, feeling for the tiny reassuring bulge of the cyanide pellet sewn into the cuff of his sleeve.

Braun stared unseeingly out the car window, briefcase in his lap. They were a few blocks from headquarters. He had no idea how he would approach Schiffer for a prisoner exchange. Schiffer would double-cross for sure.

He gave a bitter chuckle. Braun designed underground command bunkers. Concrete, not guile, was his medium. He worked with cement compositions and aggregates, he pro-duced products of varying drying ratios and strengths—he was a civil engineer, no military man, no tactical savant. And though he'd devised a ventilation system that his colleagues might call innovative, a system that could save hundreds of lives, he could not think of a single way to save one. And the one he wanted to save certainly wasn't the man in Schiffer's custody, a man he did not know. It was the man seated next to him, so infuriatingly docile, so quietly courageous.

Anger and panic resolved into an insuperable wall. He was out of time. There was no winging it, no—

Whatever your hand finds to do, do it with all your might.

The thought floated free of anxiety and despair, in some blessed neutral ground in his mind. He did not know from whence his subconscious produced it, perhaps from some catechism, from decades of Lutheran liturgy.

Whatever your hand finds to do . . .

He became aware of his hand resting upon his briefcase.

He looked down upon it as if from a great height and found himself saying, his own voice strangely detached, "Reinhart, stop. Pull over."

"Perhaps after the next intersection. There is a delivery truck—"

"Silence!" Braun thundered.

The solution came not in part, but the whole. Braun had only to study it as if studying a portrait. All of the details were there; he had but to run his eyes over them, take notice of all in front of him. His fingers curled around the edges of his briefcase and he gripped it.

A Trojan tunnel.

He looked at Rousseau. "We need to make a stop before we get to headquarters," Braun said, and his voice sounded very calm.

"Yes, sir," the driver said. "Do you still want me to pull over?"

"No. Go to my apartment immediately."

"Yes, sir."

Rousseau looked over. They had not spoken since the office.

It was all there, every detail. He had only to execute it. Flawlessly.

"I think you were right," Braun said. "We should make it look as if you had been apprehended against your will. We will need to bind and gag you."

Rousseau bowed his head. "Whatever you think best."

"I know Schiffer. If you are brought in humiliated, he will have instant supremacy over you. Things might go better." He hesitated. "Forgive me for what I am about to do."

Rousseau only gave another gentlemanly nod.

Did she love him because he came from freedom, or did she love him because he was free? The puzzle was now familiar to her, as familiar as the ache in her middle.

Brigitte and Rafael were fifteen minutes into the journey to Cabourg to see Monsieur Rousseau's brother. Rafael would not speak. He only stared out the window, pinching his lower lip in thought.

So Brigitte sought Tom.

She replayed every conversation she could remember, every word he had spoken, in order and out of order. She watched the way he twirled his hat with the self-satisfied grin, the panic on his face as he dove into her bed, the look when he made her laugh, how he seized her wrist when she touched his neck.

And the kiss. She closed her eyes. Right in front of a roomful of people, yet they were never more alone. She didn't believe for a moment Kees had kissed her. Had it been Kees, it would have been reserved, just enough to "sell it." He let her know things with that kiss.

She loved him because he was free, and she was free when she was with him.

She heard the sound of tearing paper and opened her eyes. Rafael was tearing open the envelope.

"What are you doing?" she demanded.

He drew out the letter, unfolded it, read the few lines. The paper dropped with his hand to his lap. She snatched it up.

François~
  You will do admirably.
  Forgive me.

                        ~Michel

"What does this mean?"

Rafael suddenly straightened, staring out the window. "Where are we?"

"We've not yet passed Colombelles."

He bolted from the seat.

Rafael hurried along, Brigitte at his side. She had linked arms with him once when passing a German soldier, then drifted away when the coast was clear. He started up the steps to the Cimenterie office and stopped short. The front door was ajar. His eyes narrowed. He looked up and down the street, back to the office. It was past five. They always locked it at five, even if they were staying later. He walked up the steps and pushed the door open with his fingertips.

"Hello?"

Charlotte's desk was untidy. She never left a paper clip out of place.

"Charlotte? Monsieur Rousseau?"

He paused, didn't hear a sound. Apprehension rippled his gut. He went to Rousseau's office door, pushed it open. The room was dim, but he could clearly recognize what was square in the middle of Rousseau's desk for God and Hitler to see. He stared at the transreceiver while the bottom dropped out of his stomach.

Who had used it? Why? And why hadn't it been returned to the safety of the adventure display? Wilkie would never leave it out. No one would.

He went to the desk, opened the case, and felt the box. Stone cold. It took some time for the machine to cool after it powered down. He lifted the box from its crushed-velvet slot, felt underneath—cold.

"What is that?" Brigitte said at his side.

"A transreceiver." It was a beauty of an instrument, courtesy of MI19 and the OSS. "We always keep it hidden."

"What's going on here?" a voice demanded.

They spun. Wilkie stood in the doorway, wearing a white suit, a white fedora with a dark band, and a disheveled rosebud in his lapel. He stared at the transreceiver and demanded again, "What's going on?"

"You tell me! I found this right on the desk, right in plain sight. The front door was open. No one was here." Rafael looked down at the box in his hands. "I'm too late."

"Too late for what?"

When Rafael did not answer, Brigitte said, "He believes Monsieur Rousseau has gone to Gestapo headquarters to turn himself in. An exchange for Tom."

Wilkie shook his head, dazed. "Wait—the pilot's been taken? When?"

"Yesterday morning, in Bénouville," Brigitte said. She added softly, "Though it seems much longer than that."

"And Rousseau has gone to—?" He pulled off his white hat, his face suddenly matching the color. "Oh, this just gets better and better. You are Brigitte? Well, we have a problem, Brigitte." He looked at Rafael. "I came to tell Rousseau that Century picked up a transmission from the BBC. A Lysander plane is due to arrive tonight between 1 and 2 a.m. at Le Vey. They are delivering an SOE agent and said they can pick up the pilot. They implied this might be the last pickup for quite a while."

Rafael could only stare.

Wilkie stretched out both arms, astonished. "Clemmie, and now Rousseau? Is Flame disintegrating? Diefer still missing, the pilot taken, and now Rousseau on some suicide mission to—?" He threw down his hat. "The *stupidity*! How can he think the Nazis will deal fairly? A prisoner exchange? In Caen? Since when? Has he gone *completely* mad? And where's Charlotte in all this?"

"She's probably—" But Rafael broke off, gazing at Brigitte and Wilkie as a thought struck. "Maybe he is." He put the box back into the suitcase and began to pace the length of the room.

"Maybe *who* is *what*?" Wilkie demanded.

"Braun was here. I saw his hat. Maybe Braun is helping. I wouldn't have believed it, not before . . ."

"Could Monsieur Rousseau know about the airplane?" Brigitte asked. "And that is why the box was out?"

"Maybe," Wilkie said. He looked at the transreceiver. "Maybe he tried to cancel the flight, with the pilot's arrest." But he frowned. "No, of course not. If he *did* hear the message, he would have known it was planned as an agent drop. He wouldn't have tried to cancel that."

"When did the message come?" Brigitte asked.

"Last night. Century couldn't track any of us down. They got word to me only half an hour ago. I'm missing my brother's wedding."

The room was silent, only the occasional squeak of a floorboard with Rafael's pacing.

"What do we do?" Brigitte said softly.

Rafael reached the wall, stopped, and turned. "Here's what I think: Rousseau went to Braun for help. He was desperate, he had no other choice. He wanted Braun to turn him in as

Greenland, in trade for Tom. He thought a German officer could pull it off. Maybe put some fair dealing into it."

Wilkie's shoulders slumped. "Well, what happens now? With the invasion coming any time, this pickup could be one of the last."

It was exactly what Rafael was thinking. Tom had to leave tonight.

"Then we have no choice. We have to let them know." Rafael lifted his head. "I'll tell them."

Wilkie stared. "You'll stroll right into a Nazi stronghold and—" He got under Rafael's nose. "What's the matter with you? Use your head! Anyone who goes into that building doesn't come out. If Braun is helping Rousseau, let him help. You have no idea what's really going on. You could mess things up."

"I agree," Brigitte said fervently.

"Braun doesn't know about the pickup—that I do know!" Rafael said. "If Rousseau is trying to get Tom out, he's got to get him out *now*. So we've got to let them know. We've got to give Tom a chance to make it to the pickup. It's his *only* chance."

"But we can't be sure of what Braun and Rousseau are doing!" Wilkie said, fiercely exasperated.

"Exactly. We can only be sure of what we do."

"Look, you scrawny little—do I have to say it out loud? Don't you know you are like a brother to me? I won't stand by and let you prance into that devil building on a *chance*. I won't do it!" Wilkie made an effort to calm himself. "Listen to me, Rafael, just—listen. How will you talk your way into seeing Braun? He's probably in consultation with Schiffer. Those SS are not the same lot they used to be. They're not going to let you interrupt a meeting to deliver a message. They've changed;

they suspect everything these days. They're smarter. Meaner. They're desperate."

"So are we." Rafael adjusted the wilted rosebud on Wilkie's lapel, then smiled a particularly wicked smile. He felt better. A plan was forming.

Wilkie groaned and turned away. He appealed to Brigitte. "Can you not talk sense to him? Ask him how he will make it past the guards. Ask him how he will make it past the front desk. Ask him what happened when we tried to free Jasmine."

Rafael went and put his hands on Wilkie's shoulders. "Do you know which word I am currently in love with?" He pulled himself up to breathe into his ear, "Audacity." He patted Wilkie's cheek. "We can do this, my brother. I have a plan. Braun is our best bet. We just have to get the message to him, give him a chance to make something happen. It's the only thing we can do, and we are going to do it. If it doesn't work . . ." He shrugged. "Then Rousseau is captured, Tom misses the plane, I get drunk for a week, and we'll come up with something else. But I won't spend the rest of my life wondering if a simple little thing like getting a message to Braun could have made him improvise. You're in or you're out, my brother."

By Wilkie's deflated bearing, Rafael knew he had won. At last, Wilkie said morosely, "Well, if I survive whatever scheme you have, it will be one more thing to tell my children. And if I don't—" he shrugged—"there won't be any children to tell."

"How do you plan to get in there?" Brigitte asked.

Rafael went to Brigitte and walked around her, examining her face, her figure. "Your friend far more looks the part, but you'll get his attention."

Brigitte folded her arms. "I'm not sure the old seduce-the-Nazi-guard trick will work."

"I'm not talking about a guard." Rafael looked at Wilkie's clothing, then shook his head, clicking his tongue. "You had to be wearing white. Debonair, but you'll glow in the dark."

"My brother's getting married," Wilkie said defensively. "What's the *plan*, Rafael?"

Rafael went to the transreceiver on the desk. He splayed his hands lightly on it. "You beautiful thing. You gorgeous, beautiful thing," he said caressingly. "Wilkie, my brother. Say good-bye to your baby."

Wilkie's eyes flew wide. Then he groaned. "Oh no . . . not Heloise . . ."

Brigitte, Rafael, and Wilkie stood at the corner of a building whose street connected like a wheel spoke to the wide half circle of Gestapo headquarters. The grounds of the old courthouse used to have a lawn like a park, and people came to eat lunch on the grass and on the benches. Now it felt like a compound. The lawn area was no longer tended or attended, the Great War memorials had been razed, and guards were posted at the top of the stairs near the entrance.

Braun's vehicle was parked in front, driver inside. Other vehicles lined the curb. Even this late at night, nearly 10 p.m., the place was a beehive of activity. Just a few months ago, it wasn't that way. Everyone knew the invasion was just a surprise attack away, prompting all manner of business at the swastika-clad building.

Brigitte applied heavy lipstick, but the shade was not as red as Marie-Josette would use. She couldn't tell Rafael that her seduction skills fell short. He had every right to expect a good performance: she was a—a—a *former* . . . What was wrong with her that she couldn't think the *p* word? . . . A woman who got paid for—she paused with the lipstick, startled; she couldn't even think the *s* word? She couldn't think *sex*? From prostitute to prude. She shook her head. Then she paused.

It was a return to the days before the Occupation, before her life became . . . occupied.

She knew perfectly well what had happened. Tom happened. Madame Bouvier happened. Father Eppinette happened. Love happened. It made no room for the oldest profession. It made a place for her.

She realized this *now*, quite possibly at the end of all things?

"Better late than never," she said brightly, then snapped her compact shut.

Rafael looked her over critically, then, murmuring, "Forgive me," unbuttoned her top button and pushed her blouse open a little farther. Her cheeks warmed, but she submitted to it with cold dignity. He shrugged. "You need to get his attention, little cabbage. We need that car."

She glanced down ruefully. She wished she were as well-endowed as Marie-Josette. "So this will work . . ."

His look traveled her over. "Oh, it'll work. Just do your thing, and get him to the alley."

"Do my thing . . ."

"We'll take care of the rest."

Corporal Alric Reinhart roused from his reverie and caught the book before it slid from his lap. He dog-eared the page to mark his spot, same page as when he started, and tossed the book to the passenger seat. It was a volume of Kant. Half of it went over his head. The other half made him feel wan. Kant was not what he needed right now. He needed a copy of *The Art of War*.

"Enough," he whispered, trailing the word, feeling the

saturation of it, Kant's final deathbed word. He let Kant die, then mentally grasped for *The Art of War*. He soon raised a venomous look to headquarters.

What went on in that building he could not guess, but he had to be ready for anything. Until that last-minute stop at Braun's apartment, Braun and the little Rousseau had sat in a silence so frosty it reminded Alric of the ice storm last winter that froze over trees and splintered branches. The man was terribly unhappy, and it had a lot to do with the amazing conversation earlier today.

Never before had Alric shared a beer with Braun. He was in crisis, but they didn't talk about the crisis, not then. They talked about his sons. They talked about Alric's family. And then: Alric asked about that ethereal dream come to reality, Krista Hegel.

"Krista," he sighed in exquisite misery.

She had entered the car broken and distraught; she left brave and determined. Both times Alric thought his heart would splinter like the ice branches.

She had sobbed in Braun's arms all the way to the café near the Château de Caen, and Braun, awkward but well-meaning stiff that he was, allowed her tears to soak his splendid uniform. And then: on the way back to GH, she sat with that beautiful head lifted, face freshened to a pink-and-cream glow, resolute to enter the place that hope had abandoned.

He watched the swastika. Alric's father, a resolute supporter of the crumbling Wehrmacht arm of the German military, staunchly anti-Nazi, staunchly pro–Admiral Wilhelm Canaris, under whom Father had served in the Reichsmarine, on the battleship *Schlesien* . . . Father would have had something to say about the miserable job that poor creature endured. Alric had learned appalling things from Braun.

Father would have had something to say about Braun, too,

and Alric felt his heart soar with pride. He'd had an inkling
of the sort of man he was assigned to, and it came clear after
a few rounds of French ale. And Braun later said, appraising
Alric with a new eye, that *he* had no idea what sort of man
worked for *him*. Again, his heart soared. One had to be so very
discreet about one's politics these days, to say nothing of one's
philosophy. It could cost a man his life.

He yelped at a tap on his window.

It was a girl. A pretty girl. He unrolled the window, hoping she hadn't heard the yelp. He nodded, said, dignified,
"Fräulein."

"*Parlez-vous français?*" the girl asked.

He shook his head. "Only a little."

"*Anglais?*"

He shook his head.

"I speak some German." She smiled and gave a little shrug.
"Not as nicely."

He looked at his watch. "You are aware of the new curfew,
fräulein?"

"*Oui.*" Her cheeks pinkened, and she gave a shy smile. "But
you see, I am here in town from Paris. I am . . . Oh, what is
word? . . . Lonely."

Gravity lassoed his gaze and he could not stop a lightning
glance at her cleavage. He swallowed, felt a mist of perspira-
tion, and looked away. A few nights ago, sure; but he was a
man reborn, who now lived his life for Krista Hegel. He suddenly wondered if she was related to Georg.

He said formally, "Regrettably, I am a new man, fräulein."

The girl's smile disappeared. She buttoned her top button.
"So am I."

He looked at the courthouse. "My reason to exist is in that
godforsaken building."

She straightened from the window, following his gaze. *"Le mien aussi,"* she said softly.

What a look on that face. Brown eyes large with exquisite anguish, fixed fast on the swastika. She slowly smoothed a windblown lock behind her ear.

"A guard?" he asked sympathetically.

She shook her head, eyes filling with tears.

"A little Frenchman, in there with my boss?"

Tears fell down her cheeks, and his insides went to mush. What was it with crying women? Yet maybe he had what Braun had, and she could leave all fresh and ready for battle, whatever it was.

"A prisoner," she whispered, as if she did not trust her voice to a full word. Tears rolled onto her lips. Oh, the look upon that face; oh, the wretchedness of these times.

"Exquisite," he breathed.

He roused himself.

"Fräulein," he said briskly, taking charge as Braun had: "I cannot leave my post, but you will join me at it. Come—converse with me." He got out of the car, held out his arm, and escorted her to the passenger side.

"Thank God it runs on petrol," Wilkie whispered. "But if it runs out on the way to Le Vey, we'll *wish* we had a converter box."

"Get back, you stand out like a full moon."

"Well, if you had let me stop at my apartment . . ."

"No time." Rafael's eyes narrowed. "What's she doing?"

They watched Brigitte talk to the driver. This was taking far too long. Idle moments made Rafael nervous. He needed constant action to keep his mind from any unpleasant possibility, like not getting to Le Vey at all.

"Two o'clock you said . . ."

"*Between* one and two. Look—she's getting in the car!" Wilkie hissed.

Rafael stared. They weren't going to—not right there, were they? She was supposed to lure him *here*. He wondered if things were about to get interesting. He wished he could see better. The streetlight cast a direct glow upon the vehicle, making it difficult to see inside.

"She's a bold little thing . . . ," Wilkie commented, straining for a better look. "I admire her nerve. She's not involved with anyone, is she?"

"The pilot."

Wilkie sighed. "Figures. Well, what do we do now?"

"Give her a little time," Rafael mused. This was the girl he himself had recruited. He knew all about following instinct. Maybe she had something up her sleeve, and he'd not spoil it.

27

STURMBANNFÜHRER SCHIFFER roughly grabbed Krista Hegel's chin, tilting her face up to examine it. It was wet with tears.

"You disgust me," he sneered, pushing her away. But rage surged, and he slapped her full across the face. The force sent her sprawling from the table.

A strangled gurgle from the man hanging in chains. The chains rattled in his feeble attempt to move.

Schiffer turned to him. "So you have a little in you yet. Good. You'll find our next—" But he stopped. He stared at the mottled, swollen face. One eye had swollen shut. And the other eye, all the more brilliant blue with red staining the white, was looking at . . .

He turned to Krista, weeping quietly on the ground, hand to cheek.

"So," he said softly.

He strolled to the girl and gazed down at her, tilting his head, reveling in the new surge of princely power. He lifted his head to gaze at the pilot. He smiled then, and the pilot gave another strangled cry.

Schiffer knelt next to Krista, eyes never leaving the pilot. He stroked her blonde hair, then sank his fingers into its luxurious softness and made a fist.

"Who is Greenland?"

When the two guards outside heard Krista Hegel scream, they stared at each other in shock. Johann Wallen made an involuntary movement toward the door, but the other guard put out his hand.

"Don't," Kreutz whispered. "Not unless you want to fight Russians."

"What is he doing to her?" Wallen whispered.

"She's upset, that's all. You know how she is."

"It wasn't that kind of scream."

They looked at each other.

"I could care less what he does to the Yank," Wallen said. "But I swear . . ."

"You want to end up in a Russian POW camp, singing the song of the Volga boatmen, that's your choice." Kreutz moved back to position.

Wallen swallowed. He looked at the doorknob. He looked up and down the hallway. It was empty. All interrogations were done for the day, all prisoners returned to their cells except this one. This one was special. Schiffer usually worked with Metzger on special cases, but Metzger wasn't back from Fort de Romainville. Schiffer had been on his own and seemed to relish it.

Was she simply reacting to an especially brutal tactic? He hated what she went through. Hated that the most innocent woman he had ever met was locked in a room all day with Schiffer. He knew no one like Krista Hegel. He didn't know

how she managed to retain her humanity with nothing but
hell around. She had a soul you could see straight through to
God, and when he was around her he didn't just *want* to be a
better person, he *was* a better person. He wondered if Schiffer
had ever made a pass at her. The thought brought flashes of
red to his vision. Schiffer had raped his last secretary. He knew
that for a fact.

He looked at Kreutz. "One more scream and I'm going
in there, Russian front or not. Try to prevent me—I'll make
sure you sing the Volga right at my side." He eased back into
position.

"Hey, what you do is your business." Kreutz glanced up
and down the hallway. "But whatever you do, I won't interfere." He shrugged. "Although I might make it look like I am."

Braun did not expect the Gestapo HQ to be so busy at this
time of night. There were three manned desks in the cavernous
reception room of the former courthouse. Near the desk on
the right, seven or eight frightened civilians with haggard faces
waited under guard on a few benches. It looked as though
they had been waiting for a long time. Why were they here?
Waiting for prisoners, or were they prisoners themselves, waiting for processing? They looked so . . . civilian.

The desk on the left was less busy. A balding, overweight
corporal with a pink, jovial face sipped coffee from a teacup
and chatted with two soldiers who laughed at something he
said. Braun headed for the desk in the center of the room,
where he knew any inquiries for personnel were handled. The
desk was just in front of the main entrance to the building,
a long hallway. Above this entrance hung a large portrait of
Hitler. Two guards stood beneath it on either side.

The thin, anemic-looking fellow behind the desk finished a conversation with a soldier, giving him a piece of paper, a brown medicine bottle, and final instructions to which the soldier listened anxiously. The man waved him off and then turned sour and weary attention to the papers on his desk. He glanced up when Braun approached with Rousseau. His expression did not change, even as he took in Rousseau's state.

"Tell Sturmbannführer Schiffer I have a present for him," Braun said coolly. He rested his briefcase on the desk as he tugged off his gloves.

"He is not to be disturbed."

"For this, Lieutenant, he will be disturbed."

"Procedure is procedure. I am sorry . . . sir." The man displayed a thin-lipped smile that looked more like a sneer. He glanced at Braun's insignia, then amended the appellation. "Oh, excuse me—Major."

The man might have called him Major, but he'd given no accompanying salute, meaning he had inspected the background color of Braun's insignia and chose to treat him like a civilian. For some, regard for a civilian officer hovered somewhere around regard for a private. Officially, the man's insolence could get him busted to private. Under Rommel it would.

"Tell me, Lieutenant . . . Hermann. Do you think perhaps procedure would include . . . Greenland?"

The thin-lipped smile went sickly. His look slid to Rousseau, and now the Frenchman's state apparently held more significance. He rose from the desk, murmured something like, "Right away, Major," and all but ran for the hallway past his desk.

This action seemed to alert the entire room to the Frenchman at the desk. The low murmur of noise died away completely. The two guards stationed at the front door glanced their way, curious about Rousseau. From these two he had received salutes. Braun took in their gear. Each carried a K98 Mauser rifle slung over his shoulder, each had a leather holster at the belt, likely housing a Walther P38. Same weapons as the guards past the desk, and the other soldiers in the room.

The corporal at the left-hand desk got up and sauntered over. He couldn't keep his eyes from Rousseau.

"Greenland, you say?" He nodded at Rousseau. "I know him. I've seen him around. It's Christmastime for Schiffer. How did you catch him?"

"I will discuss details of his apprehension with the sturmbannführer."

"Sure, sure, of course," the corporal said, mildly obsequious. To Rousseau he said, "Too bad for you Metzger's not here. Things are quieter when he's around. If you get my meaning." He grinned.

"Do not speak to my prisoner. Get back to your post."

The man glanced at Braun, then sauntered back to his desk.

Braun felt Rousseau looking at him. He ignored him. He couldn't bear to see the dapper little Frenchman in such a state, and that by his own hands. Worse, he knew what was in Rousseau's eyes. The gratefulness infuriated him so, it actually helped Braun do what he had to do.

Rousseau's arms were bound behind his back. In his mouth, Braun had stuffed a rolled-up sock, then tightly wrapped the belt of his dressing gown to gag him. It pulled his cheeks back, distending his mouth like a gaping fish. When it came to "roughing him up," as Rousseau had suggested, Braun could not. Michel had looked so very forlorn that he could not bear to black his eye or bloody his nose. In the end all he did was muss the Frenchman's hair, an offense surely felt as keenly as a blow.

Braun spared him a glance. The brown eyes seemed large,

disturbingly so, perhaps because he could no longer speak and spoke instead with his eyes. He wanted to say something. Braun looked away.

Schiffer pulled out a pocketknife and opened it. He yanked Krista's head back. He touched the blade to her swan-white neck.

"Don't touch her," the pilot croaked, his voice hoarse from hours of screaming. His hands were purple and swollen from pressure. Schiffer knew he'd lose use of them if he stayed that way much longer.

He put his nose into her neck to breathe her fragrance, suppressed a shudder. Marta had never smelled this good. He traced the tip of the knife up the neck, over the curve of the chin, alongside Krista's lovely jawbone, past a little mole, up the cheek, to the elegantly shaped brow. She held still, and a tear spilled over from the reddened, swimming, china-blue eyes. He caught the tear with the knifepoint.

Her eyes were not filled with terror, not like Marta's. No, righteous little Krista Hegel had eyes only for the pilot, and those eyes were filled with compassion. She shook her head slightly, imploring, and Schiffer looked at the pilot.

"Who is Greenland?"

Agony filled the face of the pilot as he stared at the girl.

Schiffer gave a little flick of the knife.

The second scream came from the interrogation room at the same time the door at the end of the hallway burst open. Wallen's rifle came up and he swung to face the door as Kreutz went to a knee and drew a bead on the shouting man clattering down the hall toward them as fast as he could.

What was happening? A Resistance raid? He was only certain of Krista's scream. Wallen gripped the rifle, pointing it first at the doorknob, and then, with a frustrated snarl, at the man running pell-mell toward them.

It was Hermann, the sallow receptionist. Breathless, he waved his hands as he approached. "Greenland!" he gasped. "I have Greenland!" He pushed Wallen aside and pounded on the interrogation door. "Sturmbannführer Schiffer!" He tried the door. It was locked from the inside. He rattled the knob.

Schiffer screamed, "Go away, you idiot!"

"Greenland!" Hermann shouted at the keyhole. "I have Greenland!"

No response.

Breathing hard, Hermann stared in bewilderment at the keyhole, then at the guards.

Krista screamed.

Wallen threw himself against the door, then stepped back and opened fire on the doorknob.

Gunfire.

Hauptmann Braun froze, locking eyes with Rousseau.

After a heartbeat of shocked confusion, the two guards beneath Hitler's portrait ran off in search of the gunfire. The guards at the front went into defensive positions, assuming a Resistance raid, and trained their rifles outside. The man on the left of the room dove under his desk, the man on the right shouted for order over several civilians who wailed, some shouting names, one of them bolting for the entrance but clubbed back by a soldier.

What happened? Had a nervous guard opened fire on the clerk, mistaking him for Resistance?

The shots had come from deep within the facility, likely the basement. Braun jerked his head at Rousseau and they followed in the direction the guards had gone.

Wilkie peered from the edge of the building. "Did you hear that?"

Rafael had heard something, but didn't know what.

"I think it was gunfire," Wilkie whispered. "You don't think . . . ?"

"Don't be stupid—he knows too much."

"Then what was it?"

"I don't know." Then, "Look!"

Brigitte half emerged from the passenger side of the car to wave wildly at them. Then she beckoned them to the vehicle with her wave.

Rafael cursed.

"She wants us to—what?" Wilkie squeaked. "Get in the car with him? Is she *mad*? I suppose you think she knows what she's doing *now*."

Rafael looked at the Gestapo headquarters. The swastika had a crimson halo about it, an eerie aura created by spotlights proudly highlighting German conquest. He looked at the car, with Brigitte urging them on. "Come on—grab the box."

"We were supposed to *ambush* the man," Wilkie groaned. "Now we're having *tea* with him. Women!"

Four shots blew the doorknob to frayed splinters. A fragment had flown into Hermann's arm, and he lay howling on the ground, rolling back and forth, certain he was shot. Wallen stepped over him and kicked the door open.

He stared through the rifle sight at the bloody mess of the Yank, then at Schiffer against the wall, and then at Krista, head bowed, weeping, a blood-filled welt rising on her neck. Her blouse was torn open. The sight swung back to Schiffer.

"He isn't worth the Volga," Kreutz said at his ear.

"He confessed, you fool!" Schiffer snarled. He pushed away from the wall, yanking down the sides of his coat. "He just now confessed!"

"You used her to make him do it." For the first time, Wallen thought that these Yanks weren't so bad. "Krista? Are you all right?"

When Krista lifted her face, his head went dizzy. Her upper lip was swollen and stood out from her teeth like a shelf. A cut at her eyebrow trickled blood in several trails. A wall of red rose before his vision, and he could barely see Schiffer through it.

"She is a German! It was her duty!"

Wallen convulsively gripped the stock of his rifle. Kreutz began to softly hum the song of the Volga boatmen.

"Johann," Krista said.

She came to his side. She placed a small hand over his on the rifle stock. She stood on her toes and whispered, as she had done to countless prisoners. The words flowed into his ear, and the wall of red wavered. She whispered again, and it buckled. Breathing hard, Wallen lowered the rifle.

"This wouldn't happen if Metzger was here," he told Schiffer.

"Is everything all right?" someone called from the hallway. A rifle nosed into view. One of the front house guards looked in. "Sturmbann—"

"Yes, yes!" Schiffer said. "Get back to your post!" To Wallen, he said, "Metzger wouldn't have gotten this confession." Pride flushed Schiffer's cheeks. He displayed the unconscious, dangling ball of battered flesh with a flourish. "Behold, my brave young soldier: *Greenland*."

"You think he's Greenland," Wallen sneered. "Even I'm not that stupid."

"Yes . . . it would be welcome news to my friend, here."

All turned to behold the strapping German officer who now filled the doorway. He pushed a bound and gagged little Frenchman into the room.

"I tried to tell you!" came the indignant cry of Hermann, who writhed, unattended, on the hallway floor.

Hauptmann Braun made use of his size, uniform, and bearing when he strolled into the interrogation room. He placed his briefcase on the table, glancing at Krista Hegel's report. He touched the report, drew it over with a fingertip, pretended to read a few lines, using the time to gather himself.

He had been unprepared for the sight of the American pilot, trussed up and dangling beneath an A-frame ladder, beaten to a slick, gruesome pulp, his bound hands purple and white; but when he saw Krista Hegel's face, he had to summon composure from the four corners of his being, he had to find it from Elsewhere, and he cried out in his heart for aid.

Whatever your hand finds to do, do it with all your might.
Stick to cement. Cement, cement.

He raised an eyebrow at Schiffer. "I regret, Sturmbannführer, with respect for your dedication to duty, that the pilot's confession must have been to protect the young woman." He glanced at the two guards, rifles gripped and pointing at the floor, unsure but ready to engage conflict. He looked at Krista. "Young lady, I know the good German stock from which you come; I fear you will protest your removal, in light of the momentous revelations about to take place—a victory for the Führer, and indeed, for the sturmbannführer—" Braun inclined his head to Schiffer—"but I request that your wounds be attended to, in order that you may swiftly return to serve the Reich in the full of good health. Perhaps one of these men can escort you to the infirmary?"

Krista placed her hand on the arm of the guard nearest her. His arm came around her, and when she looked up into his face, Braun knew his plans for Franz were over. At least the look the boy gave her in return mollified Braun. Krista was safe. Nothing could happen to her with this fellow around. Surely, this was the guard who had helped her give the pilot water.

Schiffer's face was a comedy of fluctuation. He stared at Rousseau. He stared at Braun. He stared at Rousseau. His mouth had fallen to an unflattering gape.

Braun pulled out a chair for Rousseau and motioned him to sit, then went to the door. He watched the soldier walk away with Krista, tenderly gazing down at her. He looked down at Hermann. "Get out of here."

Hermann struggled to his feet, clutching his arm, and hurried after the two. Braun turned to the other soldier. "I request for you to take up position at the other end of the hallway."

The soldier saluted smartly and trotted after Krista and her guard.

"She could have taken notes!" Schiffer scorned when Braun came back in. Braun ignored him and tried to pull the door shut. The blown-apart lock would not allow the door to close properly.

"Keep your voice down. Of course she could have taken notes." He dragged over a chair to keep the door shut, then turned to Schiffer and gave him a first taste: "You complete, and utter, and absolute fool."

Stunned, Schiffer's mouth fell lower.

Braun went to the pathetic dangling hulk. He touched the blond head, damp with blood. "Get over here," he barked at Schiffer.

Schiffer complied slowly, likely from some unpleasant instinct that told him things had radically changed.

Braun had feared the American was dead, but when Schiffer pulled a metal pin and grasped the chain to lower him, a small groan escaped the pilot. Braun flashed a look at Rousseau and saw torment in the brown eyes.

It took some time to unloose the boy. His limbs were swollen and purpled from untold hours in the cramped position. Braun cut his hands free with a pocketknife, pulled away the rod, and when he carefully straightened out his limbs, another groan rumbled, stronger, and he gave Rousseau a swift and discreet nod. He was almost certain the Frenchman was blinking back tears. Schiffer was too occupied in making sure no blood touched him to notice. The boy opened his eyes for a brief moment, they swam about, his eyelids fluttered and closed.

Braun gently massaged the boy's cruelly swollen hands. He hardly knew which position to let him lie in. Finally Braun eased him to his side, and it seemed the pilot was mercifully unconscious.

He went to the stainless-steel table and dropped into a chair at one end. Schiffer hesitated and then sat on the other end, closest to the door. He watched Braun warily while Braun regarded Rousseau, who sat at the table lost in his thoughts.

"Rousseau is not Greenland," Braun said.

Two sets of eyes flew to his face. And Braun finally allowed what he had not allowed since he had arrived in France, what he prayed to God he'd never allow again.

He unbarred the gate, swung it wide, and allowed himself to feel his ocean of hatred for the war, for what had happened to his precious son, for what had happened to his beloved wife, for men like Schiffer, who did unspeakable things to old women, young women, young men, who made *German* a word to be feared and despised. The torrent filled him until he could hardly see for hate's obscuring nature, until he tasted bile, until he knew Schiffer would believe.

"I am Greenland."

28

ROUSSEAU'S STRANGLED CRY escaped Schiffer's notice. Schiffer stared, mesmerized, at Braun.

"Open my briefcase."

Schiffer pulled over the briefcase, opened it. He looked at Braun.

"Take out the folder."

He peered into the briefcase, tilted it to the light, and pulled out a thick folder.

"Open it."

Schiffer opened the folder. He picked up a map, glanced at it, set it aside. He took the cover page and read the heading. "Project Zippy," he murmured.

"You have quite possibly blown the biggest undercover operation since Sea Lion." Braun flicked his fingers at the folder. "Please, continue."

For the first time, Schiffer looked as if someone were walking on his grave. He wet his lips and lowered his gaze to the folder. He set the cover page aside.

"You could not take my clues when I told you Rousseau was no trouble?"

Schiffer glanced over the page on which Braun had sketched his ventilation system. He set it aside, then found sketches from General Richter's subterranean command post right here in Caen. Richter commanded the 716th Infantry Division. He was a friend and had given Braun the original sketches as a keepsake. Braun had used the design for inspiration.

"Ask yourself this: Why has the name Greenland swept only the northern coast, when the name of Max, Jean Moulin, fell upon all of France—even in the Unoccupied Zone?"

Schiffer turned over the page, took another. This was the plan for the installment at Fontaine-la-Mallet, but Schiffer wouldn't know that, and it was not labeled. He appeared to study the drawing.

"Are you saying—" Schiffer cleared his throat, tried again. "Are you saying—"

"Moulin was Resistance. I am not. I am an engineer, Sturmbannführer, *the* engineer, the man you will tell your children about if Rommel doesn't execute you. I am in cover so deep, the name Greenland was connected to the French Resistance alone—as intended." He nodded at the pages. "Go ahead. One more, and you will see what you have exposed."

Schiffer paled. "Metzger arrives in the morning. He can sort all this—"

"Look at it!"

He blinked, convulsively swallowed, and took the next page. He studied the depth chart sketched in the margin and a list of computations for air pressure, sea pressure. He narrowed his eyes. He saw the sketch of the coastlines, the sketch of the connecting tunnel, the grid with a cross section of the tunnel. He snatched the map and compared the tracings on it to the sketch. He looked again at the plans for the ventilation system. And finally, he put a trembling finger on the map at Calais.

"Mein Gott," he breathed. "A tunnel to England."

"I must leave immediately with my agents, when there are fewer people to witness."

"Your agents . . ." Schiffer's eyes flickered to Rousseau, then, with undisguised horror to the pilot.

"Rousseau has served me faithfully since they raised the Todt sign over his door. His reputation as a noncollaborationist is a front. And the boy would have died to keep me secret. Lucky for you he did not." Braun tilted his head. "You have no idea who he is."

Schiffer's face said he'd rather keep it that way. And praying with all his heart the pilot did not rouse, Braun threw down the final card.

"He is the beloved nephew of Marshal Erwin Rommel."

The blow drained the last of Schiffer's bravado. He slumped in his seat.

"He requested the honor to serve under me. Yet the honor has been mine. Despite his youth, he is as fine an agent as any with whom I have worked. The zeal for the Fatherland is in his blood." He had to follow through while Schiffer still reeled. He rose, gripped the edge of the table, and leaned toward Schiffer.

"You will call in my driver," Braun said, voice dangerously soft. "You will announce to all in the reception area a great victory for the Fatherland. You will then instruct my driver to conduct myself, the boy, and Michel Rousseau to Fort de Romainville for immediate processing, and you will assign an escort of your elite guards. It is imperative that all who see believe what they see, that the man Rousseau is Greenland. I want pomp, I want circumstance, I want them to think they escort Churchill himself to the gallows."

He had no idea how they'd lose the guards. Perhaps not until Paris. What he would do then, he could not tell.

"You have cost me two fine agents, Herr Schiffer," he continued, and he strolled around the table to Schiffer. "They were irreplaceable." He looked down at him for a moment, then gave a nod at the designs. Schiffer hastily gathered them, stuffed them in the folder, and put the folder in the briefcase. "They will be transferred to Berlin, and there they will languish in deprocessing, talents wasted, and all the while those who ask questions will wonder about the one who brought the operation to a standstill."

"I thought I was doing my duty!" A fine sheen of sweat had broken over Schiffer's face. "How could I know? How could I?"

"Metzger would have known!" Braun shouted. "Everything I told you in my report on Rousseau, Metzger would have picked up! You fool! Who trained you?"

"But Metzger read the reports!"

"And you don't see him here, do you?"

He smoothed his coat, adjusted his hat, giving the impression that he was trying to calm himself.

He glanced at Krista's notes. "Burn those. Call your guards, get a stretcher. Perhaps your . . . misapprehension of events can be forgiven. But pray to God Rommel's nephew does not die. Have you seen Rommel in a rage?"

They had to land in the backseat of a philosopher.

While Brigitte hung on the German's every word, translating the drivel over her shoulder, Rafael rolled his eyes and exchanged looks with Wilkie. Rafael sat directly behind the driver, staring darkly at his head. For a little glass of Calvados, he'd slip his fingers around the man's neck and choke him to death.

"Alric says, 'That which is felt within is known, overall, without,'" Brigitte translated in awe. "He says that which is called occupation is really oppression. It holds all in . . ." She shook her head, unsure of the German word, flapping her hand with excitement. "Oh, I don't know what he means, I think he means 'thrall.' Holds everyone in its thrall, the oppressed and oppressors alike. Basically, he is saying that we are *all* under a Great Evil, French and German alike, victims everyone, and that—"

"I don't give a merry rat's—" Rafael began.

"Little Alric will be *my* victim if he keeps this up!" Wilkie erupted.

"Brigitte, is he for us or against us?" Rafael demanded.

"He is for Braun," she hissed, scowling at them for barbarians. She looked at the driver. "I think that means he is for us."

The driver turned a bewildered face to the men in the back. He likely thought he'd held them in thrall.

Rafael banged his fist on the seat. "That's it! You two deal with this moron. There's no more time." He glared at the building. "By now Rousseau may have confessed that he is Greenland. I'll request to see Braun, and if they kick up a fuss, I'll show them the transreceiver—"

Wilkie squeaked.

"—to prove that my request is legitimate." He looked past the driver to the automobile parked ahead of them. He looked over his shoulder at the automobile behind. "Be ready for anything. I wish he wasn't so packed in."

He started to grab the suitcase, but Brigitte reached over and seized his hand. She held it to her cheek, then kissed it. "Be careful."

He smiled, grabbed the suitcase, and was gone.

They watched him trot up the courthouse stairs.

"Greenland?" the driver said.

Wilkie and Brigitte froze.

"*Ja*, Greenland." He nodded. He pointed at the building. Then he jabbered to Brigitte in German, waited expectantly for her to translate.

Brigitte stared at the driver. "Braun is for us," she said faintly. "Braun is for us." She turned to the window. "Oh, Rafael. Don't mess anything up."

He stood at the top of the courthouse steps, under the rifles of two guards, hands in the air. One of them searched the suitcase, looked up at Rafael, and then motioned with his rifle. Rafael picked it up and walked into the building.

"Shouldn't he stay in the infirmary?" Schiffer said doubtfully, now quite anxious over the pilot's health. The ladder rattled as a soldier dragged it aside. The soldier helped another to lift the man by the stained drop cloth to the stretcher.

"He recognized me before he passed out," Braun said. "He knows I've been exposed. Let me put it this way: you don't want him around when he comes to."

Braun, Schiffer, and Rousseau watched them take the stretcher from the room. Braun grabbed his briefcase, then took Krista's notes and gave them to Schiffer. Schiffer looked at them blankly, then hastily stuffed them inside his coat. He started after the stretcher bearers, but Braun held him back.

"Listen very carefully. This is not over. If you cannot convince the forward group that this man is Greenland, then your life will be in Rommel's hands."

"What do I do?" Schiffer said anxiously.

TRACY GROOT

Braun put a hand on Rousseau's shoulder. Deep impressions lined Michel's cheeks from the recently removed gag; he'd only removed it when he could be sure Michel was with him. "Rousseau, you have conducted yourself admirably. I must ask a little more."

Rousseau inclined his head. "All for the Cause."

Braun looked at Schiffer, who dashed at a line of sweat on his upper lip. "When we enter the reception area, treat this man as you would have Jean Moulin."

Jean Moulin. Jean Moulin.

They walked behind the stretcher bearers. Schiffer felt the sweat in his scalp as he walked abreast of Hauptmann Braun, behind the hateful little Frenchman. Such a parade they would make, emptying into the foyer.

Metzger returned in the morning.

Sweat gathered and rolled down the side of his face.

The disgrace he would bear once Metzger learned of his failure. Had Metzger seen the boy before he was beaten, he surely would have said, "How did you not see the resemblance? He could be Rommel's *son!*"

He did see the resemblance, too late. The man was German to the core. Somehow Schiffer had known it all along. He looked far less like Rommel's nephew than he did Rommel's son.

Rommel's son, Rommel's son.

Footsteps echoed down the hallway. Sweat gathered and rolled.

Schiffer's steps slowed. He did not have to be here when Metzger returned. He did not have to be here! He would leave early—he would leave tonight! He would say he'd received orders for a transfer, and then—

377

"Are you ready to convince them?" Braun said in a low tone.

"Of course!" Schiffer exulted. Braun gave him a glance. Schiffer wanted to laugh out loud. He'd not see the look on Metzger's face! "I can do anything!"

Rafael gripped the handle of the transreceiver suitcase and followed the guard into the building. He had useful talents, he had wit, he was quick on the uptake, but most of all he had the ability to beguile. His mother said he could sell fish to a fisherman. Today he'd sell himself as . . .

Beneath the portrait of Hitler came a stretcher. Upon the stretcher was a brutalized man, whose blood soaked through the canvas.

Behind the stretcher came Monsieur Rousseau, disheveled, bound.

Behind Monsieur Rousseau was Sturmbannführer Schiffer, the man responsible for Jasmine's torture and death.

The brutalized man was Tom.

The transreceiver slipped from his hand.

The world became a place of dampened sound, as if an explosion had gone off at his ear.

He saw the joyful maniac face of Schiffer as he shouted something, displaying Rousseau to the world. Then insanity leaped to Schiffer's face. He raised his fist and pounded Rousseau's shoulder. Rousseau crumpled.

Rafael grabbed the nearest guard's rifle, hauled it to his eye, and fired.

Into dampened sound came a voice.

"Rafael," someone whispered. "Rafael."

He opened his eyes. He could do no more than that.

Welts lined Rousseau's face, like a horse's reins. Rafael wanted to touch those welts, but he could not move. He wanted to speak, but only a gurgle came out.

So he looked into the eyes that were loving him into the next world, then mouthed what he wanted Rousseau to know.

You have shown me France.

Hauptmann Braun looked at Schiffer's body and said to the man under the desk, "He was going to give me an escort, but I hate to leave you shorthanded when the Resistance is on the move. Call off the escort. My driver and I can handle Greenland."

The wide-eyed man nodded. He made no move to come out.

"See to it Metzger knows of the great victory of Greenland's capture. I'll file my report at Fort de Romainville, then forward a copy. Metzger should know of Schiffer's accomplishments." Braun shrugged. "He wasn't the one to capture Greenland— but at least he got a notorious accomplice."

The man nodded.

Pockets of two or three all over the reception room talked in whispers, staring at the bodies of Schiffer and André Besson. A few soldiers talked animatedly over the opened suitcase of the transreceiver. Rousseau had not moved from André's side. One of the women civilians wept with her fists at her mouth, two companions comforting her. Braun did not know whether she wept for Rousseau or André Besson.

A guard's bullet had taken André Besson through the throat. And because it would have been expected from him, Braun walked over to the man who had fired the shot, already recounting it to others, and said, "Well done, soldier. I'm sure I would have been next. You saved my life." Braun saluted him, and the soldier, blushing modestly, saluted back.

Braun strolled over to Rousseau, briefcase in hand.

"Well, Greenland," Braun boomed, "he was a brave lad. You've said your good-bye. Time to go." He looked at the stretcher bearers and motioned them to take up their burden once more. "Put him in the backseat." He turned to the nearest guard. "You, there—can you spare your handgun?" He jerked his head at Rousseau. "I don't expect trouble, but in light of tonight's action I told your CO to keep the escort Schiffer promised us. Might be wise for me to be armed." The guard, a little in awe of Braun and his significant charge, hurried to unsnap his leather holster and handed the Walther butt first to Braun. He took it and started to slip it into his briefcase. The soldier very slightly shook his head, with a kind glance at Braun's civilian rank. Braun put the gun in his coat pocket, and the soldier nodded. Braun winked.

He went to Rousseau and hauled him up by an elbow. He gave him a little push toward the door, told a front guard to escort him to the car, and stood for a moment over the body of André Besson.

He had given them a way out of Caen. He had killed an evil man. And as the transreceiver surely indicated, he had come here to single-handedly negotiate the release of Tom.

Good-bye, you who wished my son well.

He shook his head, as if in awe that he had escaped a similar fate, and without explanation, folded up the transreceiver under the noses of the two guards examining it and walked out the door.

"Where to?" Alric Reinhart spoke into the brittle-glass silence.

He hated to speak at all, but he needed a destination. They were long out of Caen, heading east toward Paris. He was fairly certain that was not where they should go.

Next to him sat the Frenchman in the white suit—the one they called Wilkie—head on the suitcase, sobbing silently. The French girl sat in the back with the brutally beaten man in her arms. The bulk of the man's body lay upon the little Frenchman. His feet lay upon Braun.

"Le Vey," Brigitte murmured. Such exquisite emotion on the lovely face, a confluence of two oceans: deep sorrow at the news about the feisty one, deep joy at the one from whom she could not take her gaze. The man had come to some time ago. He did nothing but look at her with his one good eye. A tear occasionally drained from the eye.

"Where is Le Vey?" Alric asked apologetically.

"North," she murmured. "Then west."

He turned the car about.

After a few moments, Alric delicately ventured, "When Kant died, he said a word: *enough*. Did the feisty one say anything?"

The little Frenchman spoke for the first time, his voice thin. "'You have shown me France.'"

Alric drew a long breath and sighed.

He ventured into the silence one last time. "You may have shown him France. You must have shown him the world."

29

THEY HAD STOPPED only once, at a village called Villons around midnight. They approached no home for aid, fearing barking dogs, but on the outskirts of town found a park with a picnic area near a bridge. The bridge spanned a canal half the width of the Caen Canal.

With Tom moaning at the movement, they got him out of the car and laid him in the grass. Alric went down to the water's edge with a flashlight he'd found in the car. He'd emptied it of batteries, filled the hollowed canister with water.

Wilkie trained another flashlight on Tom while Brigitte and Braun washed his wounds and bandaged them as best as they could with strips torn from Wilkie's shirt. They gave him water to drink from the empty flashlight, and when he asked hoarsely if anyone had powdered eggs, all felt relief.

The ordeal had exhausted him, and once back in the car, he fell asleep.

Rousseau touched Brigitte's arm. "Two can fit in the back of the Lysander. You will go with him."

It wasn't possible. She stared at Rousseau.

"I think it wise if . . . Do not tell him of Clemmie or of—"
He looked away.

To England. With Tom. Her heart soared.

She bent to him and whispered, "Did you hear that, Tom?
We will be bluebirds."

In a sky lit by nothing except the moon, they finally heard the
lonely sound of a single-engine plane.

The Lysander approached the airstrip, lit at intervals by
shadowy figures who had emerged from the darkness, swing-
ing flashlights held aloft. After it landed—and Braun marveled
at the impossibly short strip on which it had done so, surely
no more than four hundred meters—the shadowy figures
doused their lights and came running. The Lysander bumped
over the cleared ground and came to a halt. Immediately,
someone shone a light onto the plane. The rear cockpit hatch
opened and a rope ladder shook down. Someone threw down
a duffel bag.

"The SOE agent," Wilkie said, standing next to Braun. To
Braun's surprise, it wasn't a man who emerged from the plane,
but a woman. Someone came to hold the ladder, a resistant or
a Maquis, Braun didn't know the difference between the two.
When she reached the ground, the agent shook hands with the
helper, exchanged some words, then looked up at the pilot and
gave a smile and a salute.

Wilkie went to meet her, Braun at his side.

"How was the flight?" Wilkie asked in English.

"Excellent," she replied in a cheerful British accent. "Bit
bumpy on the landing. Can't complain, especially when I saw
the length of the landing strip. Had to close my eyes. You are
Greenland? I've waited ever so long to meet you."

"Wilkie. Greenland is in the car."

"Is he the agent for extraction?"

"No, he's in the car also. He has been tortured. There was no time for more than bandages to stop the bleeding. He will need medical attention as soon as possible."

"Right. I'll speak to the pilot; he'll radio in when he's over the channel. Don't worry, they'll have assistance for him straightaway. Just the agent, then?"

"And a girl."

She looked at the car and shaded her eyes. The headlights were still on. They had helped to light the strip. "Bit of a squeeze back there for two, but they'll manage. Back in a jiff." She shook hands with Wilkie and went to talk to the pilot.

"How will we get him up that ladder?" Wilkie wondered.

"I'll do it," Braun said.

Rousseau got out of the car to join Wilkie and Braun. They stood in the headlights' beam, and while they watched the SOE agent talk to the pilot, Brigitte watched them.

"Rousseau is a dead man," Brigitte said to Alric in German.

"I believe so."

"And Braun has exposed himself, has he not?"

"Yes."

"What will he do? Where will he go?"

After a moment, Alric said heavily, "I do not know, fräulein."

The SOE agent trotted back to the three. She spoke to Rousseau and took his hand in both of hers, admiration clear on her face.

Brigitte held Tom in her arms a moment longer.

She left a trail of whisper kisses on his brow, smoothed

down the damp thatch of hair, and against his swollen lips breathed good-bye.

Brigitte stepped into the headlight beam. "Excuse me," she called over the drum of the plane, "I am GP. Flame's newest agent."

The woman shook her hand. "Wren."

"Greenland has been exposed," Brigitte said. "He must leave with the other agent."

Before Rousseau could protest, Braun said quickly, "I am afraid it is true."

Wilkie raised his head. He looked at Brigitte, then said to Wren, "If he stays, he's dead."

Rousseau stared at them. "No. No, don't be—"

"Get them aboard," Wren said to Braun. "I'll tell Captain Blakeney. He'll call it in. They'll want to be there when this one lands." She winked at Rousseau. "I know how much de Gaulle wants to meet you." She trotted off.

Wilkie nearly took Brigitte off her feet with a fierce hug. "This is what he—this is what—" he tried to whisper in her ear.

"I know," she whispered back.

"He cared about the pilot. But he loved Rousseau."

"I know."

Wilkie kissed her cheek several times, then let go. He pressed his face against the sleeve of his white coat, then turned to Rousseau and put out his hand. Rousseau looked at it.

"I get no kiss?" he said dryly. "No embrace?"

"She's pretty," Wilkie said. Rousseau shook his hand with both of his, then turned to look for Braun, but Braun had gone to the vehicle.

"Help me," Braun called to the others.

※

The injured man came to again as Braun slowly carried him over his shoulder up the rope ladder to the rear cockpit. He groaned a few times as they settled him in, wedged into place with Rousseau's arms about him. He muttered something about a radial engine, then sank to unconsciousness once more.

Braun helped Rousseau tuck a thick woolen blanket around him. The space was indeed tight. Tom lay slumped against Rousseau. Only Rousseau's face showed in the swaddle of blanket and pilot.

"Can you breathe?" Braun asked over the plane's engine.

"No. And I'd shake hands but I can't move." He eyed Braun. "I hear an invasion is coming. Stay safe, Hauptmann Braun."

"You will owe me fifty francs if it is May 15."

"I will pull some strings, make sure it's the eighth. We will meet again, my friend, when this is over."

"How will you find me?"

"Through Brigitte, of course."

Braun studied the Frenchman's face, gave a little salute, and closed the hatch.

Only twelve minutes after it had landed, the Lysander bumped over the ground, gained speed, and at the last moment gained lift, leaping to clear the treetops.

They watched the spies fly away.

They turned back into the headlight beam. Wilkie slid into the front seat, Braun and Brigitte slid in back. After a smile and a salute, Wren left with the Maquis on a mission of her own.

"Where to?" the driver asked quietly, hands on the wheel.

"Bénouville," Brigitte said.

She looked at Braun, who leaned against the window. "How will I hide you?" she murmured. "You stand out as much as Tom."

Father Eppinette came to mind, and a tall bell tower with a bell that never rang. She looked at Alric the driver. Madame Vion came to mind, and a position on the grounds at the château. Wilkie . . . Wilkie could be her "pimp"! She covered a smile. He could move in with his transreceiver, take Colette's room. Colette would move in with Brigitte.

And Colette and Wilkie will fall in love.

Simone and Alric will fall in love.

Marie-Josette and Guillemot will fall in love.

And someday, Braun would reunite with his wife, and she would be restored, and his son would be healed, and then this exhausted German with the desolate face, who carried her love up the ladder, who sacrificed everything to save two enemies, would be happy.

And someday, when there is freedom, and bluebirds, they will all visit Tom and me. And we will have a son, and we will name him Rafael.

Until then, there was a lot of work to be done. There was an invasion to prepare for, a bridge to gather intelligence on. There was a sign to nail back on the door, for what might possibly be the only Resistance "brothel" in the nation. No better way to hide than in the open.

"Who will take over Flame?" Wilkie said bleakly, watching the sky.

Was the bridge rigged to blow? Had the charges been set? She glanced at Wilkie, surprised. She patted his shoulder. "Don't worry. I already have."

EPILOGUE

The tourist bus rumbled for Colleville, the American cemetery near Omaha Beach. Corporal Rick A. Harmon, a paratrooper with the Eighty-Second Airborne Division, leaned over to talk to an old man and his wife.

"You're Americans?"

"Yes." The old man smiled. "From Michigan."

"Isn't it great here?" The young soldier pushed his cap up. "Different feeling in Normandy, you know? I've been to Paris, been all over France, and they don't treat Americans there the way they treat 'em here."

"Are you here on your own, or with your men?" the old lady asked politely, in a charming French accent.

"Goin' to Colleville to look up a grave of one of my dad's buddies. We were here for a commemorative jump with my platoon on D-Day, at Sainte-Mère-Église. They dropped us in the same location they dropped the Eighty-Second, fifty years ago. It was pretty cool. Did you see it?"

"No, we were in Bénouville for D-Day celebrations," the old man said.

"Where?"

"It's a little town not far from Ouistreham—near Sword and Juno."

"What's in Bénouville?"

"A bridge called Pegasus. Used to be called the Caen Canal Bridge."

"Never heard of it."

"Not many Americans have." The old man reached to shake his hand. "Tom Jaeger. This is my wife, Brigitte."

Tom and Brigitte visited the Colleville cemetery, where, in the acres and acres of white crosses, and with the aid of information guides, they tracked down the graves of Lieutenant Kirk Oswald and Captain Bill Fitzgerald, both killed in action on June 6, 1944. They went down to Omaha Beach, and for one of his fellow fighter pilots who flew missions over Omaha on D-Day, but had never set foot in France, Tom scooped up some of the sacred ground and put it in a film canister.

On D-Day, they had strolled around Bénouville. Brigitte's home had not lasted long as one of the few Resistance brothels in the Occupation; it was burned to the ground in the fierce fight for the city, fifty years earlier. Some had called it a fitting end for the house of sin. Others, including a Madame Bouvier, were curiously silent.

They went to the place where Tom had stood in the middle of the road, caught between running forward and running back. The hedgerow where he had tried to hide was still there. So was the Mairie, the town hall that had housed German soldiers and Milice.

They went to Pegasus Bridge, renamed in honor of the British Sixth Airborne Division, which had taken the bridge with a small contingent in what turned out to be the spearhead action of D-Day. From there they could see the stately Château de Bénouville along the west bank of the canal, where Madame Léa Vion had run a maternity hospital—and where she had operated Century, a cell of the Resistance. Just past the château, the little stone chapel that had hidden downed Allied pilots still stood.

Before they left Pegasus Bridge, Tom thought about a hill in Gettysburg, called Little Round Top. Tom looked toward the sea, toward the beaches, Sword Beach in particular, the easternmost end of the D-Day operation. Had Chamberlain allowed Little Round Top to be taken, the Rebel army could have flanked the Union army; had the brave men of the British Sixth Airborne not taken and held this bridge, the operation could have been flanked with panzers on those beaches, a horrifying addition to the horror of that day.

Tom smoothed his hand on the steel guardrail, and whispered, "Thanks, fellas."

There wasn't much left they remembered of Caen. The city had been leveled in diversion attacks on D-Day and in the weeks of battle that followed. The Gestapo headquarters was gone. The Cimenterie office was gone. So was the grave of André Besson.

They visited Cabourg.

It was easy to find her grave in the little churchyard. A distant avalanche of red plastic poppies, some bright and new, some faded pink, showed the way. On the way there, Brigitte stopped at another grave and read the inscription.

A. W. Whilty
June 6, 1944
Age 19
Yours is the Earth, and everything that's in it.
And what is more, you were a man, my son!

They chose this grave to represent Rafael's and laid upon it a garland of white carnations.

Some wreaths at her graveside had the names of squadrons or divisions. Some inscriptions were jotted on flat pieces of wood, like large Popsicle sticks, and stuck into the ground. *Thank you for saving my husband. Thank you for saving my dad. Thanks for saving Grandpa.*

Antoinette Cornelia Devault
1876–1944
Connue de ses garçons comme Clemmie.

Brigitte squeezed his arm.

"What's it say?"

"'Known to her boys as Clemmie.'"

Tom knelt beside the grave. And after fifty years of rehearsing his speech, he couldn't say a word.

Next to many others on the white marbled stone, he laid an old button.

A NOTE FROM THE AUTHOR

I stood on Omaha Beach and scooped sand for Colonel Walter B. Forbes, who had flown missions over the beach on D-Day but had never set foot on the ground. I visited Pegasus Bridge and had lunch at the Café Gondrée, the first French business to be liberated after four long years of Occupation. I visited the Château de Bénouville, stood in the chapel that hid evading Allies.

I did this on July 4, the day of liberty for Americans. I found it fitting, as an American, to celebrate July 4 in Normandy.

Favorite part of the trip: I stood in the spot where Sergeant Wagger Thornton fired the single PIAT shot that stopped a panzer in its tracks en route to the bridge. Just how significant was that single shot? When German officers saw a series of explosions in Bénouville, they figured the British were present in great strength, and chose to wait for dawn and clear orders. What they had observed, in fact, was that Thornton's shot had inadvertently ignited an awesome fireworks display of machine gun clips, grenades, and shells—a display that lasted nearly an hour and caused confusion to the Germans, which prevented a decisive counterattack. Just how decisive could that counterattack have been? Rommel's Twenty-First Panzer Division, consisting of 127 tanks and over twelve thousand men, waited at various distances for orders. It was the only panzer division to counterattack the Allies on D-Day—and was largely ineffective, due to conflicting reports on the situation, due to orders that came too late . . . due to one guy with impeccable aim.

Read about Wagger Thornton's historic shot in *The Pegasus and Orne Bridges* by Neil Barber (Pen and Sword, 2009) or in *Pegasus Bridge: June 6, 1944* by Stephen E. Ambrose (Simon & Schuster, 1988). It was Ambrose who gave me the idea for this impressionistic Rahab retelling when he mentioned the brothel in Bénouville.

Chris Trueman recounts the significance of the bridge's capture on History Learning Site: "The taking of Pegasus Bridge in the early hours of D-Day was a major triumph for the Allies. The control of Pegasus Bridge gave the Allies the opportunity to disrupt the Germans' ability to bring in reenforcements to the Normandy beaches" ("Pegasus Bridge," accessed December 6, 2011, http://www.historylearningsite. co.uk/pegasus_bridge.htm). Ambrose says this: "A panzer division loose on the beaches, amidst all the unloading going on, could have produced havoc with unimaginable results." Later in his book he asserts, "An argument can therefore be made that Sergeant Thornton had pulled off the single most important shot of D-Day, because the Germans badly needed that road."

It was pretty cool to stand in that spot. So Tom did, too, however briefly.

Many characters in *Flame of Resistance* are composites of real people, while others, including Krista Hegel and Madame

Léa Vion, actually existed. The places were real, some of the businesses were real, and many events actually happened. To sort through the mishmash of truth and fiction, as C. S. Lewis says, "The spell must be unwound, bit by bit, 'with backward mutters of dissevering power'—or else not."

—T. G.

ACKNOWLEDGMENTS

Many, many thanks to the following for their kind and gracious aid in the writing of this novel; they either helped track down facts, read the manuscript, or shared memories of living under Nazi occupation: Jean-Loic Bagot, Neil Barber, Ann Byle, Ray Byle, Terry Crowdy, Katherine Dance, Brooke Dekkinga, Ryan Dekkinga, Rebecca Eerdmans, Marthe Forbes, Chris Freeman, Debby Green, Jean Groot, Rick Harmon, Jason Hill, Alison Hodgson, Melissa Huisman, Louise Lindemulder, Gerri Pipping, Jim Pipping, Jason Porter, Sergeant First Class Matthew Scherbinski, Beth Steenwyk, Jay Stone, Karen VanderVelde, Lauren Wedge, Mark Worthington, the Kalamazoo Aviation History Museum, the Michigan Company of Military Historians and Collectors, and the Pegasus Memorial Museum of Normandy.

Thanks to my beloved Guild, sisters in writing crime: Cynthia Beach, Shelly Beach, Angela Blycker, Ann Byle, Sharron Carrns, Lorilee Craker, and Alison Hodgson.

Thanks to my core competencies Kathy Helmers, Dan Raines, and Meredith Smith from Creative Trust, who, one fine day in Tennessee, were all kinds of mean to me.

Thanks to the entire team at Tyndale, including Stephanie Broene, Karen Watson, and especially Kathy Olson, who shows me all over again how impoverished a novel is without a fine editor.

Special thanks to my personal American hero, Colonel Walter B. Forbes, USAF, who graciously gave hours of his time to relate firsthand accounts and details about WWII and about a certain P-47 called *The Gal from Kalamazoo*. This Bronze Star and Legion of Merit recipient flew missions on D-Day, was shot down over France, and had a heck of a dog-fight over Germany—and the boy was just getting started. He flew a total of seventy-two missions in WWII and went on to a long and distinguished career in the Air Force.

Thanks to my kids, Evan, Becca, Gray, and Riley, for caring about what I do, and to Riley for helping with research: he cheerfully dangled from a broom handle, all trussed up, so Mom could get a visual on Tom's situation in the A-frame. Thanks, Riley. Don't call Social Services. Remember the ice cream.

Finally, thanks to Jack, my unflagging, cheerful, and inde-fatigable aide-de-camp in countless hours of research in the States, France, and England. Any errors belong completely to him.

Just kidding. Any errors belong to my kids.

ABOUT THE AUTHOR

TRACY GROOT lives in Michigan with her husband and three sons. She is the author of *The Brother's Keeper* and *Stones of My Accusers*, which both received starred *Booklist* reviews, and *Madman*, a Christy Award winner that also received a starred *Publishers Weekly* review. Luckily, she and her husband own a coffee shop in Holland, Michigan, where a caffeine junkie can find acceptability and safe haven.

Tracy is a fan of the Detroit Lions, listens exclusively to Rich Mullins and U2, is an avid supporter of nothing in particular, and in her dreams would like to host a talk show with John Steinbeck, Charles Dickens, Michael Shaara, Donald Miller, C. S. Lewis, and G. K. Chesterton. In her dreams, she'd also like to stand on Little Round Top with Colonel Joshua Chamberlain and holler, "Fix bayonets!"

In her spare time she likes to read, knit socks, watch as many movies and TV shows as she can respectably get away with, mess around on the piano, bake very naughty amounts of sweets, and take long walks, preferably in Michigan's Upper Peninsula. She also likes to write, sometimes under the influence (of sweets, caffeine, misguided notions, and wild seismic fluctuations), sometimes not.

Someday she'd like to ride through the Badlands on a Harley with "Born to Be Wild" blaring on the radio, beat Bobby Fischer at chess, and round Cape Horn in a clipper ship. Her heroes include Mary Ann Patten (who rounded Cape Horn in a clipper ship), Raoul Wallenberg, Corrie ten Boom, Jack Groot, Evan Groot, Becca Groot, Grayson Groot, and Riley Groot.

To learn more about Tracy or her books, visit her online at www.tracygroot.com.

DISCUSSION QUESTIONS

1. The author calls this book an "impressionistic retelling" of the story of Rahab from the Bible (Joshua 2). In what ways does Brigitte remind you of Rahab? What differences are there?

2. In the Bible, Rahab is characterized as a woman who had faith in what God was doing and acted on it. How do you see that theme play out through Brigitte and other characters in the story?

3. Brigitte and Tom both have preconceived notions about each other before they even meet. What are they? Have you ever done the same—judged someone before you met them? What are some of the dangers of preconceived judgments?

4. Brigitte tells Tom that the Occupation has made her glad for the things she does get. "Before, I was never grateful," she says. Have you ever faced a challenge or loss that made you grateful for your blessings? What other positive results can come from negative situations?

5. How did you feel about Hauptmann Braun initially? Did your feelings change as the story progressed? Did his actions surprise you? Why or why not?

6. In chapter 5, Brigitte asks Father Eppinette if there is a place for one like her. Have you ever asked that question for yourself, or had someone else ask you that question? How did you or would you answer? What did you think of Tom's response in chapter 17?

7. Clemmie is a grandmotherly woman who does what she can to help those who cross her path, ultimately at the cost of her own life. Have you ever known anyone like Clemmie? Have you ever had the opportunity to put your beliefs to the test, at the risk of losing something dear to you? How did you react, or how do you think you would react in such a situation?

8. Rafael believes that the more a person fears losing control, the more he or she tries to take control. Where do you see examples of this in the story? How have you seen this play out in your own life or in the life of someone you know?

9. Madame Bouvier has a sign in her shop saying she will not serve Jews. And yet she personally rescued several Jewish people from the Nazis. Do you think the sign is just a front, or is Madame Bouvier truly conflicted in this area? What are some moral or political issues that Christians find themselves struggling with today? What issues do you personally struggle with? How do you go about resolving these conflicts in your own life?

10. Near the end of chapter 5, Madame Bouvier recalls Father Chaillet's words: "Acts of repentance will not lead

to the mercy you seek, but mercy will lead to acts of repentance. God has mercy on you, child. . . . I give you one thing to do: only believe. Redemption will follow." What did this mean to you? How do you think this changed Madame Bouvier's life?

11. At different points in the story, both Braun and Michel warn about the danger of revenge. At one point, Michel tells Tom that revenge as a motive is not strong enough. Do you agree with him? Why or why not?

12. Though Krista Hegel is not able to openly share her Christian faith with the prisoners who are being interrogated, in what ways does she clearly represent Christ? How do you think you would have responded in such a situation?

13. In chapter 21, the waiter Guillemot says that "people come forward to show who they are in war." What examples of that did you see throughout the story? How could the same principle apply in other situations (not necessarily times of war)?

14. Who was your favorite character in the story and why?

15. At the end of the book, Brigitte has a wish list of happy endings for various people in the story. How many of them do you think are realistic? How important is a happy ending to you when you are reading a novel?